To Ru:

Hope you enjoy it.

Treasured Valley

from the author

Eleri Thomas

To my paternal grandmother, Catherine, whom I never knew
— but feel would have been a kindred spirit

Part 1

'How do you pronounce this name – and what does it mean?' – pointing out a house name on this 1851 census form to David, my Welsh-speaking colleague in the university history department.

'It's pronounced Glyn Aber-Cyn, William. Glin Aber Kin. Roughly translated, it means the valley or the glen of the River Cyn. Where is it?'

'In a village called Capelulo.'

'That's actually pronounced Capel..ill..o, meaning Ulo's Chapel, possibly an early saint, who founded a place of worship there.'

'Thanks, you're inspiring me to learn Welsh. These names are so very descriptive, poetical even. It's only fairly recently that I have become curious about my surname, then started delving into my family's past.'

David agreed, 'This ancestry stuff can become quite addictive once you start finding things out.'

'You are so right, I am becoming a bit obsessive about it. Thing is, I've managed to trace my ancestors on my father's side. They came from North Wales. I've even found out where my great-great grandfather's sister was buried – from a database of gravestones. I have also discovered that six generations of my family were from Welsh farming stock. As a child, my mother told me some stories about my father's ancestors. I didn't really listen then but now I wish I'd allowed myself to be inspired by these stories.' I pause as I glance at my desk diary.

'I'm speaking at a conference at Bangor University tomorrow, it's a good opportunity to explore the area. I want to find something tangible, hopefully my aunt's grave and maybe even Glyn Abercyn farm itself. I have the name now – and I can pronounce it – so how hard can it be?'

Changing the subject, I say, 'Stephen will oversee the department while I'm away. There shouldn't be anything untoward cropping up,

I think I've just about covered everything. I doubt anyone will need to contact me,' my mind already switching off from work and thinking of the endless possibilities of my visit.

As I stand up to pack away my laptop, pick up my briefcase and walk out to my car, I feel a real sense of relief to be escaping work. The vice-chancellor is breathing down my neck to complete the planning of next year's programme and the endless administrative stuff makes me hate my job. I'm so busy, I never seem to have any real time with Sarah and my boys.

Slowly, I pull out into the crawling traffic. Things have changed and I would like to distance myself from these changes. Space is at a premium. The roads have become choked. Drivers – even cyclists – use their vehicles as weapons and dangerously disregard road laws. People are packed like sardines on public transport. Pupil to teacher ratios in schools are unmanageable and what are they teaching pupils these days? They seem to want to ban anyone with a different opinion. The city is overcrowded. People are desperate for accommodation, road parking spaces, walking space, school places and there never seems to be enough hospital beds. These shortages seem to bring out the worst in human nature, manifested as a suppressed rage; people now seem less friendly and considerate of each other.

I try to filter into the main-stream traffic. A driver sounds his horn at me. Common courtesy is dead. When I was young, London was dynamic and exciting. Now it seems unwelcoming, uncomfortable and unfriendly. Strangers are suspicious when you try to strike up a conversation and choose to look at their mobile phones instead. Maybe it is me who has changed and not the city.

I often find myself ranting these days. It makes me feel better for a while but then the little irritations, the dissatisfactions with life, slowly build up again. I look back to my childhood, when values and morals seemed better – and people were kinder. I feel out of place here now, like an alien living on a strange planet. I don't belong. The city feels threatening and uncaring, everybody demanding their 'rights' whilst trampling all over the rights of others.

As I drive out further away from London, I'm engulfed with a profound sense of escape and freedom – a heavy weight lifts off my shoulders. I need to do something radical, to change my circumstances. My doctor tells me I may be suffering from a long-term, low-level depression, so I need a complete change, before I lose it completely.

Even though I think the human race and western civilisation are in decline, I remind myself that there are also wonderful instances of human kindness, shown by complete strangers to the vulnerable. This shows that there is still a strong section within society which is moral, humanistic and caringly altruistic. I yearn to be in such a place, surrounded by such people, where there is space to breathe and time to think.

Making my way northwards, surrounded by heavy traffic I finally reach the M40. I really want to retreat to some quiet, uncomplicated little backwater as I feel utterly exhausted by the pace of city life. My boys are growing up so quickly and will soon be making their own way in the world.

Somehow, as a society I feel we have lost our equilibrium with nature. I would love to have some land and become self-sufficient in food production. If more of us did this, it would be better for our planet – rather than flying in food from around the world. It would also be very therapeutic for me to grow my own food.

It's late afternoon and I finally reach Bangor and check into my hotel. For the first time in ages, I sleep well, waking refreshed as dawn breaks.

After the conference, I call Sarah, to update her. 'The conference went without a hitch. I'm going to head back along the coast to Dwygyfylchi. First, I'm going to the local churchyard to find my aunt's grave, then maybe I'll try to find the farm. I'll call you later to let you know how I get on.'

It's early afternoon and the roads are quietish as I drive eastwards. When I exit the tunnel in the granite headland, I see on my left a vast expanse of golden sandy beach, as the tide is way out. I take the next slip road exit, park on the promenade, then walk down a small jetty and onto the beach. The vast space around me is empty, exhilarating, giving me a profound sense of freedom. Walking eastwards towards the headland on the other side of the bay, I look inland and see a beautiful, post-glacial valley, snugly surrounded by a horseshoe of hills. What a glorious sight – I'm profoundly happy to discover that this place exists, quietly tucked away in this unique situation. While I'm standing and looking, I feel a strong attachment beginning to form with this place. I feel its magnetism resonate deep within my being.

I stand there for a long time soaking it up, feeling the sun and wind on my face. I close my eyes while I absorb these sensations. Then reluctantly, I realise I need to get on with my research mission and walk back over the sands to my car, convinced that this is the place where my soul belongs.

Back in the car, I potter along the coast road distracted by the sights, until my satnav guides me off at the next exit. I find myself in a lovely, semi-rural area with mountains in the background, and pull up by the local church. I grab my papers with dates and other details and get out of the car. Heading for the graveyard, a woman who is walking by with her dog, calls out to me,

'Lovely day.'

'Yes, it really is.' I grab my chance to get some local information. 'Are you a local? Would you know where Glyn Abercyn is?'

'Yes, it's up on the top road,' pointing, 'see that small white cottage up on the mountain? Well, it's just below that. It's a long white house and I think it has some land with it.'

'Do you know who lives there? I'm wondering if they would let me have a look around, as my great-great-great aunt used to live there.'

'I'm not sure who owns it now – but I think it's been empty for quite a while.'

'That's a shame, that means I won't be able to get any information about the property. Could I walk there from here? I'm keen to see more of the local area.'

'Yes, you can walk up through the golf course. Go along here a few hundred yards and you will see a kissing gate on your right, then walk straight up. Mind you, the last part is a bit of a pull! At the top, turn left, you will see a sign that says Capelulo, then in a few hundred yards and you'll see it on your right.'

'Thanks very much. I'll look for her grave first, then walk up.'

Pushing open the ancient roofed lychgate by the road, I walk eagerly up the path. The recently cut grass makes it easier to get around to read the names on the gravestones. Methodically, I walk along the rows for about ten minutes, until I spot the name Catrin Jones, about halfway down on a tall purple slate headstone. The inscription is in Welsh but it includes the name of the farm, Glyn Abercyn. I use my mobile phone to translate the inscription, which gives her age and date of death, and says that she was the daughter of Evan and Catherine. This is definitely my aunt's grave.

It has the trade tools of a carpenter carved at the top. That's unusual. Inscribed underneath the tools is the name John Jones. The translation app reveals that he was formerly from Llanbeblig and that 'he died tragically'. Who the heck was this John Jones? Here is a delicious mystery. I call Sarah, to share it.

'I've found Catrin's grave but there is another inscription at the top for a John Jones. I have no idea who he was, as far as I knew she never married. I've taken photos so I can show you when I get back. Anyway, someone has told me where the farm is, so I'm going to walk up there now. Bye sweetheart, I'll call you later.'

I set off towards the farm, already feeling at home here. Walking along the winding road, I see nice houses on my left side and what I presume is rough golf course land on the other. I find the gate the woman mentioned and go through onto the golf course. Opening up in front of me is one of the most beautiful sights I have ever seen. Looking up towards the rolling hills, I see more clearly the small upland cottage she had pointed out earlier. Below that are steep fields and fronting the fields, a long white house, majestically overlooking the valley below. That must be it. What a wonderful position looking straight out to sea. I walk uphill, a song thrush singing its four-part melody in the ancient woodland ahead of me but

5

otherwise, there is a complete, still silence. Occasionally, I stop to catch my breath and turn around to soak in my surroundings and look back out to sea. This valley is truly spectacular. On my right is a large mountain whose rocky outcrop seems to end in the sea, which is now glistening in the afternoon sunshine. Further in, what looks like a steep mountain road leads out of the valley.

I sense my ancestors all around me in this place, claiming me as one of their own, drawing me in and somehow, I feel I belong here. This feeling wraps itself protectively around me and surreptitiously creeps deep into my psyche.

Nearing the top, the heavy pull on my leg muscles makes me glad to get onto the more even road. There is no pavement, and brambles in the overgrown hedges snag on my jumper, as I'm too busy looking around me. Suddenly, I spot a road sign for Capelulo and know I'm nearly there.

On reaching the front of the farm, I stand in the road taking in every tiny detail. There is a blanked-out window in the middle upstairs, which may have been closed up because of the glass tax, or maybe it was used to hoist grain up. It's a delightful old place, seeped in history and I wonder what Sarah and the boys would make of it. Suddenly, I spot a fallen, half-hidden sign in a small shrub in the overgrown front garden. Curiously, I cross the road to read it. A 'For Sale' sign! At the bottom I see the agent's contact details and wonder if there is any chance of viewing it – to see what the inside is like. I feel my objectivity weakening and emotion taking over. Who am I trying to kid? This place is the answer I have been looking for. I admit to myself that, given the opportunity, I would love to buy it, to own it, to live in it, wallow in it – its rustic charm has cast a spell on me.

I dial the number on the board. 'Hello. My name is William Jones. I'm standing outside Glyn Abercyn in Capelulo. I saw one of your 'For Sale' signs and wondered if it is still available.'

'It's been for sale for a while now and it may be going up for auction.' My heart sings, there's a chance. 'Would it be possible to view it?'

'I'd have to find out and get back to you. I'll call you back on this number as soon as I have made arrangements.' He rings off. That was a bit vague. Would that be in five minutes or five days?

Knowing it's unoccupied, I explore around the outside. I head along a side track, which leads to a large back yard. On my right is a good-sized barn. The whole place has an air of neglect but nothing a bit of money and effort couldn't sort. On the other side of the yard, a small stream runs along then suddenly drops steeply as it reaches the back of the property and disappears underground. This drop suggests there may once have been a mill wheel accommodated there. Walking up a track, I pass an old metal gate hanging open on one hinge, through to a small paddock. From here I see two large fields, which wrap around the property at the sides and behind. I follow an old stone wall and climb up to the top of the steeper field where I sit down facing out to sea. What a spectacular view out in front of me!

Shattering my reverie, my mobile rings and I recognise the estate agent's number.

'Hello, William speaking.'

'Hello, we have an agent available. He could come over to you in about twenty minutes. Would that be ok?'

'That would be great, I'll wait for him at the front of the property. Thank you.'

My phone rings again. Work. Is there no peace to be had?

'William, it's Stephen. We've got a few problems here. First, the students are 'no platforming' the speaker we've booked for tomorrow night. They say he's too right wing and it's a bit late to book anybody else, any suggestions?'

I listen as Stephen continues his litany of disasters and slowly, I feel myself tensing. My euphoria slowly dissipates, replaced with the old familiar feeling of stress, which knots my stomach. But weirdly, during the conversation, in a detached part of my mind, I make a most momentous decision. I've had more than enough of this. I will leave my job and London to move up here. Whatever it takes.

I suggest ways Stephen can deal with the vexatious issues, end the distressing conversation and walk back down to the road, to see the agent pulling up in his car.

'Good afternoon.' The agent shakes my hand. 'Lovely day.'

'Yes, it is. I've already looked around the back and the fields. Let's go inside.'

He hands me a brochure with details of the property. Inside the heavy front door, a staircase is immediately in front of us. To our right is a small parlour. It has a quarry-stone floor and an open stone fireplace, with a very large stone lintel across the top. At the side of the fireplace, the wall is recessed as a shelved cupboard. This goes deep into the wall, possibly once a window before the adjoining outhouse was added. At the back of the room is a narrow window, between thick river boulders that were used hundreds of years ago to form its original foundations.

Thinking out loud, I say, 'This might have been a single storey long-house at some point, possibly with a low-hanging thatched roof. It's certainly very old, perhaps thirteenth to sixteenth century, and before that, maybe a fort or some sort of stronghold. Its position, looking out across the valley below and out to sea, would have given them a good vantage point for enemy approach.' The agent nods.

We walk through what must be the dining room, leading us to the back of the house.

'This is the kitchen,' says the agent pointlessly.

An ancient cream Aga sits snugly in the large opening of an original inglenook fireplace. On the floor are large river-stone flags, worn smooth from centuries of use, probably laid on top of the original earth floor. A Belfast sink with brass taps stands by a small back kitchen window. Running half the length of the back wall, by the back door, stands a large ornate, now grimy, Welsh oak dresser. Curious, I wonder why it's there – probably too big to get out but too good to break up.

Upstairs, at the back is a small bedroom and a bathroom. The height of the roof was probably raised in the Victorian era. At the front are two more bedrooms. I look out of one of the front windows. The nineteenth century glass distorts my vision – but does not take away from the spectacular view. Having now seen the inside, I'm even more determined to own this place – no ifs, no buts – I'm besotted.

It needs a lot of updating but basically, it's a sound house – just neglected. It has a good feel about it. I imagine that the spirits of my ancestors are all around me, watching me, urging me to buy it. We walk back down to the front door. 'What's the situation then? Will it be going for auction? What was the asking price before?'

My phone rings again, breaking the spell. Sarah this time. I turn to the agent, 'Sorry, I have to take this. Thanks for the viewing. I'll call you tomorrow.'

'Hello, my love, what's up?' I ask, although bursting to tell her my news.

'We've had a letter from the sixth form college. Robert's got in – but Jon hasn't. We can't let them be split up. We can't tell them one has got in but not the other. It will devastate them.'

'You're right. Maybe we should explore what's on offer for them here, in Wales.' I feel sure the letter is another sign that we should leave London and move here.

Before I can tell her about the house viewing, Sarah continues. I daren't alienate her by interrupting.

'There is another letter, with better news! They've decided to publish the four children's stories I wrote and commissioned me to write another four.'

'That's wonderful news. Well done you! A published author, eh? I'm very proud of you darling. Sarah, listen, I've found the house. It is actually for sale. I've just had a viewing with the agent. It's wonderful, everything we have ever imagined a house in the country should be, and even better, it used to belong to my family. I really think we should buy it and move here. Sorry to spring this on you but we'll talk about it properly when I get back. Is that OK?'

As I drive back to London, I imagine how the house could look once restored. I will need to get local builders in to do the structural work – but it won't have to be done all at once. We can take our time restoring as basically it just needs to be habitable. It did smell a little damp, but probably only due to being empty so long. It will soon air by getting the wood burner and Aga going and there is plenty of free wood in the ancient woodland which skirts the steeper field. I think about what the agent told me about the locality. The upland pasture, behind the farm, is used by the local sheep farmers to graze their sheep in the summer months. He said it's popular walking country and people enjoy the spectacular views high up, down into the valley and across to the coast. On clear days, you can see the hills of the Isle of Man nearly sixty miles away, particularly just before sunset. To the northwest, the island of Anglesey is accessible by two bridges. The senior school and main shopping area are only twenty minutes away, with smaller shops locally.

During supper with the family, I first describe finding Catrin's grave, then how I walked up the golf course and along the top road and found the house. I talk them through the viewing and show the sales brochure the agent gave me. They read the description of the three-bedroomed, white-washed farmhouse with outhouses at both sides and the rear, creating an encompassing farmyard. They are impressed and excited by the fact that there are seven acres of land. Then I tell them how I walked up to the top of one field and saw the amazing view right across the valley.

I hold my breath and wait, as Sarah and the boys mull over the information and study the detail, mentally willing her and the boys to love the house as much as I do. I visibly relax when she says,

'I like the look of the farmhouse. It looks cosy and snug tucked into the foothills – and looking out towards the sea. The inside looks a bit basic – but I suppose it would do while we did it up. It looks as if we could make it cosy and comfortable. You know what they say? Location is everything and it seems to have that by the bucketful. But I'd like to see it first before the auction, just in case I don't like it.'

This a reasonable request, but then I have a sudden rush of anxiety, thinking that she may not like it as much as I do.

'We'll arrange to go up to view it mid-week, if I can get a few hours off work.'

Jon changes tack saying, 'It doesn't show any other properties nearby, it looks a bit rural.' I could see which way his mind was working. 'Will you promise we can have driving lessons next year, so we can get around there?'

This is something they would never have needed in the city and I consider driving to be a life skill but can't resist teasing them, 'You'll be able to cycle to school, it's only six miles.'

'What! Cycle all that way?'

'There's a good cycle track along the coast which comes out right by what could be your new school.'

'But what if it's raining? says Robert.

'Where's the nearest bus stop? says Jon.

At this onslaught, I hold up both hands, palms out saying, 'I surrender, of course you can have lessons. I'll teach you myself, to start you off.' That matter settled, Robert, who is the older of the twins by three minutes, asks, 'Do you think there'll be a proper internet connection?

'I've checked. There's fast broadband.'

'Can I have first choice of the bedrooms? And can I have one of the outhouses to set up my drum kit?' Jon asks.

Excellent! My family seems generally positive about the idea of moving and willing to go along with my plan – or at least to give it a go. Although the boys have friends, they tend to spend time in each other's company, so leaving friends behind is not so much an issue.

I look longingly at the photos I took and show the better ones to Sarah and boys. I yearn to be back there, the place where I found the beginnings of this still, inner peace, where the people are friendly and the pace of life slower. If I don't change my lifestyle soon, I fear for my mental and emotional health. I'm not sure I can cope with the stress of my job for much longer. I don't share these fears with Sarah, I don't want to burden her – and to speak out loud of them, would make them real. Better to pull back from the brink by moving to Wales.

Back at work, I have difficulty concentrating and my sleep is disturbed by anxiety. I've decided not to tell my colleagues until I know for sure I'm leaving. Stephen tells me the student union is now complaining about the stand-in speaker and there's a Heads of Departments meeting in an hour, for which I am totally unprepared. As a deliberate act of self-preservation, I refuse to get worked up, as I would normally. Instead, I remain determinedly detached and shrug my shoulders indifferently. What's the worst that can happen? I feel a new freedom, a letting go, creep into my psyche.

People view our house over the weekend and one couple makes a cash offer, before it is even officially on the market – another positive sign for moving. While the legalities are sorted, Sarah's parents have offered to lend us the money for the farm, so we don't lose it. They have also offered to let us stay with them, once our house sale is completed.

Sarah and I travel up midweek and thankfully, she loves the property. I watch her fall in love with it before my very eyes, as we leave the house and walk through the fields at the back. Our decision is made. We accept the offer in London and we're committed.

Auction day finally arrives and as I enter the auction room, I know I am taking a huge gamble. I have no job lined up and have sold my London home. But we have some income from Sarah's books to keep us going for now. Much is at stake here. Our whole future hinges on being able to buy the farm. There's no going back. Suddenly these thoughts build into a panic attack at the enormity of what I am doing – and doubts begin to flood in. What if it is all a big mistake and I am letting go of all I have worked for? I breathe deeply and tell myself to pull myself together and get a grip. I remind myself how much I dislike my current life and how much happier we'll be in the country. I comfort myself into believing I have a good chance of getting it, as I wait for the property to come up on the list. I imagine my ancestors next to me in the auction room, watching me, willing me to buy the farm. Fanciful ideas but clearly a manifestation of my state of mind, which is bordering on the unhinged.

When they announce the property is next on the list, my heart rate suddenly speeds up and I feel a sudden rush of 'fight or flight' adrenaline. My heart thumps heavily in my chest and I wonder why the people around me seem unaware of it. The auctioneer suggests a starting price. This is it, I think, now fully focused. I glance around the room – but no one takes up the suggested starting price, then the auctioneer offers a lower one. Again, I look around. Still a stony silence. The auctioneer scans the room, gavel in one hand and looks directly at me. He knows I have made enquiries about the place. I decide that somebody needs to get the bidding started, or risk the property being withdrawn. Slowly I raise my arm to bid, as this is below what I am prepared to pay.

The auctioneer scans the room for further offers. Standing at the back, a man wearing a flat cap who looks like a farmer, lifts his rolled-up catalogue to bid. Briefly, I wonder if this is the farmer who is currently grazing his sheep on the land. I'm aware farmers need as much land as they can get nowadays to make their businesses viable. Then they sell off the farmhouses to second-home owners, who just want a nice place to escape the city now and again – whereas I am planning to escape for good. It would be a shame to see the farm split up in this way and I raise my arm again with a higher offer. The farmer comes back with an even higher bid and seems determined to get the property. I start to worry that he will outbid me, as I am nearing my limit, so I offer a bit more than I had planned. The farmer shakes his head and withdraws. Relieved, I think I am in with a chance now and hold my breath. Once more, the auctioneer scans the room to see if there are any new bidders.

Suddenly, a man in the next row unexpectedly calls out a higher price and I start to panic, as he seems very confident. Desperately, I think please don't let him have it. Reluctantly, I raise my bid once more. The price is getting silly now and I wonder why this man is prepared to pay so much. He offers a higher price again and I realise now that I have passed my limit and will have to withdraw. The auctioneer asks me if I am still bidding but I sadly shake my head and decline. I have lost it and feel sick to the pit of my stomach. The auctioneer raises his gavel, 'Going for the first time, for the second time. Gone! – to the gentleman sitting in the third row,' as he crashes his gavel down onto the sound block.

It takes a few more seconds to properly sink in that I didn't get it. I sit there stupefied and stunned. In the blur of just a few minutes, all my hopes and dreams have dissipated. What have I done? Our London home is sold – and I've promised my family we are going to move to Wales. What do I do now?

I dig out my mobile phone from my coat pocket as I leave the auction room, to break the bad news.

'Sarah, we didn't get it! Somebody was willing to pay far more than we could,' I say, my voice cracking with disappointment. 'I could have carried on bidding, maybe have got a loan for the balance, but he seemed pretty determined.'

'That's disastrous.' After the trip to Wales, Sarah has become as enthusiastic as me. She knows how desperate I am to leave London. She knows I had pinned all my hopes on it and how important it is to me to move here. She worries that I could easily slip into despondency and depression.

'What about looking for something else that's for sale while you are up there? Stay an extra day. Have a good look around, you might even find something better. Don't forget we have to be out of this house in three weeks' time.'

My carefully made plans have crumbled to pieces – I have gambled and lost. I have let my family down and feel a fool to have placed all my hopes on getting the house. I have sold our London house. Sarah has done most of the packing already and a lot of our stuff is stored in her parents' garage.

Sarah probably knows that there is nowhere better but is trying to give me hope. My heart was absolutely set on it and is now broken. After having it almost in my grasp, I've managed to lose it. The link with my ancestors is broken. It was perfect on so many levels. But out loud I resignedly say, 'Alright, I'll ask the agent what else there is.' I feel myself already sliding slowly down to that deep dark flat place.

I half-heartedly let the agent take me around a few available properties but there is nothing which comes anywhere close to Glyn Abercyn for me. It's far more than just a property – it's the home of my forebears. I soon realise that it's a waste of time looking at anything else and head back to London.

When I get back, we don't talk about it. It's too painful. The boys are keeping out of my way and Sarah is walking on eggshells. Next day, work is insufferable and my colleagues seem puzzled by my low mood – but I don't discuss it with them. I work but my heart is not in it and I worry I'm not giving justice to the assignments I mark. I feel myself getting lower by the day.

Two weeks have dragged by since the auction and it still hurts, so I use work as a distraction. I'm marking assignments in my office when suddenly the phone rings. I try to ignore it, hoping whoever it is will ring off – but it continues persistently. Angry at the intrusion, I pick it up. 'Hello, is that Mr. Jones? It's Maldwyn, the estate agent here. I'm ringing to tell you that the auction bid for Glyn Abercyn has fallen through because the bidder is unable to get his funding. We were wondering if you are still interested in buying the property and if you are, would you care to make an offer on it?'

I'm shocked. I tell myself to play it cool and say brusquely, 'Let me think about it. I'll call you back shortly.'

I can barely believe what I just heard. It's music to my ears. I have another chance to buy it. My brain switches into financial mode. I need to think about how much to offer. On balance, I decide I am in a strong position here – but on the other hand I don't want to risk losing it again. At auction, I offered more than I had planned, so decide to go back to my original limit. I call him back and make the offer.

'Thank you, Mr. Jones, I'll put your offer to the vendor and get back to you.'

I can't concentrate on the marking as I wait on tenterhooks for his call. Needing to pace, I get up to make myself a cup of tea and take it to my desk. I really want to phone Sarah to tell her the news – but I'm afraid of missing Maldwyn's call. So I sit there in a state of anxiety and hope. When the phone rings, I pick it up immediately this time. The vendor has accepted my offer. I'm ecstatic and call Sarah to tell her the good news. I feel my spirit lifting immediately and my low mood slink away. I'm on a proverbial high.

'We must celebrate. I'll pick up a couple of bottles of champers on the way home! We'll have to ask your dad for that loan – until the money comes through on our London house.

I inform my Head of Faculty about my plans. The reaction is as expected. 'What's brought all this on? I thought you were settled here.'

'I guess it might seem a little crazy, moving with no job to go to but I need a change of direction and lifestyle. I'm desperate to move out of the city and live a completely different life, before it's too late to move the boys.' I tell the head I am moving to North Wales and ask, 'Do you know any of the people who work in the university up there?'

'Not off the top of my head but I'll give it some thought. Obviously, I don't want to lose you – but if your mind is made up… you will be hard to replace. In the meantime, I can offer you some work as a long-arm supervisor for our distance learners and there's always plenty of work for a marker of student assignments and dissertations, if that's any use.'

'Yes, thanks. I can do this to tide me over but what I really want is to do research into the ancient inhabitants of the valley. I have read of evidence of them having been there.'

As the conversation ends, I hand in my letter of resignation and shake his hand. No going back now.

Next, I instruct my solicitor to act in the purchase and we complete the sale of our house quickly. Our possessions are loaded on the removal van and we stand and watch it drive away to the storage we've booked. Sarah and I wander through the now empty, echoing rooms for the last time and feel a tinge of sadness. We have spent happy years here – but I shake myself out of this nostalgia; we will start a new life – a new adventure. I lock the front door for the final time, drop the key at the estate agent's office, then we head off to Sarah's parents' house to stay there until the purchase is finalised.

Two months after leaving London, we're settled in. There is still a lot of renovation work to do but we have all the time in the world and our pace of life is now, thankfully, down a notch or two.

Of course, settling in is not without its problems as things rarely go to plan. Good and reliable builders are difficult to find, given we do not know the local traders, and this impedes our renovation. The boys don't mind too much as they have commandeered one of lofts in the outhouses and made it their own. During the rewiring and installation of the new central heating system, we have to endure a permanent layer of fine clingy dust and noise, caused by drilling through granite and the disturbance of centuries of grime.

Our reduced income means we can't carry out all the changes we'd like straightaway but there are compensations. We revel in the local water, which tastes wonderful and is beautifully soft – contrasting favourably with the hard limescale-ridden water of the south. The boys like their school and get on well with their subject teachers. I am secretly pleased that they have chosen History, English and Maths for their A-levels and their assignments receive high grades. There is some low-level bullying at school, as one would expect, but they look out for each other and are learning how to manage conflict situations.

On a gorgeous summer evening we are sitting on the bench in our small front garden, waiting to watch the flaming red sun finally sink below the horizon. The boys have gone on one of their hill rambles, so the house is peaceful. A local man is walking past our house and calls out, 'How do? How are you settling in? I used to know Owen, who lived here once,' as he crosses the road to us. We greet him and encourage him to tell us more. He introduces himself as Dennis, then continues, 'Owen lived here with his dad Thomas, very sad story really. Owen told me stories about this place but later he sold up. Last I heard he was living in the Conwy Valley. That building there used to be the local garage and petrol station.'

He knows a great deal about our farm and its history – and it soon becomes apparent that he is also a font of local historical knowledge. He suggests that we might like to join the local Historical Society, to learn more about it. I tell some of what I know: 'I started tracing my family tree and found that I had family on my father's side, who used to live here.'

After listening, he concludes, 'In that case, you must also have been related to Owen and his father, Thomas, through Anwen. Her family were big chapel people you know. Her brother-in-law used to live under the chapel along the road in the village.'

'We've found an old Bible in the attic, with a family tree in it. This must be the family you are telling us about. I guess Owen didn't check the loft before he sold the place. We should be able to get lots of information about them from this.'

I dash in to fetch my file of the family history tree and invite him to join us in the garden. 'This is what I have discovered to date, although there are gaps. You see here is my great-great-great aunt Catrin Jones, on my father's side. I've found her grave in the local churchyard and found her on the 1841 census living here in this house — which is one of the reasons we had to buy it when we found it was for sale.'

'Ah! Yes, I see. Then you definitely have two connections with the place.'

This is music to my ears. Does this mean there has been a continuity of occupation in this house by my family for many generations, both on my father's side of the family as well as my newly-discovered link through Anwen?

* * *

Thomas & Mari's Story

Thomas' grandmother, Gwladys, was quite frail now but still a force to be reckoned with. Her daughters arranged a small tea party to celebrate her eighty-ninth birthday which all were expected to attend. During the party, Gwladys presented Thomas with her large family Bible. 'I've written inside that I am giving this to you. You must look after it very carefully, it was started by my father, your great-grandfather, who ran the woollen mill in Pontwgan.'

'Thank you Nain,' Thomas said and kissed her dry cheek but was too young then to appreciate the gesture. His mother did though and carefully put it away in the cupboard of the dresser until he was older. Thomas was the only son of Catherine and Robat and they worshipped the ground he walked on, having nearly lost him when he was younger.

By the time Thomas was fifteen, he had persuaded the local quarry to take him on as an apprentice mechanic. For the first few years, being the 'new boy,' he had to fetch and carry and do the jobs nobody else wanted – but all the while he was watching and learning, picking things up almost sub-consciously. A few years later he became increasingly aware that many conversations among his workmates were turning to the possibility of another war, despite Prime Minister Chamberlain signing a peace agreement with Hitler in Munich.

Thomas completed his apprenticeship at the quarry and was officially taken on as Assistant Mechanical Engineer, as talk of a second war with Germany intensified. This was just when his mother Catherine was thinking that Thomas, having worked so hard to get to where he was, was now finally set up for life as an adult. She began to worry deeply about the talk of war, fretting that she could have her precious son taken away from her. She could not believe that it was all starting again. She remembered being bedridden during the time she carried him in the final months of the last war. She could not bear him to be called up as the last generation had been, except for Robat of course, who had been conscripted to build lookouts. They had said then that that was the war to end all wars, so why was there talk of another?

Occasionally, Thomas was called to fix farm machinery for his mother's brother, Bob, who farmed in the adjoining valley. 'I want you to have a look at this thresher,' said his uncle the next time Thomas visited. 'Either the blades want adjusting or it needs oiling. It's not working properly, anyway.'

'If you are so good at diagnosing, why don't you fix it?' teased Thomas good-naturedly, as he was very fond of his uncle.

'Too big for your boots, you are lad!' Bob wished Thomas was his son. His daughter worked on the farm with him, but she was a bit too pious and smitten by religion for his liking. She was a Sunday school teacher with her nose often in the Bible. She related everything to a proverb or a verse, which grated a bit with him.

As Thomas started to fix the thresher, Bob said, 'I'll go and make some tea.' It was quite old, powered by steam but the engine was sound. The conveyor belts and pulleys, driven by the engine, which moved the mechanical parts, had become a bit loose and needed adjustment, so he set about doing that. He was lying underneath it when he first heard, then saw a pair of dainty button-down boots, below an ankle length dress, walking towards him. As he slid out from underneath the thresher, a female said, 'It must be hot work under there, so I've brought you some fresh lemonade.' The owner of the voice was a very pretty, dark-eyed girl, with a beguiling, mischievous smile. Thomas was not really used to dealing with girls, apart from those at Sunday school, whom he had known for years. As she looked directly at him, he felt slightly uncomfortable under her intrusive, flirtatious scrutiny and thought her a bit forward when she said, 'What's such a handsome lad doing stuck underneath a dirty old thresher?' Thomas, slightly taken aback by her directness, did not know how to respond. 'Don't look so worried, I'm a friend of Bob's daughter,' pointing down the road. 'I live just down there in that house on the crossroads.'

Thomas thought she seemed an unlikely companion for Ellen, more like someone Ellen would try to convert, to save from the devil. They seemed too different to be friends. He wiped his hands on an oily rag then took the lemonade off her mumbling, '*Diolch*. Thank you very much.'

Thomas focused on the lemonade, as he'd never met anyone like her before. The girls he knew were not as forward. With her head on one side she said, 'What's the matter, cat got your tongue? A handsome boy like you, lost for words? Surely you must have plenty of girls after you?'

Although discomforted, he was at the same time flattered by her attention, as she was really lovely. Once he'd gathered his usual composure, he asked, 'What's your name then and what's a pretty girl

20

like you doing in the middle of nowhere, like this?'

'Marian. 'What's your name?'

That's all it took for him to be well and truly smitten. On his drive home, he decided that the old thresher needed a complete overhaul. From then on, he visited his uncle as often as was practically possible so that he could meet up with Marian, consequently getting into trouble with his mother for missing Sunday school.

They usually met at the crossroads after Thomas had been to his uncle's, then walked along the country lanes, crossed stiles and walked through hay fields, chatting away. She had set her sights on him and had evidently hooked and reeled him in. This quiet little romance was going on to a background of the increasingly loud talk of war, from which Thomas was temporarily distracted.

Once his uncle became aware that Thomas was courting her, he warned Thomas, 'She a flighty one and no better than she ought to be. You wanna watch yourself lad.'

But Thomas was not for listening. 'Don't be so hard on her. Maybe she's not as religious as Ellen but she's got a heart of gold.'

'Maybe, but who does it belong to?'

At work, his mates' conversation, besides girls, turned more and more to the possibility of fighting in the upcoming war. Thomas was caught up in the excitement and fervour created by the official rhetoric and the propaganda in the local cinema. Political leaders and former soldiers who had fought in the last war were telling fit and able young men about the glory of being called up to serve their country. The quarry's mechanical department began discussing forming a company.

'We wouldn't be going as cannon fodder,' said one of the young enthusiasts, 'we would be going as support – skilled engineers, building bridges and airstrips – keeping the vehicles on the road.' Thomas was liking the sound of all of this and slowly became absorbed into this realm of exciting possibilities. The only doubt which niggled at the back of his mind was that his parents would be devastated if he went away and put his life at risk.

'I might be called up,' he said idly to Marian one day, testing the water for her reaction. They sat propped up against a hay rick on his uncle's farm, eating the bread and cheese she had brought him.

She turned her beautiful eyes towards him saying, 'I'll miss you if you go away.'

'How much?' Thomas leaned forwards to kiss her pouting lips.

'This much,' as they fell to the ground together, showing each other just how much.

* * *

'Mam, I'm going to have to join up. If I do it now, I'll have more choice about which battalion I join – but if I leave it until I'm conscripted, I'll have to go where they tell me. At least this way, I can try to get in the Royal Engineers, looking after the vehicles, building bridges and runways, which is safer than being in the thick of it, fighting on the front line.'

'But what if you're not strong enough?' Catherine said, close to tears, whilst wringing her apron.

'I feel fine, but if there is a problem with my heart from the rheumatic fever, they will surely pick it up at the Medical.' Catherine remained unconvinced and continued to fret, knowing just how close she had once come to losing him. It seemed foolhardy to her for him to risk that all again. But Thomas did not want to listen, he was carried away by the excitement of it all.

Within two weeks, the quarry company had been formed, with Thomas one of the main organisers. Unluckily, or perhaps luckily for Thomas, the Medical Officer who checked him out had not bothered to study his medical records in any detail, then was called away to attend to another matter just as he was going to listen to Thomas' heartbeat. Consequently, he quickly rubber-stamped Thomas' paperwork, which stated 'Passed – Fit to Serve'. His parents were distraught when they heard.

The quarry company was soon to be transported to a camp to be kitted out and for basic training. Consequently, one bitterly cold

January morning in 1940, Thomas, who had never in his life been any further than Liverpool and had only ever been answerable to his parents, left his North Wales home, heading for an unknown army camp, hundreds of miles away in the north of England. In his first letter home to his mother, he wrote:

Dear Mam

I now have a new, stricter parent – the sergeant-major, who oversees the battalion's training. He's a hard taskmaster to please and much of the stuff they teach us seems pointless. But it's good that we lads are all able to go through this tough training together, rather than being among a lot of strangers, as we look out for each other.

By May, Thomas' unit was in the thick of it, fighting to keep the enemy at bay while their compatriots evacuated France on the beach of Dunkirk.

Their little company, now part of the Royal Engineers, was amongst the very last to leave. They lined up their trucks out into the sea, so that the troops could walk along the roofs to board the troop carrier boats further out in the bay. They watched as boat after boat sailed away, carrying thousands of soldiers into risky situations. They were sitting ducks for enemy planes overhead, which bombarded them mercilessly and many lost their lives that day, just when they thought they had reached the safety of a boat which would take them home. Thomas saw dearly loved sons, brothers, fathers, uncles and cousins blown into the air, their bodies on fire, before hitting the sheer relief of the water. The sight and the acrid smell of burning corpses on the water was forever imprinted on Thomas's mind, while many others simply drowned as their ships were attacked.

The few soldiers still left on the beach had to sabotage the remaining vehicles and equipment, to prevent them falling into enemy hands. They then had to try to escape as best they could. Thomas was lucky enough to get a passage on a small French tender, which had already gone backwards and forwards across the channel many times that day. It was a terrifying crossing for the little boats, with enemy aircraft fire narrowly missing them on many occasions. Later, they continued to sail through the darkness, hoping not to be a target. Thomas was hugely relieved to finally land safely back on home territory, still under cover of darkness and knew he owed his life to that French captain.

What a welcome Thomas received when he was finally given a few hours home leave, reports having already been received about how terrifying the evacuation had been. Unstoppable tears of pure joy fell from his mother's eyes, thankful once more that he was still alive and in one piece, at least for now.

Waking early on Sunday morning, he decided to walk over the mountain to his uncle's farm, Pont Werglodd, to clear his head of recent experiences and to seek out Marian. He set off at a fast pace, knowing the route like the back of his hand from the time spent on the hills as a child. Time was tight as he had to be back to accompany his parents for the evening service at the main church in the town later, then report back for duty that evening. His parents had been strangely unforthcoming when he had enquired about Marian the day before. 'We're not sure where she is, your uncle hasn't seen her in months, he seems to think she may have moved away. She might even have joined the war effort herself.' But then, Thomas thought, farmers, labourers and their families were generally expected to farm their land, as the Ministry of Agriculture decreed. He still couldn't understand why Marian had not written to him while he was away, as he knew she could write. Sadly, he shrugged his shoulders. Most things seemed to be out of his control during these strange times but he was determined to find out for himself, one way or the other.

Thomas was very fit from all the army training and ran some of the way there. When he got to the farm, there was nobody at home and he was annoyed with himself for not realising that they would have just left for the morning service at the Llangelynin Old Church. He cursed his lack of foresight and decided to walk across to Marian's house, a place he had never been invited to go in previously. He banged loudly at the front door with his fist – but nobody came to answer. He felt confused. Maybe they were also at the church but didn't seem the type somehow. At this very point that Thomas was seeking Marian, she was resting, having just given birth to a child, so his knock went unheeded. Had they known it was him, an effort would have been made but they were too engrossed in cutting the birth-cord and wrapping the baby in a warm swaddling blanket, to bother with callers. Thomas walked despondently away from the little cottage. It seemed that the fates were conspiring against him from knowing, one way or the other.

In his final hours of home leave, he attended the main church in town at a service for serving forces personnel. After the service, as they filed out of the church, his parents fell into conversation with another couple known to them.

'Thomas, let me introduce you to Mari, our daughter.' Thomas' mind, still fretting about Marian, thought how strange the name Mari was nearly Marian. She was not in uniform, so he asked, 'Have you joined up?'

'I'm based with the Royal Navy's Wrens in Bristol.' She did not volunteer any further information about what she did there, saying only that her work was office based. Then his mother rather embarrassingly suggested, 'Why don't you two write to each other; it's always nice to get letters when you are away from home, I'm sure.' Dutifully, they swapped details. Thomas liked her well enough but soon forgot about her.

His immediate plan was to meet up with some of his battalion, also on leave, so he made his way over to where a group of young men stood talking. They had planned to walk down to the train station together to catch the train back to camp. He then said a quick farewell to his parents, picked up his kit bag which he had left by the vestry door and joining his friends, set off, away once more from his distraught mother, who wondered once more, if she would ever see him again.

After more training in the country, his battalion was despatched to Gibraltar. He described it to his mother as *'one of the outposts of the Empire'* in his first letter home. She found out later they were there to build an aircraft runway and were based there for eighteen months. Whilst there, Thomas became well known for his inventive skills and what they could not get hold of, he could usually make out of next to nothing.

As there were quite a few men from Wales on the base, Thomas suggested, 'Why don't we set up a Welsh Society here, we could have social evenings, hold Welsh services and even have concerts.' They agreed and soon they were singing their hearts out to the familiar, comforting hymns they knew so well. The words they had previously sung at face value, now seemed to have a newer, deeper, more poignant meaning. The group also celebrated St. David's Day by organising a '*Noson Lawen*', where anybody who could, was roped in to perform on the temporary stage they rigged up. Thomas was able to accompany the singers and choirs on the piano. The concerts were hugely enjoyed by all his contingent, as well as others who drifted in to join in the celebrations.

Thomas experienced extreme homesickness at times. He had a longing to return to his familiar little village and community, where he had known only security and freedom. He longed to see and be held by his gentle parents. He even longed for the seemingly endless rain which fell there. He could just imagine them now, sitting in the little chapel, praying fervently for his safe return. These thoughts prompted him to write again to his mother, to let her know what they had been doing – at least those things he was permitted to write about, as some letters were heavily censored by their battalion leader.

Anwyl Mam
Just to let you know that I am well. We are busy ▮▮▮▮▮▮▮▮▮▮
It's hot and sunny here and I long for the cooling Welsh rain to fall onto my face. I'm with a good bunch of local lads and we keep each other going. Longing to see you and Dad again. Missing you both.
Cariad anwylaf
Thomas
P.S. Have you heard from Marian at all?

His homesickness was alleviated by a letter from his mother, which crossed with his and arrived the next day:

Annyl Fab (Dear Son)
We were very happy to receive the letter you wrote last month and are glad that you are well. We too are both well here. We have some evacuee children staying with us from Liverpool. They are little scallywags and very sweet – but they run us ragged.
Longing to have you home safe and sound once more.
Cariad annylaf
Mam

Thomas decided to write Marian a letter. He enclosed it in a letter he wrote to his Uncle Bob, as he could not remember the name of Marian's house. He asked him to pass it on to her. Later, his uncle replied that she had moved away and that he did not have a forwarding address.

Then to his surprise, he received a letter from Mari with news about what was going on. He had to finally accept that Marian must have decided she no longer wanted him and she faded once more to the back of his mind. He wrote to Mari telling her about the Welsh society they had formed and a comical account of the comedians amongst their ranks. Some of the jokers teased him about the letters he was receiving from her, announcing loudly to the barracks that Thomas had a new girlfriend.

They continued to correspond and swap the news they received from home and he enjoyed her well-written letters. He started thinking that she must now be more than a pen pal, that she must like him if she kept writing. Maybe, who knows, they could have a future together, he thought. In his quieter, more reflective homesick moments, he was moved to write some poetry and these, if he thought they merited attention, would be enclosed in his letters to Mari. The poetry was not about human love but about the enduring love and longing that he felt for his country and this bound them together. Reality about the unrequited human love he felt for Marian sank in as he realised that it was not meant to be.

After eighteen months and the runway completed, Thomas' battalion boarded a troop carrier, sailed across the Mediterranean Sea and landed in Algeria, to become part of the North African Campaign. The way the Arabs treated their women was a real shock to Thomas. He thought about Mari and wondered what she would make of this attitude towards their women, who were considered by the Algerian men to be no more valuable than their animals. He was amazed at how different humans could be in this part of the world.

The experience of war was an eye-opener for men like Thomas, who had left small insular communities to travel to many parts of the world with the armed services.

'We've certainly had our minds broadened to the peculiarities and differences in other countries,' he wrote to Mari. *'Despite this, it is a very beautiful country, especially the area of Constantine and Seif, where the operational base of the North African Campaign is located. There is a wonderful variety of fruit which grows here, many of which I have never seen nor tasted before. You would find it quite fascinating, given your interest in botany.'*

Latin had been one of her subjects at grammar school and she had written to him about flowers, plants and leaves she found, identified, labelled and pressed into a book. He drew sketches of the fruit so she could try to identify them. He felt he was slowly beginning to get to know her better through her letters, which were welcome and interesting. Finally accepting that Marian was not interested in him, he now felt Mari slowly filling up the space in his head which she had once held.

Their task in North Africa complete, the battalions lined up on the sandy beach, ready to embark onto the troop carrier ships to be transported home again. As Thomas waited in line in the sun, hot in his khaki serge uniform and plagued by sand fleas, he looked down at the white, sugary sand and noticed some beautiful little shells. They had tiger-like markings, quite unlike anything found on his beach at home. He bent down and picked up about a dozen of these and dropped them into the top breast pocket of his tunic. Maybe Mari would like these, as a memento of his time in Africa. He was thinking about her more and more and decided that when he got home, he would sound her out about how she felt about him. He even surprised himself by thinking that maybe they should discuss the possibility of a war-time marriage One thing this war had taught him was that it was best to live for the moment and seize every opportunity, as you might not live to see tomorrow.

Once the ships started crossing the channel, they realised just how dangerous it was going to be. They were sitting ducks waiting to be picked off by enemy planes. Three of the ships packed with soldiers were hit, bodies flying everywhere, aflame like fireworks in the night sky. Thomas was shocked to again witness such barbarity. He privately mourned his compatriots. He prayed for those who had lost their lives so violently and so very close to home. Thomas worried his ship would be the next to be hit but by the grace of God, he landed safely on the shores of Britain – home once more to tell his tale. The rumour spread like wildfire that, for the first time in two years, they would be allowed to go home for a few days. They knew that this was only a short reprieve in hostilities and that soon they would all be preparing for the 'big push.'

Before this, he obtained a forty-eight hour pass and was soon on a train for home, along with hundreds of others. Boarding the train in his army uniform, he flung his kit bag on the rack above his seat. He lit one of the Senior Service cigarettes he had managed to buy at the station, just before the train pulled out. He fell deep in thought again about Mari. Should he bite the bullet, he thought dramatically, before he literally took the bullet? An image of those he had seen blown up by the bombers flashed before him.

Thomas assumed that his parents must approve of Mari or they would not have introduced her to him, nor encouraged their correspondence. He did not really know her but maybe that was what marriage was about – a 'getting to know' process. By the time he reached the next main station, where the train would stop for thirty minutes, he had sealed his fate. He would send her a telegram, telling her he was coming home and asking if she would marry him. That was it, he thought, as he sent off the cable, the die is now cast, let's see what happens when I get home.

Mari, who he knew was also home on leave, received the telegram, which read:

ARRIVING HOME THIS EVENING AT EIGHT STOP HAVE FORTY EIGHT HOURS LEAVE STOP WILL YOU MARRY ME

Mari was stunned when she received the telegram. It was as surprising as it was unexpected. She hadn't seriously thought about any future with Thomas, as she was just focussed on getting through the war, until her life could start again. She had been badly let down by someone she had once tentatively discussed marriage with before the war. When war broke out, they had decided to put things on hold for the duration but it looked as if once he had joined the Navy and entered a different, bigger world, he seemed to forget her and their former commitment. She hadn't heard a word from him since the beginning of the war, although friends had told her they had seen him around on home leave. Thus humiliated, she had decided not to have anything more to do with men. She had also had unwelcome advances from some officers she worked for and had quickly learned which ones to avoid being in the same room with.

But like Thomas, it appears she was also caught up in the 'live for today' attitude, which now permeated society generally. She was giving his offer serious consideration but wanted to discuss it with him first before giving her answer.

However, all hell had been let loose once Thomas' telegram was received and read in Mari's household. She was their only child, as with Thomas, so her mother went into overdrive to arrange a wedding, given the restraints of wartime Britain. In a flurry of activity, arrangements were made, with help from Thomas' mother and father. Despite the rationing of goods and food, which were controlled via coupons, they managed to put in place all the components of a war-time wedding. The minister agreed to conduct the wedding ceremony and his wife would play the church organ. An heirloom gold wedding ring and nice material for a dress were found, along with some net for a veil. Other luxuries such as butter, milk and cream from Thomas' farm, and dried fruit, long stored away for a special occasion, were used make the wedding cake.

Mari walked down alone to the station to meet Thomas' train, determined to get a chance to speak to him on his own. As he walked out of the station entrance into the sunshine, he went up to her and kissed her lightly on the cheek. They decided to walk the long way back along the beach so they could talk. She was feeling a bit awkward with this new intimacy and said to him, 'Are you really sure about getting married? We don't even know each other properly.'

Thomas responded philosophically, 'Well, I think we have as good a chance as anybody else for it to work. I've learned these last few years that life is much too short for should haves, would haves or could haves. Who knows if we will even still be alive next week? So, I think we should live for now and give it a go. We like each other well enough, don't we?' He caught her hand and turned it into a cup. He dropped the little shells he had picked up for her into her hand, explaining where they had come from. She was really touched that he had thought of her while he was far away and decided maybe there was some hope of making this marriage work.

And so the wedding went ahead. Mari's Navy friends had booked a hotel honeymoon room for the happy couple for one night at a nearby seaside resort, a real luxury then. Her friends had clubbed together for this wedding present, because they were too far away to attend the ceremony. Later, Thomas felt that Mari was not particularly keen on the physical side of marriage and wondered if it was due to shyness. It had been very different with Mari – but then he scolded himself for even making the comparison.

Both sets of parents seemed to be pleased with the match. In truth, they had surreptitiously arranged between them for Thomas and Mari to meet that fateful day outside the chapel. Everyone had done everything they could to make the wedding a memorable day for the young couple and after their brief honeymoon, both returned to their respective bases the next day. They did not see each other again until the war ended.

Back at base, it was clear that preparations for the 'big push' were in full swing. His battalion was soon transported for the second time into France. They were shocked to arrive in a country which had been utterly and completely destroyed. They passed by the old camp they had built and been based at the first time around. They were surprised to see that the old huts were still standing, although not much else was. Thomas remembered nostalgically where buildings and farms had stood during his last time here and said to his comrade, 'Desperate for a taste of home, I remember collecting potatoes from the field of an old Frenchman. Then I called at another farm to try to find some eggs, then back to base with them carefully stored in my pockets. I made a pan out of an old petrol tin and made chips and fried the eggs in it. Boy, did they taste good!' He remembered eating many more tasty suppers out of that pan.

Thomas was sad to see the country completely devastated – as it was now. Along with American troops, they travelled straight through France and on to Belgium in September of 1944, liberating them from German occupation. But they did not stay there long. The army travelled on through to Holland, which he described to Mari as a 'land of clogs and windmills.' The enemy had scarred this land out of all recognition, but the British Army received a very warm welcome. Thomas wrote to Mari:

Annwyl Mari
'I am billeted with a family who are extremely kind to me and treat me as one of their own. We have been here for three months now and I will be sad to leave these nice people who have looked after me so well.

Cariad gorau
Thomas

By the time the letters reached Mari, some of the sentences had been heavily censored but most people at home knew that the troops would soon be pushing into Germany. Once there, Thomas saw that no one smiled. The cities had been very badly bombed, but by contrast, the countryside was strikingly beautiful, consisting mainly of agricultural land and forestry. Whilst on watch one night in a deep dark forest, he felt the hairs sticking up on the back of his neck, at a noise he had heard. He shouted, 'Who goes there?' as he cocked his rifle, the sound scaring away a small nocturnal creature, which was scuttling about in the undergrowth. The incident really frightened him. He felt a cold sweat trickle slowly down his spine between his shoulder blades and his legs felt weak and trembly. He admitted later to Mari that he had been extremely frightened during that long cold night.

* * *

The day Thomas and millions of others had been longing for finally arrived – the day victory was declared. The Germans had finally surrendered to the Allies. There were great celebrations and huge relief. The troops slowly began their return home. As Thomas travelled homewards, he wrote a poem which he put in his letter to Mari, knowing it would get there well before he did:

It's worth being exiled now and then
And to travel to distant shore,
In order to come back again
And to love Wales all the more.

After the war, they lived with Thomas' parents, while converting the old stables into a small unit for themselves. Having finished the conversion, they moved in, then fell into a daily routine. Soon it felt as if the war had never happened at all. One evening, while they were painting one of their rooms, Thomas idly asked her, 'What was it you actually did during the war?' 'That's all finished with now', she replied sharply, 'I don't want to talk about it again,' effectively drawing a curtain on all that had gone before. Thomas supposed people deal with things in different ways, so gave up trying to have any conversation with her about it. In fact, it was becoming increasingly difficult to communicate with her. If Mari didn't want to talk about anything personal, she shut down the conversation. Thomas, being so open about his experiences, could not understand her reticence, but it hadn't occurred to him that she may still have been subject to the Official Secrets Act.

He ruefully thought about how he'd turned down an offer from one of his battalion friends to join him in setting up a business when they were demobbed because Mari was not enthusiastic. She thought it risky to trust business partners, so he had not pursued it. Thomas also suggested they had a fresh start by taking advantage the '£10 Pommie' emigration scheme to Australia, keen to welcome skilled people. But Mari's mother, who was matriarchal, had persuaded her it was not a good idea.

To his friends, Thomas seemed to be getting increasingly frustrated that his plans were being thwarted at every turn. His outgoing and adventurous spirit became withdrawn and he began to spend more time in his workshop alone in the evenings, finding things to do, rather than go in the house. The more they got to know each other, the less they seemed to have in common. Apart from their love of their language and country, they seemed incompatible. He hadn't realised initially quite how so highly-strung she was, whilst he was fairly relaxed. He was more mechanically and practically minded while she liked books. Her mother had told him Mari had passed her matric with top marks. She undertook a shorthand typing course at which she excelled, resulting in her getting a job with a local solicitor. Thomas didn't know any of this when he had proposed to her and if he had, he would have realised that he was out of his depth intellectually. This is not to say that this form of imbalance never works but it was clearly not working for them. On top of this, he felt that maybe something had happened to her in the past, which had made her wary of people and close relationships.

Although she said she would like to have children, she was what he could only describe as edgy with him and he longed for the physical fun he had had with Marian. 'Where was she now?' he thought longingly.

Alone in his workshop, Thomas brooded a great deal about what he should do about the situation. He felt both frustrated and useless. During the war, he had really come into his own. Now he felt a sense of drift. He had been involved in a major world event, the likes of which had never been seen before and although he was glad to be out of it, there was still a feeling of a restless flatness. He missed the camaraderie of his company comrades, who had all gone their separate ways, mostly back to their former lives. He needed to do something with his life. He spoke sternly to himself, 'You should be glad that you came out of it un-maimed and with your life, unlike many thousands of others who never made it or who are now forever physically or mentally crippled.'

But even this self-talk failed to lift his mood. He found himself snapping at everybody, which was not like him. He desperately needed something to focus on. He thought more and more back to happier days in his childhood, when he said he would have his own car mechanical business, declaring confidently then to Bob that 'this is what I am going to do.' He thought, 'Maybe this is what I should do.' It was not just the wealthy who were buying cars now and he felt that there would be a demand if he was to provide a service.

One morning he was having breakfast with his mother and Mari. The large dresser provided the domestic backdrop, as he announced, 'I'm going to start my own business. I want to use the big shed nearest the road as my garage. I'll extend it a bit and dig a pit, so that I can examine and work on cars underneath. I'm going to teach you to drive, Mari,' he said turning to her, 'so that we can run a taxi business as well.' Thomas' father had bought him a small Austin car as a present on his safe return home. Mari and his mother just turned and stared at him open-mouthed, initially lost for words. 'Where did this come from?' Mari asked. 'I got the idea from my friends bringing their cars to me to be fixed. Well, I thought, I may as well get paid for this. I just want to do something, are you with me or not?'

'Yes, of course,' replied Mari, I will set up the book-keeping side of things, while you can do the practical work. I quite like the idea of learning to drive as well,' as a slow smile spread across her face. Thomas thought it was worth it just to see this reaction and he thought, if we work well together, it might yet bring us closer. Enthusiastically, Thomas' mother added, 'And I will look after the farm, so you two can concentrate on getting the business going.'

Enthused, Thomas spread the word locally, then set about extending his garage and building an inspection pit. Mari told him, 'I bought accounts books and have ordered invoices and headed paper. We need to work out how long each job takes and how much you will charge per hour, then draw up a price list of how much to charge customers for jobs.' Thomas said to Mari, 'We should also sell petrol and paraffin – but pumps cost a lot of money.' Mari suggested, 'A petrol company might fit one for you, as long as we agree to sell their petrol.'

This is when she came into her own, thought Thomas and he was glad that she was on board with him. Even before the business name was put up on the front of the garage door, word had spread and people had already started calling at the new garage, asking for Thomas to fix this or that.

The pair worked every hour God sent and were soon running a very successful business. They worked well as business partners and this kept the lid on his disquiet about other aspects of their relationship. They subsidised their livelihood with products from the smallholding, such as milk, butter, eggs and vegetables. They bred litters of pigs, reared turkeys for Christmas and kept a few sheep and cows. Thomas' mother ran this side of things, as she always had, while his father did odd jobs as a stonemason. Thomas often thought about how he loved his home, the little farm, surrounded by mountains at the back and looking out to the sea at the front. This place held all the good memories of when he was a small boy and he was happy now that his business was doing well.

One day, as he worked outside on a car, Happy Charlie came

walking along the road. 'Good day to you,' he said as he came over to Thomas for a chat. Happy Charlie was a very popular local figure, a gentleman tramp. He had a 'far-back' accent, a bushy moustache, wore a flat cap and in winter, a large brown coat. Gardening twine held up his corduroy trousers. He did odd gardening jobs for people and was reputed to live in the old quarry. Some say he came from a very wealthy, important family – but was unable to cope with everyday life. He was said to be very clever but that he had been shellshocked during the war. 'They keeping you busy, Charlie?' asked Thomas. 'Yes, plenty of work around here, when I want it.' Thomas knew that people also fed him when he worked for them and gave him milk, eggs, blankets and old clothes. 'How's business? he asked Thomas. 'Keeps me out of mischief,' he said smiling. He liked old Charlie, who always had a good word to say for everybody. As he watched him carry on down the road, Thomas thought about how he had been messed up by the war. Then Thomas realised that, in a way, the war had also messed up his own life. He had everything he could want, except a warm loving marital relationship with his wife. Again, he felt guilty as his thoughts drifted towards Marian and what his life might have been had he not had his 'seize the moment' idea while travelling home on that fateful day.

Five years after the war ended, Thomas' mother became very ill with the asthma which had plagued her all her life. Luckily, through the new National Health Service, she was treated for free, not as in years gone by when they had had to beggar themselves to pay for medicines and doctor's fees. On a cold, damp, winter's day, Thomas sat on a chair, next to her bed. Despite the comforting fire in the bedroom, his mood was one of despair. It was a pretty little fireplace with Victorian tiles surrounding it and the floral wallpaper was as familiar to him as the back of his hand. While he listened to her laboured breathing as she struggled to take in air, Thomas said, 'Mam, I need you,' holding desperately onto her hand as if he could keep her there with him. He desperately wished for her to live, as she had done for him when he had nearly died of rheumatic fever all those years ago. He could not imagine his life without her. She had always been there; his lodestar. He needed her affirmation. But despite all his pleading and the medical treatment she had received, it was evident that she was fading away and drew her last breath in the small hours of the night. Thomas felt his mother's loss and love keenly, leaving a huge gap in his life. His father soon seemed to lose the will to live and his health began to deteriorate. 'There's nothing else for it, we'll have to move in next door, he can't look after himself.' Mari responded by saying, 'So you now expect me to look after your father as well as clean the house, run the farm, do the washing and run a business?' This harshness, so soon after his mother death, drove yet another nail into the coffin of their relationship.

Things were fraught between them. Mari felt resentful about having to see to his father and frequently complained to both of them. It was fortunate that his father was becoming deaf, so he did not have to listen to the comments she made under her breath. He thought that Mari now also regretted the hasty decision to marry, as she could have had an easier life had she married a professional person. But couples stayed together, for better or for worse. Divorce was not an option, neither could they afford it; it would certainly be frowned upon by the chapel people. They just had to get on with it. The old adage of 'marry in haste, repent at leisure' often came to his mind. During the war he'd had a 'seize the day' attitude but now it was 'rue the day'. He desperately wished he had not rushed things – there had been no real need. He wished he had done a lot of things differently and taken up the opportunities he'd been offered, as he would not now be stuck in this unhappy situation. Her angry parting shot as he walked away was, 'What if you are out on a call and somebody wants petrol and I am stuck here helping your father?'

* * *

Ten years after the war ended, Thomas and Mari were still childless. Thomas comforted himself with the thought that it was ten years before he was born to his mam and dad. He thought if they didn't have a child, it couldn't be helped, what would be, would be. The business continued to tick-over and he was always in demand to fix the cars he knew inside and out. He was in the middle of yet another argument with Mari about who should feed his father, when suddenly the outside telephone bell on the garage rang. Thomas went to answer it and picking up the receiver said, 'Hello, Garage,' – there being no 'how can I help you?' then.

'I've broken down,' said the caller. 'I'm outside a small farm called Pont Werglodd, I think that's how you say it, in the next valley. Can you come out?' Thomas took the details and thought idly, that's by Uncle Bob's farm. I quite fancy a ride out to there, get away from her for a bit. I might pop in to see him and Ellen. 'I'm on my way, I'll be about fifteen minutes.'

He called out to Mari, 'I'm going to a breakdown, shouldn't be long.' Mari rolled her eyes, thinking about how she had been left alone to run everything again.

Thomas drove through the little village then up the steep pass, dropped down then turned right towards Llechwedd. As he drove along the narrow country lanes, he felt good to be back in the familiar area, where nothing much seemed to have changed at all. Except everything was about to change.

The sun was shining. Golden pollen-laden catkins were dangling down from their branches in the hedges of the fields. Wild spring daffodils were growing abundantly on the grass verges and whole grassy banks were covered in delicate yellow primroses. Celandines and daisies provided a colourful mix in the newly growing grass, while birds flitted between hedges and trees, carrying little twigs, sheep's wool and straw, to build their nests. He soon located the broken-down car on the single-track road. 'Hello, there,' Thomas called. 'What happened? Did it just stop, or was it gradual?'

'Just came to a dead stop.' Pointing to a gate down the road, he said, 'A man from that farm came out to have a look, then said I probably needed a mechanic. He told me where there was a phone box and recommended that I called you. This place is miles away from anywhere,' as he looked around, wondering how he was ever going to get back to civilisation and a main road again. Thomas lifted the bonnet and after checking a few things, soon had the car working.

'There you go, good as new,' as he closed the hinged bonnet and clipped the rubber bungs back onto their hooks. As well as the call-out charge, the man gave him a hefty tip. He must have plenty of money, thought Thomas, nevertheless grateful. As the man drove away, having been pointed in the right direction, a voice from behind called, '*Thomas bach, sut wyti?*' He turned and saw his old uncle leaning on the farmgate by the entrance to his farm. He had been waiting for Thomas to finish fixing the breakdown, then beckoned him to come to the farmhouse.

Thomas parked his car nearer. 'Long time, no see,' he said as he walked up to his uncle. 'How are you all?' Sadly, he noticed how much his uncle had aged since he had last seen him.

'Not too bad, considering we are getting older, just a bit of rheumatism now and then,' his gnarled old hand which gripped the walking stick, giving testimony to that.

'How's Ellen?' asked Thomas.

'She's out in the fields somewhere, gone to look for mushrooms, she'll be back soon.' As Thomas entered the kitchen, he saw a young lad there. He knew they had a lad living there and assumed that he was an evacuee who had stayed on because his family had been killed in the war.

'Go out now, see if the hens have laid' his uncle told the boy, 'I want to talk to Thomas.' His uncle then looked at him directly from under his bushy eyebrows. 'I'm glad you came today,' he said seriously. 'I have something to tell you I should have told you a long time ago. It's been on my mind a lot lately.'

'Sounds serious, what is it?'

'Well,' said his uncle, 'Do you remember Marian? You were sweet on her once.'

'Yes, of course, but the war got in the way and we lost touch. You told mam that she had moved away from here.'

'She did lad,' said Uncle Bob, 'but she left us a little parcel before she went — a *plentyn siawns*.'

'What do you mean,' said Thomas perplexed, wondering why he was talking about parcels and illegitimate children.

'Well,' he began again, 'About nine months after you got called up, we had a knock on the door one morning. We opened it and Marian was standing there, with a bundle in her arms. 'Here,' she said thrusting the bundle at me, 'You have him, he's your nephew's after all. With that, she turned on her heels and walked away from the farmhouse and straight down the road, without a backward glance. We have never set eyes on her since. We just stood there flabbergasted. We looked down at the bundle and saw the poor little mite, then the penny dropped that she had given birth to your son. The baby she thrust upon us was yours.'

Thomas was dumbfounded. He grabbed the side of an old settee to steady himself. What could he say? He shook his head from side to side, unable to believe what he had just been told. His uncle started talking again, 'Later, I went to her house, but her mother said she had gone to London to take up a position as a parlour maid. She said she already had too many mouths to feed and didn't need another one. She had told Marian the same thing, who apparently just took it into her head to dump him on us.'

What his Uncle was saying was devastating but at the same time weirdly pleasing. But with the shock of it, he felt the blood drain from his face and his hands started visibly shaking. What on earth was he going to do? His uncle got up and busied himself with making Thomas some sweet tea from the kettle on the hob.

He continued, 'Once we got used to the idea, we just got on with rearing him. He's a nice lad, looks just like you did at that age. I talked to your mother about it and she didn't know what to do about it all either. You had gone away to fight for your country by then and so she couldn't ask you what should be done with him. So, we all agreed that we would raise the boy here; we didn't tell anybody who his father was or anything, and people just seemed to accept him. People thought he was an evacuee who never went back home. To be honest, he's been a big help these last few years as we've got older and then when your auntie died.' He wiped a sudden tear from his rheumy eye at the thought of this. 'Ellen took a while to get used to him, muttering darkly about being conceived 'out of wedlock' and all that stuff but he soon melted her heart and she's alright about him now. He can carry on staying here and as he gets older, he'll be able to help her to run the farm when I've popped my clogs. I can't see Ellen ever marrying.'

'Well I hope that's not for a long time. I don't care about what Marian went through but how could she be so heartless as to just abandon him like that? If only she'd just told me, my life might have gone in an entirely different direction. How am I going to tell Mari that I have a son?'

Bob shrugged his shoulders, then added, 'He hasn't really asked much about where he came from, he's been told that his mother had to go away to work. She doesn't write or send any money home, even to her mother. Probably forgotten all about him by now. I think she wanted her own life and didn't want to be saddled with a baby. She would have had a tough time if she'd stayed around here, – an unmarried mother would have been quite a scandal in this small rural area. He didn't even have a name when he came to us, so we decided on Owen.'

What was he going to say to Mari about him? She would blame herself now for her childlessness. How will she cope with knowing that? It will break her heart and might just tip her over the edge, as he had come to realise that she 'lived on her nerves' and was prone to frequent mood swings.

'What shall I do, Uncle? I had no idea. Why didn't Marian write to tell me?'

'I suppose she just brought him here on the spur of the moment, because her own mother wouldn't look after him,' his uncle replied. Sadly, shaking his snowy white head, he continued, 'Well, why don't we just let things be for now? The lad's happy enough here, it's all he's known. At least you know about him now, so I've got that off my conscience; I wouldn't like to go to my Maker not having told you. I won't tell him you are his dad, I'll leave that to you, when you think the time is right. He's doing well at school, his last report said he is very good at sums. He likes tinkering with things, seeing how they work, just like you did when you were a boy.'

As Thomas came out of the front door to leave, he paused and took a long look at the lad, who was kicking a ball about in the yard. 'He does look a bit like I did,' he thought. 'Poor lad didn't ask to be born. I suppose if mam had told me about him, I may never have married Mari, but I still might not have been able to find Marian. Maybe she wanted a new life and did not want to be found. What a mess! Funny how life throws up these strange twists and turns when you least expect them.'

To give himself time to think and in no rush to get home, he pulled into a quiet layby. He took out his pack of untipped Capstan cigarettes, pulled one out and absentmindedly tapped one end on the pack, to compact the tobacco. He lit it with his petrol lighter, drawing deeply on the first pull. As he slowly exhaled, his head was so full of this new information that he took no notice of the wonderful panorama which stretched out below him. The sandy, tidal estuary of the large Afon Conwy below was almost empty with the tide out, but little channels of run-off water joined the main body of water that continued to trundle its snakelike way out to sea. Over on the opposite riverbank stood white-washed cottages and a large prosperous looking farm with a forested area to one side. The mid-morning sun was now burning the mist off the river, and wispy spirals escaped upwards from between the pine trees, creating an ethereal other-worldly atmosphere below him – but all this beauty was wasted on Thomas; his mind was elsewhere. He sat there wondering what having a son would mean for him once Mari knew, as there was no way he could keep this from her forever. His father was in very poor health now and had recently told Thomas that he was leaving the farm to him in his will as expected and that there were some savings as well. His parents had both obviously known about the lad, so why hadn't they told me, Thomas wondered; after all Owen was their grandson? There was no point confronting his father now given his fragile state, what good would it do?

But Mari was a different matter. What would she do once she knew about Owen? Would she leave him? He certainly couldn't run the business without her. It was not as if he had been unfaithful to her but she would blame herself for their childlessness. He wound down the car window and flicked out the cigarette end. Despairingly, he ran both hands through his hair and thought again, 'What a mess!' Why didn't his mother tell him before he married Mari? Or even when she was dying? There seemed to have been a conspiracy to keep the information from him while he was away in the war, which was not difficult. They obviously did not want Mari's parents to find out about Owen, so had kept it to themselves to enable the wedding to go ahead.

Despite the dilemma, part of him was inordinately pleased he had a son. A secret smile spread across his face and he felt a flutter of excitement on being a father. It gave him a feeling of continuity, otherwise, what was his purpose in life? Maybe he should take his uncle's advice and let things lie for now. Maybe when Owen was older, he could take him on as a trainee mechanic, if he was that way inclined. Bob had said he liked mechanical things. Would Mari guess he was his son? There was a resemblance. But procrastination won the day. He knew he didn't have to decide now, he had a while yet to think it through. With that indecisive thought, he got out to crank up the engine of the little A7 car and set off for home.

Life went on. The business continued to thrive. Then a few years later, Thomas said to Mari with his heart is his mouth, 'I think we should consider taking on an apprentice, to help me with the workload. There're more jobs coming in than I can cope with now, as more and more people are buying cars. What do you think?'

'How much would you have to pay him?'

'Not much while he was learning, I suppose.'

'It takes about four to five years to do an apprenticeship,' Mari said. 'I suppose we should think about it if we don't want to start turning work away.'

Amazingly, that was all it took. A simple conversation to open up the possibility of finally getting Owen here under his wing.

Thomas wasn't very comfortable about deceiving her, but he felt he also had to do right by his son.

Next weekend, Thomas went over to his uncle's farm. Uncle Bob was now quite unwell and bedridden, and his daughter, Ellen, was caring for him. Ellen, who was unlikely to marry, would inherit his farm. She was after all quite capable of running it. But how would she manage, Thomas thought, if Owen wasn't there? On the other hand, she might soon have to pay him a wage and she may not be able to afford to keep him on. Owen would then have to start searching for work elsewhere and Thomas realised he might lose track of him. Owen had just had his fifteenth birthday and was turning into a handsome, mature and self-reliant young man. He was certainly no longer a child. Thomas was shocked that he now looked even more like him and wondered if it was such a good idea to take him on; surely Mari would see right through it. 'Well' said his uncle, his watery blue eyes full of sympathy, 'If she asks, you will just have to tell her the whole story then wait for the fall-out. If he doesn't go to work for you, I feel he will soon want to spread his wings and go from here anyway. Not much of a life here, is it, for a young lad living with an old man and a spinster? Ellen will inherit the farm, so he might decide that he has nothing to stay here for.' But then, Thomas thought, if he told Owen that he was his father, how could he expect him to keep quiet about it once he was working for him? Procrastinating yet again, he decided he would not tell him just yet. Better to wait until he was a bit older and more mature to deal with it maybe. But what if later, he became angry with him for not telling him sooner?

They called for Owen to join them in the farmhouse. 'Thomas here's got something to ask you lad.' Owen seemed surprised to be summoned and wondered what on earth could they want with him. He stood there in front of the older men, looking so undeniably like one of them, it was frightening. Pulling himself together, Thomas started, 'Uncle tells me you're good at fixing things and that you like mechanics.'

The boy nodded enthusiastically. 'Yes, I do.'

Thomas continued, 'I was wondering if you would like to do a mechanic's apprenticeship with me in my garage.' He swallowed deeply and held his breath for Owen's reply.

He was getting to quite like the lad, he wasn't cocky and full of himself like some young men are, the ones who wouldn't be told anything. He seemed to be quietly considering the offer, whilst both older men waited with bated breath for his reply. Turning to Bob, he said, 'Would that mean I would have to leave here? It's the only place I've known and how will you manage without me? I know I'm not proper family, but you have brought me up from a baby. You have always treated me with love and kindness, as if I was your own son and have given me a good life.' He paused. 'But I suppose nothing stays the same forever and I should now start to think about what I want to do with my life.' Thomas, let out his breath then looked at his uncle and saw that he had become tearful. Turning to Thomas, 'I do like working with mechanical things, don't know where I get that from, but I would really like the chance to become a proper qualified mechanic and earn my own way. So yes, I would like to take you up on your offer. Where would I live though?' Thomas hadn't really thought that far.

'You can live in the small cottage next to the garage, which we converted after the war. You can't be walking every day from here, for sure.' So that was it. It was settled. Just like that.

'I will come and pick you up next Saturday, then show you the ropes. You'll have to work hard mind you; we can't carry any passengers – except in the taxi of course,' Thomas said jokingly. 'I'll have to teach you to drive as well.' Owen smiled, pleased with this prospect.

'Don't worry,' said uncle, 'if Owen can drive my old tractor, he can drive anything.' Turning to Owen, he said with a catch in his voice, 'And don't you worry about me and Ellen lad, we'll be fine. We hope you will come and see us sometimes though,' he said emotionally, at the thought of never seeing Owen again. But it was high time for the boy to spread his wings; he had done his best by him. His work was now done.

And that's just how it happened. When he introduced him to Mari, she did a double-take and said, 'There's something of a look of you about him, are you sure you're not related?' She knew that Owen had lived with Thomas' uncle so assumed that was the family resemblance. Thomas did not respond but bustled Owen out of the house saying, 'Come on, I'll show you the workshop,' hoping she wouldn't dwell on that thought. She did not mention the likeness again, but Thomas was never sure if she was suspicious or not, as she was so very good at hiding what she thought and felt. Maybe she thought that if she pushed it, she would not like the answer. So, sleeping dogs were left to lie.

The young man quietly integrated into the work and family life of Thomas and Mari and proved to be a great asset. All the customers liked him. Thomas could see that he had the right attitude to run his own business one day. That thought then hit him like a 'bolt out of the blue.' The fact that they still didn't have any children got him thinking of his own mortality. Who is going to run it when I get too old or if I get ill? If Mari had to run it and hire another mechanic, there would be little profit left over to live on. He had no idea then how insightful and prophetic that this train of thought would turn out to be.

Thomas never discussed Owen with his father. He was old now and would fret if Thomas was to start remonstrating with him about keeping Owen's existence secret. Thomas suspected that his father soon realised that Owen was his grandson but never let on, nor did he tell Mari. This particular skeleton was hidden very deeply at the back of the closet.

* * *

A few months later, a local solicitor walked up to Thomas' garage to pick up his car, which had been serviced. His appearance was that of a typical country gent with his plus fours, mustard yellow waistcoat, Harris Tweed jacket and stout brown brogue walking shoes. 'Nice little business you've got here. Doing well?' Thomas nodded, thinking that it was none of his business.

'Do you rent or own it? Is the farmhouse, the adjoining cottage and the land surrounding it yours?' Thomas confirmed he had inherited it all from his father, who had died recently.

'Are you going to carry on, or sell it when you get older? You don't have any children, do you?' Thomas was somewhat taken aback by his bluntness and considered him a bit forward.

'I don't know, haven't really thought a lot about it.'

'Well you should,' said the solicitor, in his public-school accent. 'Damned complicated for those you leave behind if you don't make a will, especially if the estate goes to probate. It could also be subject to Estate Duty. Your wife might have to sell up to pay it. Best to get it sorted now, believe me, then you'll have peace of mind.'

'Come and see me in my office tomorrow morning at ten o'clock, we'll discuss it then,' he called from the open car window as he drove away.

Thomas' mind was in turmoil. Maybe the man's right. I should get my affairs in order, remembering just how precarious and unpredictable one's life could be during his time in the war.

Next morning, Thomas set off for the solicitor's office, telling Owen he was just going down to the town to fetch something and wouldn't be long. Thomas thought that it would be a good opportunity to share his burden, get some advice – as he was at a loss about what he should do.

'This conversation is confidential, right?' Thomas started, setting the tone.

'Of course,' assured the solicitor, 'do you have something you want to confide?

'Well, it's like this see,' said Thomas, squirming a bit on the hard office chair. 'Before war broke out, I was courting a local girl, who unbeknown to me, had a baby by me. She literally dumped him on my uncle and cousin, who raised him very well. I only found out about him a while ago but have recently brought him into the business, as an apprentice.'

'I see,' said the solicitor, intrigued. 'This is not as straightforward as I had first imagined. I take it your wife doesn't know about your connection to this young man?'

'No, neither does he. But she may have her suspicions. As you may have noticed, he looks a lot like me. I suspect she considers it 'a can of worms' which she'd rather not open. She's not easy to talk to, prefers to leave difficult things be, rather than deal with them.' Thomas had noticed recently that this trait of hers had been getting much worse. 'You see, by blanking them out, problems did not exist. Or maybe she knows but is in denial.'

The solicitor looked at his hands, fingertips together forming a pyramid shape, pondering this information. 'There are two possibilities,' he said gravely. 'One, you tell her now and deal with the consequences, whatever form they take, or two, you say nothing and make out your will to him and let the consequences take care of themselves when you are no longer around. Which is it to be? I assume you want your son to inherit your business. You have a few options. You could leave your wife the farm, or entail the farmhouse, cottage and land to your son and let your wife live in the farmhouse for the duration of her natural life. A form of trust can be established by deed of settlement, which would restrict your wife selling the property, which would then be passed onto your son on her death.'

Thomas, always fair minded, moved uncomfortably in the chair and said, 'It would seem a bit mean to just hand the business to Owen. Mari helped me build it up from scratch after the war; it wouldn't be there but for her keeping the accounts in order.'

'Well, you could entail the farm to Owen, allowing your wife to stay for the duration of her natural life as we discussed, and leave the business between the two of them. That way, she would have a steady income and somewhere to live and he would have a bookkeeper.'

Thomas pondered these options, while the passing silence was broken only by the loud oppressive tick of the large clock on the wall, pressing him to decide. Realising this decision would affect the two most important people in his life, he took the cowardly way out, saying 'I don't think I could face the fall-out, which could mean that she would leave me, and it might just tip her over the edge, as I think her nerves are fragile. Let sleeping dogs lie, I say.'

So, the solicitor drew up the necessary documents and a week later, Thomas went in to have his signature witnessed on the will. He felt satisfied now that he had legally settled the matter, as it could have been an almighty mess otherwise. On his way down the steps from of the solicitor's office, he bumped into a former member of his old company. Companionably, they lit up cigarettes and chatted for a while, then his mate said to him, 'Have you heard about Edwin, the one who wanted you to go into business with him after the war?' 'No,' said Thomas, 'Is he alright?' 'He's more than alright mate, the business he started is now worth millions. He always had his head screwed on right, did that one.'

Another opportunity missed, Thomas thought ruefully. Best not to dwell though. He bid his friend farewell and went on his way, back to his garage. He comforted himself that he might not have enjoyed the world of big business anyway. The bigger the business, the bigger the problems and the small problems he already had were more than enough for him. The old adage came to mind again as he walked to his car, 'marry in haste, repent at leisure.' He often thought about this; it rang so true for him and he berated himself once again for being so impulsive in asking Mari to marry him on that fateful day on the train.

Owen was a very quick learner. He soaked up information and knew everything about all the new cars manufactured: their cc, their acceleration and top speed, as well as type of engine. He and Thomas had many good conversations about cars and the days passed by companionably, doing services, selling petrol and running taxis. Thomas was feeling happier than he had for a while. A real bond had developed between them as they worked, but he instinctively pulled back from this matey camaraderie when they were in Mari's company.

The years passed by and the business continued to thrive. Thomas was now in his forties. Owen had finished his apprenticeship and was now treated more like a partner in the business. One day, they were both working together on the local GP's car when Thomas complained to Owen, 'I've got such a bad headache – I can hardly see properly. You carry on, I'll go and get some aspirin.'

But it didn't get better, it got worse. Mari sent him to bed, as he was unable to stand up or walk properly, without bumping into things. 'If you're no better in the morning, I'll call the doctor.' As it happened, the doctor had decided to walk up to fetch his car, which he had been told would be ready. When Mari saw him approach the garage, she said, 'Thomas seems to be really poorly. He can't seem to keep his balance and has a very bad headache.'

'Probably a bit of 'flu, there's a lot of it about' said the doctor. 'Give him plenty of fluids and keep him warm in bed.' Mari thought it was a bit more than that but deferred to the GP's superior knowledge, as she did not want to be seen as over-reacting.

Next morning, he was no better and she worried during the day. By the following day, she thought this is very serious. His right eye was a bit crossed and his left arm seemed to hang limply by his side. She called the surgery and was told that the doctor on duty would call in on his house calls round. At about eleven o'clock, the now very elderly doctor who had treated Thomas years ago for rheumatic fever, walked into the house and went straight up the stairs to where Thomas lay. He checked his heart, declaring that it seemed very weak, which could be as a result of his childhood illness, or another inherited weakness. He also thought that Thomas may be bleeding from the brain – but the presenting symptoms would need a specialist to diagnose them. He immediately called for an ambulance and Thomas was rushed off to the nearest hospital's Casualty Department and later transferred from there to a neurological hospital further away.

He had suffered a brain haemorrhage and a stroke had paralysed him down his right side. Had he been taken into the hospital when he first became ill, the specialist said, it may have been possible to do something – but it had been left too long. Thomas would no longer be able to work. He did not have any control over his right arm and could only just walk with the aid of a walking stick, so Mari now had to care for another invalid, having already looked after his father. She wondered how the business could carry on but between her and Owen, it did seem to tick slowly along. They were unable to take on the volume of work they had done and some of their regular customers began to go elsewhere.

Sadly, a few years later, Thomas began to feel ill once more. He had been thinking a great deal about his own mortality recently and decided he must let the lad know the truth before it was too late.

One chilly spring morning, he waited for Mari to set off for the village shop, then shuffled his way towards the garage, where Owen was working on a car. As he entered, he called Owen's name. 'I want to tell you something I should have told you years ago, please don't be angry with me.'

'What is it?' said Owen, immediately alarmed.

'You are my son, Owen.'

Owen took a step back, shaking his head in disbelief and denial. 'You're lying, if you were my father you would have told me years ago.'

'Please just listen to me, I need to explain things and I don't feel too well.' Owen stood staring stonily at him. 'I was courting your mother, Marian, just before war broke out. I was called up suddenly and we lost touch, she never wrote to me, she took herself off to London. Before she did, she took you as a new babe in arms to my uncle and told him and his wife to bring you up. I didn't even know about you myself until years later and by then I was married to Mari and was afraid to tell her. We were still childless; I knew she would blame herself and I didn't know what she would do.' He stopped for breath, as all the talking and standing was literally draining the life out of him.

'I really wanted to tell you – but I was too afraid. Then, when I heard you were good at fixing things, I thought up this plan. The business needed to expand and in order to get you here, I offered you the apprenticeship.' He paused again for breath then continued, 'It was a great day for me when you started here. I am very proud of how you have turned out. You are a real credit to me. It was good to have you here, close to me all these years. You have brought me more joy than I ever believed possible. You are the one good thing in my life and I love you dearly,' he said, looking directly into Owen's eyes. 'I don't think I have much time left in me now. I want you to know I am leaving you – in more ways than one', he quipped ironically, 'the cottage, the farmhouse, the land and a half-share in the business. But Mari must be able to live in the house, for as long as she wants. You and Mari will have to work it out between you about how you run the business. But I want to warn you, she may never forgive me and probably won't take it well. She could take it out on you.'

Thomas was by now absolutely drained. His face had gone a deadly white and his lips had taken on a blue tinge. He reached out his other arm to hold onto the workbench and was slowly collapsing in a heap onto the floor as his legs gave way, when Owen reached out and managed to catch him. As he held him around his shoulders, Mari walked into the garage. Owen shouted to her, 'Call 999 – quick – he's collapsed!'

Thomas was suffering a massive heart attack. His heart, already weak from his childhood illness, finally gave up and he passed away that evening, having never regained consciousness. It was difficult to tell if Mari was upset or not. She went through the motions of arranging the funeral, which was very well attended, as Thomas had been a popular local person. Bob was too unwell to attend but Ellen was there, and Owen was glad of her support. He looked down as the coffin was lowered into the cold ground, tears rolling down his frozen cheeks and he wished his father had told him years ago. As he stared at some hardy snowdrops which had stalwartly pushed their way bravely up through a recent covering of snow and were now trembling in the cold east wind, Owen wished he had known his father for all of his life. But the bond they had formed while being together would have to suffice as his only memories; he knew that they could have been very close, had circumstances allowed it.

During the few days Mari had shut the garage following Thomas' death and funeral, she attended an appointment which had been sent to her by the solicitor's office, to hear Thomas' will read out. As she entered, she saw Owen already sitting there, and said, 'What are you doing here?'

As she sat down, she glared at him and then said to the solicitor, 'I didn't know he'd even written a will. When was this, why hadn't he told me?' The solicitor, realising the extreme delicacy of the situation said, 'Please sit down. I have something to tell you.'

When he told Mari that Owen was Thomas' son, she was angrier than she had ever been in her life. The paranoia which had been growing inside her was finally confirmed. 'Bringing that cuckoo into my nest,' she spat, 'that was really sly. He can damn-well clear out before I get back,' she said, now glaring at Owen. She thought the pair of them had probably been laughing behind her back the whole time.

'Owen has only just found out himself,' said the solicitor. 'Thomas never found the courage to tell you or him until very recently. In fact, it was on the day, moments before he actually collapsed and suffered his fatal heart attack, that he told him. But you can't throw him out I'm afraid; the property is entailed to him. You can live there for the rest of your natural life though, and half the business is yours, so you will have an income. You are going to have to learn to get along with him or walk away from it all,' said the solicitor.

'This is intolerable,' Mari said, as she stood up, knocking over her chair and stormed out of the office, slamming the front door so hard that the stained-glass panes rattled. The real reason for her anger was the fact that Thomas had had a son, which now clearly proved she was the reason they had been childless. She could not believe that Thomas had deceived her all these years. The gossips would have a field day now. She found it all extremely hard to accept and the shock was slowly tipping her over the edge, as Thomas had always feared it might.

Owen just sat there. Mari's venomous comments had made him wince and had felt like physical blows to his body. Now she had left, the solicitor said, solemnly, 'You are now the owner of a house, a cottage, ten acres of land and the half owner of a small business. You are basically set-up for life. I'm not sure what she will do now but she can't throw you out.'

Owen walked slowly back to the garage in a sort of daze. He was aware that a huge responsibility had been placed on his shoulders. He had to keep the business as a going concern but Mari's response at the solicitor's office did not augur well. He was right to be concerned; Mari had gone straight to another solicitor's office to seek legal advice on how to oust the imposter. Whereas before, she hadn't taken much notice of him, she now focused all her pent-up anger and hate towards him.

Mari saw Owen as the person who had stolen her life's work and her home. She would never work with, nor could she bear to be anywhere near him. When she told her solicitor this, he said, 'It appears your late husband wanted the situation to carry on as before, with you and Owen working together. However, if you can't see your way to doing that, the only way for you out of this situation is to sell your half of the business to him.'

'How can he buy the business? He has no money. He came with nothing and can leave with nothing.' The solicitor looked at her gravely. 'You are going to have to accept the situation sooner or later. I can write to Owen suggesting he buys you out but it's very difficult to set a price on it. It will be what you are willing to accept in the end. You know the business, what do you think would be a fair price – what sum would you be prepared to accept?' Impulsively, she plucked the figure of £1,000 off the top of her head, knowing that he would never be able to pay her.

'Very well, I will write to Owen with your offer. But where will you live if you won't live there? You are entitled to stay at the farmhouse for as long as you want to, it is your home. But Mari was too proud to even contemplate this, given the loss of her status as its owner. To save face, she said, 'I have decided to move into my elderly mother's house to take care of her. You can write to me there' – and with that she stomped out of his office.

The next day, Owen received the letter from her solicitor, with the offer for him to buy her out of the business. 'How on earth am I going to do that?' he said out loud to nobody in particular.

He thought hard about it during the day, as he worked on the cars. He decided he would telephone Thomas' solicitor to ask for advice; there was no one else he could turn to. He wasn't even sure if £1,000 was a reasonable price or not, it seemed a bit high to him. But then he thought, she has lost everything else and the money would give her some security. He closed the garage just before one o'clock, sat at the knee-hole desk in the office, picked up the black Bakelite receiver, then dialled the solicitor's number. He was put through and told, 'I was just off for my lunch, can't it wait?' Very quickly, Owen told him about the letter and asked his advice. 'Let me think about it, I'll be in touch,' he ended brusquely, not wanting to be late for his afternoon game of golf.

Owen attempted to work on the bookkeeping in the evenings after closing. He thought he could do it for a while but would eventually need to get a bookkeeper. Again he wondered about how he could buy Mari out. She hadn't been near the place since the reading of the will. He decided, as tomorrow was Sunday, he would go to visit Ellen to talk about it. At Thomas' funeral, she had invited him for dinner the following Sunday. He needed a break from the place for a few hours and taking Thomas' car, which he realised was now his, he set off. On arrival, it was comforting to be back in the snug kitchen with Uncle Bob and Ellen to talk things through.

When he returned later that evening, there was a strange, forlorn feeling about the place, as if it had been violated. His small cottage seemed in order but when he tentatively opened the unlocked front door of the farmhouse, he realised that it was completely empty, apart from the old kitchen dresser which was too big to move out. He guessed that Mari had been here with somebody while he was out. Well, he thought, let her have it, it's only bits of wood. I can let the place as it is, get some rent for it to pay for the loan I will need to buy her out.

When his solicitor called next day, he told him what Mari had done. 'Technically the furniture was yours, you could bill her for it.'

'No, she can have it. What advice do you have on buying her out?'

'It's clear she does not want to live in the house. She is entitled to the rent from the farmhouse, but she is not asking for it, so I would keep quiet about that. I would ask for her to relinquish all rights to the house, in writing. My advice is that you buy her out for the figure she is asking. You can raise a loan with the bank, using the property as security. Make an appointment to speak to Mr. Jones at the Midland Bank, I'm sure he will help you. Let me know when you have the loan, then I will send a document to her solicitor for her to sign, relinquishing her claim to the property. She will then be given a cheque for £1,000 from us via her solicitor.'

Owen was amazed at how easy it was to raise the loan. The interest rate was not too bad and he soon found a tenant for the farmhouse who was also able to help him out part-time. The last he heard of Mari was that her already fragile mental state had been made worse by the situation with the will, her paranoia resulting in a nervous breakdown. Had Thomas still been alive, he would have been very sad but not at all surprised.

* * *

A year or so later, having also buried Uncle Bob by then, Owen was down in the inspection pit when he saw a pair of boots walking into the garage. As if history was repeating itself, he heard, 'What's a handsome lad like you doing down a pit?' He climbed out and saw a smartly dressed woman in her early forties standing before him. 'Can I help you?' he asked, wiping his hands on an oily rag. 'You certainly can. Are you Owen?' His suspicious, narrow-eyed nod confirmed he was. But he felt uncomfortable about the way the woman was scrutinising him. 'Well,' she said with a flourish, 'I am your mother. I thought it was about time I came to find you.' He felt his knees go weak so he stepped into the office where he thankfully sat down on his swivel chair, in a dazed state. She followed him. 'So, this is all yours then?' as her gaze took in the box files, invoices on bulldog clips, the till, the desk and the ancient paraffin heater in the corner.

'What do you want?' Owen said venomously.

'That's not a very nice way to speak to your mam, is it?'

'You're not my mam, you dumped me when I was two days old,' angry now that she should just turn up and then tell him how he should speak. Pensively, she said, 'I loved your father, you know — but he went away to the war and I never heard from him again. What was I supposed to do? I couldn't look after you. After that, I learned not to trust anybody.'

'He didn't even know about me for years; he told me that you just vanished and that you never tried to get in touch with him.'

Marian had returned from London for her mother's funeral and had learned through the grapevine that the 'evacuee' at Thomas' uncle's farm had done very well for himself. He had gone to work for Bob's nephew, Thomas, and had inherited everything when Thomas died. She put two and two together and confronted Ellen, who, unable to lie, confirmed that Owen had indeed inherited Thomas' farm and his business. But she warned her that Owen was not wealthy, he had a big loan to pay off and had to work very hard to keep the business going.

'Don't you think you could be a bit nice to your old mam after all these years then?'

'What do you want? Why now? You could have got in touch with me any time in the last twenty-odd years — but you didn't.'

'I wanted to so much but didn't know how you would be with me. Now I know I was right to hesitate.'

Just then, a bell rang, which warned him someone had pulled onto the forecourt for petrol. Glad to be able to escape, he went out to serve the customer. When he had finished, the man signed for the petrol and drove off. Owen, respite over, had to face her again. She was still there and obviously had no intention of being discouraged by his unfriendly reaction.

'Just what do you want?'

'I wanted to meet my son,' she replied.

Angrily, he said, 'Well, you've met him, now you can go. I have managed very well without you so far; I can carry on doing so.' Although a small part of him wanted to let her in, he did not trust her not to let him down again. He reasoned she could have written to him years ago via Ellen. She had always known where he was.

This hostility was obviously not the reception she had expected when she had planned to grace him with her presence. She wondered what she could do to soften him, as she could usually get around most people. She really needed some money. Suddenly, she decided there was no use sitting there arguing, best to retreat tactically. She would go back to her mother's house, where her brother now lived, and let Owen think about it all for a couple of days. She was fairly certain he would go and see Ellen to talk about it, so she could see him there, when this news had sunk in and he had cooled down a bit.

On Sunday, as predicted, she saw Owen going into Ellen's for his Sunday dinner.

'I don't think Marian's a nice person,' even though she did not like speaking ill of anybody. 'She can be sweet as you like to get what she wants out of you. I didn't want to tell her about your inheritance – but she wheedled it out of me.'

'It's not your fault Ellen,' he said,

As Owen patted her hand reassuringly, she said, 'I don't know what she's been doing all these years – she was always a bit flighty but she seems to have a hard edge to her now. She must want something. Maybe money. That's why she came to her mother's funeral, probably thought she might have been left something but wasn't, so is now trying you.'

Although at some level, Owen wanted to get to know his mother and give her the benefit of the doubt, his guard was well and truly up. Ellen was not normally one to judge another harshly and he valued her good sense. On the other hand, Ellen might be jealous of Marian and resented the fact that she had gone off and left Owen for them to raise. He felt very conflicted and decided to have an open mind for now.

Once Marian judged they had finished their Sunday roast meal, she made her way over, knocked, called 'Coo-ee,' and brazenly walked into the farmhouse kitchen. 'Oh good, I'm just in time for a *panad*, as she sat herself down at the dinner table. Owen and Ellen exchanged looks at this overfamiliarity, as she took a cup from a hanger and poured herself a cup of tea. 'Well, this is cosy isn't it, haven't been in here for years,' as she scanned the room disdainfully. 'Not changed much has it?'

'What do you want Marian?' – he was determined not to call her Mam. 'Nothing really, as I said, I wanted to get to know my son – but you are making it very hard for me, especially with my health being like it is, an' all.'

'What's wrong with you then?'

'It's a bit delicate to be honest, not something I'd like to discuss publicly but if you could see your way to giving me a bit of money, I can get myself sorted out.'

Owen's heart hardened as he said, 'Just as we suspected. You didn't come to find me out of any motherly motive or obligation. I'll give you fifty pounds, it's all I can spare but don't come back for more, because there won't be any.' With that he slapped some bank notes onto the table, having already anticipated that that was what she was after.

The two women sat open-mouthed, but not for long. Marian quickly stood, snatched up the money and bustled out of the farmhouse. 'What on earth did you do that for?'

Owen replied, 'Don't you see, this just proved why she was here. It's a small price to pay for getting rid of her. If I had trusted her, I would have been disappointed. I've saved myself from that. We won't see her again.' Ellen saw the sense of this and stood up to clear the table. 'I'm just glad that my father isn't here to see all this.'

* * *

Owen ran the business successfully for many years but eventually thought about retiring. He had seen the writing on the wall; the supermarkets were now selling petrol and he could not compete. A motorway was being planned along the coast and less traffic would be passing along the old road now.

Then Ellen died and left Pont Werglodd to Owen in her will. He was the only mourner at her funeral, which he had arranged, and later went to the house. The place felt strange and empty with neither Bob nor Ellen there. As he was sorting through her personal letters, he found one written in a very formal style, dated not long after Marian had returned for her mother's funeral, the time he had given her the money. It read:

Dear Miss Jones

I am writing to you regarding Marian Roberts, as I found your address with her personal belongings. I am sad to inform you that she passed away two days ago, as the result of a medical procedure which went badly wrong, to be indelicate, a 'backstreet abortion'.

I cannot tell you how sad her passing has made my wife and me. Marian had worked faithfully for our family for many years and we will miss her dedication and common sense. We were unaware that she was with child and had we been so, we would have done all in our power to support her – but she was a very private person. Maybe she felt she could not confide in us, so took matters into her own hands.

I will post her belongings to you, which include a small Bible, with an inscription, 'To Marian, from Ellen,' who, given the date, must have been her Sunday School teacher when she was a young girl. Maybe this was you?

Please accept our deepest condolences. We had a private burial at our local church, as she had said many times she had no desire to return to her native Wales.

Yours most sincerely
Major James Braithwaite-Browne

Owen put the letter down, guilty tears running freely down his face. If only she'd told him, or if he had listened properly, he'd have found out what was going on. But he was young and unforgiving. If he had known, he'd have looked after her. The thought that he had given her the means which had led to her death was unbearable. She could so easily have stayed with him, then she would not have had to resort to such a drastic course of action – she would still be alive. Maybe she felt he would have judged her, having had him out of wedlock as a young girl, then to have fallen pregnant again on the cusp of middle age. He wondered who the father was. He realised that he could have had a sibling, a family, and would not have been so lonely. Now he felt a deep regret at having been so hard on her.

Owen eventually decided to retire and moved to the familiar surroundings Pont Werglodd. He was comforted by the happy memories it held of his childhood. When he was packing up at Glyn Abercyn, he didn't go up into the attic where the old Bibles belonging to Thomas' Nain were stored. If he had ever been told about them, he had long since forgotten.

He never married. Maybe his experience of being abandoned at a few days old, his first-hand experience of Thomas and Mari's unhappy marriage, as well as the trauma of his natural mother turning up out of the blue years later, had made him very wary of relationships. But after finding the letter with Ellen's papers, he now realised he had wasted the one opportunity he had to know his birth mother by rejecting her. He did have the occasional dalliance with some of the local women but that is all it was. He could not bring himself to really trust any of them. He had had a successful business, owned property and money – but still he was not truly happy and had no real expectation of being so.

Part 2

S arah and I are enchanted with our new home – our little country idyll. Our new lifestyle makes us relaxed and happy – our former existence seems a long time ago now. This is our new identity. Our old life seemed to have been a necessary step to get to where we are now, the place we belong. Our lives have woven into the fabric of the place and there is a profound feeling of our being in the right place.

However, I begin to sense a new detachment in our boys – a breaking away, as teenagers are wont to do. This makes us feel sad – but we see it as a necessary passage into adulthood and are grateful that this is happening in this safest of places and not on the streets of a city. Some days, after their chores and when the weather is fair, the boys walk up into the hills to wander for hours and bivouac overnight. This new independence means they are less reliant on us as parents, so I fear that on this level, our usefulness is coming to an end.

The builder is still working on our new kitchen. We have chosen units in keeping with the character of the cottage. The large oak dresser is fully restored and looks magnificent up against the back wall of the kitchen. Beeswax has given it a protective high polish and it has a pleasing patina, despite the underlying black rings of long-ago ink bottles. The antiques restorer remarked on the high quality of the workmanship and shows me the discreet place where the initials J.J. and 1865 are hidden.

The weather is warm, so the boys sleep in the stable loft and the drum kit is mercifully muffled in the barn. Sleeping there is a great adventure for them – they enjoy the independence it gives them. This also gives Sarah and me time on our own, as well as some peace and quiet in the house!

Today the builder decides to reset and cement some loose bricks in the wall around the kitchen inglenook fireplace. As he lifts one of them out, he says, 'Looks like there's something stuffed behind here.'

We peer over his shoulder as he pulls out a dusty old cloth package, which he gently places on his portable work bench. Then he pulls out a small wooden box. Pointing, he suggests 'You'd better open it.' It is locked but the builder manages to pick the lock open.

Gingerly, I unwrap the cloth which begins to disintegrate as I unfold it. We are astounded by its contents. A gent's antique rose-gold pocket watch, together with a waistcoat chain and winder key, as well as a small heart-shaped gold locket. This has a very delicate gold chain and the initials C.J.and J.J. and 1866 engraved on one side. In the box is a bundle of old letters. Excited, I say to the builder, 'Maybe, these belonged to my forebears. They were living here around those dates. My great-great-great grandfather's sister was called Catrin Jones, so this locket may have been hers. But then again, there are lots of Joneses in Wales!'

Despite my cautiousness, there is huge excitement about this find – a tangible link to the past. Gently, I open the back of the pocket watch and see on the inside are engraved the initials J.J. and 1810. 'Given the date, this can't be the same John Jones who is buried in Catrin's grave, but it might have belonged to his father or grandfather. To have owned a watch of this quality at that time suggests that the family then was not without means.' There is an assay mark, a crown and the number 18, as well as other marks which I cannot see clearly with the naked eye, as they are quite worn.

By contrast, the locket looks new and unworn – but the gold has dulled over time. I open it to find a lock of dark hair inside, so quickly close it again so as not to spill it. Resisting the temptation to study them now, 'I will look at these again when I have more time. Exciting as this find is, we need to prioritise getting the house straight, so I will put them away safely for now.'

The boys are disappointed but return to their jobs, while I carefully wrap both pieces in clean tea towels. Along with the box of letters, which are in a better condition, I place them all safely in a drawer of the large dresser.

* * *

The old cream Aga is fully restored. The heating specialist says this model was made in the nineteen-thirties but was probably converted from coal to oil in the late sixties. It is now warming the entire kitchen and most of the downstairs area. We cook stews and casseroles on it and it provides an endless supply of hot water – useful with two, newly body-conscious teenage boys!

The existing bathroom was a Victorian addition. Originally the privy would have been outside in a small shed, with a hole cut out of a plank of wood, over the nearby running stream. Bath nights would have been in a tin bath tub in front of the fire. The ceiling is tongue and groove, popular with the Victorians and recently back in fashion. All it needs is a coat of emulsion, which I will get the boys to do. The roll top bath is re-enamelled and looks impressive with its shiny new livery of modern, old-fashioned style taps. The pedestal washbasin is in reasonable condition. It also has new old-fashioned taps and the plumber has managed to get the old cast iron flush cistern to work, with the aid of a brass chain and porcelain pull handle. The overall effect is exactly what we wanted. The plumber wants to get into the attic to check the water tank, so he lifts the hatch to climb up there, then shouts down, 'There's a pile of books up here, some of them are really big.' We ask him to pass down one of the big ones and excitingly it turns out to be a leather-bound Family Bible. On the first page appears to be written the names and dates for the Jones family. Something else to pore over when time permits. I wipe the dust off its leather front cover and carefully store it away in a cupboard of the dresser.

As the boys are in their stable loft for the summer, there is now no urgency to do up their rooms. The house is renovated enough for now, with many of the interesting old features preserved.

* * *

Tonight, we sit in the pervasive, comforting warmth of the ancient Aga as a summer storm swirls forcefully around the house, causing sudden gusts of strong intensity. I have today received a copy of my aunt Catrin's will, which I applied for to the archive. Also laid out on the kitchen table are the pocket watch, the locket and the box of letters we found a few weeks ago, behind the loose brick. Forensically, I examine the engraved date and the stamps on the pocket watch with an eyeglass. I see a crown with lion passant and wheatsheaves which confirms the watch is very much older than the locket. I am convinced the locket belonged to my aunt Catrin. But why had she hidden them away and whose hair is in the locket? Could it be J.J.s?

According to Catrin's will, she left the farm to her nephew, William, my great-grandfather. The letters are interesting. The top one is written to Catrin by 'sister' Mary, who appears to actually be her sister-in-law. In it she informs Catrin how her husband, also called William, died young. I say excitedly to Sarah, 'That must be my great-great-grandfather. Maybe I was named after them, William seems to be a family name. The address is Kendal in the north of England. My great-great-grandfather was living here on the 1861 census but not in 1871, so he presumably left to live in Kendal. Now I understand from Mary's letter why they left and Catrin took over the farm instead of her brother. Mary says they ran a business up there. I've just googled the address on the letter to find it was once a transport café. How fascinating! That may have been the business Mary wrote about. Poor Catrin must have battled on alone here until she died in her eighties. Later, the farm was sold to the other side of my family in 1921, when Thomas' family bought it. I also need to study the house deeds the solicitor gave me, as there will be a mine of information about ownership in them.'

Happy hours pass as we re-examine our treasures in the cosy kitchen. Suddenly we realise how late it has become, so I wrap the precious items up once again and we slowly climb the stairs to bed.

We now have a basic working routine around the farm. The boys created a good vegetable patch and the seedlings are shooting up, encouraged by the warmth of the sun and the gentle rain. We are not too ambitious, just basic salad ingredients and new potatoes. The nutrients in the virgin soil are good, so the plants thrive but need protection from ravaging rabbits. The boys had fun making a scarecrow to frighten off the jackdaws, which peck at the soil.

We have acquired a sheepdog from the animal rescue shelter. Her name is Bess. She is well trained and assessed as being about three years old. She loves wandering the hills with the boys. Strangely, she has no interest in sheep – a bonus in this area where they graze freely on the common land up above the farmhouse, but quite likes gathering us all together in one place. Maybe her previous owner had trained her to leave them be, as a farmer will shoot a dog if he sees it chasing sheep. Sadly, I have heard tell of flocks of sheep being driven over the edges of old quarries to their deaths by out-of-control dogs.

We have a few chickens and ducks, which supply us with lovely fresh eggs. Our current project is planting a small orchard next to the stream. In our make-do portable greenhouse, we had a glut of green tomatoes, so have made a delicious green chutney, which we stored away in the pantry.

Seed potatoes planted a few months earlier are yielding a good crop. They taste delicious baked outside in wood coals then filled with lashings of salted butter. The vegetables and salads are a great success and save us a fortune on our grocery bill. We feel inspired and plan to be more ambitious in next spring's planting. The boys are also building up a decent woodpile to keep our sitting-room log burner supplied during the winter months.

We ramble together for hours over the tops of the surrounding hills and are continuously discovering new places. We know our way around the tops of the mountains quite well now. Occasionally we see the remains of a roundhouse or a cairn and often walk over to the west of the Carneddau Mountains to look at the ancient circles there. I am told that the largest circle is called Meini Hirion.

This morning, as a break from marking essays, which is my bread and butter income now, I walk along the road to the small village chapel which my family have used for generations. The door is unlocked, so I press the highly-polished, smoothly-worn brass door latch and enter. I sit down in the quiet stillness on one of the highly-polished wooden pews and I think about the strong faith which had motivated its construction. Looking up, I see ancient cobwebs hanging languidly in the high rafters. There is a slightly musty smell in the air and I think about all the lives which have passed through here over the ages. This chapel would have been the epicentre of community life for a long time.

My mind drifts back to my own wedding and I fondly recall how Sarah and I met at a friend's wedding, as many people do. I first spotted her when she and other guests were being shown to their seats by the ushers. She looked very striking and I hoped to get a chance to chat to her later. I watched her during the service until my friend nudged me and whispered, 'Stop gawking, eyes forward, pay attention!'

At the reception, with the official part over, people began to relax, shedding ties and tight shoes as a band began to play. The group Sarah was with, went off to dance but she stayed at the table, with her shoes kicked off as she people-watched, happy in her own company. With a modicum of Dutch courage, courtesy of the champagne, I walked across to her and asked, 'Is it ok if I join you?'

'Of course. I'm giving the dancing a miss – these new shoes are killing me.'

'My name is William – I'm a university friend of the groom.'

'I'm Sarah – the bride is my first cousin.'

She looked even more striking when she smiled, which lit up her whole face. I felt immediately at ease with her and hoped maybe she felt the same. We found we had a great deal in common and as we lived fairly close to each other, we agreed to meet up the following weekend and the rest, as they say, is history. Our marriage is very happy. I am one of the luckiest people alive, especially now that we are starting a new phase of our life together – in our new house which has been occupied by my ancestors for centuries.

Jon and Robert attend their new school and are coping well with the A-level work. They tend to spend their time in their den but Bess is happiest when we sit down together for our evening meal.

One evening after supper, having visited the chapel, I decide to research a bit on the other side of the family that the local historian who had known Owen mentioned, the ones I have come to call the Chapel Family. I say to Sarah, 'I wonder what Thomas' maternal family was like. It says on the house deeds that they purchased here in 1921, so Thomas must have been three when they moved here from the house next to the village chapel. That means the farm was once again occupied by my ancestors, albeit from a different branch!'

* * *

The Chapel Family's Story
(Stori Teulu Tŷ Capel)

'Use that goose wing, it's better for getting right into those corners,' Gwladys instructed her younger daughter. 'The place has to be spick and span for Robat and Catherine's wedding tomorrow.'

The caretaker's accommodation, which they called Ty Capel, lay snugly beneath the little village chapel, which was level with the road. This was because the land the building was on sloped down towards the flatter valley floor. This gave Ty Capel an open aspect out over the fields and out to the sea. The caretakers, Cledwyn and Gwladys, had the responsibility of maintaining the fabric of the building and preparing it for services, for which they were paid a nominal sum from the Sunday collections. On Saturdays, the females of the family diligently cleaned the '*set fawr.*' Here, on a raised dais, sat the chapel elders, indicating their authority and assumed wisdom. They sat on individual deacon chairs with cushions, long ago flattened by generous posteriors. These elders were not revered for any materialistic possessions they owned, nor for any class they belonged to – but for their wealth of religious knowledge, gleaned from decades of studying the scriptures. Their collective knowledge on matters of good and evil, saints and sinners, was often called on to pass judgement. They could be fair but not always, sometimes blaming the victim for their own demise and shaming them in front of the congregations. It was considered a good deterrent to others.

Cledwyn and Gwladys were parents of two daughters and two sons. It was Robat, the younger son who was to be married. Gwladys, the matriarchal head of the household, was a force to be reckoned with, a stout lady, with disapproving frown lines etched deeply into both sides of her usually pursed mouth. She ruled her roost with a metaphorical iron rod, based on her unshakeable belief of right and wrong – and woe betide those who erred outside her imagined parameters of righteousness. She expected absolute obedience from all her children, even long into adulthood and her husband did not risk crossing her if he could possibly help it. It would have to be something he felt very strongly about to risk disagreeing with her. Although strict, Gwladys had a heart of gold and would help or do anything for anybody. The dog, Spot, a small white terrier with a black eye patch, knew when to keep out of her way and when to chance getting up on her knee for some fuss.

But today was Friday and everything must be perfect for tomorrow. The women covered their long skirts with large calico aprons and tucked unruly hair into mop caps. They used beeswax or lavender polish on the pitch-pine pews, leaving not a speck of dust anywhere. Traditional thick red felt runners, printed with a black-patterned edge, somewhat softened the hard-wooden bench pews.

Chapelgoers provided flowers for the altar, carefully arranged on Saturday afternoons, ready for the next day's services. A competitive, passively aggressive element existed, to try to upstage the previous Sunday's contribution, in the hope that the preacher would comment on them – and name the donor, during the service. Too bad if you were on the rota for December, as all you had to offer then was holly with shiny red berries. But these low-level hostilities were suspended when it was a wedding. The whole village was involved one way or another, flower arranging, cleaning, gardening, singing, dressmaking and food preparation. There were to be no holds barred with this wedding, the stakes were high and important reputations were at stake.

And today was the day before the 'big day.' Gwladys informed the others, 'Mr. Jones should be here soon with the flowers. He'll probably bring his own vases, he won't think ours are good enough', she sniffed disdainfully, 'but if they look lovely, I won't mind. There will be a communion during the service, so get on with washing and polishing those communion glasses. Make sure there are no smears on them,' she barked from the vestry. Her daughters rolled their eyes at each other; they knew what needed doing without being told. But there was no point arguing. Before the service tomorrow morning, they would fill the little glasses with communion wine and carefully carry them in their special silver trays, with little round circles cut out to prevent them from spilling. Then they would place each one into an individual round metal holder, screwed into the back of the pew in front. As they were all teetotallers, the wine was non-alcoholic. It symbolised the blood of Christ and tiny little cubes of white bread, representing the body of Christ, were passed along the pews on large oval silver platters. In this simple chapel, there was no parade of shame requiring them to troop up to the front altar to have wafers paternally placed on their tongues by a priest, nor to drink out of the communal cup in the High Church or Catholic tradition. Communion here was a far more private affair between the individuals, their maker and their consciences.

Only those who had been formally 'Confirmed' participated in this ritual. Drinking the wine, then reverently placing the bread on their tongues, they bowed their heads in silent, secret prayer, before the preacher began his. In a strong resonant voice, he would ask them to pray for starving children in far off lands, a local parishioner who was bed-ridden, a child with an incurable illness, a family who had had a bereavement; the list of those who suffered seemed endless. But these prayers were merely a warm-up for the fire and brimstone sermon which was to follow.

Gwladys was the older daughter and former housekeeper to her prosperous wool-manufacturer father, in the tiny hamlet of Pontwgan. Melin Pontwgan housed industrial looms, which made traditional Welsh blankets, rugs and flannel. The looms were driven by a large mill wheel, powered by the River Roe. When the river was in full flood and the looms clattered loudly, it was often impossible to hear anything else. Gwladys' mother had died young, leaving her to bring up her younger siblings, which may have shaped her now domineering personality.

Gwladys first met her husband, Cledwyn, at a non-conformist outdoor revivalist meeting, as most young people in their communities did then. He was an agricultural labourer, a well-built and stocky man. He grew up in the Swan Cottage Inn, Rowen and occasionally over-indulged in strong spirits but Gwladys was not going to put up with that if she had anything to do with it. She persuaded him to join the religious Temperance Movement, where he signed the 'Pledge to forsake the consumption of alcoholic beverage in order to receive salvation.'

Cledwyn was a handsome man who dressed in the usual black of that time, which contrasted sharply with his impressively bushy salt and pepper sideburns. When Gwladys announced her intention to marry Cledwyn, her father was not impressed as he did not think that Cledwyn was quite good enough for her. But Gwladys had no intention of being left a spinster in her father's household; she was determined to have her own life and family.

Her two younger sisters had married well and the only son helped their father to run the mill. In her father's opinion, Cledwyn's only saving grace was that he had become a Methodist lay preacher, as the newly converted often do. Many of these were considered the celebrities of their day and revered for their oratory skills. During Sunday sermons, their passionate words could stir a congregation to feel great emotion and righteous indignation. When Cledwyn preached it was probably the only time that Gwladys could not interrupt nor contradict him.

Cledwyn did not have much choice in the matter of marriage; Gwladys had decided that they would marry, so that was that. One spring day, they walked the two hours to the Conwy Register Office, carrying under their arms their best clothes in brown paper parcels tied with rough twine, to save from getting muddy. As they neared the town, they quickly changed behind a conveniently high hedge into their Sunday best, with their backs to each other, of course.

The Registrar diligently performed the official ceremony, a marriage certificate was produced – and a photograph taken as additional proof of their marriage. When they posed, they did not smile, due to the seriousness of the occasion, which required dignity and gravitas. The puff of smoke emitted by the camera, hung acridly in the air for a few minutes and made their eyes water. Then, to mark the special occasion, the newly married couple went to a local tearoom and treated themselves to tea and scones, which Gwladys described as mediocre. Then they set off back to their respective homes, repeating on the way the same quick change into their everyday work clothes. They were a 'no fuss' couple who had decided they would have their union blessed later in chapel. The registry office marriage was made necessary because they had been offered the custodianship of the new Glyn Chapel in the next valley. They were extremely pleased, realising that there, they would be set up for life to raise a family. Cledwyn would also be expected to preach there when a circuit preacher was unavailable. A week after the ceremony, they moved in there together to begin their married life, taking what little they had on the back of a cart.

Life carried on pretty much as they had planned and once the daughters reached marriageable age, they found respectable men from the congregation – one was a music teacher, the other the local schoolmaster. Robat and Roland, still unmarried, served apprenticeships as stonemasons. They were guided, or one could say instructed, by their ever-pragmatic mother to save most of their wages to eventually get married. It took a long time to save what she thought was enough so both were well into their thirties by the time they settled down, which for Robat would be tomorrow. But there would be no paltry registry office wedding for Gwladys' son.

Robat was marrying Catherine, who lived with her parents, sister and brother, on a large hundred-acre farm further down in the valley nearer the sea, called Dyffryn. Some of their fields ran right up to the clay shoreline, which was gradually being eroded by the force of sea. There was a long-established clay-brick factory based there to fulfil the local need for quarrymen's houses, used alongside the locally quarried dressed granite.

Robat saw Catherine mainly on Sundays and during the weekly choir practices. He and his brother Roland were innately musical, as were most of the family; music and singing played an integral part in their cultural and social lives. Roland conducted the choir, whilst Robat accompanied on the piano. Their sisters, who had natural soprano and alto voices, sang duets together. Every performance was polished to absolute peak perfection before the public was permitted to hear it. Their choir, which competed in the many town and inter-chapel musical festivals and eisteddfodau, was highly regarded and won many silver cups. There was a long-simmering rivalry between them and a choir of the next town. Things came to a head after one competition, which the rivals believed they should have won, and attempted to steal the cup off Robat. A chaotic melee broke out in the main town square – but he managed to hang on to it while making a tactical escape. The story was then widely reported in the local newspaper, with Robat portrayed as the local hero!

One Sunday afternoon, suddenly out of the blue, Catherine, plucking up all her courage, demurely said to Robat, 'My mother is asking if you would like to come for tea this afternoon after Sunday School.' She had built herself up to ask him and turned a slight shade of pink. Afternoon tea was a popular ritual then, partaken between a Sunday Roast dinner and a light supper of bread, pickles and cheese.

Catherine had had her eye on him for some time now but knew that if she waited for him to make the first move, she would forever remain a spinster. She reasoned that she would not lose face if she said it was her mother who was asking. Robat saw right through the mother's invitation ploy but did not let on, as he was inordinately pleased. He replied with a grin, 'I would like that very much,' adding, 'Shall we walk down together and have a '*sgwrs*' on the way down?' She had not included Roland in the invitation, which must mean that it was only him she liked. Robat had been reticent to approach her because her parents were wealthy farmers, wealthier than his anyway, but once again, religion and music opened doors through which to cross the imagined class divide. They lived at a time when class dominated everything but the lines within Welsh society were less rigid than their English counterparts. People who were poets or preachers were academically or musically gifted, and people who worked hard to help those less fortunate, such as evangelists or missionaries, were more likely to be respected. It was what you did, and did to the best of your ability, rather than what you had, which was valued.

Robat found it hard to concentrate for the rest of Sunday school class, where they were both teachers. He watched the fingers of the large chapel clock slowly crawl towards home-time, while Catherine gave him shy looks from across where she was teaching her class. To pass the time, he asked his class to write down as many of the Ten Commandments as they could, on their wooden-framed slates, using their slate pencils. This took them quite a long time and gave him some time to daydream about what was to come.

On their walk down to the farm, they chatted away as if they had known each other all their lives, which they had but previously only as friends. Catherine's younger siblings, realising what was happening, walked on ahead, just out of earshot. They giggled mischievously, realising that they would have lots of fun teasing her later.

Catherine's mother, Mary, laid on a spread of paper-thin slices of homemade bread and butter, fruit scones, slices of rich Madeira cake, and a large pot of strong tea. Robat was not unduly impressed; it was normal fare – as most Welsh farmers' wives were excellent bakers. Robat did not feel particularly scrutinised by Mary, given that he was probably here to be given the 'once over.' She was far less intimidating than his own mother for sure. Despite her giving off a slight air of gentility, he felt quite comfortable in her presence. Catherine's brother was excused to go help his father with the afternoon milking, so Robat was left at the mercy of the women. Having two sisters himself, he was not too fazed by this; he knew how to behave around them. Catherine's mother then handed him a side plate saying, 'Please help yourself to what you fancy.' This made

Catherine giggle nervously and soon any tension had eased. That day was the start of their future together. They courted, as couples did, and assumed that they would marry. Robat told her that he had saved up enough money for them to rent and furnish their own home, so they set a date.

Many of the congregation, not invited to the wedding itself, attended the service sitting discreetly in the back pews of the chapel. Other locals gathered outside the little chapel, ready to throw rice and wish them luck, as it was a big occasion for a local person to get married. Women stood in the road outside so that they could gossip later with others who had not been there. Then they could say, 'I was there' and be in with a chance of catching the bride's backwards-thrown bouquet of yellow roses.

It was a lovely 1908 summer's day and the wedding party did not have far to go. The setting was stunning, the weather glorious and the women looked elegant in their Edwardian dresses. The Wedding Tea was held in the pretty garden of the chapel house below. On Gwladys' orders, it had been manicured to within an inch of its life. Lazy bees buzzed by, flitting between pale pink hollyhocks, vivid blue delphiniums and mauve lupins, not really bothering the guests, just intent on collecting the abundance of pollen. Thrushes and blackbirds sang earnestly in the nearby ancient woodland above, mainly unheard over the chatter of those assembled in the garden. Trestle tables, covered with pristine, stiffly starched cotton tablecloths, heaved with all sorts of deliciousness.

'Everybody please help yourselves to food. Pots of tea coming just now,' announced Gwladys, clapping her hands as she barked like a sergeant-major, in her element, overseeing everything. The spread was soon devoured by those who had been invited – and some who had not – but no-one seemed to mind too much. Nephews ran themselves ragged, playing tag in their long short trousers, getting themselves hot and bothered. Their mothers scolded them when they got dirty, rubbing furiously at their muddy, grass-stained knees with snowy, beautifully pressed white handkerchiefs. Robat's sisters and helpers ran backward and forward to the kitchen, endlessly fetching fresh tea in large brown enamel teapots. No alcohol was served, as the family and most of the congregation were teetotallers but there was fresh lemonade or ginger beer for the children supplied by Aunty Meg from Bedol Bach. The occasional speech was made, predicated by men tapping loudly on their china saucers with teaspoons, for attention. Then Cledwyn tapped his saucer. 'Thank you to everybody here today to celebrate the marriage of our son Robat to Catherine. We welcome her into our family and give her all our best wishes. I'm sure she will keep Robat in order!' – to the sound of laughter and the embarrassment of Robat. After that it was open house. Many made the long oratorical speeches which they were so fond of inflicting on others. Some guests seemed to enjoy them, entertained by a story well told, especially at the groom's expense. Robat's past misdemeanours were duly aired to be soundly sniggered at, especially the stolen silver cup story – but his valuable contribution to the musical life of the village was also soundly commended.

Catherine's parents, who were a handsome couple, had agreed to let Gwladys arrange the reception in the chapel garden. By rights, it should have been held at Dyffryn Farm, but they did not mind. They were shown great deference by Robat's family and other guests, due to their perceived higher social status as farm owners but they themselves did not stand on ceremony. Catherine's mother, Mary was from a very old and distinguished family from Eglwysbach, in the next valley. Mary was still petite and pretty, despite her hard life of a farmer's wife. She looked very striking in a mauve, high-collared, mutton-sleeved dress, with a slight bustle and a short train. She wore a small hat which sported a magnificent ostrich feather, stuck at a jaunty angle. Catherine's father also cut a very dashing figure. He was by trade a master carpenter but had thrown himself wholeheartedly into the farming life. He was tall, well-built and his dark good looks were enhanced by his luxuriously thick moustache and sideburns and laughing eyes. Mary realised that as well as losing her daughter, she was losing her best dairy worker but felt happy that Catherine had married a man she so clearly adored. Robat was marrying into a hardworking family, conscientious and obsessive about cleanliness, particularly in their dairy. They had a large dairy pedigree herd of Friesians and grew arable crops. Their dairy provided milk and butter for the local TB sanatorium nearby and this contract had given them a good steady income over many years.

'Everybody gather round for the wedding photograph please' shouted the official photographer. Herding them all into one place, mindful of their status and who should be standing where was no easy matter but he captured the mood of the day beautifully. The photographs stood proudly on the mantlepieces of many family members for years to come.

The couple settled down to life in the house next to the chapel. It was a bit too close to Robat's mother for Catherine's liking – but she decided she could probably put up with that. In time, hints began being dropped about why there was no 'patter of tiny feet.' Catherine, surrounded by the offspring of her in-laws, felt the familial pressure of their childlessness. Eventually, the family gave up, realising that they were being insensitive and the couple themselves accepted that they would probably remain childless. It was God's will, therefore not meant to be.

However, after about ten years of marriage, Catherine began experiencing morning sickness and her breasts felt tender. Having listened to the childbearing woes of Robat's sisters, she suspected she might be expecting a baby. When Robat returned from work that evening, she said to him, her eyes swimming with happy tears, 'I hardly want to believe this – but I think there might be a baby on the way.'

He sat there, his mouth open in sheer disbelief, then ever sensitive to her feelings stuttered cautiously, 'Are you sure about this? You don't want to be building up your hopes for nothing.' He had heard some women could suffer from phantom pregnancies and because he loved her so much, could not bear for her to be disappointed. 'It seems a bit unlikely after all this time but not unheard of, of course,' – giving her hope.

A few hours later, Gwladys was at Catherine's back door. 'Cooeee,' she blustered in, her massive bombazine bulk filling the kitchen. Catherine looked around for support but Robat seemed to have quietly melted away, so she was left to her mercy. She began unsubtly, 'I hear you believe you're with child. You'd better describe your symptoms to me, then we'll see if you need to see a doctor or not,' she said bristling with importance, whilst folding her arms over her ample bosom. In those days, nobody wasted money on doctors, unless it was a matter of life and death. Besides, bringing babies into the world was woman's work. Despite her mother-in-law's interrogation, Catherine was relieved to have her suspicions confirmed.

'Now,' said the sergeant-major, looking directly at Catherine through her small steel rimmed glasses, 'You must look after yourself, you are no youngster and it could be hard for you. Tell Robat that he must leave you alone now – we don't want to take any risks. You know what I mean don't you?' she dropped her voice, heavy with innuendo and looked at her so intently with her periwinkle-blue eyes that Catherine dropped her gaze in embarrassment at what her mother-in-law was implying, as one did not normally hint, never mind speak openly about such private matters.

Over the next few months, Gwladys popped into Catherine's kitchen regularly. She brought round all sorts of concoctions and treats such as egg custards for her to eat. 'This is to build you up, it's full of iron.' she said importantly as she handed Catherine a glass of foul, disgusting looking liquid. She drank it, despite its taste, as she trusted her completely.

It was 1918, the end of the First World War, when at full-term, Catherine struggled – but gave birth to a healthy baby boy she named Thomas. Even the threat of Spanish 'flu and the exceptionally cold and heavy snowfalls that winter could not burst Catherine's bubble of pure joy. She had spent her confinement in virtual isolation, for fear of the baby contracting anything harmful. She was besotted with the little chap, who she instantly adored. She had plenty of baby advice from her mother, mother-in-law and sisters-in-law. In turn, they cleaned her house until it shone, even though it didn't need it. They did all the baby and other washing, starched and ironed sheets and shirts with their piping hot black cast irons which were heated on the range. She was very grateful for all of this but thankfully glad when they all left for the day to prepare their own evening meals. Then she had her baby all to herself to gaze at adoringly. Her joy was immeasurable – but nobody then knew what the future would hold for Baby Thomas. By rights, he should have been named after his paternal grandfather Cledwyn – but his sisters had long ago appropriated that name, thinking that Catherine would not be needing it.

All was well for the next year, the happiest time of her life, until her father told her, 'I'm afraid your mam is very ill. There is nothing the doctors can do for her. They've tried bloodletting, digitalis, mercuric compounds and even opium but her condition is incurable. I don't know how I'm going to manage without her to be honest. Your brother has made it clear he's not interested in the farm, so there is only Mary Jane to help me now and she can't run the house and the dairy. There seems no point in carrying on with it, I think I'll have to sell it eventually.'

Catherine was understandably shocked. They had kept the bad news to themselves until now so as not to worry her but felt that as it was becoming critical, she needed to know.

Mary slowly slipped away one evening at the age of fifty-four. Her husband, her two daughters and son were by her bedside. The death certificate cited Bright's Disease, as well as Exhaustion. Mary had chosen to be buried in Eglwysbach churchyard with her father and mother. The grave was near the church door and next to the family vault of her famous ancestors. After the funeral service, where the singing was hauntingly beautiful, a sad dejected round-shouldered family followed the coffin and vicar out to the freshly dug grave. The icy ground numbed their fingers and toes and froze their faces as they stood there in the weak winter sun – the cutting east wind adding to the bitterness of the day.

They gathered for the funeral tea at the family farm. They talked of a life well-lived, comforted by the fact that she was now in the arms of her Maker and no longer suffering. None of this however, touched her husband John, who was beyond comforting and he snapped at anyone who peddled platitudes. By sheer chance, Mary's brother, Tom, who was her youngest sibling, was also at the funeral. Being a younger brother, he'd had no chance of inheriting their father's farm, so possessing an adventurous spirit, he had left his home many years ago and emigrated to Patagonia. He had recently sold his farm there and was now en-route to a government grant of land in Canada, stopping off to visit his sister and her family on the way. He was thankful that he had been able to spend a few weeks with her before her death. He, however, was resolutely unmarried and childless, so did not feel the need to stay rooted to one place – but wherever he went, he carried with pride his Welsh identity and heritage deep within himself.

Soon after the funeral, Catherine's father went into a steep decline. 'What's the point,' he said to Catherine, 'she was too young to die. What am I going to do without her?' He was in a dazed state of loss and bewilderment as they had been together a long time and were devoted to each other. Robotically he carried on working on the farm, along with his younger daughter, Mary Jane, who had replaced Catherine in the dairy making butter and cream. She had a young man who would marry her in an instant – but her father would not allow it and she could not bear to upset him. His heart was now no longer in the farm, it all seemed pointless without Mary at his side and his son was uninterested in taking over. He passed away soon after, a broken-hearted and disappointed man.

The farm was consequently sold and the proceeds of the sale were split three ways between Catherine and her two siblings. For her younger sister, Mary Jane, it was the opportunity to marry the man she had been engaged to for many years, and their brother put his share into his business in the north of England.

Catherine and Robat were still considering what they should do with her share when one day the farm, Glyn Abercyn, just along the road, unexpectedly came up for sale. It was as if it was meant to be.

They cautiously approached the agent and made an offer and there was great excitement when it was accepted. They soon settled into their new life on the smallholding, with Gwladys thankfully now a little further away! They kept a few animals and grew vegetables while Robat continued his work as a stonemason.

Their son Thomas seemed destined to be an only child. Catherine considered him her miracle child and he was bestowed with more love than one small child could possibly contain. It also seemed to flow out of him. He was charismatic and instantly liked by both adults and children – especially older ladies, who he unconsciously charmed. You couldn't say he was spoilt but he really didn't have to go anywhere or do anything if he didn't want to. He was not academically gifted – but he was very clever in a creative and practical way; he could turn his hand to making or fixing anything and was endlessly fascinated by how mechanical things worked. He would sit on the stone walls of local farms during harvest, studying the tractors pulling harvesting machines cutting corn in the fields while the threshers separated the corn from the stalks. He would then volunteer to help build the hayricks, so that he could get close to study the machinery, to understand how it worked and how it could be made more efficient.

School days were not a happy experience for him. Obviously, being from a Welsh-speaking family, he spoke only Welsh, so struggled to learn English when he first entered infant class. But he was not the only one. An allowance was made by the British National School Board for these infants, but when they were a little older, they were forbidden to speak Welsh at school. They were punished for doing so, by having to wear a piece of wood on a string around their necks, with the words 'Welsh Not' written on it. They also had to stand with their supposed 'shame' in the corner of the classroom facing the wall. The piece of wood was then thankfully handed to the next child who inadvertently spoke Welsh. The last child left wearing the 'Welsh Not' board at the end of the school day was soundly caned. As Thomas thought in Welsh, the Welsh words had a habit of slipping out and he was often the wearer of the shaming stick. He never told his parents about this, as he knew they would be down at the school straight away to complain about the brutality – and he did not want the other children to call after him, 'tell-tale tit, your tongue shall split, and all the dogs in town, shall have a little bit.'

Thomas looked just like any other boy of his age in that between-war era. He wore long shorts of worsted wool, held up by either braces or a dual-coloured striped elasticated waist belt, hooked together by a metal s-shaped clasp. His knee-length grey socks were hand-knitted in itchy Welsh wool by his mother or Gwladys, his Nain. These were held up with elastic garters, tucked in under the fold-over at the top. His shirts, also homemade, had collars which often curled up at the ends. When threadbare, the collars were unpicked and sewn back on inside out. He wore sleeveless, home-knitted jumpers, usually grey or even a Fair Isle pattern if the knitter was particularly skilled. When he had outgrown the jumper, the wool would be undone and reknitted into a bigger size with some extra wool. His hobnailed boots could be heard coming from a long way off as he walked home from school on the smooth concrete road surface, which was particularly good for roller-skating. His trouser pockets held his trusty Swiss Army penknife, his champion conker with string running through it and knotted one end, a catapult to fire at anything which moved, and a gent's handkerchief carefully ironed by his mother. This item was seldom used, as his sleeve was quicker! This was all he needed. He had lost his two front teeth and his hair was cut in the then style of 'short, back and sides' but this little scrap of humanity meant the world to his doting parents.

Thomas also liked to watch the village mechanic fixing cars. 'It's a carburettor, it's what the petrol feeds through. Go and fetch me a small screwdriver, so that I can adjust the flow.' Elwyn liked having young Thomas there, he was good company and very keen to learn. He was handy to run and fetch tools for him and brewed him endless pots of tea. Thomas knew the make and model of every single car in the valley and who owned them, which wasn't difficult as there were only three or four at that time. Elwyn had a 1925

Crossley, which he used as a taxi to bring people and holiday-makers up the steep hill from the railway station into town. Thomas knew it could reach 75mph top speed but as a taxi, it never got above 30mph. The local doctor had an Austin Seven Swallow Saloon to make home visits, and the magistrate, who was rich anyway, owned a 1928 Vauxhall, which Thomas thought was a bit too swanky, believing that its looks were better than its performance.

'When I am grown up, I am going to be a mechanic and I will have my own garage.'

'I don't doubt that you will, my lad, you know almost as much as I do.'

Thomas knew the names of most of the parts of a motor engine and for the plethora of mechanic's tools. He liked nothing better than to sit and ride in a car when it was being moved about the garage forecourt or taken on a post-service run to be tested. He enjoyed discussing the engines with the owners of these cars, who were often bemused by his knowledge, given that he was only just ten years of age. When he sat alone in these cars, he fantasised about working on them, driving them and one day even owning one. He spent a long time thinking about which type of vehicle he would buy, given the choice and the money of course.

Thomas walked along to the garage in the village whenever he could get away from his chores and feeding the animals on the family's smallholding. They kept two cows, a pig, some hens and geese. In the summer months, his mother took in holiday visitors, hill walkers and travelling artists and was very pleased when one quite well-known artist painted her a picture of their farmhouse, which now hung in pride of place in the parlour.

They had a substantial vegetable plot which grew all sorts of root and salad vegetables. Priority was given to grow food, but they grew a few flowers to put on the altar in the chapel when it was their turn on the rota. They had an orchard, often raided by Thomas when he was hungry.

* * *

One unforgettable morning, Thomas' mother went up the stairs to wake her precious son to get him ready for school. This was unusual, as Thomas was normally up and about very early, usually to raid the bread bin or to fetch the hens' eggs for breakfast. 'I don't feel very well. Can I stay in bed today?' said Thomas, lying pitifully in his bed, his face flushed with fever and layered with a light glistening of sweat. She placed her hand on his forehead and was alarmed to feel just how hot it was. He was burning up with fever and croaked that his throat and joints were hurting. When she checked his chest, she was alarmed to feel a rash of small bumps under his skin. Catherine called down urgently to Robat, 'Go quickly and fetch the doctor, Thomas is burning up.' Gwladys soon appeared and after checking him, the look on her face confirmed that Thomas was gravely ill. The doctor confirmed the diagnosis of Rheumatic Fever. He advised, 'Wrap him with cold wet sheets' – even though Thomas was shivering. He then continued gravely, looking over the top of his half-moon spectacles, 'Plenty of fluids and keep the room darkened to protect his eyes. The fever needs to break and if he survives, he may be left with permanent damage to his heart muscle, affecting its ability to pump. But I must warn you that there is a high risk he may not pull through.'

His seriously worried parents paid the doctor half a crown for his visit and followed his instructions to the very letter. On hearing about Thomas' illness, the whole village, including the few non-religious, fell into a low depression. They willed him to live with all their might. The congregation of the little chapel prayed fervently on their knees, asking their God as they had never asked before, to make him better. A sombre mood descended on the little community. It held its collective breath for news of Thomas pulling through. They accepted that older people died eventually but this was not the proper order of things, Thomas was just a child, and a sweet child at that, who had his whole life in front of him.

Catherine sat by his bedside continuously, gently holding his hand, as if she could transfer her own life force into him to battle the demons which had invaded him.

'My dear sweet boy. You are my very life,' she said. Sudden tears frequently banked up on the rims of her eyes, distorting her vision in the same way the flawed glass in his bedroom window did. The shadows in the sick-room, thrown up by a single candleflame, were magnified by the tears into flickering grotesque, burlesque shapes. These she ignored, knowing them for what they were, as she pleaded endlessly with Thomas, 'You are my reason to live. I cannot imagine my life without you now, I waited so long for you to arrive. Please don't leave me,' her cracking voice forcing the words out of her chocked-up throat. In the small hours of the night, a desolate sounding wind picked up and tormented the corner of the roof outside with its whistling – competing with Thomas' laboured, raspy, uneven breathing.

The women came to help, making beef teas, which through his delirium, they tried to coax in between his lips, but he choked on it and it dribbled down his neck then soaked into the already sodden bedsheets. Four times a day they wrapped him in cold wet bedsheets, to cool him down to make him more comfortable – but Thomas knew nothing of this, as he slept his fevered sleep. Sleep is a great healer, a time when the body can focus its attention on fighting the infection, a time when it isn't busy with the business of being awake.

All continually prayed fervently to their God to spare him. The doctor called regularly to check up on him. He refused to give them any shred of hope and every time he left the bedside, he had a grim, tight-lipped, turned down mouth.

After an agonisingly long four days, the fever suddenly and inexplicably seemed to burn itself out. Thomas stopped tossing and turning and his sleep became restful. Still he slept on, his consciousness seemingly lodging in another place, unreachable by those who sat around his bed hoping. Catherine looked down at this scrap of a boy. She noticed that his little body was becoming emaciated, his bones protruding through his skin. He looked so pitiful that her tears started flowing again.

On the fifth day, as Catherine sat by Thomas' sick bed gently dabbing his dry, cracked lips with a soft, damp flannel, she heard a low murmuring from his throat. It was as if his consciousness was attempting to return from that other place, fighting its way back and struggling to reconnect once more with his body. Catherine, called to Robat,

'*Turd yma*. Come here. Thomas is making little noises, maybe he's going to be alright after all,' she said hopefully. She held Thomas' hand gently as she stroked his forehead, saying, '*Cariad bach*, come back to us please.' If his recovery was totally dependent on her love and her will for him to live, he could rely on those in spades. After about an hour, his crusted eye lids slowly began to flicker, as he tried his best to open them. A small smile played on his lips as Catherine said, 'Thomas, Mammy's here. Open your eyes '*pwt*,' I think you are going to be alright now,' she said, as this slow realisation began to dawn on her. Robat put his arm around his exhausted but exhilarated wife as they sat there, lovingly gazing at their little son. But who knew what damage the treacherous infection had wrought on his frail, shrunken body?

Thomas soon drifted back off into the comfort of his deep, irresistible sleep but for now, he seemed to be out of immediate danger. His relieved parents walked exhaustedly down the stairs to the kitchen. Catherine walked past the old dresser which stood against the back wall of the kitchen. It had been there when they moved in many years ago now and had probably stood there for many decades before that by the look of it. But she thought it was beautiful, just as its original owner had thought a long time ago, when a skilled carpenter had made it for her. It looked splendid with her grandmother's cheerful blue and white transfer plates standing upright, like soldiers at attention in rows along its shelves. Its background presence made the kitchen a special, comforting place to be. In truth, it was a bit too grand for a kitchen with its fancy ornate brass-handles – but it was impossible to move into the parlour, which would have been a more suitable setting. It had stood there as a silent witness to many a family drama over the years.

Catherine was exhausted but ecstatic. She picked up the big black cast iron kettle and filled it with water from the single brass tap above the porcelain Belfast sink. Thank goodness, she thought, she no longer had to go out to the well in the yard to fetch water. She carried the kettle over to the black range, removed the round top which covered the fire below it, and placed the kettle solidly above the fire to boil. Having fetched cups and saucers from the dresser top and a loaf of bread from the bread oven, she placed these on the kitchen table beside the home-made butter and gratefully sank onto one of the kitchen chairs to wait for the water to boil. Robat went out the back door to the farmyard to check on the animals and came back with a basketful of newly-laid eggs and a pitcher of fresh milk for their breakfast.

'These look like double-yolkers,' said Catherine, taking the basket from Robat, 'I'll scramble them in a pan and maybe we can tempt Thomas to eat a little.' Gwladys soon appeared and there was jubilation as the news of Thomas' recovery spread around the village. The collective gloom lifted from the little valley and people began to smile once more. The longed-for news brought joy to their otherwise mundane day. One of their own was out of danger at last.

A few days later, Robat carefully carried his precious cargo, Thomas, downstairs, to sit by the comfort and warmth of the kitchen range. Thomas had always loved this kitchen and looked around the familiar space. It was the hub of the whole farm and it felt good to be there. The large table in the middle was used for many things. Bread-making, jam-making, bottling, butchering, shoe cobbling, to name a few and it was worn smooth by decades of hard scrubbing. The irregular shaped flagstones on the floor were worn smooth by the endless traffic of feet and ruthless daily scrubbing. The little back window which was fitted deep in the thick stone walls of the house, let some light in. High above the range, a clothes drier hung, hoisted up by a pulley. It was full of the weekly wash, slowly drying and airing. This routine was reassuringly comforting for Thomas, as Robat gently put him down on one of the high-backed settles next to the range. He tucked a Welsh blanket around Thomas, which had been woven in his great-grandfather's woollen mill and handed him one of his favourite adventure books to read while breakfast was being made.

Thomas may have been out of danger – but he took a very long time to fully recover, so missed a lot of schooling. He was housebound for weeks. Too weak to get up by himself, he had to be carried up and downstairs.

When the doctor next called round, he was very pleased to see he had recovered and said 'I have listened to his heart to check for any lasting damage but as far as I can tell there isn't any. Maybe it will become more apparent when he's older. I will check him regularly though. He's lucky to be alive at all.'

A few weeks later, as Robat settled down to read Thomas' favourite bedtime story, Robinson Crusoe, he suddenly asked his father out of the blue, 'Dad, what did you do in the war? Were you a soldier? Did you fight the Hun?'

'Well, son,' putting Robinson Crusoe to one side, 'in 1916, conscription started, which meant that all able-bodied men were called up to enlist, except of course, those who were in essential occupations. Your Uncle Roland and I were not sure what to do then, as we were farmers as well as stonemasons. Most of the young lads hereabouts were mad to go, even young lads not yet fifteen. They thought it would be exciting to fight the enemy. Your uncle Roland and I were much older of course. We thought hard and prayed about it and decided that although we didn't believe in killing people, as it says in the Bible, we should go to make enquiries, as people had started dropping hints about cowardice.' He stressed this last word darkly, giving Thomas a sideways look. But Thomas did not feel inclined to ask him what he meant, as he knew his dad was the bravest man in the whole world. 'When we arrived at the Recruitment Office, I don't know if it was co-incidence or what, but the sergeant-major behind the desk barked at us, asking our occupation. When I answered that my brother and I were both stonemasons, he said, 'Ah! You are exactly what we need. Go and report to that man over there,' pointing his swagger stick in the direction of the corner of the room. We were baffled and disinclined to ask the foreboding sergeant-major why we could not be recruited in the usual way, but we made our way over to the indicated corner. 'Right lads,' said what seemed to be a gang-master. 'You are just what we need, it's your lucky day, you're not going to France – you will be working with me.' Having taken our details, he handed us some official-looking paperwork. 'Report to the Battalion's billeting office tomorrow morning at 7 am sharp. Bring your trade tools. Everything will be explained to you then.' '

Thomas lay there open-mouthed as Robat recounted his story. 'We made our way home. We had no idea what would be going on tomorrow – but the sergeant-major did not look the type to argue with. When I got back, I told your mam what had happened and said, 'It's all a bit odd, we weren't given a uniform or anything, just told we wouldn't be going to France and to be there early in the morning.' ' He paused to recall. 'She was puzzled but secretly relieved. Maybe the army thought we were too old. She was glad I'd had a reprieve, as she had prayed to God that I would not have to go to the Front. Next morning, we set off really early, so we could be at the office at 7am. We got a ride from a carter for some of the way, so bought ourselves some breakfast and a cup of sweet tea in a café, before reporting to the office. The gang-master was already outside with a horse and cart, loaded with bags of cement, sand and stone, as well as a handful of labourers. I felt sorry for that poor nag, as it had quite a load to pull. I hoped for its sake that we weren't going up any steep hills. Anyway, he told us to climb onboard and we set off towards the North Shore. On the way, he told us that we were going to build dressed granite lookouts on the headland, so that soldiers could be posted there to scan the bay for enemy submarines and ships. But all that was 'hush-hush', and we were sworn to secrecy. We learned later that three German officers had escaped from captivity a few miles away and had made their way to the headland to rendezvous with a German U-38 submarine boat. They didn't get there in time for the first night, so tried again the next, but the U-boat could not see their signal. When they failed to make contact the third night, they knew they had missed their best chance of escape, so they started walking towards London but were picked up on the road by the authorities.'

Thomas' mouth was wide open in amazement and he was sitting up, full of rapt attention; he had never heard anything so exciting in his whole life. He thought, wait until I tell my friends about this. Robat continued, 'Because of this incident, the Home Guard had decided that they needed to have look-outs on the peninsula, and we were to build them. That's the reason your uncle and I never went overseas to fight. You could say right place and the right time' said Robat, concluding the story. 'Time to go to sleep now boy. *Nos da.*' Thomas snuggled down beneath his sheets, hugging this new, exciting information to himself, imagining it all as it would have happened while adding a few of his own embellishments.

Months passed before Thomas finally returned to school. The teachers treated him more kindly than they had previously – maybe they had been warned that his heart could be weak. He was well behind his classmates with his schoolwork. Clearly intelligent, school for him was something to be borne – a means to an end. He had accepted that he needed to be able to read and do his arithmetic if he was to be a mechanical engineer. He was not really interested in religion, history or PT, the last because he soon became breathless, but never seemed to have breathing problems when he was out wandering about on the hills. He was happiest when he was busy making or fixing something; or reading mechanical brochures and books with diagrams. Ideas just seemed to pop into his head. When housebound during those months of his convalescence, one of his uncles, concerned about his lethargy, had bought him a Meccano set. This consisted of strips of metal with holes in, plates, wheels, axles, levers and girders, held together with nuts, bolts and screws, using a screwdriver and spanners. Thomas had spent hours in his own little world, making things such as cars, trucks and cranes. Many were extremely inventive, his concentration and focus excellent. His intelligence clearly had a practical bent. Thomas gradually became stronger and held onto his wish to become a mechanical engineer.

The local garage in the heart of the village had once been the blacksmith's workshop, which had serviced the horses and coaches that carried passengers over the pass to the nearest towns and villages. Over time it had somehow morphed into a motor vehicle garage but had many other uses over the centuries. Elwyn could still make metal parts if he needed to. Catherine did not try to stop Thomas going to the garage, she was just grateful that he was still alive.

When Thomas turned fourteen, Elwyn said to him, 'Do you want to have a go at driving that thing?' pointing at an old tractor in the yard. 'Gwil, Tyddyn Du brought it in to be fixed but when I told him how much it was going to cost, he asked me if I wanted to buy it off him, said it wasn't worth fixing. I've got it to go. It's a 1920 Austin ploughing tractor. See, it has rubber tyres on the back but only steel rims on the front. I'll clean it and paint it up a bit then sell it for a profit. You can help me do it up if you want.'

Thomas stood there with his mouth agape. He had never, ever driven anything. Before Elwyn could change his mind, Thomas had run across the yard and was sitting in the purposely shaped metal tractor seat, now padded with rough farm sacking.

'Right,' said Elwyn, when he had caught up with him, 'This thing has two forward gears. The clutch is awkward, you might have to play around a bit to get it into gear.' Thomas climbed down so that Elwyn could get on it, to show him how it was done. He asked Thomas to crank the engine at the front and it soon spluttered into life. As he tried to get it into gear, it made a dreadful grinding noise – but he lifted his foot up and down on the clutch a few times, then finally got it in. Very, very slowly, the tractor started to move forward. Thomas was fascinated. There was no risk of it getting out of control, as all that had to be done was to knock the lever out of gear and pull up the handbrake. It moved slowly across the yard, the metal wheels crunching the gravel as it went, then Elwyn brought it to a halt half-way across. 'I'll show you how to get into reverse now.' he said. Soon the vehicle was slowly reversing back the way it had come. Thomas was mesmerised and impatient for Elwyn to climb down, so he could have a go. Elwyn got out of the seat but stood behind on the back box while Thomas climbed back up into the driver's seat. This was Thomas' very first experience of driving a mechanical vehicle. He was ecstatic. His legs only just reached the pedals, as he perched on the very edge of the metal seat. He could not help smiling, whilst trying to look serious, as he coaxed the clutch to engage first gear. He felt the wheels gaining traction and it began to move slowly forward. He felt a sheer, utter delight. He drove it carefully across the yard, as Elwyn had done, then on his own managed to find the reverse gear. 'You're a natural,' Elwyn declared, 'you'll be better than me soon.' Thomas grinned from ear to ear when he finally bought the tractor to a halt. 'Can I do it again?' he said. 'I'm definitely going to be a mechanic when I grow up.'

'Then you still need to work hard at school, lad. You'll have to be good at reading instructions. Work hard on your sums 'cause you'll need to learn about measurements and things, as well as working out the bills for your customers.' Motivated and absolutely certain what he wanted to be when he was grown up, Thomas started working a bit harder at school to catch up with his peers.

Part 3

We have finished our evening meal and the boys have gone up to their rooms to do homework. Sarah and I sit in the kitchen chatting and finishing off our bottle of wine. We smugly agree that we are now living the life we had craved while in London. Sarah tells me she has finished her next book and will call her publisher tomorrow to tell her. I have marked a stack of student assignments and am feeling extremely relaxed while I look around the room and think how cosy it is.

The wind, which is intensely gusty, makes the rain lash across the windows. These gusts seem to come from nowhere, channelling their way up the valley, which seems to act as a funnel. Sarah and I found some blue and white transferware crockery in a local antique shop, which looks magnificent on the dresser shelves. Once again, I pull out the treasure trove we found in the hole in the wall. We often do this on such nights, encouraged by any new clues we discover. Acutely aware of the fragility of the contents, I place them carefully onto the kitchen table. First, I pick up the locket. 'The engraving C.J. and J.J. suggests it probably belonged to Catrin Jones and the date of 1866 is also the date of John Jones' death on the headstone. I guess John must have given it to Catrin as a sign of his commitment – but I wonder whether he died before or soon after he gave it to her – presumably before they could marry. Catrin was living here in the 1861 census but was the only occupant. John must have got here after this date. She died in 1921, so was alone for all those years. Just imagine that. The lettering on her grave is much more modern than John's inscription.' Turning it over, I open it and see again the lock of black hair inside. 'I bet this is John's hair, Catrin could have put it in the locket after he died tragically, as it says on his grave. I wonder if it's worth getting it DNA checked. Probably not, as he was not actually family – but he was clearly important to her. Imagine if they had married, I might have had a lot more relatives!'

I turn the locket over to look at the other side and its delicate gold chain. 'I don't believe that this locket has had any wear at all – I'll give it a quick polish to get rid of the tarnished bits. There, it looks splendid cleaned up.'

'The gent's antique rose-gold pocket watch is a much earlier piece. It really is a splendid specimen. I imagine any owner would have been proud to wear it.' Very gently, I open the back lid of the ancient timepiece, looking through my eye magnifier, saying, 'The inscription reads J.J. 1810 so it may have originally belonged to John Jones' grandfather. The waistcoat chain and winder key attached both look original.'

'There are also letters here written to Evan Jones, who was Catrin's father – but it's getting late now and my eyes are tired.' I carefully put the letters and the gold pieces away for another time.

As we climb the stairs, I suggest, 'Maybe we should walk down to the church cemetery tomorrow to have another look at Catrin's grave to see if we can glean any more information.'

* * *

Catrin and John's Story

They first became aware of each other as co-worshippers at the small village chapel which was the very heartbeat of the community. Its members tried to live good Christian lives and the Ten Commandments they had learned by heart as children were regularly inculcated into their souls, through the stirring narrative of their non-conformist preachers. They worshipped them, nearly as much as the God they paid homage to, several times a week. Lay preachers of that time brimmed with an evangelical zeal and enthusiasm which could stir the congregation's religious fervour. The haunting hymns they sang in the minor keys filled the high space in the rafters with beautiful, divine music, while cathartically cleansing and comforting their souls.

It wasn't always easy to live by the New Testament's scriptures, which required them to turn the other cheek. Some preferred the

Old Testament's edict of an 'eye for an eye' when a neighbour trespassed on their land, stole their crops, poached their game or rustled their sheep. The forgiveness of sin, their own and those of others, was at the very core of their Christian faith. There were degrees of sin of course, some were considered more acceptable than others. But they were generally kindly, caring people with an over-developed sense of propriety. Being respectable was high on the list of aspirations and the good character and reputation, their own and their families', was of paramount importance.

When John had finally left his home in Llanbeblig on the western peninsula which stuck far out into the Irish Sea, all he possessed, apart from his skills, were the clothes he stood up in, a backpack, a large piece of canvas, a billy-can, a skillet and the tools of his trade.

'We're going to miss having you around lad,'

'And I will miss you all. You've raised me from a boy, an orphan – and I will always be grateful to you for that, as well as the skills you have taught me. I understand that you can no longer afford to feed an extra mouth, you have already fed me enough! I will write to let you know how I get on.'

'We were only doing our Christian duty, John. Here take this.' The tearful carpenter's wife handed him some bread and cheese – and other provisions for his journey, wrapped in a clean cloth. With that, he set off at a good pace, his intention being to walk eastwards along the length of the coastal path, searching for work.

His first choice would to be part of another project, building a big house for the gentry. He liked to see things go from being a flat abstract plan on paper, to becoming a completed building. He called at sites along his route but there was nothing for him, due to a general slump in the building trade. He knew his other option was to join many of his countrymen who were emigrating to other lands – but he could not quite make the break with his roots. However, that was always an option if he got really desperate. He had no money for a fare but thought he might be able to work his passage out, as a ship's carpenter. But he would have to make his way to Liverpool for that. That would be an adventure! He had read stories in the local newspaper about groups of religious people who planned to emigrate to farm in the Patagonian area of Argentina. It seemed a radical thing to do but their motivation was to keep their Welsh culture and language; to live the farming life they loved, to worship as they chose in their non-conformist chapels. He could empathise with these sentiments and knew that he would be a useful addition to help set up their new colony. But still he hesitated; his country was the only link he still had with the family he had lost. He did not want to set himself adrift completely from his roots and was reluctant to break his bond with his country.

Although John's family had only ever spoken Welsh, he had learned to speak English whilst working in the big house. The children of the house, who were younger than him, liked to spend time talking to him and watching him while he worked. The daughter had her own governess and liked playing the role of teacher to John, who was her willing pupil and a quick learner. John had had some schooling while his parents were still alive. He had also learned to read and write Welsh in his Sunday school class at the local chapel. There they practised their letters on slate, using a thin slate pencil wrapped in paper to keep their fingers clean. It was easier to rub out any mistakes on these, unlike expensive paper.

When the carpenter's family had first taken him in as a child of ten, he had worked as their house servant. This was to prevent him being taken into the local workhouse after being orphaned and made homeless in a cholera outbreak. But John liked going to the carpenter's workshop. He watched the meticulous way he drew his plans and worked out measurements with a stub of pencil, which he kept tucked behind his ear. Occasionally, John was asked to sand down various pieces of wood and felt satisfaction as the wood turned smooth under his shaping hand. He soon came to love this work and the smell of the oils in the pitch-pine wood-shavings.

The carpenter soon noticed the intensity with which John watched him work. He saw John run his hands lovingly over, almost caressing the shaped surfaces of the wood and realised that John would make a much better carpenter than a house servant. Although always willing, John was not cut out, nor did he have the temperament, for servitude. So he took him on as an indentured apprentice, helping him with the work in the big house. With no official sponsor, the carpenter taught him out of the goodness of his heart. John was not paid for his work but given his board and lodging free. During this time, he learned his numbers and came to love geometry, for which he had an innate aptitude.

Over the next few years, he more than justified his master's faith in him but as work began drying up, he realised it was time he made his own way in the world. This realisation was both scary and exhilarating at the same time

His own family slowly had faded from his memory. He found this distressing at times – but one childhood memory stood out, untarnished by time. He remembered a feeling of utter peace and security while being lulled to sleep by his mother's melodic contralto voice and still remembered the words of the song. At times of desolate loneliness, he sought out that haunting memory to comfort himself.

He was a loner. He had decided to depend on himself alone. He did not risk getting too close to anybody, in case he was let down again. He could not bear to go through the utter grief and pain he had suffered when he had lost his entire family in a matter of days. Why he had been spared was still a mystery. Maybe God had a special plan for him.

John was well-built, his upper body and arms were muscular from years of working with wood. He was tall, slim-hipped and had the dark-eyed, olive-skinned look of his Celtic ancestors. He wore thick, well-worn trousers and a work jacket woven from home-spun Welsh wool, with leather patches at the elbow and strips reinforcing the cuffs. His clothes were shabby and had been heavily but neatly repaired many times. They kept out the cold, and the oil in the worsted wool of hardy Welsh sheep kept out the damp. His shirt, now grubby, was collarless, held together at the neck by a single brass stud, once owned by his long-dead father. His heavy, hobnailed, steel-toed boots, given to him by his former employer, should last for many years. His grey socks were knitted by his former employer's wife. Apart from the tools of his trade, his only valuable possession was the large gold fob watch, which had also belonged to his late father, and his father before him. It hung on a link chain with its winder and was tucked carefully away in the small watch pocket of his charcoal grey, serge waistcoat. He treasured this watch above all things. He was proud how it kept time with impressive accuracy; he wound it religiously every evening, at the same time, with the same number of winds, so as not to overwind it. It was his only link with his family. His initials were engraved inside the lid of the watch. Luckily for John, he had been named after his father and grandfather before that – but it was the engraved date which revealed its true age, despite its present ownership.

On enquiring yet again, a stranger suggested, 'Why don't you try the new quarry which has opened up in the hills above Dwygyfylchi? They might be hiring.' So John was now heading inland in that direction. In between walking, he had been given rides on various farm carts and wagons, by people wanting to be helpful as well as those wanting company. Suddenly, he heard a horse's hooves behind him, then a voice, 'Want a ride?' John accepted gladly, as his load was heavy and the weather hot. The driver, who John quickly realised was fairly drunk, soon nodded off. The horses seemed to know their own way home but even so, John thought it best to quietly take over the reins from the driver, in case the horse got spooked by something and bolted. In the quietude, to the hypnotic clip-clop, he remembered as a small child his mother had warned about the evils of drink. He guessed that this chap had probably nipped into a local tavern after delivering his load of flour to a baker and spent some of his earnings on strong drink. It was lucky that it was John he picked up, as another person might have relieved him of the remainder of his money.

As the wagoner neared his destination, he suddenly woke. 'Oh, I must have just nodded off for a minute or two.' The sleep seemed to have sobered him up, as he was now quite coherent. John asked for directions to the local quarry. 'You just carry on walking through the village over there,' pointing to some cottages along the road, 'then turn right up between the two inns,' with which he presumably was well familiar, 'then follow the track all the way to the top, bearing left of the river as you climb up, then you will see the workings up ahead of you. Mind you, it's a couple of miles up to there.'

John was hopeful of work as he headed for the quarry. He was glad of the skills he had learned during the long years as an apprentice carpenter, as it meant that he had the means to earn a living. He was also glad he was free to travel to find work, which he may not have done with a wife and family. He knew the quarry would not need a skilled worker. They might only want him to hew wooden props out of tree trunks, to reinforce the roofs in the quarry tunnels but as an ambitious young man, he hoped this might lead to something better. What he really wanted was his own carpentry business one day. His apprenticeship with the old master carpenter had involved making doors, door frames, sash windows, cupboards, floors and skirting boards in the big house built for the local gentry. He had had to learn many intricate skills, such as carving mouldings and fine furniture making.

Walking towards the small hamlet of Capelulo, he followed the driver's directions. Turning right, he walked up the Nant, alongside a large river. To be sure, he asked others the direction to the New Quarry, arousing the curiosity of the locals. This was to be expected in a place such as this where everybody knew everybody else, as he stood out like a sore thumb.

The quarry was some way up the side of a mountain. Quarry workers walked the steep climb in the morning, then back at night – but thankfully downhill. During the winter months, they walked there and back in the dark, although their eyes soon adjusted. They could almost find their way blindfolded if necessary, having walked the route so often. When low mists, which came down suddenly, closed in around the mountain, they needed their good sense of direction. But in the long light days of summer, when it was often still light until eleven o'clock at night, some workers cultivated small potato plots next to the track, to augment the family's food supply. Anything planted above ground would soon be eaten by sheep or rabbits – but potatoes were safe from these raiders. The ground was rich and loamy, and together with the soft, frequently falling rain, the potatoes' shoots soon appeared. In a couple of months, the potatoes were generally ready to be dug up. Following the well-worn track, John noticed these random potato patches and was impressed by their resourcefulness.

Finally, he arrived at the quarry and asked a young lad, 'Can you direct me to the site manager's office?' Once there, he said, 'I am a carpenter by trade and am looking for work. Do you have anything here for me?' The manager replied, 'I would be glad to take you on – but it will only be on a temporary basis making props, ladders, fences, platforms and sleepers for the rail tracks and suchlike. Occasionally to repair tools and the trucks used for bringing the stone out. So, there's enough work for now if you want it.' He then stood up, saying, 'Come, I'll show you around the quarry and point out what needs doing. If you like the look of the job you can start in the morning.' The manager went on to explain, 'The miners generally work in gangs of about six men. They mine a certain section and are paid so much per ton for what they bring out. These gangs are made up of fathers, sons and brothers. The younger sons are employed as 'rubblers', which means clearing away the rubble left behind from the mining. The slate slabs brought out are then taken into the dressing sheds to be split and shaped into roof tiles. This is very skilled work and they really know their stone. You would be responsible for erecting wooden props in the tunnel's entrance and their general maintenance, as well as all the other tasks I mentioned earlier. For this, I will pay you five shillings a week.'

'I'll take it on and will start tomorrow,' said John, touching his flat cap in acknowledgement of the offer.

They shook hands warmly on the agreement. The pay was low but it was better than nothing and would keep him going for a while.

Being early summer, John decided that to save himself the long daily walks and paying rent somewhere, he would camp on the mountain. The tent he had used during his journey from home was a sheet of canvas, draped over an across pole, held up by two uprights. This kept the rain out but not much else.

He chose a sheltered dip, close to a nearby stream. He decided he would go to the village on Saturday to buy food, as well as soap and shaving cream, to be decent to attend chapel on Sunday.

John had already walked a long way that day and hunger soon began to claw at his belly. Once he had put up his tent out of sight of casual passers-by, he set some rabbit traps, so he could have some supper. He had been brought up in the countryside, so was adept at feeding himself from the bounty of the land and rarely went hungry for long.

He walked a little further up-stream, to get the lie of the land. The stream had been dammed naturally by boulders, creating a dark, deep pool. There wasn't a living soul for miles, so he stripped and had a quick dip to wash away the dust and dirt of the journey. The coldness took his breath away but was, at the same time, invigorating. He swam and moved about quickly to keep his circulation going, washing himself as best he could without soap. He got out feeling refreshed, then lay on the grassy bank to dry off. The sun began to drop lower in the sky and he felt the first stirrings of an evening chill, so quickly dressed. When he had more time, he would return to the stream to tickle the big fat trout he had seen lurking in the shallows.

Picking up dead wood as he returned to his camp, he lit a fire. Once established, he put a billy-can of water to boil. As he waited, he walked back to the traps and sure enough, one had caught a leveret. He carried it back to his camp and quickly skinned, gutted and cut it into small pieces with his penknife. He speared these with a metal skewer he had in his rucksack and once the wood turned to coals, he placed the skewer above to slowly grill. To his billy-can he added some small potatoes, which he had been given by a farmer when he had a lift in his cart. He decided he would also plant some seed potatoes, maybe he could borrow a spade from work one evening. He then mixed flour and water into a bread dough and placed this in his skillet on top of the hot coals. After a while, he turned the dough over, to cook on the other side. This would be his breakfast and lunch tomorrow with any left-over leveret. Content for the time-being, he knew that he could stay in the tent through the summer.

John sat, satiated by his evening meal. He looked around him and noticed old furrow lines, only now highlighted by the very low sun casting long evening shadows. These furrows looked very old, indicating ancient cultivation of crops on this land at a different time in history. He wondered if the climate had been warmer then and if people had lived permanently up on these hills, instead of on the valley floor, as they did now.

The large, red glowing ball of the sun sat on the hazy, shimmering horizon. Slowly and imperceptibly, it began to sink while a strong red line reflected across the water, widening as it neared the shoreline. John was mesmerised. The sky above then started to turn into every imaginable shade of red, purple and orange, lighting up the wispy fine-weather clouds, making them look like little bursts of flame. He sat very still as the sun finally disappeared, then the red sky deepened and became even more fiery. He let the still atmosphere, which felt like the quiet sacredness of a church, soak into him. He imagined that this place, at earlier times in its pre-religion history, was a place where nature and the stars had been worshipped, by people who knew the true value of their location.

The spectacular sunset and the mackerel sky portended that the weather would remain fine. Having work meant he did not have to worry about money for a while and he was eager to start work in the morning. He banked up the fire with more wood to keep it going, then carefully wound his father's watch to be sure of knowing the correct time when he woke. He guessed it would start to get light about four o'clock and decided to lay more rabbit traps before leaving.

When he awoke just after first light, there was a damp film of dew on his clothes. He quickly relit the fire from the now dying embers, warmed up some of the flatbread and brewed strong tea in his billy-can. Having washed his face and rinsed his can in the stream, he picked up his carpenter's tools and started walking towards the quarry path just before six o'clock. He met up with other workers who had started walking from the village earlier. He introduced himself but they already knew that a new man would be joining their ranks. They did not break their step as they walked but warmly said, '*Croeso,*' knowing that he would be making the mines, therefore their lives, safer.

Despite his usually solitary leanings, John enjoyed the camaraderie of these men and he was soon accepted by them. It seemed that it was up to him in what order he did the work, so asked his fellow workers, 'What do you think needs fixing first?'

'Repairing the props by the tunnel entrance; last week they got knocked by one of the slate carts which came off the track.' Another said, 'The handles on some of the spades could do with a bit of attention as well.' John began his work, mindful that their safety was now his priority and responsibility.

At midday break, he ate some of his flatbread, while the others tucked into coarse bread smeared with lard and drank buttermilk. They only earned a few shillings a week for their labours and many supported large families on this. During the breaks, he preferred to listen than talk, as he learned a great deal more that way. He began to realise which men were worth listening to and which to humour or ignore.

Time passed quickly as John felled the small pine trunks. Once he had cut them to size, he trimmed off the branch nodules, then used a two-handled cutting scraper to remove the bark, making the trunks smoother. Using a large lump hammer, he hammered the posts into position, removing the old posts as he went, which had begun to rot at their bases, due to constant standing water.

With his first day's work over, John left with his workmates. He split off from the main path to make his way back to his camp. 'See you tomorrow morning' they called as he walked away from the group.

He soon lit a fire with wood shavings saved from shaping the supports and other dead wood he had gathered. He placed flattish stones around the fire to get hot and made some more flatbread. He also placed some remaining pieces of leveret on the stones to gently cook. Later he checked the traps and hung the caught rabbit in the nearest tree for next day, hoping the crows would not get at it.

Again, John watched the sun set over the horizon in front of him. Sitting there, he felt like the king of the world. The sky provided another beautiful kaleidoscopic show of colours, which deepened as the sun sunk. He felt then at peace with the world and himself. Presently, he rose to search for more firewood to bank the fire with, when to his left, hidden under the ferns, he discovered what seemed to be an almost complete ring of very large stones covered in lush moss. He wondered if this had once formed the round base of the primitive shelter of people long dead.

As the months slipped by, John realised this outdoor lifestyle could not last much longer. Soon he would need a warm, dry place to stay in come the late autumn. He had carefully saved his wages, spending only minimally on the basics needed to survive. He hid his money in a secret place in case somebody stumbled across his camp. This seemed unlikely, given its concealed position – but once the bracken turned brown, his cover would become compromised. There was the risk that someone would notice the smoke rising from his campfire caused by damp wood and become curious. It was time to enquire about permanent accommodation.

John now regularly attended the newly-built Methodist chapel in the village. He had fallen into conversation a week or so before with one of his workmates who had explained, 'The chapel was the idea of one of our founder members, tragically deceased. The land was donated by a wealthy local gent, whilst others gave money, materials and their labour.'

The result was a plain, simple building, as befitted their religion, their main extravagance being the harmonium to accompany the beautifully haunting hymns. He went on, 'As a congregation, we are of course pleased and very proud of our new chapel which also gets used for many other community purposes.'

John liked the unpretentious feel of the people and the place.

Surreptitiously, he cast a professional eye over the pitch-pine pews and carvings on the pulpit, as well as the oak deacon's chairs, where the elders of the chapel sat. He acknowledged the skill and craftsmanship which had gone into making them.

Over time, John got to know more members of the congregation; many were his quarry workmates, while he was on nodding terms with others. He was warmly welcomed but being reserved by nature, he did not give away too much personal information. His fellow workers knew he was camping out on the mountain, so most of the congregation was aware of his living arrangements. Being a small but well-meaning community, it was difficult to keep personal business private, despite his best efforts. What they did not know about him, he assumed they made up through speculation, which soon became fact at the mouths of gossips.

The weather had cooled and the driving rains of autumn began to penetrate his make-do shelter. Although still warm, he sometimes woke at dawn in very damp clothes, making him shiver. So after the next Sunday service, he asked a fellow chapelgoer if he could recommend suitable lodgings. He said he would make enquiries. The following Sunday, he was approached by one of the elders, who said tentatively, 'A member of our congregation, a young woman, can offer you a place to stay, in exchange for a few hours labouring on her smallholding. She says you can sleep in the loft above the stable, rent free and meals included.'

John knew who the elder meant, having seen her before at the Sunday services. She was a single smallholder, whose appearance reflected her lifestyle. Her body was strong, slim and sinewy from relentless, physically hard work. Her striking dark looks, accentuated by the outdoor work on the farm over the summer had given her skin an attractive healthy glow. However, since her father's tragic accident, he was told Catrin rarely smiled. Her life was hard, a constant struggle – but she knew she was better off than many. She had somewhere to live and the means to provide for herself. She transported her farm produce to market, using her docile Welsh cob and cart. Catrin was very self-sufficient, eminently capable but reticent by nature. Her upbringing and religion had inculcated her with humility; she believed it was wrong to be proud, pushy and opinionated.

When the chapel elder had approached her with his proposal, she had mixed feelings. She agreed it would be a mutually beneficial arrangement. She also believed that as it had been the elder who had proposed the idea, the arrangement would not be frowned upon by the rest of the congregation as chapel people would be scandalised if she'd had a single man living under the same roof in the farmhouse itself. Although not entirely comfortable with the arrangement, she knew she was not coping and that she needed the help with the backlog of maintenance work; the fabric of the farm buildings had become run down, neglected and in need of major repairs.

Next day, on the walk to work at the quarry, John told his fellow workers, 'I have been offered a place to stay above the stables at Glyn Abercyn, in exchange for a few hours farm work.' He waited for their response. One of the wiser men nodded agreeably, 'This arrangement would be good for both of you.' Another, younger one, could not resist the temptation to tease, 'mmm…living very close to a single, unmarried woman, who owns her own farm! I wouldn't mind being in your shoes.' John frowned, choosing not to respond to this disrespectful comment.

John and Catrin met early one evening to discuss the arrangement. Both were self-conscious and awkward during the conversation. She led the way to the stable and pointing up to the loft said, 'This is where you can sleep, do you think you would be comfortable?' Glad at last of a dry place to sleep at night, he replied with a smile, 'I am sure I can make it very cosy.'

Outside once more, Catrin walked around the farmyard pointing out the repairs which needed doing. 'Will you be able to fix them?'

'There does seem quite a bit of work to do but I am sure I can soon get it into good shape,' he assured her. 'Well, that's settled then, you repair the buildings, help with the animals and in return, you get a place to stay and your meals. You will have to do these jobs before you go to work in the mornings and again when you return in the evenings, as well as on Saturday afternoons. Sunday is a day of rest of course but the animals still have to be tended and fed.'

'Yes, this will suit me very well,' said John, thinking he could save his wages from the quarry job and maybe one day he could rent a small place and start his furniture making business. But that dream was a very long way off. Catrin then left him and returned to the house, while John climbed up to the loft to look around the little space he was to occupy. He would certainly be more comfortable here than in a tent on the mountain in winter!

It did not take John long to get settled. He constructed a narrow sleeping pallet from old planking he found nearby. He blocked gaps in the walls with stones and old newspaper. He found an extending wooden ladder, so climbed up onto the roof to fix the roof slates which had slipped. With the heat rising from the cob stabled below, he would be very cosy here during the cold winter months. This place was heaven-sent, given that the weather and the days were closing in. After work the next day, he packed up his camp and moved most of his belongings down to the farm and soon made his quarters comfortable; the rest he would fetch tomorrow.

Catrin's attitude had become quite negative. She expected the worst to happen – as a form of self-protection from further disappointment – but praying to her God at bedtime, she told him she was grateful for what she had. Her daily routine rarely varied, except on the days she went to market. She rose when it was still dark outside, washed herself by candlelight from cold water in the large jug on the washstand then dried herself with a rough towel. She drew a comb through her unruly hair and pinned it up out of the way. She dressed quickly, pulling on her woollen vest and drawers, a bodice and long woollen stockings; added numerous petticoats, which she then covered with her black, everyday homespun woollen dress. She slipped on wooden clogs, then threw her woollen shawl around her shoulders, tucking the ends into her belt, before making her way down the narrow wooden stairs to the cold, dark, stone-walled kitchen. The kitchen fire often went out overnight, especially when windy and the wood quickly turned into cinders. She would ask John to take the cob and cart up to the marshy area on the mountain to dig out a cartload of peat turfs which would burn more slowly.

Lighting the oil lamp which stood on the kitchen table lit up the kitchen with a warm comforting glow. She donned her calico apron and tied the strings in a bow at the back. Riddling out the kitchen range, she carried the ashes and cinders onto the paths, then relit the fire, ready for another day. The range was impressive. One side held the open fire, with the hotplates across the top. The other side was a baking oven and below that, a proving oven. Above it, was a mantle shelf with some tapers and a pair of Staffordshire dog ornaments. Above that was the wooden clothes airer, operated by a pulley system. With the fire lit, the kitchen was a warm cosy oasis. Plentiful in the ancient woods which skirted the field were fallen branches which made good logs, but the woodpile was running very low and winter fast approaching – another job for John.

Catrin filled the large black kettle from the well and put it on the stove to boil, then went out to the cowshed to milk her cows, now gently lowing, their udders uncomfortably full. She rubbed her hands briskly to warm them and sat on her three-legged milking stool, then rested her head on the cow's flank for warmth as it munched contentedly on the fresh hay she had put into the feed-holders. The mesmeric squirting sound of the milk filling the wooden pail relaxed her and they yielded a good bucketful, with enough spare to make some butter. Catrin covered the pail, then led the cows out into the open fields to graze on the lush grass. Carrying the precious milk to the small dairy behind the main farmhouse, she poured it into a wide-brimmed, glazed, earthenware pot. As she did, she recalled as a small child they had a dairy maid called Gwen, who used to let her help in the dairy, which was how she learned to make the delicious butter and cheeses. Carefully Catrin covered the earthenware pot with a muslin cloth, weighed down with colourful glass beads to protect from flies, and left the cream to rise. Later, she would churn the cream into butter and put some by to make the cheeses she sold in the local market. The buttermilk left behind from the butter-making was used for drinking and baking – with any spare given to the pigs.

Catrin noticed that John had already let the cob out to pasture before he left for work. As usual it had headed straight for the stream which ran through her property. From now on, John would be responsible for the cob, given the stable was his territory.

On her way back, Catrin checked the hen shed for eggs. She let out the birds and threw them some corn which they cropped from the grit in the yard. She gathered the few, still warm eggs, which she carefully placed deep in her apron pocket. She used them for cooking and baking and sold them to people who called at the farm, as well as at the market – these were a good steady source of income. Next, she checked the pigsty. She fed the pigs mainly on turnips and vegetable cuttings but also let them out into the field where a very large oak tree was dropping its acorns. They loved grubbing about in the undergrowth in search of them. It was a free source of food which added flavour to their meat. She had had rings put in their snouts to stop them disturbing the pasture. Occasionally, she would slaughter and butcher one, then salt some joints, which she hung on hooks above the fireplace to smoke.

As the day lightened, Catrin looked heavenward to check what the weather had in store. She saw a rain squall slowly working its way inland from the sea. She reckoned she had about ten minutes before it reached her so went to her vegetable plot and quickly dug up carrots, potatoes and leeks for the evening meal. John was soon to learn what an excellent cook she was.

Every springtime, she planted seeds and vegetables and any glut, she pickled or sold the surplus. She was plagued by rabbits, which dug their way in under the wire fence to eat her plants. Another job for John to set some rabbit traps, she thought, walking quickly back to the house just as the rain started. The kettle was now boiling furiously so she made a pot of tea, then got some oats to make porridge, which she left to gently bubble on the stove.

Catrin had a very proud and independent nature. She did not realise what a strong woman she was doing all this work on her own

– she thought only that it needed to be done. But she now accepted she needed a bit of help around the place and was so glad that John was now there.

She kept a small flock of hardy Welsh mountain sheep, which provided her with meat. Occasionally Catrin would slaughter one of the older sheep and sell off the mutton joints, keeping some for herself to make delicious stews. She made candles and soap out of rendered sheep fat and fire ashes, adding herbs such as lavender to use for personal washing. She also sold her lavender soap and small muslin sachets of lavender to use for storing clothes and bedding.

She spun their wool into yarn during long winter evenings and used this to knit her under-garments and stockings. She also took some to a local fuller to clean and then to a wool manufacturer, who weaved the yarn into flannel for her, from which she made outer-garments and blankets. This naturally-produced material was excellent and hardwearing. After shearing, Dafydd's son from the adjoining farm took her flock along with his up to the high summer pastures and brought them down again when summer ended. In return for this, she gave him one of the lambs as payment. This arrangement worked well for both parties as she did not have the time to shepherd them. She sold off most of her yearling lambs, keeping the occasional one or two ewes for breeding. Her Welsh sheep dog, Pero, went with her neighbour to round them up and seemed to know which ones were his. He had been trained by her late father Evan and was also good at guarding the property from strangers.

Once the grass in the hay field was harvested and stored in the barn as winter feed, large wild field mushrooms grew in the corn stubble. Catrin picked these at first light and fried them gently in butter for breakfast. She sometimes sold them at market if there was a glut. Eating these was one of life's little pleasures.

As her porridge bubbled, she saw that more showers were on their way, so she ran out again to let out the geese, which freely roamed the farmyard. Their eggs were used for baking and gave cakes a lovely golden colour. She also sold these in the market.

Having completed her outdoor jobs, she made her way quickly back into the farmhouse through the backdoor – again just as the rain arrived. She made bread every other day and set to work to make the dough, so that it could prove for an hour or so in the range. Once she had done this, she finally sat down to eat her porridge, followed by a cup of strong tea. This was therefore the relentless pattern of Catrin's life. Pero, who slept in one of the outhouses, had sneaked into the kitchen and hidden under the table. He was getting a little older now and enjoyed the warmth from the fire.

Towards the end of the next day, his ears pricked up. He'd heard hob-nailed boots approaching from the road, then down the side of the barn. Even before John appeared, he was barking furiously. 'Easy boy' said John, trying to quieten him down, as he clung desperately onto the rest of his belongings. He attempted to hold out one hand for the dog to sniff but Pero was more interested in snapping at it. Catrin came out of the house, shouting for the dog to be quiet but he carried on barking, so as to have the last word. Finally, considering his duty done, he slunk away back to his warm bed of sacking in the corner of the barn.

Catrin and John greeted each other once the din had stopped. 'I have made some stew for supper if you're ready to eat.' John, who was ravenous and exhausted after his full day's work and the walk down from his campsite carrying the rest of his belongings, said 'I'll take these to the loft then come straight back.' The smell wafting from the kitchen made his stomach rumble. In the loft he saw that Catrin had left him a woollen blanket, an old sheet and a striped blue and white pillow, stuffed with goose feathers. He headed to the back door, removed his boots, then entered the kitchen. 'Thanks for the bedding. Much appreciated.' She nodded to the sink, 'You can wash your hands there.' He dried them on the roller towel close by. They both felt slightly disconcerted at the unfamiliar domesticity and he sat down at the kitchen table feeling self-conscious. A steaming hot plate of mutton stew was placed in front of him and Catrin sliced him a large piece of the loaf she had made earlier. 'This is good,' he said after a few mouthfuls. 'A welcome change from damper bread and rabbit stew.' Despite his awkwardness, he was glad to be sitting in her cosy, warm kitchen,

A small smile played on her lips as she said, 'It's a long time since I shared supper with anybody. It's going to be a regular thing now, so we had better both get used to it. Talking of rabbits, you know how to lay traps then?' He nodded. 'The place is riddled with them this year and they play havoc with my vegetable plot.' Nodding whilst swallowing a mouthful, he replied, 'I'll set some tomorrow when I get back from work. I'll put them where the animals won't get caught up in them and you will need to watch where you are walking.' She then volunteered, 'There is an ancient gun in the shed. It's wrapped in an oiled cloth' but John shook his head at this suggestion.

As he wiped his plate clean with the last of his bread, he said 'Diolch. That was just what I needed. Thank you.' He scraped the flagstones with the chair legs as he quickly stood up saying, 'I'll go and sort out my sleeping quarters while there is still a bit of daylight left.' She gave him a stub of a candle, then he was gone – and the room felt suddenly very empty again. She carried the plates over to the sink to wash, inordinately pleased that he had enjoyed his supper.

Late summer and autumn brought an abundance of fruits and berries. She baked fruit pies, flans, cakes and tarts. She made preserves, jams and pickles. Rosehips were made into syrup for winter cough mixtures, as well as into salves to treat joint pains caused by damp weather. She had learned all these skills as a girl from her own mother. Her beehives provided the 'sweet nectar' for spreading onto the homemade buttered bread and at the Conwy autumn seed fair, she sold pots of honey, which tasted of the mountain heather from which the bees gathered their pollen. This fair was quite a social occasion for the local people and outlying farmers. Stalls lined both sides of the main street, which led to the castle, and sold a wide variety of goods. They met up with people they had not seen for a while and exchanged news about their families and farms. They bought seed for the next season's crops, as well as any miscellaneous household goods which they needed.

The orchard produced cooking and eating apples, as well as pears. In the autumn, Catrin wrapped unbruised fruit in squares of old newspaper and carefully placed them in wooden boxes, to store in the dry, dark loft of the house. Bruised windfalls were made into chutneys and sauces. Hazelnuts and beech nuts grew in abundance in the hedges which grew along the stream, near her neighbour's boundary. These she also stored in the loft, placed well out of the reach of any vermin which might winter there. In the flatter, slower-flowing area of the stream, grew watercress and mint. She used these in her cooking and sold bunches tied with coarse brown twine at the market.

Catrin took in tourists and travelling artists in the summer, attracted to the valley to capture its scenic beauty on canvas. Who could blame them for wanting to do this? She also loved her home and could not imagine living anywhere else.

Subsistence farming was a way of life for many smallholdings in the area but there was usually at least one wage coming in. Catrin did not have this luxury – she knew she had to make the place pay – but it was a constant struggle. Her day began well before first light and ended only long into the evening, when she finally collapsed in her bed. This was Catrin's world, the world into which John had now entered.

He settled quickly and soon got into the rhythm and routine of the farm. Catrin did not really have to tell him what needed doing, he seemed to know instinctively and got on with his tasks quietly and efficiently. John was still wary of Pero when they came across each other in the farmyard. The dog occasionally sneaked up behind him to nip at his ankles. Gradually the dog came to accept him, bribed with a few sneaked-out food morsels, and when he realised John meant no harm, he kept him company when he carried out his jobs around the farmstead.

John found doing the two jobs exhausting but the wonderful food he was rewarded with when he sat down to eat with Catrin was worth it. Camp-side food was replaced by manna from heaven. Catrin, found pleasure in cooking for someone else again and getting used to having him around. As well as getting the farm buildings into shape, John made many improvements. He thought of better, more efficient ways of doing things and soon Catrin began to wonder how she had ever managed before he came.

At the end of the following summer, 'Bad news boys, they're going to be laying some of us off,' said the foreman, 'The quarry industry is being hit by a general recession. Demand for our product has dropped worldwide. So, the owners will tighten the rules at work and will demand more work for the same pay.'

Relationships between the workers and the owners deteriorated, intensified by the differences in language, culture, religion and politics. The quarry owners were English and Church of England, whilst the workers, many of whom spoke only Welsh, were non-conformist working class. The owners tended to look down on the Welsh workers, seeing them as an inferior class and refused to even listen to their perspectives. The workers called for strike action, as they had learned their compatriots had done at other quarries nationwide. From some there was heady talk about emigration, to establish their own colonies and farms, build chapels to worship in peace, without having to pay the hated tithes for upkeeping the Church of England, churches they did not attend. John listened to this emotive talk of moving overseas but was himself reluctant to leave. He would just have to wait to see what happened.

He was one of the first to hear. As he was last in, he was the first out, so began to work full-time on the farm. There was plenty to keep him busy there and he did not like being idle. This made things even easier for Catrin and she began to increasingly depend on him, handing over more of the outside tasks to him and told him, 'I'm sure my parents would have been very proud of how ship-shape the farm looks now,'

Occasionally, on a long, beautiful summer evening, John walked down through hayfields of tall summer grasses, where wildflowers such as buttercups, cornflowers, cow parsley and poppies grew. The heat of the day created a wonderful earthy scent to greet him as he strode through the grasses. Later, he would find his trouser turn-up full of seeds and dust. Once at the shoreline, he watched the lazy plop of small languorous waves; at other times, the pounding, powerful waves churned up by recent storms. There he watched the sun slowly sink down while sporadically picking up pieces of driftwood for the fire – but more often than not, he walked up onto the hills behind the farm, where he had first camped. He thought of it as his own thinking place, while watching the sun sink below the horizon, then watching as the sky burst into its kaleidoscope of vivid colours. At these times, he felt the nearest thing to true contentment – but fretted about not making any real progress in his life. He was in a comfortable rut, a sort of limbo, his former ambition of owning his own business now no longer seeming a possibility. The sudden realisation that he was also becoming fond of Catrin was as frightening as it was unexpected. He admired her quiet courage and her independent spirit in keeping the farm going before and since his arrival, despite the hardships. He respected her knowledge and skill in running the farm as a viable business. His role had only been to improve the basic fabric of the farm as she did not need his help in running it – but nevertheless, he felt useful.

Summer came and went again, then the first real storm of winter blew in from the Atlantic in the west. It lashed the valley with rain and tormented the trees until they gave up their gold and red leaves. As Christmas approached, John again wondered what he should do. Catrin could certainly not afford to pay him for his labour but he was grateful to be well fed with a warm place to sleep. On his bed, he glanced gratefully at the quilt Catrin had made with feathers, plucked from her geese. He felt sorry for his former quarry co-workers who had to live in miserable cold hovels, with no money coming in and dependents to feed. He knew many parents went to bed hungry to feed their children, while he was able to live off the bounty of the farm.

He thought again of moving on to find work elsewhere but from what he read and heard from people passing through the valley, there was a general depression and work was scarce. If he left, he could end up like them, skeletal forms tramping the roads looking for any

116

work just to eat, then sleeping rough in cold barns or ditches. He knew he was fortunate – but he missed the company of men and the camaraderie of his fellow workers. He thought back fondly to their mid-day break, while discussing politics, gossiping and making jokes. Their inherent love of music was an integral part of their being. They had often sung in unison on the long walks to and from the quarry. They often sang for no reason at all, except for their love of the music they made, which reflected both the joy and the sorrow in their souls. Of course, John enjoyed this when he went to chapel services. Hearing the soaring sopranos, mournful altos, tuneful melodious tenors and the deep bass voices singing in such harmony felt like they all melded into one sound. These voices came into their own when singing the haunting minor key hymns of their mother-tongue, which echoed the pathos of their lives. Each Sunday the little children had to recite a verse by heart from the Bible in front of the congregation, as he had done as a child. Sometimes when inspired by the beauty of his surroundings, he would write poetry to express the thoughts and emotions he could not talk of. He never disclosed these to anyone, as he did not feel they were good enough in comparison to the wonderful prose produced by some local people – but it was cathartic for him to put 'pen to paper.'

Suddenly, after a year, the strike ended. When workers returned to work, it was for the same or even less money than they had earned before; all the sacrifice and suffering had gained nothing – the quarry owners had won but there was no work for John, at least not yet.

Catrin had a niggling feeling that some of the chapel people did not consider their situation quite respectable. Nobody said as much – but she was finely tuned into nuance and the way her people thought. Some delighted in making mischief and spreading gossip; some probably thought they should do the right thing and get married, or that he should move on. The problem was that although she now realised she had become very fond of him, she had no idea how he felt about her. She thought that he must also have picked up on the innuendos of his male friends and was considering his situation.

Once the notion of their becoming a couple had occurred to Catrin, she started to fantasise about their lives together. Being a farmer, she knew all about reproduction in animals – but she had no mother, sister, or even close friend to talk to about the relationship between a man and a woman. There were inevitable gaps in her knowledge – but she spun her fantasies all the same. She wondered how it would feel to lie next to him in the double bed which was her mother and father's; what it would feel like to be held by him and to have the sort of closeness and intimacy she knew she now craved with him.

Next evening at supper, Catrin, curious about his early life was told, 'I lost my whole family to cholera, I don't know why it was just me that was spared. I suppose I feel guilty I survived. I soon decided after that to only depend on myself through life. It was hard losing my mother, as I was only ten at the time and I still miss her kind guidance and love.' He teared up, then, 'I suppose this made me wary of trusting and depending on people, in case they also left me. I can see why people get married though.' This moment of intimacy was an opportunity to tell her he was getting fond of her, yet he held back, as he did not know how Catrin felt and had neither the courage nor the skills to ask her – while she felt that she had been too forward and had intruded into his sorrow.

Her feelings grew more intense; she could not contemplate him being absent from her life. It would leave a gap, which he had amply filled. Neither of them had family, except for her long-absent brother, and she felt the loneliness and desolation of that keenly. Her only family now were the chapel-goers with whom she felt at peace and happy. She loved Sundays. Her faith was strong and when she sang the comfortingly familiar hymns, she felt her spirit rise, her clear soprano voice blending in unison with the others. It was the one day in the week given over totally to the worship of God – her day of rest. It provided respite from the endless drudge of farm work and gave structure and meaning to her week. When it was her turn on the rota, she fed the visiting Sunday preachers, as some travelled many miles to preach at the little village chapels. Later in the day, she provided a high tea of very thinly sliced bread and butter, cakes, '*bara brith*,' scones with homemade jam and cream, together with a large pot of strong tea, before they left to preach the evening service. John thought best not to join them on these occasions. The conversation would occasionally turn to her situation and she keenly felt the insinuation that the arrangement was not quite proper. Easy enough for them to judge, she thought, but how would she manage the farm if he was not here and how else could she earn a living? She glanced down at the brass clasps on the big black Family Bible on the small table next to the kitchen shelves, which held her grandmother's blue and white plates. She wondered if her brother's name would be the last name entered in it. Did he have any children? Generations of names – parents, grandparents, great-grandparents – were all recorded there, along with their birth, marriage and death dates. But was this the end of their line?

As her father had not made a will, she wasn't sure if she or her brother now owned the farm. Maybe she would have to prove to the courts that her brother was dead, before being made owner. As the law presently stood, if it was hers and she then married John, he would become the legal owner. That did not seem right. There had been young men who hinted that they would consider courting her but not anyone who she felt she could become fond of nor respect. How could she be sure they were not only after the farm? But she felt sure that John was not the type of person to marry just to gain its ownership.

Both eventually concluded separately that they must either marry or he would have to leave. Did he think enough of her to commit his life to her and the farm? Maybe he was afraid of being trapped in a relationship of convenience which could easily turn into resentment and dislike.

He was aware that if she was to marry, he would own the farm. It seemed unfair for a woman to lose everything she owned when she got married. The law needed changing but might not for years, as legal wheels moved very slowly. He had read stories about men marrying their wives to get access to their money, only to spend it all then desert them. Others simply drank or gambled away their fortunes.

John knew that materially, he had far more to gain but emotionally, possibly a lot to lose. He was relatively young with skills which could earn him a good living. But the reality was that he had become too comfortable where he was and the thought of uprooting and starting all over again was daunting. He valued security, stability and certainty now, having been orphaned when so young. He knew he must take the lead in the situation and resolved that he would decide after Christmas.

* * *

Christmas was fast approaching, a time to celebrate the birth of Jesus Christ which meant frantic preparations in the chapel. There were the usual carol services as well as a nativity play put on by the children of the village. Catrin had prepared the geese and plum puddings over the previous months and was now readying them to sell at the market. To Catrin, John appeared to be both thoughtful and restless. Maybe what he was doing did not now fulfil him. He had told her how he loved making beautiful things out of wood and so decided to offer him a proper space to work in.

Apprehensive that he might think she was tempting him to stay, she said tentatively one morning as they ate breakfast, 'I was thinking that maybe you should start your own woodworking business.' Alert, his head jerked up from his plate of food. 'I have heard you talk about how this was always your ambition. If you like, you can use the old outhouse next to the road. There's quite a bit of space inside if you clear out the old junk.'

John was genuinely shocked but inordinately pleased by this unexpected offer. He had a fleeting thought that it meant getting even more established at the farm but nevertheless he responded positively to her suggestion, his mind racing ahead. 'I think that it is an excellent idea. I could give it a go. There would be plenty of room in there for a work bench and for storing a stock of wood, as well as for displaying sample pieces. Being by the road would make the business more visible and bring in passing trade.' Catrin smiled happily at his obvious enthusiasm.

John immediately set about clearing out the unused farm building. He found some oak that had been stored which he kept for making something special. He moved his tools into the shed and made himself a sturdy workbench. He would never need to return to the quarry now having been given this chance to make his own furniture. He would ensure it was a success. When he had fitted out the shed to his satisfaction, he fetched Catrin to show her what he had done.

'I've also built myself a sleeping area at the back, so I'll bring my stuff down from the stable loft.' Catrin said, 'It all looks very professional, a proper workshop and it's good to see you so passionate about it.' An awkward silence hung in the air between them, as it sometimes did. Both knew that something needed to be said but neither could articulate to the other their innermost thoughts and feelings.

To repay her kindness, John made her a beautiful rocking chair out of the oak, so she could relax by the fire at the end of the day. Proudly he carried it to the kitchen when it was finished and carefully placed it down next to the cast iron kitchen range. She clapped her hands together in delight as no one had ever made her anything quite so beautiful. She admired his craftsmanship and knew then that her parents would have approved of this man.

John was glad that she seemed so pleased, shown in the beautiful smile she gave him. She told others about it and when they saw it, insisted that he made one for them. Soon he had so many orders for furniture that the money was flowing in steadily. With the money he bought good quality seasoned wood. Soon it felt as if he was supplying the whole area with furniture, as his reputation as a master craftsman grew. Before long, he was asked to make a coffin. Initially he baulked at this suggestion but then thought if it helped the relatives to think they were giving their loved ones a good send off, then why not? But being so busy once more pushed the decision-making to the back of his mind.

One evening, when all her chores were completed and John had retired to his shed, Catrin sat in her rocking chair by the dying embers, wondering again if John would now stay for good. Sitting in her new chair, her eyes wandered over her surroundings. She thought about how she really loved this place; she felt safe and secure here but at times like this, she missed her parents very much, she needed their wise counselling. She remembered the evenings she and her mother sang together, her father accompanying them on the old harmonium in the parlour. She stared absently at the glow of fire in the range, fed by the logs of a recently felled tree, giving them enough wood for a year. It heated the water to fill the tin bath on bath-night in front of the fire. The large black cast iron kettle was permanently boiling on the top and the large black stock pot was simmering full of stock bones and vegetable scraps. Her old work boots, toes still damp from the field earlier, were drying in front of the fire, stuffed with newspapers. Her water had to be pumped up from the well, fed by underground streams running off the mountain, in this country of seemingly endless rain. Looking up, the familiar thick oak lintel capped what was formerly a large open inglenook and now housed the range. A row of brass preserving pans stood on a high shelf above the lintel next to a small window, sunk deep in the thick stone walls of the farmhouse. Pretty curtains cheered the place up and the cosy window-seat held a long comfortable cushion stuffed with goose-feathers. The kitchen ceiling was low but only a very tall person had to duck his head. Lime-washed walls still looked fresh, despite black smoke which sometimes billowed out from the range when the wind blew down the chimney, and the relentless tick-tock of the large mahogany wall clock measured her life as it ticked away, with still nothing resolved.

There had been a mill on the stream side of the building when she was little. Mechanical remnants still lay in the tangled brambles and corn-seed lay under the floorboards inside. There were now two large commercial mills in the valley where farmers took their corn to be turned into flour. She still slept in the small back bedroom of her childhood, warm because it was above the kitchen range. The window frames of the front bedroom windows were deep-set in the walls and often battered by the westerly winds which drove the rains in over the sea and lashed loudly against the glass on stormy nights. Imperfections in the ancient glass distorted the outside view. Catrin could not remember the last time the small pretty fireplaces, surrounded by tiles, had been lit. Maybe John should put the chimney brushes up in case the crows had built nests up there but she quickly changed her mind, as it might embarrass him to enter the bedchamber. She then imagined what it would be like to lie with John in her parents' iron bedstead. The very thought of waking up with him next to her, feeling his warmth, hearing him breathe, sent a frisson of excitement through her. Then she scolded herself for having wicked ungodly thoughts – but this was how it would have to be if he decided to stay. They would have to marry. Given the success of his business he may now feel more equal to asking her. Catrin continued knitting absentmindedly by the dying embers, her hands never idle, even when she was resting.

There was a deep cupboard behind the small pine door opposite the proving oven. She guessed it must have once been a window, which allowed a good view along the road and up the steep pass. This would have been before the extension at the side was added, where all the farming implements were now stored and once housed the milling equipment. She knew the house was very old and full of history; it must have had many uses over the centuries. With the introduction of the seventeenth-century Window Tax, owners had bricked up all unnecessary windows. She remembered her father telling her about this, saying that the tax had lasted for 156 years but was finally repealed in 1851, just a few years ago. She knew that the farm had a much larger acreage once, with the flatter fields below the road put down to arable crops and sold off during bad times. Her mind, which was never still, often wondered how things might have been. It was a small luxury she allowed herself but as usual lately, her mind always drifted back to the same seemingly unsolvable problem. And still the clock kept ticking mercilessly on.

She decided she would go along to the little chapel tomorrow. Its door was always open for those who needed the quietude which endured there. She would pray to God for guidance for the answer she craved. Suddenly she felt an irrational flash of anger at her brother leaving her to manage the farm alone. If he had inherited, she would not now be burdened with its future. Then it would not have mattered who she married. Sometimes it all felt so complicated and was far too much responsibility. What if she was to marry John, then her brother returned to claim the farm?

John's furniture business grew and Catrin was glad to see him so engrossed in it. She could see he loved working the wood; first he would look at which way the grain ran through the wood then incorporate it into the shape of the piece he was making. He worked the surface until it was perfectly shaped and smooth when he ran his hand over it; then he would rub the nurturing oil deep into the grain. He was clearly a perfectionist. Soon, he needed the assistance of an apprentice to do the more mundane tasks, just as he had originally, when learning his trade. He mentioned this in general conversation with some of his customers and within hours, a young scrawny lad had turned up at his workshop, asking to be taken on. It was agreed that he could have a trial period and the lad would sleep in the stable loft vacated by John.

John secretly planned to make Catrin something really special as she would not take rent off him. She had inherited a dinner set of beautiful blue transferware from her Nain, Elizabeth, which would look impressive on a decent dresser. He knew it was probably too grand for a kitchen, probably more suitable in a parlour. It would be decorated with fancy wooden columns and brass door and drawer handles. He cut out all the pieces in his workshop then planned to assemble it in the kitchen, as it would be difficult to get it in to the house through either low door. Working in the evenings, it took him a few weeks – but he wanted it to be perfect. Proud of his work, he carved his initials and the date in a hidden part. While putting the pieces together, he had covered it with a white sheet, so Catrin could not see it until it was finished and she was banished from the kitchen in the evenings while he worked on it. Catrin had an inkling of what he was making but she was astounded when finally, he flamboyantly removed the sheet off the finished item. It was exceptionally beautiful. He had not used any screws and she marvelled at the skill which had gone into making the dovetail joints which held it all together.

She ran her fingers along its surface and carved columns saying, 'It is truly an impressive dresser, the best I have ever seen. I want to thank you from the bottom of my heart. I am so proud of it. Now I will have to carefully wash my Nain's dinner set, so I can display it properly on the dresser shelves.' John had made the shelves to match the exact sizes of the plates, so that they fitted snugly and safely.

Catrin washed and dried the plates to her satisfaction and carefully placed each one on the shelves, standing them upright. The large meat platters on the very top shelf looked very impressive. On the shelf below she put the dinner plates. The next shelf down held the middle-sized breakfast plates and on the bottom shelf were the small side plates. On the cupboard top, she carefully placed her vegetable tureens with their under-plates and the sauce boat jugs with their little pot ladles. She stood back to admire it and thought it was the most beautiful thing she had ever seen or owned. These dishes were only used on special occasions. She was full of awe for the talent of this man who stood beside her looking justifiably pleased with himself. She felt very emotional then, and wanted to hold his hand but was unable to. John did not know what to say either. And so, another opportunity passed them by. Instead, he quietly left to return to his workshop – his own safe space.

Taking some fresh flowers, Catrin walked down to her parent's grave the following Sunday afternoon after chapel service. She trod carefully and respectfully between the other graves, recognising many of the names and the farms to which they belonged.

Later, 'Did you enjoy your walk down to the cemetery? Was it tidy down there, have they cut the grass recently?' Mundane questions, not the ones she wanted to hear. 'All was as it should be,' she replied, instead of saying, the visit had been no help whatsoever and that she was unhappy that her life was not moving on as it should do.

Soon John was providing furniture not only locally but over a much wider area, his reputation as a skilled master carpenter spread. He had orders to make furniture for many of the new local chapels which were springing up due to the Revivalist movement, and he took on more casual labour. He decided that it was only fair that he started to pay Catrin some rent for using the outbuilding – but she would not hear of it, preferring, she said, to continue to keep to their arrangement for him to help on the farm. Both too proud to admit that they were fond of each other, the situation continued, unresolved.

John said to her casually one day, when they were at ease with each other, 'Do you know, you don't smile enough?' He sometimes teased her in order to make her laugh and when she smiled, her beauty reached her eyes. He had been thinking that this was where he should settle, he was happy here and everything he needed was here. The business was doing well, so he now felt that he was more on a par financially with her. If they married, nothing much would change except that he would live in the house and sleep in her bed. He did not know if he felt passionate about her; he was fond of her and thought that maybe love could grow; after all, there had always been successful marriages of convenience. The gentry did it all the time. Until now he had always had 'one foot out of the door' but knew that the time had come to make a commitment. He just needed to work himself up to asking her.

Earlier, Catrin had said to him, 'When you have some spare time, which is not often I know, will you turn over the small piece of land which runs along the stream, close to the back boundary of the farm.' She continued, 'I think it would be a good place for growing some potatoes in the spring. Turning it over now will let the winter frosts break down the soil and get it ready for planting.' John acquiesced saying, 'I could do with a break from the woodworking, I will go and look at it.' He knew the area as the small meadow, which was skirted on one side by the small stream. He spent some time that evening clearing away some of the larger boulders and replacing them on the already existing dry-stone wall.

Having cleared the land of stones, the next dry day, he led the cob with the plough blade to the meadow. He debated which direction he should plough in. As the plot was slightly sloping, he decided it would be best to plough against the slope, to hold in moisture in case there was a dry spring, and to prevent the soil being washed away if it was a wet one.

There were other large boulders lying around the periphery of the meadow. He wondered if this was why it had not been ploughed before. Many had been used to build the dry-stone walls which divided the fields but some were just too big to move. He speculated that there may have once been a building here, probably a very long time ago. He wondered who had built it and where those people had come from. As he looked more closely, some stones appeared to have been shaped by a stone-knapping tool, giving John the sense that they were ancient.

John and the cob started ploughing over the sods and by mid-morning, had completed a few rows in the rich loamy soil. On turning the horse around to start the next row, his eye caught a glint of sunshine on metal in the last row.

'Whoa!' he said pulling on the rein to bring the cob to a halt, then pulled up the brake. He walked over to where he had seen the shiny object. Bending down, he cleared the soil from around it and saw that it was a yellow metal. He cleared more soil away from what appeared to be a beautiful ancient neck collar. He was shocked by what he had found and carefully put it down to one side. Digging a little further down, he discovered smaller ornamental gold items underneath and fragments of what he thought must be animal skin, long since rotted away. He assumed that this piece of land had never been turned over before, otherwise this would not still be here. He remembered Catrin telling him that the farm was much bigger once, so there had probably been no need to plough this small meadow. He took the neck ornament over to the stream and gently let the flow of the stream wash the soil off it. It was hardly tarnished. He guessed that this was because the soil was peaty. He saw the design was unlike anything he had ever seen before but which, at the same time, seemed familiar. It seemed to be knots within entwined knots and he thought this would be a nice pattern to carve on a piece of furniture. Suddenly he remembered he had seen similar patterns on some old Celtic crosses in churchyards. He wondered where this hoard had come from originally and how long it had been buried, who had put it there and why? What was the value, both monetary and historic? He wondered if they had belonged to ancient inhabitants.

John looked furtively around to see if he had been observed but there did not seem to be anybody about working. He decided to put the collar back in the ground with the others, marking the spot with a few boulders to give himself more time to think about what to do next. John literally buried the problem. He felt a little bubble of nervous pleasure in his stomach, knowing that he had a secret that nobody else in the entire world knew about.

Just what was he to do? He told himself he should tell Catrin immediately – it was her land. Did that therefore make this her property? As he was cautious and secretive by nature, he decided not to rush into anything, until he had had time to think it through properly. He knew nothing of the law regarding hidden treasure. It had been found on private land, so would the Crown be entitled to claim it? He did not like the idea of the English Crown taking it off them and displaying it in an English museum. He had never been to a museum – but he had heard of such places. If he started asking questions among the locals, they may become suspicious. They could even think he had stolen it and he might be arrested. Yes, he thought, best to leave them where they were for now. He turned over the rest of the area, so that Catrin would not ask why he had only turned over some of it – he did not want to have to lie to her.

By the time he had finished his ploughing, it was beginning to get dark, so he cleaned and stored the plough. He fed, groomed and settled the cob for the night saying gently to her as he brushed, 'It's a good thing horses can't talk, my lovely.' Then he made his way to the farmhouse for his supper, usually bread, cheese and pickles, washed down with a mug of strong tea, followed by a piece of fruit cake if he was lucky. During the meal, Catrin asked if there was anything bothering him. She had become unsettled by his change of mood, thinking that he might be about to tell her that he was leaving, but afraid to hear him say it. He said he was just thinking – but felt very uncomfortable about not being completely honest with her.

To deflect, he said, 'I wrote to the family who brought me up to tell them how I was getting on and how my business has taken off. That was more than a month ago and I have not had a reply. They must have moved or are both dead.' Catrin guessed that he must be feeling sad that the last link to his childhood was dead, so did not question further. By not telling her of the find, he had again missed an opportunity to share his new knowledge which could have formed a bond between them, stymied as he was with his over-cautious personality.

After a restless, sleepless night, John had decided. He would write to a university to ask if they had an expert who knew about ancient gold ornaments, but worried that they might just turn up at his address. He reasoned he was not doing it this way because he wanted to keep the stuff for himself, he honestly thought it was best not to disclose the find just yet, or it would all get out of control. He wondered if he could write anonymously through a post office box number but concluded that this would cause suspicion at the local post office. In this place where everybody wanted to know everybody's business, they would wonder why he needed a post box, when he already had an address. Eventually, he decided he would go to the post office in the nearest market town, where he was not known, and correspond from there.

The following Saturday afternoon, he donned the new clothes he had purchased a few months ago and put his gold watch into the small pocket in his waistcoat. His business was doing well and he presented himself as a man of substance. He set off with the cob and cart, ostensibly to buy some more timber, as well as some bags of flour for Catrin. He hadn't drafted a letter to the university yet; this needed a lot of planning what to write. His first step was to set up the post office box.

It was a beautiful sunny day and he felt excited about the journey. He had got to the top of the steep pass and was dropping down into the next valley, whilst thinking about how he had come to love the rhythms and feeling of security Catrin's farm gave him – a feeling he had not felt for years. He was gratified that his business was doing so well and that his skills were appreciated. His new position had changed the dynamics between them somewhat, at least in his eyes, as opposed to the part-time farm hand he had been. He remembered falling in love with this valley when he had first arrived looking for work and camping up on the hills during the summer. It all seemed so long ago now. Since then, the valley had surreptitiously worked its way into his very core – he felt that he belonged here now. He recalled sitting very still by his tent in the evenings while the atmosphere vibrated with ancient antiquity. Ancient people must have shaped the once wooded landscape and he speculated, may have some connection with his recent find. Instinctively, he knew that all who had ever lived here had loved the place with a passion.

As he mused, it suddenly dawned on him, like the proverbial bolt from the blue, that in the middle of all the endless activity of his life, he had slowly fallen in love with Catrin. He hadn't recognised it before for what it was – but it was suddenly clear to him that it was there in everything he did for her and her for him. He realised that she must feel the same way about him. Stunned by this sudden realisation, he pulled the cob and cart over to the side of the track, so that he could process this massive realisation. For sure, this feeling between them had been growing slowly and surely over time. He was certain now that he wanted to be there all the time, helping her, talking to her, planning with her and to be the most important person in her life. He decided there and then what he would do. He would speak to her about how he felt as soon as he got back and if she felt the same, he would ask her to marry him. He knew how important the farm was to her and even though legally it would automatically belong to him if they were to marry, he would reassure her that he did not want ownership, just the privilege of living there with her and to carry on with his business.

John could not understand this unfair marriage law. He remembered the old carpenter telling him about the Welsh laws of Hywel Dda of the 10th century when men and women were legally equal. But Wales was now subject to English law. He thought it may have had something to do with them not wanting to split up the large estates between their children, so the eldest male always inherited everything, leaving other male siblings to enter the church or the army. It seemed unfair and alien to him, coming from a culture where most people's experience was that the mother was the head of the family. As far as he was concerned, Catrin worked as hard as any man, harder than most. He was determined to reassure her that the farm would always be hers and if they were lucky enough to have children, it would pass to them. It felt good to have finally made his decision. A heavy weight had been lifted from him and he looked forward to a long and happy life with Catrin.

John knew that by not committing previously, he had been unconsciously protecting himself by not allowing himself to get too close to her. His business had given him a new confidence and he decided life is for living. Losing his entire family had made him far too wary of commitment. But he could not go through his whole life in that way. If you were lucky enough to find the right person, then you needed to commit to and love that person and be loved and needed yourself. They could be quietly married in the Register Office in the town, as neither of them had any family. Later they could have a blessing in the chapel. Having now made the most momentous decision of his life and his mind finally at peace – knowing his future would be here with Catrin – he clicked the pony's reins and set off once more for the town, feeling more light-hearted than he had for a very long time. At last, he was now certain about the future and if there were difficulties, they would deal with them together.

On arrival in the market town, John tied up the cob outside the general store. He purchased his timber and the flour, and safely stowing them on the cart, walked towards the post office to enquire about a post box. On the way he saw a little jewellery shop and pondered the significance of that. Without realising that what was buried in the ground at the farm was far more important and valuable than what was on display in the window of this shop, he stopped to have a look. He decided that he would buy something precious for Catrin, as a token of his feelings for her. She did not wear any jewellery, she probably considered it too vain – but he thought that she might wear something nice on special occasions. But most of all, he knew that it was the significance of him wanting to give her something, as a token of how he felt, which was important.

As he entered the shop, an old service bell which hung on the inside of the door, rang out loudly. A wizened old man with snow white hair, slowly stood arthritically upwards. He leaned with one elbow on his well-worn counter top for support, then greeted John warmly by shaking John's hand, with his free hand. He commented on the clemency of the weather before asking how he could help. John asked to see a small heart shaped gold locket, which hung on a fine gold chain, to the side of the window.

'Ah', said the man, 'you want to buy it for your cariad?' He pulled it out from the display, then showed John how the little locket opened into two halves. He explained that a memento of a sweetheart could be placed inside it. As John examined it, the man offered to engrave their initials onto the back of the locket. John asked how much the locket cost, to see if he had enough money with him. He did not have quite as much as the jeweller was asking but he said he would let him have it for what he had and engrave it for free. John, relieved, waited and watched while both Catrin's and his initials were engraved, intertwined on the locket, as well as the year. Then the old man polished it and wrapped it carefully in a soft piece of cloth. John paid the man and placed the package in a small pocket in his waistcoat, next to his father's pocket watch. He felt elated as he left the shop. This locket was a declaration of his love and a token of the way his life would be lived from now on. As he headed for the post office, he found a spare copper in his other trouser pocket, so purchased a local newspaper from a boy.

Remembering about the hoard, he suddenly realised that he could ask a solicitor about how to go about dealing with it, as he knew they were sworn to confidentiality. He was standing there deep in thought about this new idea, when he was suddenly jostled by a passer-by, which made him drop his newspaper. As he bent down to pick it up, a skittish horse nearby kicked out her back leg and its hoof struck him hard on the side of his head. He lost consciousness immediately and crumpled like a marionette whose strings had been suddenly cut. As he lay in a crumpled heap on the cobblestones, blood started to trickle down the side of his face from his temple, causing a pool to form on the pavement. People gathered around him. A man shouted urgently for someone to fetch a doctor. Another put his folded-up jacket under his head, to make him more comfortable but this seemed pointless as he looked dead. The local doctor soon arrived, pushing his way urgently through the onlookers. He knelt beside John and felt in vain for a pulse on his throat. He closed John's eyes, which had a look of surprise in them, then solemnly pronounced, 'The man's dead. Does anybody know who he is?'

People began asking each other. One of the stall holders came forward and said he thought he must be the worker from the smallholding in the next valley, as he had recognised the cob and cart when John tied it up earlier. Somebody went to fetch the horse and cart. Two strong men lifted John's body up off the cobbles, one by his shoulders and the other by his legs, then gently placed him lengthwise onto Catrin's cart. They covered him with the cart's tarpaulin. The doctor then gave a young lad a coin to drive the cart back to the farm.

When John did not return to the farm by mid-afternoon, Catrin became anxious, as he had said he would be back for his dinner. As travellers from the direction of the market town passed her property, she asked them if they had seen him and the cart, or if they were aware of any accidents along the route. The last coach driver she asked, told her, 'I saw a man in the market-place lying on the ground.

Seems he had been kicked in the head by a horse but I'm not sure if he was still alive. I couldn't see any injuries on him but a kick from a horse can be fatal.'

'What did he look like?'

'He was a dark, well-set man.'

Grabbing the gatepost for support, Catrin felt sick to the pit of her stomach and knew instinctively that it was John. She checked his shed and all his possessions and tools of his trade were still there, so he had intended to return. She sunk onto a half-finished chair surrounded by wood shavings as the devastating realisation sunk in. She glanced up at a coffin and thought how prophetic it was.

The sun was beginning to set as she sat waiting outside in front of the farmhouse. She did not notice the beautiful sunset to her left, she was far too distracted with worry, looking continuously eastwards towards the pass. Eventually, she noticed a horse and cart slowly making its way down. As it was starting to get dark, she could not be sure if it was her cart. When it reached the village, she finally saw it was hers, with a young lad driving it. The old cob knowing its way home, pulled up alongside her in front of the farm. She saw that the cart's tarpaulin was covering the shape of a man, his body and face hidden from sight.

'The doctor asked me to drive the cart home Miss,' said the lad as he climbed down from the driving seat. On hearing the horse, John's apprentice came over to the cart from the workshop to see what was happening.

Catrin's worst nightmare had come true. She felt her legs buckle under her but quick as a flash, the lads caught her before she swooned to the ground, then guided her gently into the house. They carefully sat her onto her rocking chair in the kitchen in front of the fire, as she was shaking with shock. They placed a blanket over her. They did not want to leave the cart in the road so the boys went out to lead the horse and cart around to the back of the farm and into the stable with John's body still on it, as they did not know what else to do.

Her grief seemed to pierce straight through her heart into her soul. She knew she would never recover fully from her loss. Raw sobs racked her body until she felt she could not breathe. Before this happened, her dreams had some hope – but now there was nothing. Just a barren empty nothing in front of her. The heart-wrenching keening coming from the kitchen shattered the still air. It was the sound of a heart breaking into a thousand pieces, which could never be put back together again. She yearned for him with all her being – but now it was too late. She cursed and hated herself for her former reticence and foolish pride. She would never now experience his warm love.

The lad was hanging about wondering what he should do. The apprentice would need his help if they were to carry the body into the parlour, which was the normal procedure. He entered the kitchen, screwing his flat cap in his hands. 'Shall we bring him in Miss? I need to start walking back soon.' He had not been paid to do this but he could not just go and let the apprentice deal with it all. Catrin's face was drained of any colour, which contrasted with her bloodshot eyes. She nodded her assent, too choked up to speak. As they came in carrying his body, she pointed to the table in the parlour at the front of the house, which she had covered with a sheet. His sad job now complete, the lad started on his long walk home.

After an hour or so, Catrin's more practical side took over. She decided that she alone, regardless of any propriety, must prepare his body for a Christian burial, so that he was ready to meet his maker. It would be her first and last act of love for him. She gently removed his clothes, thinking how beautiful his body was. Years of working with wood had made his upper body muscles hard. She would now never lie alongside him and feel his comforting warmth, there was now only a lifeless coldness. She poured warm water into an enamel bowl and gently used a flannel to wash down his body. She washed away the caked blood from the side of his face, which had run down from the injury and noticed the blueish-black bruise on his temple and bent to kiss it. She then washed his beloved, handsome face and bent down to softly kiss his lips, blinded by tears which would just not stop flowing, expressing the enormity of her loss.

John's apprentice went to the workshop. It occurred to him then that John had unwittingly made his own coffin. He gave the raw wood a fine coat of beeswax and polished it up to a fine gloss. He brought it into the house on a trolley and moved it awkwardly into the parlour of the house. He left it there, standing up on one end. He felt that even though the body was now covered in a clean white sheet, he was imposing on something very intimate. As he left, Catrin told him to go to John's cupboard to fetch a clean shirt.

With his help, she dressed John in his best clothes he had been wearing, lifted and placed him in the coffin, then lifted the coffin onto the table. The apprentice then quietly slipped away. He decided he should go and tell one of the chapel elders what had happened, so that she would not be completely on her own.

Catrin could not bear to put the lid on the coffin, it was too final. He looked perfect lying there and at peace. She stroked his hair and ran her fingers along the angles and contours of his handsome face. She comforted herself with the thought that his death would have been instant, he would not have suffered any pain. She wondered what she should do with his cherished pocket watch. Could she keep it as a memento of him, knowing it had been his most precious possession? She knew he had no living relatives to leave it to and that his adoptive family had not written back to him. She decided that she would ask one of the chapel elders about it. As she carefully put it back into the watch pocket of the waistcoat, she noticed a small bulge in the pocket below and gently pulled out a small package, carefully wrapped in a soft material. Her curiosity got the better of her. As she unwrapped it, she saw that it was a beautiful small gold locket hung on a fine chain. She saw that it was hinged and gently opened the two halves. It was empty but had an engraving on the back, with C.J. and J.J. intertwined and 1866. Suddenly the significance of this became crystal clear to her. Clasping the small locket to her chest, she finally crumpled to the floor, bereft and overwhelmed again by the intensity of her grief. She now knew that he had loved her after all and it seems he had intended to give her this locket as a token of his love.

Exhausted and drained, she rose and went to look lovingly at his face once more. As she gently stroked it, she said, 'Thank you, my love. I loved you too. Thank you for my beautiful locket, it will always remind me of you' and added bitterly, 'and the love we were never to share.'

She fetched a small pair of scissors from the drawer of the dresser, then returned to his coffin. Very gently she cut a small lock of his hair and through the distortion of her tears, carefully placed it inside the locket. This was a tangible piece of him she could hang right next to her heart, to open and look at – whenever she could bear to.

Later, the same chapel elder who had arranged for John to work for her, came to the farm. He sat down in the parlour with her and tried to comfort her by quoting relevant texts from the Bible – but these fell on deaf ears, she was way beyond comforting. From her reaction to his death, the elder realised that she must have loved him very much. She silently showed him the locket and he shook his old white-haired head in sadness at what could now never be. 'Did he have any family we can contact?' She shook her head sadly. When asked, he told her, 'Keep the watch, you were obviously the nearest to family that he had.' Strangely, this acknowledgment comforted her.

'Will you please make the funeral arrangements? – I want keep him here with me until the funeral.'

'Of course. I will let you know when all is ready.'

The funeral took place a few days later in the village chapel, then afterwards he was laid to rest in the local cemetery. The village people, as well as his former workmates and customers, turned up at the chapel in their hundreds. Catrin had not realised he was so popular. Possibly the tragic circumstances of his death and the fact that he was so young, prompted their sympathies. Whatever the reason, those whose throats were not choked with emotion, sang their hearts out that day and gave him a good send-off to his maker. Catrin hoped that John could hear them, as he had always loved the chapel singing. She found that she could not sing, as her throat choked off the sound each time she tried.

By the time the funeral was over, raw grief had slowly turned into a numbness. She felt nothing. She functioned because she had to and went through the necessary physical motions automatically. Her head was in another place and her heart empty. Later, as her grief turned into anger at her loss, she could not bear to look at the pocket watch and locket, which brought the raw grief and tears back afresh to the surface. So, she placed them for safety, behind the brick near to the bread oven. She decided she would get them out when the passage of time made it possible for her to look at them again without sorrow.

She went to his workshop, lovingly touching the tools he had touched. She went into his sleeping space and held his clothes to her face to breathe in his scent which gave her comfort, then took them into the house. Later, she decided to clear out the drawers of a little desk just in case there was any correspondence from family. But she knew he had none – but her. She found a folder of poems he had written which she decided to take and read. Then she opened the bottom drawer and her hand touched a locked black metal box. It was heavy and when she shook it, it rattled. Intrigued, she searched for a key and finally found one in a small drawer inside the desk itself. Gingerly she unlocked it, with a feeling that she was intruding into his privacy. But she reasoned, if she didn't deal with it, then who would? As she opened it, she was astounded to see that it was full of sovereigns and shillings. He must have been saving all his money from his business. But what was she to do with it? He had no relatives for her to pass it on to. Well, she thought, I can't leave it here in case somebody steals it. Tucking it and the poems carefully under her shawl, she walked back to the house. She wondered what would John want her to do with it – then placed it safely in the hole by the range while she thought about it.

After John's death, there remained an unhealable hole in her heart and a big void in her life. Everything seemed joyless and pointless. She grieved endlessly for him and for the life she might have lived. She never married and robotically, year after year, went about her chores on the farm. The apprentice helped her out on the farm and carried on with the furniture business John had so skilfully built up – but it soon fell away. The pieces he made did not have the beauty nor the 'soul' which John's had. So he made a basic living, making everyday utility pieces of furniture and the occasional coffin, for which demand never seemed to abate.

Many years later, Catrin received a letter, which had been forwarded by the local solicitor. It read:

My Dearest Sister . . .

Catrin immediately thought that she had been given this letter in error, unless of course it was from her brother. But it was certainly addressed to her at the farm. She looked over the page at the signature and saw it was from a woman called Mary. She was baffled but read on:

You will be surprised to receive this letter from me after all these years of silence. I have very sad news for you. Your loving brother, and my dearest husband, William, has passed away, at a tender age. He had seemed in good health but the cause of death was listed as 'sudden and catastrophic heart failure,' which according to the coroner, appears to be an inherited condition. I wonder if it's better, or not, to have known about this condition beforehand. I don't think William knew, as he would have been a little more prepared. It has been a difficult time, but we are now 'out of the woods' and 'coming out the other side,' so to speak.

He went quickly and did not suffer too much. His funeral took place here in Kendal two weeks ago.

As an involuntary sob rose in Catrin's throat, she put a clenched fist up to her mouth in shock and dismay, while mumbling to nobody at all, 'My own dear brother is dead – and I was not at his funeral to say goodbye.' She read on:

I know we were unkind not sending you word all these years as to how and where we were but he was a very proud man and forbade me ever to do so. Well, he can't stop me now and I think you have a right to know. I will not return to my former home in the valley, even though my elderly mother still resides there. My son, also named William….

'They had a son!' Catrin exclaimed, again speaking into thin air. 'I have a nephew whom I did not even know existed.'

…and I will stay on here to continue with the small business we have built up. It is not much but enough to earn us a living. Do not try to persuade me to return, I would find it too humiliating to show my face in a place which I left in disgrace. I do not know how much you know but we left because I was with child and we knew that your father would never condone William's behaviour and he did not want us to be married. Sadly, we had no other children. William is a fine young man and is now running the business and I help a little with accounts.

I am very sorry that you have lost both your parents, and now your dear brother. Life can be very cruel. I realise that your life must have been very hard over the years, as I believe you did not marry. I only found out about your situation recently, when I wrote to the solicitor. I expect you were keeping the farm going for William, in the hope that he would return – and I am sorry to disappoint you in this matter.

If you need to contact me, please do so through the solicitor. He has been instructed not to reveal my address, but he will pass on any letters he receives, to me.

Yours affectionately
Mary-Aimee

'Oh! So, you have chosen that I am not to know my nephew.' She thought angrily, 'I am not as I thought, alone in the world. I actually have blood family but am not allowed to know him.'

She fell, defeated onto the rocking chair John had made for her, while she screwed up the letter in one hand. This was another cruel blow on top of all the others she had received through her life.

'Well', she said out loud, 'I will not reply to this letter. If I am not to know my nephew, I will not acknowledge your letter.'

Later, she placed the letter along with all the other important letters, including those her father Evan had received. She wrapped them all carefully, and together with the locket and the fob watch, placed them for safekeeping in the hole behind the brick by the fireplace, just as the former occupants of the house had done for centuries. She never replied to her sister-in-law, Mary. She decided that what will be, will be, as she could not control what happened to the farm after she died. Perhaps, she thought hopefully, her nephew would come here to farm in time if she left it to him in her will. She felt sure that if he saw it and its wonderful position, nestled at the foot of the hills, he would not be able to resist falling in love with it, but the farm did not even get the chance to lure him in.

As she got older, she did less and less on the farm. She kept just one cow and a few chickens to feed herself. Over the years she used up the sovereigns to live on, which she thought is what John would have wanted her to do.

They say Catrin eventually died of a heart irretrievably broken. The apprentice stayed on for a while after her death to look after the animals. Catrin's solicitor contacted her sister-in-law to inform her of her passing and that Catrin had left everything in her will to her nephew – but it seemed that he did not intend to return to the area and instructed the solicitor to sell the farm or let it to a tenant farmer.

So, the farm hoarded its precious secret a little longer.

Catrin, who had never done anything scandalous in her entire life, left instructions she was to be buried with John. This caused a great deal of consternation amongst the chapel people – but she had decided that if she could not be with him in life, she would at least lie with him in death. She had instructed the solicitor to make sure that this, her final request, was carried through; she had made him swear 'on oath' that he would make sure her last wish was respected, which despite the strong local opposition, he did.

Part 4

Sarah's books are selling really well and provide us with a steady income. Her publisher recently commissioned her to write another set of six. Wild creatures which live in and around the farm, such as hedgehogs, moles, toads and foxes, give her inspiration. She spends hours in the small back bedroom we have converted into an office, because the light there is good as the sun works its way around the back of the property during the day. She is very talented. Not only does she write the stories but illustrates them all herself. As she works, the room is kept warm by the heat rising from the Aga below.

As a break from work, we sometimes walk along the deserted beach when the tide is way out. Bess loves to disturb the flocks of seabirds. They move out of her way but soon settle again on the shoreline a little further along. As we walk towards the east headland, I like to imagine the very first settlers entering this vast sandy bay from around that headland, then looking up and seeing a beautiful, uninhabited valley in front of them.

The carpenter has finished repairing the wood frames of the outbuildings and today is starting on the wide oak floorboards upstairs. He lifts a section which needs re-fitting and we are astonished to find some very old, dehydrated corn seeds lying in between the rafters. These will have lain there for centuries after falling down between the gaps of the wide planks. This convinces me the farm once had a mill attached, which explains the long drop in the stream's flow at the side of the property, where a water wheel would have been housed. This could also explain the blanked out centre window at the front, through which they probably winched sacks of seed for grinding into flour between two large sandstone grindstones. These delicious little discoveries are the clues to the various uses of our house over centuries. These clues are all around for someone with a fresh as well as a trained eye; we believe there is still much more to discover here. The main renovations are almost complete and given the beautiful home we now have, it was well worth all the dust, noise and inconvenience.

This evening I decide to look again at the letters we found, specifically one written to Evan Jones by his cousin, Hugh William Ffowcs. I have discovered that the Ffowcs were an eminent and wealthy family in the area. Our more recent branch of the family hails from the hamlet of Eglwysbach, so this is where I will begin the next part of my family tree search.

According to the 1841 census, Evan Jones was living at Glyn Abercyn, so I assume it was he who initiated the mill. Hydropower was at its peak in this period and the valley floor was mainly laid to wheat fields. Evan's daughter Catrin was six years old but her brother was born later. The census tells me that Evan was born in 1809 in the Parish of Eglwysbach and his wife, Catherine, was born on a farm on the banks of the Afon Conwy in 1808, so I wonder how he ended up in Glyn Abercyn. My next trip must be to Eglwysbach village and the local churchyard to see if I can find Evan's grave.

* * *

Evan & Catherine's Story

Catherine and Evan were of a similar age. They had formed a close bond since he had moved to the farm with his mother, as a young boy. Evan cannot remember much before then, except for a vivid memory of walking, full of trepidation, down the farm track one dark evening, very hungry and utterly exhausted. Catherine and Evan usually spent any spare time from farm work together, fishing, talking or both at the same time. There was great fishing to be had on the salt-marsh banks of the Afon Conwy, where the sheep grazed. The netted, migrating salmon made a change from the usual beef and lamb.

Catherine got on better with Evan than she did with her own brother, Richard. She also got on well with Evan's mother,

143

Elizabeth, who was endlessly patient with her father's vile temper and mood swings. When her father had told her, 'I'm going to marry Elizabeth,' Catherine thought it was a bit sudden after the death of her own mother but made no objections. She did not feel Elizabeth would be replacing her mother and she rather welcomed another female in this house of men.

Richard was more like his father in temperament and comforted himself by believing that even if his father had any children with Elizabeth, being the eldest son, he would still inherit the farm. In the meantime, being lazy by nature, it was useful for him to have Evan around as he eased his own workload. Although he and Evan were of a similar age, they tended to keep each other at a respectable distance. Richard considered Evan to be a bit of an imposter and he was jealous that Evan got on so well with his sister. But then, Evan got on well with everybody and everybody liked him, which irked Richard.

Evan had the ability to turn his hand to anything and was a very quick learner. He often daydreamed of having his own farm one day – he would certainly do things very differently from how things were done on this one. But he knew this would never happen and accepted he would probably be an agricultural labourer all his life. However, he thought, when he was older there was nothing to stop him leaving here and making his own way in the world, except he would be reluctant to leave his mother at the mercy of her bad-tempered husband. He was often nasty to her, did not appreciate her and certainly did not deserve her. Evan swore to himself that if he ever saw him raise a hand to her, he would strike him, regardless of the consequences. In his estimation, a man who could strike a woman was the lowest of the low.

Years went past and the children grew into young adults. The strong bond he and Catherine shared, morphed into more than friendship. Although they never spoke about it, Evan was sure she felt the same. He had become a very handsome young man, whilst Richard was plagued with disfiguring acne and a surly manner, which caused him to actively despise Evan. The old farmer watched Evan and Catherine like a hawk and would have been glad to tell the lad to clear off, if he hadn't been so useful. He knew Evan was a far better farmer than his own son, who did no more work than he had to and had to be told to do anything. Evan, on the other hand, embraced responsibility and worked out efficient ways to do things. He was far too valuable to lose.

One day, Evan was busily filling in the potholes in the farm track. They had become rutted over time by a combination of cartwheels and recent heavy rain. As he lifted his head to see where the next hole was, he spotted a young lad walking down the track towards him, whistling a tune he recognised – but could not name. The lad, who was wearing a sort of uniform, said 'I am looking for an Evan Jones. Do you know where I can find him? I have a letter for him and must give it directly and only to him.'

Evan, taken aback and somewhat bewildered said, 'I am Evan Jones. Are you quite sure it's for me?'

The boy looked him up and down as if to say it could not possibly be him. 'You do not look important enough to receive a note from a solicitor,' he said.

A solicitor? Evan, wondering how to persuade the unconvinced lad, said, 'I can go and fetch someone from the house to prove it if you like.' However, finally convinced and not willing to waste any more time, he handed Evan the missive.

The post boy turned on his heels and walked quickly away, his mission accomplished. Evan looked down to read his name on the front of the envelope, made of a thick luxurious white vellum paper with a bright red wax seal on the back. He stood there stunned, looking around him, then again at the letter in his hand, noting how his grubby fingers contrasted sharply with the virginal whiteness of the paper. He felt important and humbled at the same time, to receive such a letter for the first time in his life. With the tip of his index finger, he slowly felt the rigid, official-looking red wax stamp. He decided the contents must be very important indeed for somebody to send it to him personally. He wondered if he should show it to somebody but then quickly decided against it. It could cause trouble and he didn't need any of that. Tucking it safely into his shirt breast-pocket for now, he decided he would try to read it later, although it might take him a while to join the letters into words. After supper, he would take a candle stump up to the stable loft where he slept, to try to make sense of it.

For the rest of the day, Evan found it very hard to concentrate on his work, impatient as he was to read the letter. Finally, after a supper of bread and cheese, he made his way up to his loft. He quite liked having this space all to himself; it gave him some peace and independence from the others, even though it was very cold sometimes. He kept his place and himself scrupulously clean and every morning and after work each evening, he scrubbed and sluiced himself down under the water pump in the yard.

Evan lit his candle from the outside yard lamp, then carried it up the loft ladder, carefully cupping it with his hand to protect the flame. Once seated, he looked down at the letter and with his now clean hands, gingerly broke open the red seal and unfolded the letter, which read:

Dear Mr Evan Jones,
Please attend the office of Jones and Sons Solicitors, in Market Street,
Llanrwst, tomorrow, Thursday at 2pm.
I respectfully remain your obedient servant,
Caradoc Humphrey-Jones Esq, Solicitor

Well, Evan thought, that didn't take much reading but what on earth is this about? He had certainly never had an 'obedient servant' before in his life! He panicked – would he be able to go tomorrow? Could he get there for that time? What pretext could he use to leave the farm? He knew the farmer was riding a couple of horses over to be traded tomorrow, so would not be around to see him leave – but there was a risk he might see him in town and shout at him to get back to the farm. He could tell his mother that he needed to go to get feedstock and take the old cart. Whichever way he did it, he would have to get there somehow, as it sounded very important. He hoped he was not in any trouble with the local police but could not see how he could be as he rarely left the farm. He thought that Richard might try to stop him going, so he needed to have his story ready. Otherwise, he decided, he would just go and not explain to anyone. He would ensure all the animals were seen to first and make sure to be back for milking.

However, he need not have worried, it was easy to leave unnoticed. He put his Sunday clothes into a parcel in the cart and on the way, pulled over into a small track and quickly changed into his best clothes. He continued his journey, feeling strange to be in his Sunday clothes on a working day. But it was a bit of a strange situation altogether and he had absolutely no idea what to expect when he got there. People assumed he was important when he asked directions to the solicitor's office, so respectfully directed him and tipped their caps. He pulled up his horse and cart outside and tied the reins to a convenient lamp post. He caught sight of his reflection in a shop window – not recognising himself. He spat on his hands to flatten his thick, unruly hair – but it had a mind of its own, so he stuck his flat cap back on.

Evan stood in front of the solicitor's office door, having first read the brass name plate. In a state of high anxiety, he took his cap off again and stood there wringing it between his hands, then pulled the bell. He wondered if they spoke Welsh or English; his English was not that good but passable. But he need not have worried, the solicitor himself came out to the reception area and greeted him cordially in Welsh, *'Dewch i mewn.'* Pointing the way to his office, he said warmly, 'Thank you for attending the appointment at such short notice.'

Evan looked around in awe at the room he had entered. Never in his life had he seen such a room. His eyes swept over the two large leather armchairs on either side of a magnificent oak knee-hole desk, which had shiny ornate brass handles on the drawers and a green leather top, engraved around the edge in gold filigree. A mahogany-surround fireplace, with beautiful tiles around the hearth, gave out a comforting heat. Plush golden drapes at the window reached to the floor and were tied back with golden rope to let in the afternoon light. The office walls were lined with shelves filled with hundreds of gilded law books and ledgers. Evan concluded that this solicitor must be a very learned man to have all this knowledge at his fingertips. He was urged to sit in the leather chair facing the desk, as the solicitor sat down opposite him. The solicitor began, saying 'I have some very sad news to tell you but also some very good news.'

Evan sat transfixed on the edge of the chair, still twisting his cap as the solicitor continued, 'Sadly, your father has died.' Evan looked at him in utter bewilderment and blurted out, 'But I don't have a father.' The solicitor replied smiling, 'Indeed, you did have a father and he has left you a considerable amount of money in his Will.' After a short pause, Evan asked, puzzled, 'Are you sure you have the right Evan Jones, it's a common enough name? I don't think it can be me you mean.'

'It most definitely is you. Your mother's name is Elizabeth Jones. It was your father who told me where you were both living, which is why I was able to send you the appointment letter.'

The solicitor let this information sink in. Evan was now in complete and utter shock. He did not know what to say or how to react – he just sat there open mouthed as the solicitor continued, 'Your father's name was William and he wanted to make sure that you were well provided for. He left you enough money to set you up for life, maybe to buy a house – or a farm even, if you want.' Evan slowly let this electrifying piece of information sink in and with his young man's trusting nature, started to very slowly believe that what the solicitor was telling him was true. He had never properly discussed who his father was, as his mother always managed to change the subject whenever it came up. He decided there and then that he would demand she discuss it with him, as he suddenly needed to know more about this man who claimed to be his father and who now felt more real to Evan dead than he ever had alive.

Dragging his thoughts back to the present, Evan said to the solicitor, 'I would dearly like to leave where I am now and have always dreamed of running my own farm. I think I would be good at it but although I know about farming, I do not know anything about the world of business and property, so would not even know how to begin to go about it.'

The solicitor reassured him, 'I will be able to advise you about that side of things,' and added humorously, 'But I would not know how to begin running a farm!' Evan nodded his acknowledgment to this wry comment then asked, 'What acreage of farm would I be able to buy? How would I go about finding one?'

The solicitor replied, 'Your father has left you enough money to buy a decent sized farm of quite a few acres and to buy stock and equipment to start you off in business.'

After a pause to let this information sink in, Evan asked, 'Do you know of any such farms for sale?' Taken aback by the question, the solicitor carefully considered it, then told him, 'I have recently been dealing with the estate of a deceased man in the next valley and I'm sure that the farm will soon be coming up for sale. I am the executor of the will and have been told by the benefactors to sell the farm, as they would prefer to have the money.'

He went on to describe it to Evan, saying, 'It is in a lovely, elevated position, overlooking the valley floor and out towards the sea. It has about fifty acres of land, some hilly, suitable for sheep grazing behind it and arable land in front for crops. The farm itself needs a bit of work done to bring it up to scratch but nothing that a resourceful young man such as yourself could not tackle. The previous owner had suffered chronic ill-health and the place is now very run down.'

Evan then said excitedly, 'The more I hear about this place, the more I like the sound of it. It seems perfect but I don't know the first thing about whether this farm is workable or not, nor about how to go about buying it. Is this something you could do on my behalf?'

The solicitor was warming to this young man, he liked his positive attitude and adventurous spirit, so decided he would help him. 'Although the situation is a little unusual, as it would normally be sold through an agent, I could ask the beneficiaries if they would be happy for me to sell it directly to you. If they are, I will go ahead and arrange it all for you. I will get a valuation first, then I will contact the beneficiaries offering them what I believe would be a fair price. You will need to sign a piece of paper giving me 'power of attorney' to act on your behalf legally in this matter.'

Evan felt daunted by the legal language and knew he was completely out of his depth. The solicitor could be telling him anything and then keep the money for himself. But he had no choice but to trust him. He reasoned that if he did lose his fortune, he had never really had it in the first place. Anyway, he decided to trust him as a professional solicitor who would not ruin his reputation for the price of a farm.

After a short pause, the solicitor said, 'But are you absolutely sure that you want this farm? Did you not want to see it first? Maybe have a look at some others which are for sale? Evan then said, 'It feels to me like it is all meant to be. First, I am left some money by a father I never knew I had – then this farm becoming available. I can't imagine having all that money in a bank account, I don't even have one. I think I should put my inheritance straight into buying my own place, keeping some to one side to get me started. It seems my father wanted to see me settled and secure, so I should fulfil his wishes.'

Suddenly curious again about his benefactor, he asked, 'Can't you tell me anything about the man, my father, who left me the money?'

'That's not really my place, you must ask your mother. But one thing I feel sure of, he would have approved of you and it is a shame he never knew you. He would have supported your decision to buy the farm, as he was a very astute businessman himself. You are a very lucky young man and I hope you do well.'

He then wrote on a piece of official paper and said, 'As per your instructions, I will proceed with the purchase of the farm and contact you as soon as it is all completed. Please sign this document giving me the power to act on your behalf. I cannot say how long the process will take but it should not be more than a few months.'

Everything then seemed to have been said and the solicitor

stood to indicate that the meeting was over. 'Congratulations young man on your good fortune, you will hear from me in due course.' They shook hands cordially and an elated Evan was shown out of the office, feeling as if he was walking on air. He was unable to quite believe this incredible thing that had just happened to him. It seemed that his dream of running his own farm might come true after all.

On his way home, Evan realised he needed to carefully plan how he would handle it all. He decided to carry on as normal for the next few months, as if nothing had happened. But as soon as he received word that it was all signed, sealed and legal, he would go, just walk out of there and it would be the happiest day of his life. He wondered what to say to his mother. Should he tell her, or wait until it was official? Should he take her with him? He would certainly prefer if she left with him but she may decide that she could not in conscience leave her husband, miserable as he was, as she had made a promise before God. There was a risk that once Evan left, the farmer would make her life even more unpleasant. But alternatively, if he risked confiding in her, she might tell her husband about his plans or let it slip by accident. If that happened, the farmer would throw him off the farm immediately. No, I will go when I am ready, he thought. Also, if she did not know, the farmer could not blame her for not telling him. He would bide his time and keep this wonderful secret to himself for a little longer.

Evan knew he might feel lonely on his own at his new farm. He was used to being around people – his only quiet time was up in his loft. And what of Catherine? He knew he would miss her. Maybe she would go with him but of course they could only do that if they were married. He could not think of anyone he would rather spend the rest of his life with. His moving out could bring things to a head – but he wasn't sure if she wanted to marry him. Her father would be against their union. Evan was certainly not good enough for his daughter and even more than that, he would be devastated to lose two productive workers in one go. It wasn't part of Evan's nature to be vindictive – but he believed it would serve him right for being such a thankless bully. He would not be able to run the farm without them, so would have to dig deep to pay a farm hand a decent wage. Why should he expect Catherine to continue to stay on the farm working for him indefinitely? It must have occurred to him that one day she might marry and leave. Then he thought gleefully that Richard would have to do some actual work for a change!

About a week later, having gone over and over in his mind what had happened and exhausting himself through thinking, Evan felt he could no longer keep the news from his mother. The first conversation would be about his father; he would no longer be fobbed off. He had not pressed her before, as the subject seemed to upset her. Now as a young man himself, he needed to know. He assumed he had been wealthy to leave him so much money. Would she be surprised by this legacy? Had she been in touch with him? His departure from the farm would need careful planning. His mother would need to be sworn to secrecy about the inheritance.

It had dawned on him recently that she was very good at keeping secrets; the truth about his father for one. Suddenly, like a piece of a jigsaw falling into place, he remembered a man who came to the farm a few years ago, who spoke to his mother in the parlour, then left very suddenly, before he even drank his tea. She was very upset for a long time after that and Evan wondered then if this man was his father. He certainly had a similar look to him, as he could still picture him. He would ask her about that visit and its significance.

When they were finally alone and he was sure they would not be overhead or interrupted, Evan told his story from the beginning. 'A few weeks ago, I received a letter from Jones' Solicitors.' Her face registered shock at this, as she thought he was in some sort of trouble. He went on, 'It was an appointment letter for the next day in his chambers. He told me I had been left a great deal of money in my father's will.'

Her response was totally unexpected. She began crying uncontrollably, which he realised was due to the news his father was dead. He waited for her to calm down, then looked into her swollen, red-rimmed eyes, saying to her gently, 'Mam, I really need to know about him now, please tell me.' She said sadly, 'Now that he is dead, it is probably safe to tell you.'

He waited for her to blow her nose and calm herself before she began. He sat quietly next to her and listened to the sad story and was amazed at her strength and courage.

Changing the subject, he said, 'It will soon be legally settled and the farm will be mine. Will you leave here and come with me?'

'If I could not leave my husband for William, then I cannot leave him for you.'

This was expected, as she took her marriage vows very seriously. But, Evan thought bitterly, the farmer had not kept his promise to cherish her.

Evan was sure that his father had loved her dearly. He had never married another. It was a comfort to him that he had been conceived in love and that his father would have married her had it been possible. It would have been so good to have had a father. He and his mother would not have had to live with the miserable farmer all these years. Their lives could have been so very different but he could see she did what she thought was best at the time.

As their conversation ended, his mother told him, 'I found an important looking letter amongst my mother's personal possessions after her death. It had my name on it – but I hadn't seen it before and it had never been opened. Evan asked her to fetch it, to see if he could read it to her. When she returned with it, he read out aloud,

My Dearest Sweetest Elizabeth

I trust this letter finds you well, as I am in body – but not in mind or heart, which are both sorely broken into a thousand pieces. My father has forbidden us to marry, which is my one true desire in all the world – he has threatened to disown and disinherit me should I do so, as he says it would bring shame onto our family.

It grieves me not to be able to see you again and only God knows if we will be together one day, if circumstances change. At present, it is impossible as I cannot wish ill on my father, nor go against his wishes. If I did, we would all be homeless and I would not be able to provide for you.

Know that I love you with all my body and soul and long for us to be

together again. Please be sure to let me know where you are, if you move from the little homestead.

Yours always, lovingly and longingly
William

As he read it, Evan realised that his father was not then aware that his mother was with child and wondered if this would have made any difference. His mother and father must have loved each other dearly and he knew they would have been together, had it been possible.

His mother burst into tears, realising the contents of the letter and cried, 'Why did my mother not give me my letter? I could have gone to William for help when we left the cottage. Our lives would have been so much better.'

When she had left the cottage for that last time, she could have sent word to William. He would have cared and provided for them both and she would not have ended up with the dreadful, loveless life she had endured during her years on the farm. Tears ran crookedly down her cheeks, mimicking the rain as it tracked crookedly down on the glass outside. The keeling of her newly broken heart echoed the low haunting moan of a coming storm, mimicking her loss and deep sadness. Evan, seeing her so broken, again begged, 'Please come with me, you can just leave him, he won't know where to look for you.' Although tempted, she replied stubbornly, 'I made a Christian vow before God, for richer or poorer, for better or worse. It's been mostly worse, but if I left him now, it would be to break the promise I made before God.'

'Do you think Catherine should leave with me?' Elizabeth did not seem surprised he asked, inadvertently revealing his feelings for Catherine as he did so. She had suspected for some time that they had grown close. She cautioned him, 'Her father will do whatever is in his power to stop her leaving. Go there on your own first. When the dust has settled and you are established in your own right, come back and ask for her hand in marriage.' Elizabeth did not want him to have to suffer, as she had, by having to live her life without the one he loved.

'How am I going to explain your inheritance to him without exposing my story that I was a widow? If he finds out, he will throw me out.' This seemed unlikely to Evan, as no one else knew the truth except his mother, the solicitor and him. Evan said, 'That is no bad thing. Maybe you should leave with me?' But stubbornly, she would not budge. 'I can say that a distant relative through your father's side has left you money – this would not be far from the truth. God knows what he will do if he ever finds out the truth about who your father really was – and that I lied to him – he is sure to be violent. That would be the time to leave him.' If you survive the beating, thought Evan, but he had to be satisfied with this.

Evan carried on as normal for a while longer. His work ethic prevented him from not working hard but his mind was elsewhere, longing for the time when he could leave and strike out on his own to his new, freer life.

On receiving the long-awaited letter a few months later, Evan announced, 'I am leaving the farm for good, today – you can do your own work.' The farmer was predictably furious and red in the face with anger. Evan did not tell him he had his own farm but said, 'It's time I made my own way in the world. I've worked here for nothing for long enough.' The farmer shouted at him, 'You ungrateful little runt! I took you in when you and your mother were desperate, I fed you and housed you and this is how you repay me.' As he spoke, spittle flew everywhere, as he was apoplectic with rage. Evan began to wonder if he was actually mentally unstable. He was worried his leaving would cause the farmer to take it out on his mother. So he said quietly but with menace to the farmer, 'If you ever ill-treat my mother, I will hear about it and you will have me to deal with.'

The farmer was visibly shocked to be spoken to in this manner. In his mind, he had taken him in, out of the goodness of his heart. He shook his fist at Evan's back as he walked away, warning him never to come near the farm again. 'With pleasure,' called Evan over his shoulder.

Evan walked proudly away from the farm for what he thought

was the last time. The farmer would not come looking for him, he would know there was no point. His new farm was far enough away for the local gossips not to find out where it was. He just carried on walking away down the track, while the dog barked furiously, much the same as on the day he had arrived there. At the end of the track, he looked back just once and saw a forlorn looking Catherine standing by the front door.

Having left behind his hand-me-down work clothes and now dressed in his Sunday clothes, he felt elated as he walked towards his new life. He had an appointment with the solicitor and was lucky enough to be offered a lift with a farm cart going to the market. Inside the impressive office once more, the solicitor informed him that all the legal paperwork was complete. The deeds and documents of ownership were ready on the desk and Evan was asked, 'Please put your mark here on this document, then the farm will officially be yours.' Evan said, 'I can do better that that, I will sign my name. In the signature, would it be right and proper for me to take on my father's surname, as an acknowledgment for all he has done for me?' The surprised solicitor replied, 'You can call yourself whatever you want.' So Evan picked up the pen, which he carefully dipped in the ink pot. He had been practising writing his full name as it had appeared on the solicitor's original note but added his father's surname before his.

'Just one more thing – will you please purchase the plot next to my father's family tomb? I know I will never be allowed to be buried with him – but I'd like to be buried next to him.'

The solicitor was growing more impressed with this clear-thinking young man and knew he would do well in life. He would not squander this wonderful opportunity he had been given. He agreed to follow through this request, then ceremoniously handed over the keys and the deeds of the farm to Evan. 'I suggest you go and open a bank account, so that I can pay in the balance of the inheritance money.'

Evan agreed to do this straight after their meeting. The solicitor handed him a purse of coins, to buy a horse capable of pulling a cart over to his new farm in the next valley. 'I have arranged the purchase of all the basic provisions and utensils you will need to get yourself established in your new home. These are already loaded on a cart which now awaits your collection from the general dealer in the town.' Evan thanked him and shook his hand, as the solicitor added warmly, 'If you ever need my help, please don't hesitate to get in touch.'

Evan carefully tucked the deeds and the purse safely in an inner pocket, then set off towards the market, calling into the bank on the way. He was a good judge of horses so knew what to look for. There was a livestock market in town that day and a horse trader invited Evan to inspect his horses. Evan needed one with a mild temperament and strong enough to pull a heavy cart. Having haggled on a cob for a while as the solicitor had advised, Evan managed to negotiate a lower price and got a saddle included. The men then shook hands on the deal. Evan, growing quickly into his new role, decided that he really enjoyed haggling and decided that he might even become good at this buying and selling business.

He then went to inspect the cart. When he saw it, he thought it would serve its purpose, although it needed a coat of paint to smarten it up – but the wheels and springs looked as if they still had a bit of life left in them.

He returned to pick up the horse from the dealer. The horse dealer walked over with Evan to the general store and placed the saddle in the cart for him while Evan hitched the horse to the cart. Shaking his hand, he again wished him all the best in his new venture.

Evan called to the store's pimply-faced assistant to keep an eye on the horse and loaded cart, while he went to purchase working clothes. He kitted himself out, choosing what he thought a prosperous farmer would wear. He had never had new clothes or boots in his life. He had only ever worn 'hand-me-downs' after the farmer's son had outgrown them, so it was a real treat to buy new clothes which fitted properly. Fully dressed, he looked in an old misted-over, full-length mirror, which stood in the corner of the clothes section of the general store. It was only then he really saw himself properly for the first time in his life and thought he didn't look too bad. He guessed he was already his full adult height, so the clothes should last him a long time. Carefully placing the deeds and purse into the inside pocket of his new long coat, he asked for his other clothes to be parcelled up. He then bought some bread, milk, cheese and eggs for later.

As he turned to walk back to the wagon, he spotted a man selling sheepdog pups, tightly crammed together in a wicker basket. He thought he would need a dog to train to round up sheep. He asked the man, 'How much are your puppies?' pointing to a pup which was completely black but for a white patch on his nose and white on its feet. 'What's the mother's character like? How easy would it be to train this pup?'

Realising the man could be telling him anything, he opted for the one he had first pointed to, which seemed intelligent and lively. Evan passed the man a coin, then carefully tucked the pup into the other deep inside pocket in the lining of his heavy long coat. It soon settled down to sleep, comforted by Evan's body warmth and the murmur of his heart. He returned to pick up his horse and fully-provisioned cart, ready to set off for his farm.

Evan had directions to the farm, from the solicitor – the journey appeared straightforward. He had been warned about the steep track finally leading down into the village, but first he had to travel up the gentler slope from this side of the valley. Climbing up onto the wooden bench at the front of the cart, he picked up the reins, gently flicked them and shouted, *'Dôs'* – to the horse. Carefully, he steered the horse and cart through a few narrow, cobbled streets of the market town but was soon out on the open road to freedom!

His excitement grew as he travelled on his momentous journey to his new life, comforted by the weight of coins in his money pouch to cover his immediate needs. He had never had such a feeling of elation and joy in his entire life. He wondered what state the farm would be in but one thing he knew for sure, he would find out before this day had ended.

After a while, he felt the puppy wriggling so pulled the cart over to one side, so it could relieve itself on the grass verge. It found a drink in a rainwater puddle, then they soon set off again to the farm.

The solid brown cob's hypnotic clip-clop was the only sound to be heard as they journeyed up the gentle sloping track towards the next ridge. Evan watched the light feathering on the cob's lower legs and fetlock, lifting gently in the breeze of its steady gait. The market town was far behind, they were now in the open countryside. He saw only the occasional distant farmhouse, wispy smoke rising from the chimneys, as the afternoon drew out. Low, shrubby heather bushes of various types grew on both sides of the mountain track, intermingled with bilberry bushes. Later in the season, these would provide a welcome roadside snack for hungry travellers, once their red berries had ripened into a juicy, deep purply-black. Out of this low shrubbery grew rowan trees, which had avoided being eaten by sheep as saplings; their creamy-white, multi-flora blossom heads getting ready to turn into the bright red berries which wintering redwings and fieldfares would feast on frenziedly in the late autumn. As Evan neared the top of the slope, he saw that the track entered a small pine copse, with high dry-stone walls on both sides, indicating that he would soon be travelling through a walled estate. From the directions he had been given, he knew he was nearing Bwlch Sychnant, where the steep pass down to the village would begin.

As he neared the walls, he thought again how lucky he had been to be able to buy his small farm. The inherited money from his father had allowed him to escape life-long servitude. His decision to claim kinship to his father by adopting his surname was a good one. Given his father's status and class, Evan thought it courageous of William to officially acknowledge him in his Last Will and Testament, before God, that he had an illegitimate son, despite the scandal and shame this might cause his family.

How different their lives could have been had his father found his mother when they first left the cottage all those years ago. How different if his Nain had given his mother William's letter when she should have. And then again, if his mother had not married that miserable man, she would have been free to leave with William when he had come looking for her that day. So many ifs, lost opportunities, and so many actions with dire, unhappy consequences. But his father had finally done right by them in his Will. The solicitor had explained that his father's older brother, Hugh, had inherited the bulk of his father's fortune and just a small part of it had been left to Evan. The solicitor had also told Evan that Hugh had a son, Hugh William, who was his first cousin. It was highly unlikely that they would ever meet, but it was strangely comforting to think that he did have another blood relative out there somewhere, apart from his own mother.

Driving through the wooded area between the high walls of the estate, the atmosphere was very different and it felt as if he had entered another, ethereal world. The horse's hooves now echoed loudly. Blackbirds and speckled thrushes sang but the sound of tiny wren's high-pitched, excited chirping dominated. Small, unseen rodents scrabbled about in the dry, brittle undergrowth of rotten leaves and dead bracken. From up high, shafts of sunlight fell in between the upright pine trunks, highlighting the myriad of insects in the sun's rays. Just before driving out of the trees to begin the final descent, Evan noticed a garden door built into the stone wall and wondered who would use it. Maybe it was a way in for estate workers who lived down in the village.

As Evan reached the start of the descent down the steep pass, he decided to pull over to the side and put the cart brake on, so he could look at the valley below. This was his valley now. Home. His farm and new life were not far away. The scope of its beauty took his breath away. The track ran down one side of a ravine between two mountains and further away, he could see green fields stretching out along the valley floor for miles and the navy blue of the sea beyond. The valley floor was nestled snugly in a horseshoe shaped range of hills, with the open part of the horseshoe facing out to sea. Mindful of the weight of the load on the cart, he then cautiously proceeded down the hill and saw the valley starting to open out in front of him after passing an overhanging rock on his left. In this narrow section of road, he saw holes in the rockface, where explosive black powder had been used to blast out some of the rock face to widen this vital road which joined the two valleys. To his right, he saw a long expanse of sandy beach wedged between two large rocky headlands, jutting out to the sea. Low tide was the only time people could travel along the exposed beach in front of the headland. He assumed that made this newish track he was on more vital and left people less dependent on the vagaries of the tides, weather and treacherous sands. In the distance on the left, he could see a farm, situated near the road, basking in sunshine and nestled snuggly into the foothills of the mountain and knew then this was his farm. Cautiously he continued down the steep pass, frequently applying the cart brake to prevent speeding up. This road was not for the faint-hearted! You needed to keep your wits about you, especially the stagecoaches which carried passengers in and out of the area.

On the last section, Evan passed a long farmhouse on his left, then gratefully dropped down into a small sleepy village of stone-walled cottages huddled protectively together, built where the land finally levelled out. A coaching inn came into view, set back a little from the road, so he decided to pull in to have some fare before travelling any further. Pulling the horse and cart up in front of the inn, he tied the horse's reins to a large metal ring fitted into the side of the wall.

A boy appeared from nowhere saying, 'Can I mind your horse and cart, mister?'

'How do I know you won't drive off with it?' he replied laughingly.

'Sir, I been brought up to honour the Bible and know wrong from right and know that it's wrong to steal.'

'Where's your home, boy?'

'I have no home now sir. Bailiff threw us out. Mam was very ill with the cough, so couldn't work and went into the workhouse – but I thought if I went in, I might never come out again, so I ran off. I like the open spaces, see.'

Evan felt sorry for the lad. 'Your story is familiar – but we were able to find work, as my mother was well. Yes, mind my horse and cart then and don't let anyone touch it.'

'I'll guard it with my life.' He shrugged, 'there's nobody about anyway.'

It was dark and quiet inside the Cross Keys as he entered. Two old men sat in a gloomy corner, hunched over their tankards. One sucked at his clay pipe, in an effort to relight the damp tobacco in the bowl with a lit wax taper. They glanced up briefly in Evan's direction, then judged him to be of no account. Turning their attention back their ales, they wrapped their hands protectively around the pewter pots, as if afraid someone would snatch them away. Evan said to the landlord, 'A pint of your finest ale if you please and food.'

Once he had been served with a steaming mutton stew, he engaged the host in conversation about the local village. When asked about his business in the area, Evan proudly announced, 'I am the new owner of Glyn Abercyn Farm, just along the road, and intend to farm it myself.'

The two men looked up, interested now but silently judging him as a bit young to have the ownership of a reasonably sized farm. The bartender shook his hand cordially, '*Croeso*. It will be good to see the old place lived in and working again. You will find it's a bit run down but it's nothing a bit of hard work can't sort out. The previous owner lived there alone and was ill for a long time before he finally passed away.'

Evan exclaimed wryly, 'I am well used to hard work.'

The proprietor continued, 'The roof is new though. There was a fire a few years ago, so it had to be replaced. They raised the height of the new roof, which gives more headroom in the upper rooms. We don't know what caused the fire – the owner was away at the time – but his quick-thinking farm hand let all the animals out of their pens, so they were safe from burning.' He added laughingly while remembering, 'It was quite a sight to see all the animals running amok around the village, going into gardens, causing damage and hilarity, until they were eventually rounded up, just before dark. The old farmer seemed to lose his will to live after that, saying that all his years of hard work building up the farm had literally gone up in smoke. He must have had some money stashed away though, as he quickly repaired the roof – but his heart wasn't in it after that and he went downhill fast.'

Evan thought maybe he should get a farm hand and wondered if the lad outside would want the work. He would ask him when he went out again. He looked as if he hadn't eaten properly for days. Poor mite.

'Barman, can you please ask one of your hands to take some mutton stew out for the urchin?' Surprised, the man agreed, 'Aye, I don't know where he's from, he suddenly appeared a couple of days back. Seen him rummaging in the midden pile. Don't know where he sleeps.'

'I might offer him some work to help me get things started on the farm but,' added laughingly, 'I will have to fatten him up a bit first!'

Evan felt a slight stirring on his chest and the sound of soft whimpering. Gently he lifted the pup out and placed him on the coaching room floor. He asked the proprietor for a saucer of milk and watched as the pup contentedly lapped it up. As he watched he enquired, 'Do you know of a reliable and honest local who could run the household for me?' The innkeeper rubbed his chin doubtfully, so Evan added, 'I'll leave that with you then.'

Replete from his good meal, he placed a coin on the bar. He then picked up the pup, tucked him back into his cosy place and walked outside into the welcome sunshine.

The boy, who was still holding the reins, doffed his cap and said, 'Thank you, sir, for sending the food out for me. It was very kind of you.'

'Right lad, if you want some work, you can come and help me on my farm.' He did not need asking twice and he had already climbed onto the back of the cart as Evan set off on the final leg of his journey, to his new life on the farm.

The farmhouse – its name written on a whitewashed granite boulder which formed part of the garden wall, stood there like a sentinel looking out over the valley towards the sea. Evan halted and just sat on the cart looking at it. The front gate was bounded both sides by lime-washed stone walls, which enclosed a small front garden. This was divided in two by a gravel path which ran directly up to the heavy front door. Being early spring, there was already colour provided by daffodils, primroses and a few bluebells.

Evan felt elated but humbled – this beautiful place was now his home. He looked skyward and thanked God and his unknown father for his blessings. Although he had the large black key to the front door ready in his hand, he decided to check the property outside first and leave the house to last. In truth, he was procrastinating, overwhelmed by the enormity of it all and wishing that his mother or Catherine was there with him. In the event there was only him and the urchin boy – two loners restarting their lives.

The lad, Harri, jumped down then opened the five-bar gate at the side. Evan drove the horse and cart through and along the side of the farmhouse, passing what must be the barn. He pulled into a cobble-stoned farmyard at the back of the house. The horse gratefully drank from a large granite horse trough now in front of it. Evan climbed down off the cart, removed the puppy from the inside of his coat and carefully placed it inside the cart on a blanket.

Turning to Harri, who was stroking the puppy, he said 'You can off-load the cart, put the food stuff and blankets by the back door, then the rest of the stuff in the barn.'

In his new work clothes, Evan looked every bit the part of a farm owner. Slowly he walked up the farm track towards the two sloping fields which surrounded the back of the property, savouring the moment. He walked through a small meadow by the stream, then followed the dry-stone boundary wall up to the top of the steeper field and looked down onto his little kingdom. The farmstead looked serene in the early evening sunshine. As well as these fields and the flatter ones in front of the property, he owned some walled friths higher up on the mountain, for use as summer pasture. The stream divided the fields, providing water for grazing animals. Evan noticed an ideal catchment area for branding and dipping sheep. He would also keep a few cows, a couple of sows and poultry, but first he must get the place ship-shape. A good crop of grass this summer would feed his stock over the winter months, giving him a steady supply of meat. He was aware of the huge responsibility of making wise decisions – but he liked a challenge.

A patchwork of green fields of various hues filled the valley floor below, petering out near the shore. Beyond this was the wide expanse of a sparkling blue-green bay. He thought that this valley was the most beautiful place he had ever seen. He already had a real affinity with the place and felt the first stirrings of really belonging somewhere. He would make a success of this so his father would have been proud of him. Then he heard his mother's voice in his head, telling him to go down and get on with it, there was plenty to do. Again, he wished she was here with him – but she had made her choice.

Reluctantly, he headed back down towards the barn, past what looked like poultry sheds, their old timbers silvery-grey and weathered with age. The top half of the barn door, its once-red paint now blistered and peeling and faded by the sun into a deep flat dusky pink, swung open easily at his tentative push. He looked over and saw there was a heavy metal bolt on the inside of the lower door, which he slid open and stepped inside. A musty smell of mice and old dust hung in the air. He saw a range of farming tools hanging on the wall. Some had been rusty for a long time, their oak handles powdery with woodworm. Once sanded, sharpened and oiled and their handles replaced, these tools would be useful again. This would be his first task, as decent tools were essential to do a good job. The place exuded a rundown, unloved air, which he would change. He would breathe new life into it with his young man's energy, making it the very epicentre of his existence.

Next to the tools, he saw a squared-off timber framed section. It was covered in chicken mesh and he guessed it was for hatching chicks, as he could see a dusty old oil heater in the corner. A metal poultry guillotine was screwed onto one of the thick timber uprights, hewn out of tree trunks by builders of a by-gone era; these ancient uprights ably supported the barn's roof. The barn floor was laid with large granite flagstones. A raised granite ridge separated off about a third of the barn floor, behind which the winter grass feed could be stored, the ridge preventing it from spreading onto the rest of the barn floor. It was a good solid barn with plenty of ventilation provided by the long slits in its stone walls, which prevented the hay going mouldy during the winter. The original builders had clearly known what they were doing.

Evan walked along to the lean-to cowshed. It had three milking stalls. The inside walls were hung with years of dusty cobwebs and needed a good clean out and a generous coat of lime-wash. Above the stalls was a wooden-floored loft area, useful for storage. Leaning onto the other end of the barn was the stabling, with room enough for a cart to be stored alongside the horse's stall and more flooring above. This suddenly reminded him about the horse, still tethered to the cart in the farmyard. He called to Harri, 'Let's get the horse unhitched and stabled, then we can push the cart in.'

Harri filled the metal hay holder attached to the wall with some hay he found in the stable, then settled the horse into the stall for the night. Together they then pushed the cart in next to it.

Evan then left Harri by the back door holding the pup and walked back down the side-track to the front. Inserting and turning the large black key into the keyhole in the heavy studded oak door, it unlocked easily, then the door swung fully open. The low sun, now at the west side of the house, flooded into the front hall as he entered. Long settled dust motes, disturbed by both him and the accompanying updraught, soared then floated aimlessly around him. Illuminated in the concentrated shafts of sunlight, they began to silently float down to settle once more.

Once in the hallway, Evan turned the small, somewhat dented brass doorknob of an oak plank door on his right. Entering, he saw an ornate fireplace in what must be the parlour, probably seldom used and only on formal, special occasions. The damp smell of the unused, unaired, unoccupied room rose up but it was nothing that a good fire could not fix. The walls had been lime-washed once upon a time but were now dingy with age, except where pictures had more recently hung on brass hooks from a wooden picture rail. These showed up as lighter, rectangular shapes. Large spiders, judging by the size of the cobwebs, had been industriously spinning them in the dark mildewed corners for decades, although it was doubtful that there was anything here for them to catch and eat given the windows were tightly shut, only the soot from an occasional hearth fire landed on them.

The floor was laid with worn granite flagstones which needed a good hard scrubbing. Some light entered in through the small-paned front window, misty and thick with years of grime and mould. Returning to the lighter main hall area, he looked up a steep narrow oak staircase. Resisting the climb, he lifted the brass latch of the door on his left instead. This led into a sitting area with a large open stone fireplace. It had a large brown river-stone lintel running across the top, sunk into the stonework of the wall. The fireplace was flanked by two black-oak settles, again thick with dust and clearly not considered worth removing during the house clearance. Evan made his way towards the back of the house where the kitchen ran its entire length. At one end, a large black cast-iron cooking range took up most of the width of the wall, rusty with lack of use and in need of black-leading. A long wooden table, smooth and uneven from years of scrubbing with a hard brush or scouring stones, stood lengthways in the middle of this room, on an unevenly worn flagstone floor. Down a small step on the other side was a scullery, which had a small narrow window where large boulders had permitted.

A shiver ran through Evan as he stood in this chilly, damp side of the house, where the sun of the day had not penetrated. He slid across a large heavy bolt to open the back door and called to Harri, 'Go and get some dead wood for the fire. There's plenty at the top of the field.'

He needed to get the stove lit. He hoped that the chimney was not blocked by birds' nests, so he burned old papers, to make sure the chimney was clear. Thankfully, the smoke rose freely, pulled upwards by a good draught.

As he waited for Harri to come back with the wood, he walked across the small yard. He heard his hob-nailed boots echoing off the walls of the buildings, loud against the background of intense silence all around him. Just when the silence was becoming oppressive, he heard a song-thrush singing its musical repertoire in an elderberry tree close by, its earnestness making him smile. He took a quick look inside the small outbuilding and saw that it was shelved with slate slabs and counter tops and assumed that this must be the dairy where butter and cheeses were made.

The puppy, missing the warmth of Evan's coat, started to whine as Harri returned and piled a bundle of wood next to the range. Evan said, 'He likes you, what shall we call him?'

'I think Macs would be a good name.'

'Macs he shall be then,' said Evan noticing a slow smile of pleasure from the lad, at being asked.

Evan piled the dead wood, the result of previous winter storms, on top of some kindling. He used an old tinder box left at the side of the range and some ancient spills. Once the fire had caught alight, he found an axe on the cart and started chopping some of the larger branches while Harri brought the provisions in. Piled on to the kitchen table were bags of flour and oats, vegetables, lard, jars of jams and pickles, as well as household soaps, blankets, pots and pans and a large black kettle to boil water on the range. Evan went out to prime the ancient water pump in the yard until the water eventually ran clear. He filled the kettle and carried it back to put on the range to boil. He felt in need of a good wash – but the water would take a good while to boil. He gently placed Macs on one of the blankets in front of the range to keep warm and wondered if it had been too young to leave its mother.

Then he gave the lad some of the bread and cheese he had purchased earlier in the day and handed him a blanket. 'You can sleep in the loft in the stable. Take Macs with you if you want – you can keep each other warm.'

Evan felt nervous about carrying the pouch of sovereigns the solicitor had given him so started exploring around the fireplace for a hiding place. People generally hid money in such places in case a casual person walked into their homes when they were out working in the fields. Sure enough, he noticed one brick which seemed a little different and gently slid it forward. When the brick came away, he found a cavity behind it, empty now but perfect to hide the pouch. On a whim he decided to also put in the solicitor's letters, farm deeds and the letter his mother had given to him written by his father William, to make sure they were safe.

With daylight fading fast, he went to explore upstairs. Climbing the narrow staircase, he reached a wide-boarded wooden landing with doors leading off. Opening one of them, he entered a front bedchamber, where an old iron bedstead without a mattress stood up against the back wall. He remembered his mother saying it was better to burn a mattress if a person had been ill or had died on it, so as not to spread disease. Used to sleeping above the stable above shuffling animals, a bedchamber would take some getting used to. He would have to buy a feather mattress and wondered where he could get one, as these things were usually inherited – or made on farms from the moulted or plucked feathers of poultry. Maybe a farm sale would be a good place to start, somewhere he could get other household items and furniture as well.

Set deep into the thick stone wall was a window seat. He sat and looked out into the dusk through warped glass panes; they distorted the view of the fields and sea, which was slightly disorientating. On his arrival in front of the property, he had noticed a blanked-out window in the middle of the house upstairs and wondered if it had been used to winch up sacks of grain to the upper floor, especially as he suspected that there had been a mill at the side of the building. The other upstairs rooms off the landing were similarly floor-boarded, with tongue and grooved ceilings, but devoid of any furniture. Slowly he went downstairs to check on the kettle, stopping first by his front door to look out towards the sea in the dusk. The large red sun was now halfway down below the line of the horizon and sinking fast, casting a long red ribbon-like band across the surface of the calm water. Since living on the farm on the other side of the valley, he had not actually seen the sun going down over the sea for years and he stood there, mesmerised. Once it had sunk completely out of sight, he noticed that the wispy clouds in the sky above and around dramatically turned into a blood red colour. He felt a sudden rush of love for the place working its way into his soul. He would make the farm work as he was determined he would never leave this beautiful place; he only had to step outside his front door to see this beautiful spectacle of nature.

Shaking him out of his reverie, he heard the kettle lid begin to bounce and rattle as the water came to the boil and splutter on the range. He fetched a white enamel bowl, a block of carbolic soap and a rough towel from his supplies. He filled the bowl with the hot water for a stripped-down wash, then enjoyed his supper of bread and cheese in front of the range.

It was a long, eventful day which would stay with Evan forever; his first day as the independent owner of his own farm. Overcome by fatigue, he lay his blanket down on the floor by the warmth of the banked-up kitchen range, threw his heavy coat over the top of him and fell into a deep exhausted sleep.

The next thing he knew was the puppy's raspy tongue excitedly licking his face. 'Bore da,' said Harri, who had collected more wood and let the puppy in through the back door. It was just after dawn and starting to get light. The water in the big black kettle was still warm, so Evan added wood to the fire to bring it to the boil once more. While waiting, he went out to the pump for his morning wash.

Harri had already led the horse out to graze in the steep field and Evan felt sure he had made the right decision in taking on this urchin lad who used his own initiative. Evan had made a cursory inspection of the boundaries the previous evening, so knew it was safe to let the horse out. He set Harri some tasks around the farmyard and made his way back to the house to find a slightly-built girl waiting for him outside the back door. 'My name is Elin, sir. The innkeeper said you are looking for a housekeeper. I can come every day to wash, clean and cook, if that is what you want.' She could not be more than fourteen years old. Noticing his doubtful expression, she assured him, 'I have helped my mother bring up my six brothers and can turn my hand to anything. My father has had an accident in the quarry and can no longer work, so my family needs the money.'

'You don't look that strong – but I will give you the benefit of the doubt. I will pay you five shillings a week to start with.' No sooner had he said this than she busily gathered up some cleaning rags, which included a large goose wing for getting into dusty corners, and headed up the narrow stairs saying, 'I will clean the place from top to bottom, you won't recognise it by the time I have finished. Once I have cleaned the kitchen, I will put this stuff away,' pointing to the provisions still piled on the kitchen table.

Bemused by the feisty Elin, Evan was suddenly ravenous and called Harri to breakfast. They finished last night's bread and cheese then washed it down with hot sweet tea while Evan thought about which jobs to tackle first.

Over the week, Elin made great progress with the cleaning and persuaded Evan to limewash the internal walls. Soon, she had even mastered the oven in the old range and began to produce delicious crusty loaves, which filled the kitchen with a wonderful aroma. Each day she prepared a midday meal for Evan and Harri and a cold supper, before she left for the day.

Evan concentrated on repairing and painting the broken windows and doors of the outbuildings, mending tool handles and servicing equipment. Harri trimmed hedges, cut logs for the woodpile and kept the stable clean. With all this activity, the place began to take on a new lease of life, losing the uncared for, run down staleness. Soon there was an established daily routine, which started at daybreak and went on until dark and Evan knew he had been very fortunate in finding both Harri and Elin.

While working on replacing fallen stones on the wall in the small meadow, Evan said to Harri, 'Cat got your tongue today?'

'I was wondering about my Mam.'

You're not alone there, thought Evan. 'Do you know which workhouse she is in?'

'Yes, she's in the one in Llanrwst.'

'Well, I tell you what we'll do, we'll write them a letter to ask after her.'

'Oh! Thank you, sir, I'd just like to know one way or another,' obviously fearing the worst.

'Don't call me sir,' said Evan feeling uncomfortable. Ruffling the boy's hair, he said, 'Mister will do.'

That evening, Evan, having purchased paper, pen and ink, settled down to write the letter. He wasn't very practised but persevered. Next day, he took it to the village Post Office. They waited for a reply - but none came. So, Evan decided that he would call personally at the workhouse to enquire, next time he went to Llanrwst.

After a few more weeks of carrying out repairs, Evan believed that the farm was ready to buy in stock. He sought the advice of Dafydd, who had been farming for decades on the adjoining farm. 'The number of sheep is roughly ten per acre and the best livestock market is in Llanrwst in the next valley.'

He did not tell Dafydd about his links to Llanrwst. He did not relish bumping into Catherine's father and brother there, as they might create a scene, but on the other hand, he would be very happy to see Catherine. Then he remembered he had promised Harri he would call at the workhouse.

Dafydd, a deeply religious non-conformist, had added, 'You do realise that you have to give a tenth of any crop you produce in tithe tax to the established Church? The church considers it the act of giving the first fruits of our labour to God, which goes towards the upkeep of their church buildings. It makes me so angry that I am forced to pay this tax. I don't see why I should pay for the upkeep of a Church I do not attend and to an idolatrous religion which I do not hold with.' Although Evan had vaguely heard about this, the old farmer had always dealt with the paperwork, so it had not previously concerned him. He felt outraged that he would now have to give away crops, produced through his own hard work, to an entity he also did not believe in – but felt powerless to do anything about as it was ecclesiastical law. Many other people agreed with Dafydd and a groundswell of protest was slowly building up against it. Although Evan was not then overtly religious, he had a strong sense of justice and over the years, Dafydd's strong faith came to influence Evan, who became more religious as he got older.

There was an obsessive quality about Evan's personality which demanded that everything he did was to the best of his ability; failure was unthinkable, as it would not do justice to his father's memory. He was lucky he did not have to pay rent nor mortgage out of his income – only wages and those dratted tithes. But his mother had taught him to be frugal, never wasteful. These values were ingrained in his nature and even though no longer poor, this trait would ensure that he prospered. He knew that as a farmer, the rest of his life would now be dictated by the needs of the farm animals he was soon to buy, the weather and the abundance, or not, of his crops.

As it was still spring, he knew he had plenty of time to prepare food stocks for next winter. He fixed, oiled and sharpened the blades of an old plough he had found abandoned in a patch of stinging nettles and bramble. He and his cob ploughed together as a team, turning over row after row of rich dark soil in the lower fields creating a feast for the birds. He planted a field of potatoes, known to be good for cleansing the soil of a field left fallow, then planted a field of turnips, as winter feed for the animals. Dafydd had told him that there was a deficiency of lime in the soil in the area, so after ploughing, he carefully distributed it onto the fields suitable for crops.

'Harri, I'm putting you in charge of the kitchen garden. Mulch-in the horse manure to make the soil fertile ready for seedlings. You can also look after the herb garden and see to the orchard.' This would ensure a steady supply of food for the house as well as herbs for medicines. Although Evan was no mechanic, he also decided to try to rebuild the mill, to grind the corn when it had been harvested. Evan thought it would be good for Harri to help him on the project. 'We're going to fix the waterwheel and get the mill working. All the metal workings seem to be there. I found the badly rotted wheel abandoned in one of the outhouses. Some of the wooden blades need replacing but first we'll oil the cogwheels, see if there's any life in them after being rusted for so long.'

They worked solidly for a few days, then it gradually ground into life. The milling would be undertaken close to the power of the wheel, on the upper-level space, so they strengthened the floor where the pulleys were fitted and fixed the winch which would be used to lift the sacks of grain. Evan then ordered two grinding stones and the internal machinery needed to work them. He was pleased with how inventive and practical Harri's thinking was. 'I'm going to put you in charge of running the mill as well, once the grain starts coming in in the autumn, so I'll start paying you a proper wage.'

The lad thought how proud his mother would have been of him having such a responsibility and felt himself choke up at Evan's faith in him. Evan and Elin were now his family and she spoilt him like she did her younger brothers.

With the farm finally ready, Evan set off for the livestock market. He bought poultry, which he loaded onto the cart in their cages. The larger stock animals would have to be walked over by paid drovers but from then on, he would breed his own animals and drive them himself back to the market. On his way back, he called at the workhouse as promised and was informed that Harri's mother had passed away soon after being admitted. He would have to confirm Harri's worst fears. He bought a cone of toffee for the boy to try to cheer him up.

Evan intended to make good use of the bounty of nature to feed his animals. He planned to buy a gorse threshing machine, to provide winter feed. There were plenty of gorse bushes up on the common land above the farm. He would ask Harri to collect the gorse with the cart. His pigs could gorge on the acorns, soon to drop in the ancient woodland adjoining his land. In early summer, he would drive his sheep up to the friths with Macs, if he was trained by then, to fatten before bringing them back down to shear and brand later in the summer.

Evan set off for home with his purchases. On his return, Macs bounded over to greet him. He saw that Elin had baked a meat pie with a lovely golden crust for supper but first he off-loaded his point-of-lay hens into the prepared sheds, then put the ducks and geese into their shed. The geese would make excellent guards around the farmyard. Hopefully, the poultry would settle down in a couple of weeks and start laying. He had already dammed a part of the stream further up, to form a small pond for them and would let them all out tomorrow morning to get used to their new surroundings. Tomorrow, the dozen sheep, two pigs and four milking cows would be driven over and down Bwlch Sychnant by the drovers, then his farm would be fully stocked at last.

The house was now habitable, he had livestock coming and he had Elin, Harri and Macs for company. But he needed a wife, Catherine, to work with him and be his life companion on the farm. He noticed that Harri and Elin had become good friends reminding him of his younger friendship with Catherine.

Early next morning he said to Elin, 'I will be needing a dairy maid to milk the cows and make butter, cheeses and cream to sell at market, once the milk starts coming in. Do you know of anybody who can do this job?' She was pensive for a moment before replying, 'I have an older cousin who learned to do all that sort of work in the dairy of the estate at the top of the Bwlch Sychnant. She was very good at it – but she left their employ because the son of the farm had wandering hands and tended to trap her in the dairy.'

Elin blushed slightly at her own boldness at saying this and would not meet Evan's startled gaze. She mumbled as she scuttled away, embarrassed, 'I will go and see her to ask her,' as she had already said too much about Gwen. Evan chuckled softly to himself, thinking that this cousin of hers sounded quite spirited so would probably fit in well. 'If she does a good job, she will be left in peace to work.'

Evan's mind wandered back to the stock he was expecting. A feeling of anticipation was rising in him. The sheep and cows could be let straight out into the fields – but the pigs would need to be driven into the pigsty, which had already been cleaned and laid out with fresh straw. He would need to get rings put through their noses before he could let them out in the fields, or they would dig everywhere up. He also thought that next summer, once the new lambs and the ewes were strong enough to go out to the mountain pastures, he would need to find a shepherd who could stay up there to mind the flock for the summer. This had been a normal pattern of the farming practice since the first settlers had tamed and domesticated local wild animals and was still a viable option for fattening stock. There were gangs who went from farm to farm shearing the sheep of their winter coats. He must ask Dafydd. But he had already cleaned up and sharpened a pair of rusty old shears he had found in the barn if he had to do it himself. He had also found an old branding iron with intertwining initials. Using this to brand his sheep would make them identifiable as belonging to his farm, when all the farmers went out for the mass gathering in summer. But he had plenty of time before he needed a shepherd and he certainly wasn't going to go back and ask Elin; she had already had enough embarrassment for one day!

Evan had purchased a feather mattress for the brass bed. Elin had made some curtains for the window, cushions for the window seat and a rag-rug for the floor. He thought it surprising how quickly a woman's touch can make a place feel homely. Despite his new-found comfort, Evan woke in the early hours, way before the sun rose and was suddenly, uncharacteristically filled with panic and self-doubt. What if the animals he had bought were diseased? What if they were not good breeders? What if the hens and ducks failed to lay? Having thoroughly scared himself, he broke out in a cold sweat. After a few minutes, he heard his mother's voice in his head saying sternly, 'Pull yourself together Evan, this is no time for self-doubt, just get up and get on with it.' The anxiety gradually receded. He rose from his bed and made his way outside to the water pump. The icy water he splashed on his face invigorated him and he was soon back to his confident self.

Later that morning, he heard the far away sound of animals bellowing and bleating, so knew they were on their way. He looked

176

up towards the pass and sure enough saw them being driven down the steep track. Sound carried a long way in the valley, echoing and bouncing between the mountains. Given a still day with no wind, he could sometimes hear children's voices in the small hamlet below his fields, a mile away.

With the arrival of the animals, stage two of his plan would be complete. He picked up his shepherd's crook, whistled to Macs and quickly made his way towards the village to meet them. It was quite a spectacle for the village people to witness and Macs wasn't much help. Children ran about gleefully, thinking they were helping but made things worse by spooking the animals. Women stood in the doorways of their small cottages laughing at the animals' antics – some were very determined to escape so deviated down a side-track to the river. But the drover's dogs were ready for these renegades, bringing them quickly back to the main flock by nipping at their heels. As they neared the farm, Evan waved his shepherd's crook, indicating to the drovers that all but the pigs could go into the fields and the farm gate was already open. Next, the pigs were guided along the track into the pigsties near the farmyard. It was all managed with smooth efficiency and soon the farm gates were firmly closed with the animals safely inside.

Elin brought out home-made beer with bread and cheese for the drovers, then they set out on their way. Not long after, Elin's cousin Gwen, the milkmaid, turned up at the farmhouse. 'I hear you are looking for a dairy maid,' she said looking at Evan warily. He said, 'Ah Gwen, Elin has told me all about you,' at which point Gwen glared at Elin, hoping she had not told him too much. Evan said generously, 'If you are half as good a worker as Elin, the job is yours – and you will be left alone to get on with it,' he couldn't resist adding with a grin. 'You will be totally in charge of the running of the dairy. Everything will have to be kept scrupulously clean of course and you must let me know what equipment I need to purchase. You will start your day by milking the cows, keep aside enough milk for the household, then process the rest for butter, cream and cheese.'

Evan was impressed when Gwen then suggested, 'I could also take pails of milk on a yoke, to sell in the village, as I know the local man is pretty unreliable and his milk usually on the turn.'

She scrubbed the small dairy until it was spotless, then asked Evan to limewash the walls. Then she got Harri to rearrange and clean out the cow stalls. Quietly and efficiently she got on with her job and Evan hoped they would soon be selling their products to see some return on his investments.

When constructing the duck pond in the small meadow by the stream, Evan had noticed the footprint of an old round dwelling. He was passingly curious, but the stones were now needed for the dry-stone wall he was building, so he placed the large lichen covered stones onto the wall. Flat on the ground were two longer stones as well as some flatter ones inside the circle. He used the tall ones to form a gateway into the next field.

On fine evenings, Evan allowed himself to rest and reflect. He sat outside on his garden bench watching the sun slowly sink below the horizon. He often compared this new life with his old one at the other farm, where his mother still lived. Here he made his own decisions and if things went wrong, he only had himself to blame. He remembered how the old farmer used to blame him for everything and was not averse to slapping him around the head if he happened to be within arm's reach. Evan winced at the humiliation he'd had to suffer at his hands and was eternally grateful to his benevolent father, who had enabled his escape. Relaxing after his supper that evening, he saw that his plan had finally fallen into place; the farm was well-run and orderly – and he was gradually being accepted locally as part of the community. There were tacit agreements with the other farmers that they would help each other, particularly at harvest time.

He thought of Catherine often and longed to see her again. Some of the local women – or rather their fathers – had dropped hints about him courting their daughters but he knew that Catherine was the only one for him. The two had a rapport he had never felt with any other human being and he felt sure that when they met again, they would simply pick up where they had left off. He would seek her out once the hay was in. There would of course be great opposition from her father. Evan would prefer to have his blessing but was not going to beg him for her hand. He now felt equal to her father but knew he would only ever be seen by him as an ungrateful upstart.

The summer months rolled relentlessly on. The weather had been kind, the harvest good and many locals came to help. They were rewarded with a midday snack of bread and cheese and later Elin prepared a celebratory harvest meal in the kitchen at the end of the day. It was the first time for Evan to see all the chairs filled around his kitchen table and he felt as one with these people.

Hay sheaves were now safely stacked up in the barn. The orchard's apples had been picked and carefully wrapped in newspaper and stored in wooden boxes. Windfalls and blackberries had been made into pies. Nuts had been picked and stored. Jams and pickles were made and carefully labelled and stored. Cheeses had been wrapped in muslin and put away in a cool dark place. The sow had had a litter of pigs which he was fattening for Christmas. The heifer had had twin calves and the sheep flock had doubled in size. Evan lifted potatoes, which he stored in hessian sacks, and had a pile of turnips stored in a cool section of the barn. The grain from the lower fields was stored ready to be milled. All preparations were now in place to see them through the winter months. Now was the time to seek the truth from Catherine.

He visualised various scenarios in which he could meet her; in darker moments he panicked she may already be married. He considered writing a letter – but her father could get hold of it. Evan was desperate to see her face to face, so he could see the truth there.

Next Sunday, dressed in his best, he set off early on his cob over to the next valley. Once there, he tied his horse out of sight and gave a small boy a coin to mind it. He skirted around the back of the church, then stood in the shadow of some ancient yews, surrounded by lichen-covered gravestones of people long forgotten, then he watched as black-clad attendees filed in. He soon caught sight of Catherine with her brother and father then covertly watched them walking in through the lych-gate entrance. As he did, his heart began to thump loudly in his chest and his pulse drummed loudly in his head. Noticing his mother was absent, he felt anxious.

When the tolling bell finally stopped, he quietly slipped into a shadowy pew at the back, just as the warden shut the church door. He had hoped that Catherine would sense he was there but how could he expect her to? Surreptitiously he watched her during the interminable service. She looked so very lovely in her best cloak and bonnet and he was impatient to talk to her.

Evan settled down to listen to the sermon but felt discomfited by the formality of the service. Although Catherine and her family still attended the established church, he knew that many people were now becoming disillusioned with it. Non-conformity had a significant influence in Wales and was gathering momentum. Travelling preachers were converting them to Methodism at open air services. They rejected the idolatry of the established church for a simpler type of worship. Evan recalled Dafydd telling him that the Bible had been translated from Greek and Hebrew into Welsh by William Morgan and that it was first printed in 1588. This translation had raised the status of Welsh to a literary language and because people thought in Welsh, they expressed themselves more naturally in their own tongue. He was still pondering this when he suddenly realised the congregation was rising for the final hymn. Then slowly, the choir began to file out, followed by the vicar. The rest followed, talking as they went to others they probably only ever saw on Sundays. They were in their best clothes and on their best behaviour. Respectability was everything – but hypocrisy lurked just below the surface. Shuffling along, they patiently waited for their turn to shake the vicar's hand on exiting the church.

Evan spotted Catherine moving down the centre aisle towards him. Her lovely face stood out in the sea of bleak faces. She was very near now, filing out behind her father, who was looking straight ahead. He willed her to look in his direction. She glanced sideways and saw him. He saw the flicker of recognition in her eyes and the sudden blush in her cheeks.

By the time he got outside, she was standing to one side. Her father was deep in conversation with another farmer, so she quietly slipped away into the shadow of the trees and Evan followed. When they faced each other, Evan could see the sheer joy of love radiating from her and knew then that their special connection had endured.

Autumn rain started to fall, so Catherine put up her umbrella, which kept their faces hidden from others. They both spoke at once in their haste to spurt out all they had kept bottled up inside for so long. This in turn made them giggle nervously. He said, 'We don't have much time to talk but I want to know if you will marry me and come to live with me on my farm?' Catherine, too choked to speak, nodded her agreement with joyful tears brimming in her eyes, then running freely down her face. He wiped one gently from her cheek.

Swallowing, she said lovingly, 'I have been waiting for so long to see you again, to hear from you – and for you to ask me to marry you.' She added with a cautious note, 'My father will do everything in his power to stop us, so you must be very careful. He doesn't know where you are and believes you are working locally, doing odd jobs.'

Evan said urgently, 'I will have banns read out over three Sundays at my parish church, so that your father will not know of the announcements. We cannot use any of the Conwy Valley churches as he would find out somehow. I will go to see my solicitor to make arrangements. You will need to be ready to leave at very short notice. Call in at Jones' solicitor's office each time you go to the market, I will leave instruction about the arrangements with him there.'

Suddenly, her father was approaching them, his face like thunder. Evan quickly slipped away leaving Catherine to his mercy. Cupping her elbow, her father pulled her roughly towards the gate. Evan heard him muttering furiously to her, 'I don't want you ever talking to that ungrateful upstart. Do you understand me? Get on that wagon now.'

Evan could well imagine the curses he would be making under his breath as they made their way to their cart and felt sorry for her when her father got her home. She, his mother and even the animals would feel his wrath for days to come. This was something Catherine would have to go through but by the grace of God, it would not be for too much longer – there was now an end in sight. During the period when the banns were read out, he did not think anyone would guess it was them as their names were common enough.

Her father gradually dropped his guard but as a punishment, he forbade her from leaving the farm. It was only three weeks later, believing his threats had worked, that he relented, when Elizabeth said she urgently needed Catherine to fetch her some things from market.

Evan, euphoric that Catherine wanted to marry him, visited his solicitor to formulate a plan. He firmly believed people should be free to marry who they chose, without family interference, especially since finding out about his parents' unhappy experience. Although legally Catherine did not need her father's consent, she knew this would mean nothing to him. He would expect her to do her duty and remain at home, looking after him and his son – conveniently forgetting he had a wife.

The wedding had been planned for the next market day. Catherine felt uncomfortable about being deceitful but there really was no other way. She would leave the farm ostensibly to go to the market but go to the solicitor's office. When Catherine finally managed to get to the solicitor's office, she learned that the wedding had been arranged for the following week. Knowing the plan, she returned home and spent the entire week in a nervous state of anxiety, mingled with excited anticipation. Her mother's jewellery box contained only one piece of value – her wedding ring. So that she did not leave this behind, she slipped it onto a chain and hung it around her neck, carefully tucking it inside the bodice of her dress. This made her feel closer to her dead mother and quietly, in her prayers, told her all about Evan and their plan to marry. She knew she would feel happy for her, unlike her father, who would be ranting and raving once he found out. She had always loved Evan, first as a friend and latterly as a sweetheart. He had always been kind and considerate to her and she had missed him more than she could have imagined, since that fateful day when he had left.

The day arrived. Catherine, acting as normally as possible in the circumstances, put on her everyday bonnet and cape and set off for the market town, with her straw shopping basket over her arm. She went directly to the solicitor's office as instructed and was greeted by the solicitor's daughter Dorothy, a Sunday school friend, who whisked her away into a small side room saying, 'I have a surprise for you in here. We decided we couldn't let you get married in your everyday clothes, so Evan asked me to buy you something suitable. I hope they are all the right size.' To Catherine's surprise, a beautiful trousseau was laid out for her inspection and a charming wedding outfit hung up next to it for her to change into. 'The dress will be perfect for your hourglass figure. Then there is this beautiful paisley shawl to drape on your shoulders,' she drooled enviously, fingering its fineness and fringe, 'and to finish off, a pretty little silk bonnet with ribbons and a beautiful hand bouquet of lily of the valley. Oh! I almost forgot, I also bought some wedding slippers,' – placing them on the floor for Catherine to slip on. 'I hope you like it all, I had such fun choosing everything. You should have seen the faces of the people in the shop. When I was trying them on, the local gossips thought it was me getting married. Caused quite a stir it did!' They giggled at this. Dorothy knew instinctively what Catherine would choose and fortunately they were roughly the same build. She wouldn't have wanted anything fussy, just quietly understated and tasteful.

Overwhelmed and overcome with emotion, Catherine threw her arms around Dorothy because she was choked up by the kindness and speech had deserted her. She was overwrought by it all and clung onto Dorothy a little longer for comfort. Evan's thoughtfulness in providing all this for her to make it a special day confirmed that she was marrying a dear, considerate man.

Before leaving home on the fateful day, she had intimated to Elizabeth that she may not be back but to not say anything to anybody as it might not happen and also not to worry as she would be safe. She had written a short note and told Elizabeth where to find it if she did not return.

183

Dear Family,

At the end of this eventful day, I will not be returning to the farm, as I will be with Evan.

By the time you read this, we will be married.

I hope that you are not angry with us that we did not tell you – but hope we will have your blessing.

Your affectionate daughter, as ever

Catherine

By the time it was read, it would be much too late to stop proceedings as the deed would be done.

Her father exploded with rage when he read out the words. Elizabeth's hand went up to her mouth in shock but then had to suppress a happy smile which threatened to spread over her beautiful face. She was glad they had the courage to defy her husband and would marry for love, as she had been prevented from doing.

* * *

Catherine looked beautiful in her wedding outfit. Looking now at her reflection in the ornate cheval mirror before her, she was astounded by her appearance. Her jaw dropped in amazement. What a transformation from a dowdy farmer's daughter. 'I wish my mother and Elizabeth were both here,' she thought.

When Dorothy returned to the room, she stopped in her tracks at the sight of Catherine, saying tearfully, 'Catherine, you look so very lovely – Evan is a very lucky man.'

The solicitor knocked tentatively at the door and entered. He smiled admiringly when he saw Catherine but ever the pragmatist, quickly ushered them into a waiting carriage. Soon they were on their way to the church; from this moment on, Catherine's life would be changed forever.

The carriage travelled up the side of the valley towards the walled estate, as Evan had done some eight months earlier. On the way down the steep pass on the other side, Dorothy pointed out Evan's farm to her. A quick glimpse showed it nestling in the distance, like a sentinel looking out over the valley below. Catherine then thought to herself: from today, I will spend the rest of my life here in this valley with the love of my life. At this thought she felt a frisson of excitement and a sudden nervous shivering spread throughout her body. Dorothy noticed her hands were shaking and held them warmly in reassurance. When the carriage had almost reached the village at the bottom of the pass, it turned sharply right, down another track, then around a wide bend, which skirted a dry-stone wall. Further along, Catherine noticed through the trees on her left a mill with a waterwheel attached. This was powered by the large river, which the road was now crossing by way of an ancient stone bridge. The river was on their right, then veered off in a northerly direction on its way to the sea. The carriage continued through farmland along a road dotted with a few cottages, until it pulled up outside the church.

Dorothy and Catherine looked at each other, as if to say, this is it. They climbed down from the carriage and walked towards the church's lych-gate, built with a small slate roof to shelter undertakers bringing coffins to funerals. However, they did not loiter under the gate nor reflect on its darker functions. Today was a happy occasion and they walked quickly towards the church door. Soft music was playing as Catherine reached the doorway – but a more jubilant piece struck up as she began to walk slowly towards the altar. Evan was already standing at the front of the nave waiting for her, his face full of love, seeing no-one but her. Catherine glanced to the side and saw two young women and a young lad seated in the front row. Catherine took all of this in; it was a day she wanted to remember in every precious detail forever.

She finally reached Evan's side in front of the vicar. Unused to being the centre of attention, she blushed slightly. Evan noticed and thought it made her even more beautiful. Determined to have a wedding to remember, despite no parents being present, Evan had spent a great deal of time working out every little detail. His only regret was that he had not been able to marry in a chapel.

Portraying a sense of the importance of the occasion and of his own role in the proceedings, the vicar announced, 'We are gathered here today in the sight of God Almighty to join Evan and Catherine in holy matrimony. If anyone knows of any reason why these two people should not be joined in holy matrimony, let them speak now or forever hold their peace.'

Evan and Catherine both looked back towards the church door, half expecting her father to come bursting in – but there was only a reassuring silence. The vicar continued, 'Evan Ffowcs Jones, will you take this woman, Catherine Evans, to be your lawful wedded wife?'

'I will' – and added to himself, 'With all my heart and my soul.'

Catherine was then asked, 'Catherine Evans, do you take this man, Evan Ffowcs Jones, to be your lawful wedded husband, to have and to hold, through sickness and in health, from this day forth?'

'I will' she said. Evan tenderly slipped a slender, rose-gold wedding ring onto her marriage finger. The vicar declared them man and wife and Evan kissed Catherine lightly on her lips, then they went to sign the register. Evan proudly named his father on the certificate, wishing that he had experienced the same happiness by marrying his mother, Elizabeth. Elin and her cousin Gwen were then invited to come forward to act as official witnesses. They signed with the signatures they had been practising for weeks.

The irrevocable deed was legally done. Evan and Catherine had exchanged vows, they were now man and wife and there was nothing that Catherine's father could do about it. They felt a huge sense of relief and looked forward to married life together – but still expected some sort of repercussion, once her father realised she had left for good. Apprehensively, Elizabeth would be breaking the news that Catherine had left and was now married to Evan, expecting that he would demand to see Catherine's letter and would become apoplectic with rage.

They travelled back to the farm on Evan's horse and cart, specially decorated with flowers for the occasion. They were a handsome couple and along with Elin, her cousin Gwen and Harri, presented as a happy, jovial wedding party. Some locals had gathered outside the church to wish them well and throw rice at them as they rode away.

Back at the farm they enjoyed a celebratory wedding spread, prepared earlier by Elin and Gwen. After they had eaten and all had been cleared away, Elin and her cousin left for the day, leaving the happy couple alone, as Harri took himself off to his loft in the stable.

Catherine went upstairs to one of the back bedrooms to change out of her wedding finery, back into her everyday clothes, which she had in a small canvas bag. When she descended, Evan took his new wife by the hand and showed her around the rest of the farmhouse. Upstairs, in the bedroom at the front of the house, the iron bedstead, with its new feather mattress, was covered with fresh white cotton sheets, a large bolster pillow and a colourful red and blue Welsh tapestry bedspread. There was a short silence as they shared a shy smile, thinking of what was to come later. Next was a washstand with a marble top, with a pretty blue and white washbowl and a water jug. Fresh towels and a special bar of lavender soap had been placed on the grey marble top. Against one wall stood a handsome chest of drawers with a set of ebony hairbrushes on top. Evan told her he had recently picked up these impressive pieces of furniture at a local auction, held at one of the big houses.

As they walked back down the stairs, there were no longer dust motes floating around the hallway – Elin had banished them all. They walked hand in hand out of the front door, through the farm gate and along the track to the farmyard at the back of the house. Evan introduced her to the wildly enthusiastic sheepdog, Macs, who gave her a good welcome and they became firm friends. They inspected the pig pens, the milk stalls and then the barn. She looked over the animal stock with an experienced eye saying, 'You've done well.' Evan was encouraged but was not looking for praise. 'The place was quite run down when I first got here. The doors and window frames needed work doing to them. I wanted to get everything done before you came, so that we would have a home we could be proud of.'

Catherine did not realise Evan owned the farm until they sat down together on a grassy ledge at the top of the field, looking out towards the sea. Carefully he explained the whole story from the beginning. He told her about the boy bringing the solicitor's letter and his unexpected inheritance with which he bought the farm. She was shocked but happy, as it seemed to have turned Evan into the confident and outgoing man she loved.

Catherine was enchanted with the farm. She loved the way it looked out to sea and the way the hills behind seemed to wrap themselves comfortingly around the valley. She smiled sweetly, her head to one side and stroked his face with the back of her hand, 'You are such a dear kind person and I am so blessed that you are my husband.' Pure contentment was just to be there with Evan.

'I am glad to escape from my father and his bad temper. I know he will explode with rage when he finds out what we have done and I wouldn't be surprised if we get a visit from him one of these days, when he finds out where we are. And find out he will, one way or another. I wonder how your mother will explain about the farm. He will probably think you are running it for somebody.' She continued pensively, 'I already miss your mother and hope that, in time, she might join us. But she told me many times, when I asked her why she put up with him, that she had married my father for better or for worse and her vow was made in the sight of God. I said to her that you definitely got the worse bit anyway, because he's not going to get any better!'

Evan loved her wry sense of humour, her kindliness and her quiet courage. Not many women would have risked all as she had today. He recalled the time he and his mother had first arrived at her farm. Only Catherine realised they were tired and hungry, and despite her father, had brought out bread and cheese. He thought he had first fallen in love with her at that moment because of that act of pure kindness.

'It feels so good to have you with me at last.' He could not help going about with a silly grin on his face. 'I feel a true sense of completeness and belonging and know I can tackle anything now, so long as you are here with me.'

Later, when he took her hand and they climbed the stairs to the bedroom, he took out her hair combs and her hair fell about her shoulders. He lifted one of the ebony hair brushes and gently brushed her waist-length, chestnut hair. They made love that first night of married life, both shy of each other at first but feeling that all was at last as it should be. Then both were soon sound asleep, exhausted but exhilarated by their love-making – and by the enormity of the day.

A week later, a horse and cart pulled up outside the front of the farmhouse. Catherine's father and Evan's mother sat stiffly on the bench of the cart, which the farmer had already turned around, obviously planning to leave quickly once he had Catherine on board. Word had got through to him about the general area Evan was in. Then he asked locals in the village about the farm's whereabouts.

Evan was busy working in the top field and saw a cart pull up. As soon as he heard her father's voice, he raced down the field. Threateningly, her father shouted, 'Catherine, come out of that house at once and get on this cart now. You will feel the back of my hand if I must come and drag you out. You have disgraced me. I have come to take you home where you belong, not here with this scoundrel.'

Evan ran in through the back door. On seeing how scared Catherine was, he said, 'Stay in the house, I will go and deal with him,' and went out of the front door to confront him. He looked at his mother who seemed exhausted and he waited for the farmer to stop yelling. He told him firmly, 'Catherine is my wife now and is not going anywhere with you.' Then with a more conciliatory tone, 'I hope that you will give our marriage your blessing but this is where Catherine lives now – you had better get used to it.'

He saw his mother trying to suppress a smile and he felt sure she was proud of him standing up to the tyrant. Few had ever spoken to him like this before, except Evan on the day he left the farm. His new-found confidence, developed along with his newly independent status, made him an equal to this man and he was no longer prepared to be intimidated by him. 'You are both very welcome to come in for something to eat.' But her father shouted angrily, while wagging his finger at him, 'I will never set foot in the house of an upstart. I regret the day that I ever took you and your mother on, if this is how you ungrateful wretches repay me. Damn you to Hell!' forgetting that Evan had worked on his farm for years for nothing and his mother had tolerated his bad moods. But all he saw was his daughter disobeying him. Still in temper, he flicked the reins sharply across the back of the horse causing the cart to jerk forward, then rode out of view and out of their lives.

* * *

Despite this unpleasant scene, life for the married couple settled into the seasonal routine of a farm. Given there was so much else to think about, the incident was pushed into the back of their minds. Everyone had the tasks they were responsible for and they all worked extremely hard. Catherine preferred to work outside with the animals and having Elin in the house made this possible. The farm became prosperous. Surplus products were taken to market and sold so well that they had to overproduce to meet demand. The sheep flock increased above all expectations and high prices were achieved on stock they took to market.

The spring lambs had grown strong and their mothers were sheared of their heavy wool coats. Evan and Elin's younger brother Tom, the new shepherd, as well as his now excellent working dog Macs, took the flock back up the mountains to their summer pasture, where they could be left to graze on the grasses, bilberry bushes and heathers which covered the hills. Evan loved the feeling of freedom of the wide-open spaces up there. They drove the sheep high up into the hills and walked for hours, getting them used to what was their territory, so that they would remember next year where to wander. They built a crude shelter in the corner of one of the friths, so Tom could stay up there during the summer to guard the flock against rustlers and foxes.

Whist looking for a lost sheep near the summit of Tal-y-Fan, Evan once came upon a pile of rocks, deliberately placed on top of each other to form an elongated cairn. It looked like it had been in that desolate, isolated place for centuries. Maybe it was a grave but who would choose to be buried in non-consecrated ground, thereby risking their immortal soul? Or maybe it was built by an ancient people who had lived on these hills way back in history, long before Christianity arrived.

Another time, walking along the Caerneddau range to the west, he came across a very large circle of tall, standing stones, some still upright, as well as other, smaller circles nearby. Some were covered in eons of pale green circular lichen. Again, he wondered what purpose this circle had served. Who had erected it? Could it be connected to the cairn, he wondered; the standing stones must have been quite a feat of engineering to transport, then set into place. The sun was just dipping down over the sea as he sat to rest on one of the stones. He noticed a long, bright shaft of sunlight filtering in through what seemed to have been an entrance of two uprights with a stone across the top of them. As he watched, the beam settled onto a large rectangular stone, at the centre of the circle. He then realised these stones had been deliberately placed to capture this effect. A shudder of fear ran down his spine as he guessed it could have been used for pagan worship and sacrifices. Disturbed, he called Macs, who was lurking some way off and they quickly walked away from what he felt was a sinister place. From then on, he avoided the circles of stones and never mentioned nor discussed it with anybody.

* * *

Life on the farm progressed uneventfully until one day a note was delivered for Catherine. It was from Evan's solicitor and read:

Dear Mr. and Mrs. Jones
It is my sad duty to inform you that Mr. Evans passed away this morning.
As I drew up his will, I am aware that the farm has been left to Mrs. Evan

Jones' brother Richard, which may make Mrs. Elizabeth Evans' future at the
farm untenable. I advise you to travel over to the farm to attend to her well-being
and to make funeral arrangements and such, at your earliest convenience.
Yours respectfully,
Caradoc Humphrey-Jones Esq, Solicitor

Catherine read the note out loud to Evan. This was an
unexpected shock. Her father had been an omnipotent presence
since childhood; he had seemed indestructible. Briefly disorientated
by the news, they sat dumbfounded; they did not care that he had
died but needed to ensure that Elizabeth was alright with Richard
now in charge. As if of one mind, which was often how they worked,
they prepared to travel to the farm. Their own farm was in good
hands, and as they left, Catherine asked Elin to prepare one of the
bedrooms, as they would be bringing Evan's mother back.

On arriving at the farm at midday, they were met by the now,
very ancient, bad-tempered sheepdog, reminding Evan of the time he
had first arrived there as a young boy, destitute. Inevitably the place
invoked unhappy memories – but he pushed these to one side to get
on with the purpose of their visit.

Catherine said, 'This place is tinged with both happy and sad
memories. I was born and spent my childhood here and can
remember my mother here.' She had left as a young, single woman
and had now returned with the dignity of a respectable farmer's wife.
Her brother came out of the farmhouse and was barely civil to them.
They accepted that this was grief and anger talking. He saw
Catherine as someone who had deserted them, a view drilled into
him by his father's bitterness towards her; he had also had to work
much harder since they had both left. 'What do you want? You're
not welcome here. Don't think you can just come here and have any
claim to the farm, he told me he has left everything to me. You can
have nothing.' Turning to Evan he said, 'And you can take your
mother from here, I have no need of her.'

At this, Elizabeth appeared behind him in the doorway, dressed
from head to toe in black, one hand holding onto the doorframe. She

looked very thin and pale and clearly in shock. Catherine knew Elizabeth was worried for her future, now her husband was dead. Catherine asked, 'We would like you to come and live with us. You would be very welcome.' Turning to Richard she asked, 'Have you made any funeral arrangements yet? Is there anything you want me to do?'

Elizabeth remained silent, afraid to answer Catherine. Richard had made it abundantly clear to her earlier that he no longer wanted her there. Replying to Catherine, Richard spat out, 'You've probably done enough damage already. He worked himself to death because you weren't here like you should have been,' clearly without any self-awareness that his own lazy behaviour may have contributed to the sad situation.

Wounded by her brother's attitude, 'In that case, if we can't help, we'll leave you to it. The dresser pots are mine, left to me by my Nain, so in due course, I will send a carter to collect them. I would like to attend his funeral – he was my father after all. Perhaps you'll be good enough to let us know when it will be held.'

Catherine turned back towards Elizabeth and said, 'Get your things together, you are coming with us. You should have left years ago.'

Elizabeth turned to go inside, whilst Richard shouted after her, 'And don't take anything which doesn't belong to you.' Wounded, she stopped in her tracks, then retorted, 'You are your father's son alright. I will take only what is mine, God knows that I have worked hard enough all these years for it. I want nothing to remind me of my time in this wretched place.' Richard stormed off towards the stables, as Evan and Catherine sat on the cart waiting for Elizabeth to come back out to join them, then set off for home.

Evan was glad to give his mother a home at last. It had taken this to prise her away from this unhappy place and he hoped to bring some joy into her life once more. He wanted her to again be the person she had been so very long ago when he was a child, before she was ground down by life. He thought that if his father was looking down on them, he would be glad that at last she was going to be properly loved and cared for. His generous legacy had enabled that.

They were never informed by Richard about the funeral and they left behind that part of their life. When asked, Richard refused to tell Catherine where their father was buried but she guessed it would be with her mother. She also suspected that her brother would now make a big effort to find himself a wife, another poor woman to work half to death. He certainly was not capable of looking after himself or running the farm.

Elizabeth settled into life on Evan's farm and into the local community. She began to blossom, away from her dead husband's toxic presence, although her nervousness never left her, so deep had it worked into her psyche. She gladly took over the running of the household with Elin.

A few months after Elizabeth's arrival, Catherine began vomiting as soon as she rose in the morning. Evan was perplexed but Elizabeth suspected that she was with child, though waited for Catherine to tell her. Then realisation slowly began to dawn on Evan. When he and Catherine sat out one lovely summer's evening on the front bench outside the farmhouse, watching the sun sink below the horizon, Evan held her hand very gently, looked her directly in the eye and asked her, 'Is there something you want to tell me?'

Catherine dropped her eyes to her lap, almost overwhelmed by the intensity of his look, which seemed to see right into her. She loved the intimacy they shared and knew that their lovemaking had resulted in conception. She said, 'Yes, I am almost sure that I am with child. It has not been confirmed by the doctor; your mother knows about these things and will be a great comfort to me over the next few months. I am so glad she is here.'

Evan was ecstatic. His life was becoming truly complete. All the people he loved were right here with him under his roof and soon there would be a new addition to his little family – a proper family. Someone to inherit the farm from him and carry on the family line. He vowed solemnly to Catherine that he would always be a good father to his son or daughter – who would not grow up without their father as he had done, nor with a cruel father as Catherine had done.

Catherine continued working on the farm, right up to the birth of her child. One fine spring day, as she carried a pail of milk from the dairy, she was suddenly gripped by a violent pain, which caused her to cling onto the gate post she was passing at the time. She waited for it to die down before gingerly making her way towards the house. As she reached the back door, she was gripped by a second pain spasm, just managing to stumble into the kitchen where Elin rushed to her aid. 'Come, sit down here on the settle by the fire.' Then, 'Elizabeth, quickly get the bedroom prepared for childbirth.'

The pains grew in intensity as the pain-free space between them became shorter. A few, very long hours later, after a fidgety Evan had been banished outside to the fields to work, he heard his mother calling him from the back door. He rushed down to the house, greeted by the news, '*Hogan bach del*, - a beautiful baby girl. Mother and baby are well, go up and greet your daughter into the world.'

Elizabeth, now a 'Nain', importantly led the way up to the bedroom. Evan was visibly relieved to see Catherine was alright, partially sitting up nursing the baby. She gave a tired but happy smile, radiant with achievement and relief that the terrible ordeal of giving birth was over. Evan sat down gently on the edge of the bed next to them and was instantly mesmerised by the sight of the tiny bundled baby. He touched the baby's fingers gently and his little finger was instantly gripped by the baby's hand. This made him smile and say, 'I think she likes me already! We should call her Catrin, cariad.' So Catrin she became. A son, named William after Evan's father, was born three years later. This completed their little family – content with what they had been blessed. Their only sadness was the death of Evan's mother Elizabeth a few years later.

Evan, having purchased the plot next to his father's family tombs, arranged for Elizabeth to be buried there as she would have wanted, next to William, if only in death. He told Catherine that when he went, he also wanted to be buried there with her. Evan often rode over to the churchyard in Eglwysbach to take flowers to place on Elizabeth's grave and it comforted him to talk to her, as if she could hear. They had always been close, having gone through so much together, especially when he was younger. He was glad that he had been able to make her later life comfortable and happy.

By the time Evan was late middle-aged and his children grown adults, he was a well-respected and well-established pillar of the local community. Elin and Harri had since married and gone to run a farm of their own. Evan liked nothing better than having visiting preachers to eat at his table after the Sunday service. They discussed evangelical and philanthropic subjects, as he was quite knowledgeable on these matters. During one such discussion, he voiced his concern about the local village children having nothing to do on Sundays but get into mischief – but the nearest chapel was a long walk for them. He believed that they should be taught the scriptures and learn to read and write in their own language. They had already started running a Sunday school in a small cottage up the Nant but soon it wasn't big enough. So, he decided that the village must build its own chapel and a committee was formed to look into this.

Evan had grown more religious as he grew older and there was something which disturbed his peace of mind. He did not like the new vicar, judging him to be sneeringly arrogant and pompous. It ate away at Evan that he still had to give the Established church one tenth of the value of his crops for the upkeep of the church building and the vicar's salary, whether he wanted to or not. They said the money was needed to rebuild the church – but Evan would rather be spending it on his chapel. The church's agents annually inspected his farm crops, then told him how much he had to give them. The crops were then taken and stored in the tithe barn next to the church. But then the Tithe Commutation Act was passed, which meant he had to give them the value of his crops in cash instead. This of course saved the church having to sell or store the goods. There were some very prosperous farms in the district and Evan felt sure much of it was being syphoned off to the church's hierarchy. It almost acted as a disincentive to him to be productive and he begrudged what he was forced to give. In some districts, the enforced payment of tithes was so loathed that many people were protesting on the streets and sometimes these protests led to violent riots.

Village children, who normally worked on farms during the week, still roamed the streets aimlessly and played outside the three public houses on Sundays – and he strongly believed that the devil found work for idle hands. He also believed that alcohol was a scourge on the poor families, whose men spent hard-earned money on it instead of on food for their families, who often went hungry. It could also turn some men violent, their victims often other men, their own wives or their children. He believed that the new local chapel could serve the double purpose of congregational worship and the education of the children, as well as adults if they chose, to learn their letters. Some of the local gentry did not think that educating the poor was a good idea, as it would only lead to insurrection and to poor people believing that they were all equal to their betters. They believed that everyone had their place or station in life. But in Evan's world, all souls were equal before God.

When he lobbied the local gentry, one of them agreed to sign over a small, otherwise useless sloping corner parcel of land which he owned. They drew up plans, supplies were ordered and building then started – all was going to plan nicely.

For Evan, putting his money and energy into building the village chapel was a way of thanking his God for his life of fulfilment and contentment. But recently this peace of mind was being threatened. All was not idyllic at home. His son William had grown into an opinionated young man, whose views differed from those of his father. Evan believed William needed to learn some humility. He remembered as a young man, he had had to learn quickly to be self-dependent and firmly believed that his way was the right way.

'The trouble with you, is that you don't know when you are well off. I had to work very hard when I was younger – and it was only by the grace of my father that we have this farm.'

Unfortunately, like most fathers and sons with similar personalities, they disagreed. Fathers think that their sons know it all, while sons think that their fathers are too old to know how things are now. Their arguments were frightening in their intensity. Their hostilities did not come to blows but their arguments were aggressive with an underlying threat of violence. Daughter Catrin and her mother usually kept out of the way when they argued.

'I will marry her and there's nothing you can do about it.'

'But I don't approve of her – she's English and she attends the papal church.'

'But you are not marrying her, I am.'

Evan held strong views about his non-conformist, Protestant religion. But what Evan did not realise was that love does not see religion, culture or language, it just sees the need in the soul of the other. Slowly but surely, Evan's intransigent attitude towards her alienated William further still from his father.

William thought that his father building the village chapel, which was nearly finished, was a vainglorious waste of money, which was eating into his eventual inheritance. Catherine normally managed to reconcile the two after an argument – but that was getting more and more difficult, because William was becoming increasingly headstrong and disrespectful to his father.

Things finally came to a head one day. William, stabbing his finger into the kitchen table to emphasise his words, said to his father, 'I will not be dictated to as to who I will marry and marry her I will, with or without your approval.'

Furiously, Evan shouted back 'In that case, you can say goodbye to inheriting the farm when I am gone.'

At that, William stormed out of the kitchen and stomped up the stairs slamming every door hard as he went. He packed a few belongings, tying them into a bedsheet then left the house, also slamming the front door behind him. Evan was visibly shaken by this but believed William would be back once he had cooled down.

Later, doubts about how he had handled the whole situation began to creep into his mind. He thought back to when Catherine's father had disapproved of him as a husband for his daughter – but they had married regardless. Then he thought about his father, William, who had been forbidden from marrying Elizabeth. It seemed that history was repeating itself time and again, leading to more unhappiness as parents tried to impose their wills on their children. He had been harsh with William and decided to soften his attitude. But unfortunately, he never had the opportunity to reconcile with his son.

Days, then weeks passed with still no sign of William. They wondered where he could be. Evan made tentative enquiries locally about William's intended, only to find out that she had also left the area, her whereabouts unknown. This realisation that they may have left together was a massive blow to Evan and Catherine and they never quite got over it. It seemed to have knocked all the reason for living out of them. Catherine adored her son and missed him more with every single day that passed. She longed to see him again. Evan blamed himself for her sorrow, as she sunk lower and lower into sadness and depression. Due to their despondency, their daughter Catrin was left to take on more and more responsibility for the work on the farm.

Chapel people whispered amongst themselves that the girl William was courting was expecting his child. William had known that his father would never condone what he would consider this disgraceful behaviour, of conceiving a child out of wedlock. This was the reason for William's defensive manner. He had wanted them to marry quickly to save face but Evan had unwittingly managed to scupper him at every turn. The threat of losing his inheritance was the last straw. He thought he had nothing to lose or to stay for and they would have to make their own way in the world. William's fiancé had a relative who farmed in the north of England. He was looking for someone to help him, so they had headed up to that part of the country with their few belongings for a new start. But this story never reached Evan and Catherine and they never heard from, nor of them again. Evan was endlessly remorseful and regularly prayed fervently on his knees for forgiveness. The ugly scene with his son played over and over in his mind and he saw now where he should have acted differently and said less harsh words. Even his dear sweet Catherine had no words of comfort for him, as she was herself bereft. He seemed to lose interest in his beloved farm and even agreed to sell off the lower fields when approached by another farmer.

There was a huge emptiness in his life. Even the thought of his almost completed chapel could not raise his spirits – but he carried on building because his obsessive nature would not let him leave incomplete anything he had started. He blamed his son's fiancé for the break-up of the family. He could not look his neighbours and fellow worshipers in the eye because he felt such a failure. He could not sleep at night, tossing and turning in his bed, his uneasy mind tormenting him in the deepest, most unforgiving dark hours of the night. He should have swallowed his pride, accommodated his son's wishes and done things differently. He should have been less unbending with the lad. After all, he could see now that his son was trying to establish himself as a man but that he, Evan was still treating him as if he was a boy, preventing him from making his own decisions into adulthood.

A few months later, Evan received an important looking letter but not from the solicitor this time. He was baffled, so took it into the house for Catherine to read out loud to him. Catrin, was working out in the fields so was not party to the contents of this letter. Neither did she have any input into the decision which Evan made, sunk as he was in his misery, without a single thought for her or the future. Catherine read:

Fy Anwyl Nhefndar (My Dear Cousin)
You will be surprised to receive this letter from me – I am your first cousin Hugh. I think we are aware of each other but have never met, nor communicated. I am the son of Hugh, brother to your father William. My mother died giving birth to me and I was sent away to Bala, to be raised by a childless relative. I do not know the details of this or why I was not raised in my father's house. I suspect that my father blamed me for my mother's death – I was never told as much – but children have a way of sensing these things. However, do not feel at all sorry for me for I have had a very good life with my dear surrogate parents, as well as an excellent education. This education has enabled me to open a grammar

school for local boys, for those whose parents can pay, as well as some scholarships for those who cannot.

Catherine paused, looking wide-eyed at Evan, before continuing,

I felt obliged to write to you as I do not believe we were treated equitably by our respective fathers, and as I have a strong sense of right and wrong, as well as of justice, it does not sit right with me. On my father's death, I inherited the bulk of his estate, which was substantial. I believe that your father also left the bulk of his estate to my father, bequeathing you only enough to buy a small farm and it is this that I do not feel was fair. This injustice has been on my mind for some time. Therefore, I want you to receive half of the large fortune, for indeed it is, which was left to me. I have no need for all this money. I have no wife, nor children to support and my financial expenditures and needs are few.

Catherine's eyes were even wider on reading this and she looked across at Evan who was squirming with discomfort and embarrassment.

I ask that you write to me to advise me of your response to this suggestion, you will do me a great honour to acquiesce to my request.
Respectfully, your cousin
Hugh

Catherine slowly let the letter drop to her lap as she stared at Evan, who said, 'More guilt money from beyond the grave. What a very strange request. I will pray to the Lord for guidance on this matter.'

With that, he left the room. This offer of money from his cousin did nothing to lift his spirits. Later, he said to Catherine, 'It feels like it is a sort of compensation for losing our son – but no amount of money could replace him. In happier times, I may have accepted it to build the chapel for the Glory of the Lord but that is all accounted for now and we have succeeded without it. Had William been living at home, I may have accepted it and given it to him, to buy his own farm. There is no sign that Catrin will marry soon, or I would suggest it be her dowry. But I have no use for it and wish it had not been offered. I feel I have already been lucky enough to receive money bequeathed from my father, it seems wrong to accept another gift of money at this stage of my life. I need for nothing now but for the return of my dear son, which money cannot buy. I will write to Hugh a reply thanking him for his kindness of thought but will say I have no need of it. I will say use it on my behalf for the benefit of the poor people in your area, or to provide more scholarships for the boys of the poor in your school.'

Little did he know that within a few years, his daughter Catrin would have been very glad of it, but he was not at that time even considering his own mortality, nor her future.

The deep reflective sorrow that never left him showed in his face as his smile now never reached into his eyes. The joy had gone from his life. Things finally came to a head one sad day. Whilst Evan was finishing off some corner stonework on the new chapel and getting it ready for its inauguration and consecration, he suffered a massive heart attack and fell backwards off his tall ladder. They say he probably died before he hit the ground, some would say of a heart broken emotionally as well as physically.

Ironically, after all his hard work and effort, the only time Evan was able to use the chapel, which was his legacy to the village, was for his own funeral. After the well-attended service, he was buried in the same plot as his mother, in the cemetery of the church he had attended as a boy and laid to rest next to his paternal family's tombs. The headstone proudly declared for all to see that he was 'one of them.'

Part 5

S arah continues to spin her spell-binding stories for children. The new series has been published and sales are steady. We have made some good friends locally and have plenty of people visit us from our old life, who are often reluctant to leave our new-found paradise. I lecture part-time at the local university and mark assignments for my old university. I have applied for research funding into the ancients and await a response. Together, our combined incomes allow us to live comfortably at the farm. We do not need to spend much now, except on the twins' university education and running the house. We do not buy anything we do not really need, which is very liberating, and manage to keep our old car in good running order.

The boys got the university places they wanted and are well into their studies. I enjoy debating their subjects with them. They still prefer to use the stable loft during the holidays – but if it is too cold, they soon decamp into the warmth of the house.

The place is in great shape now. We half-heartedly considered converting one of the outhouses into holiday accommodation to increase our income – but we do not really want strangers around. We enjoy quietude and think of the farm as our own peaceful sanctuary, resenting intrusion. So life moves on for us in our contented way. I am forever thankful that we made our bold move from the city, although the boys have since returned and are now in their final year.

The only cloud on the horizon is Sarah's health. For the last few weeks, I have noticed that she can seem lethargic and vomits when she gets up in the morning. When she feels like this, I bring her a cup of tea and encourage her to lie in and rest for a while. It occurs to me that she might even be pregnant and although she is still of child-bearing age, this is not part of the plan!

I finally persuade her to see the GP. She tells him of the morning sickness; he checks her and says, 'I can dismiss any diagnosis of pregnancy. Do you have any other symptoms?'

'On some days I have really bad headaches when I wake in the morning and sometimes when I stand I lose my balance and get pulled over to the right.'

The GP frowns at this, clearly becoming a bit more concerned. 'I am going to make a referral for you to see a consultant neurologist.' This indicates to me that the situation is a lot more serious than we originally anticipated and we exchange worried looks.

I have been looking at the symptoms on the internet. I know this is unwise, as one can easily imagine all sorts of things which may not be true. But from what I read, it could be a blood clot, which can be treated if caught early enough. I don't tell Sarah this though, so as not to alarm her – but since seeing the doctor, I am deeply worried. I am absolutely terrified about what is happening to her and frequently wake from sweating nightmares. I just cannot imagine my life without her in it.

The day of the dreaded appointment with the neurologist arrives so we set off for the hospital. During the consultation, the neurologist is asking Sarah questions and undertaking some basic tests. Then he tells us that she needs an MRI scan and calls the radiography department, who will carry it out in about an hour's time.

While we wait for the scan, I comfort myself by thinking that they are being really thorough, as we head to the hospital canteen. 'Fancy a cup of tea?' I ask her. Neither of us has any appetite for anything other than a cup of tea. It is stewed and luke-warm and we sip absent-mindedly. We are distracted and distressed. I can't believe what is happening – just when we are finally settled in our utopia. Sarah says, 'This is serious, isn't it?' 'Seems to be,' I reply, 'but we don't really know for sure yet, do we?'

Following the scan, we make our way back to the waiting room, before being called into the neurologist's consulting room. He sits at his desk with the sombre expression of somebody about to impart devastating news. He says empathetically, whilst pointing to the scan on his laptop, 'This dark area here indicates a dense mass of abnormal cells to one side of your brain, evidence of a large brain tumour.'

I turn to look at Sarah and watch as the colour visibly drains from her face. I hold her hand tightly. I break out in a cold sweat and feel myself reeling, as the room spins uncontrollably around me.

I mutter, 'What's the cause?'

'This can happen when normal cells acquire errors in their DNA, then mutations allow cells to grow and divide at an increased rate. We need to do a biopsy, to identify whether this is cancerous or benign, as this will dictate treatment. It will have to be done under general anaesthetic, so I will arrange for you to be admitted into the hospital. We will call you when we have arranged an appointment.'

He may as well have announced Sarah's death sentence. I hold her tight and say into her ear, 'Oh my darling, I can't believe this nightmare is happening. What are we to do?'

The consultant quietly leaves the room to give us privacy while we absorb the devastating news, which will touch so many people on so many levels. I feel myself panicking and am falling to pieces in front of Sarah, at the precise moment she needs me to be at my strongest. There are no words adequate to articulate our extreme horror at what is happening to us and I look down at my hands which are shaking.

After this initial display of weakness, I tell Sarah 'I'm going to 'man up'. I need to be strong for both of us, to deal with this dreadful situation.' She does not respond. Presently, we get up and walk out of the hospital to the car like zombies, neither of us wanting to articulate the all-pervasive thoughts, invading and spinning madly in our heads. Sarah has still not uttered a single word since being told the bad news. Will there be further bad news to come, once the biopsy has been performed? I dread telling the boys about it but decide that I must call them to come home immediately.

Once those fateful words are spoken by the doctor, every single element of our lives changes. In that one single moment it is as if somebody had clicked their fingers. Our former reference points having gone by the board, we now have to adjust to living with a whole new set of points, rules, possibilities and probabilities. We cannot plan for anything, except an uncertain, unhappy and devastating future.

Morosely, I wonder if things would have been different had we not moved up here – but objectively decide that these things are usually percolating away inside a person for years before there is an outward manifestation, or physical evidence. So no, I do not believe the move is to blame – just an unfortunate coincidence. I know that the level of radon is high in this area – but I think I read that is more likely to cause lung cancer, through breathing in the particles. Surely, Sarah would need to have been exposed for years for it to affect her so suddenly and profoundly. Whatever the reason, it is now the harsh, cruel reality of our lives.

I do not remember much of the journey home as my mind is working overtime elsewhere. Sarah is exhausted by the hospital visit and I lead her upstairs and help her lie down on the bed. Gently I tuck her in under the duvet and at a loss for anything else to say, I offer to make her a cup of tea but receive no reply. I feel utterly desolate, powerless and useless. I don't know what to do as I have never had to deal with this sort of emotional trauma before.

Sarah appears to be in some sort of catatonic state; she has still not uttered a word since we were given the bad news. She is obviously in severe shock. I feel the need to talk to her about it; I need to know what she is thinking but these are my needs, not hers. It feels like she is blocking me out, letting me go already.

To feel useful, I go to make her a cup of tea anyway but when I get back, she is fast asleep, either from exhaustion, or as a symptom of the condition. I have never before known her to sleep during the day. Maybe sleep is a form of escapism from her new, harsh reality.

I sit down by the bed and watch her as she sleeps. When she finally wakes, I tell her that I intend to ask the boys to come home and she shouts, 'No, I forbid you to do that. They must complete their final year studies. We must not spoil their life chances by dragging them here because of me. They have their own lives to live now and will need to pass these exams to get good degrees, otherwise they will undo all their hard work of the last few years.'

I am alarmed by the vehemence of her tone and think it may be a symptom of her condition. She has never spoken to me like that before in all our years together.

'But the boys will want and need to know. They will want to be with you.' She looks me directly in the eye, 'I am absolutely adamant about this William, you must not contact them. You can only call them if I get much worse, and anyhow, we still need the results of the biopsy, it might be benign and treatable.'

Sarah suddenly smiles as she visualises her sons' futures, 'Robert told me during the last half-term break that he has met a girl at university and hopes that she is 'the one' – so maybe he will have someone to support him if anything happens to me. As for Jon, I can't see him ever settling down.'

And so, because I love her, I collude unwillingly with her, a thing I later come to bitterly regret.

A few days later, we are heading again to the hospital for the biopsy. The sample has been taken to the path lab. Slowly she comes around from the anaesthetic but is weak and washed out by the procedure.

We survive an anguished few days and are now on our way back to get the biopsy results from the neurosurgeon. 'As I suspected, the tumour is an aggressive form of cancer, which is probably also making its way through to other parts of the body. Sadly, there is absolutely no hope that we can treat this – or of your being able to survive it. Treatment might extend your life just a little if you decide you want to try it.'

Sarah's reply is a categorical, 'No. I've thought about it and decided that I don't want to undergo any form of treatment. I will let it take its course but would be glad of pain medication later, if it becomes unbearable.'

I know I love her more in that moment than at any other point in our life together. I am so proud of her quietly brave spirit that it makes me feel utterly and completely humble – and fighting back tears which now spring up easily. Plucking up courage, I choke and swallow hard on the question I really don't want the answer to, 'How long?' and am told brusquely, 'Weeks, at most.' A death sentence then.

Once home, with Sarah tucked up in bed asleep, I try to deal with my unbearable anguish by keeping busy doing the chores. I find a modicum of comfort and distraction in being busy, which helps to keep down the panicky feeling, always near the surface, from rising in me.

Later – 'Please Sarah, I've thought about this and think we really should let the boys know.' Again, she becomes extremely angry with me for even asking, spluttering out the words, 'I know what is best for them. They must not be told until they have finished their final exams, it's only a few weeks until then, and only if I get much worse.' I mutter, 'This is already much worse.'

I try to tell myself that maybe it's better for them to remember her as she is, not how she will be later, when she will be ravaged and her condition worse, but I know I don't really believe that it justifies not telling them now.

Over the next few weeks, Sarah deteriorates to the point where she has to use a walking stick to prevent her falling over whenever she gets up. She is vomiting a good deal more and her head really hurts when she coughs, sneezes or bends over to do something. She is getting her words muddled and becoming confused at times – and she can be quite horrible to me. I make allowances, as change in personality can be one of the symptoms. Whereas before, she could smell strange unidentifiable smells, she is now losing her ability to smell at all and occasionally can't focus her vision properly, so just closes her eyes. These symptoms are gradually becoming more pronounced and permanent – and the pain is getting slowly worse. Still she refuses to have any treatment, apart from painkillers just to take the edge off. Despite her stubbornness about not telling the boys, she is so utterly courageous, which makes me love and respect her more and more, if that is even possible. But I feel there is also a part of me which is dying alongside her.

Finally, despite her strong wishes, she has become too weak to object and argue. With a heavy heart, I call the boys to break the bad news and ask them to please come home. By this time, as she had wished, they have finished sitting their exams and travel home immediately.

Their reaction to the news is a mixture of hope and disbelief – but once they digest what I am telling them, they turn their grief and anger, shockingly, onto me. Physically I flinch from the force of their fury and believe their treatment of me is grossly unfair. Can't they see that I am also suffering? I am losing my soul mate.

Robert shouts, 'How long has she been ill for? Why didn't you tell us sooner, we would have come to her straight away?'

'Mum was absolutely adamant that I wasn't to tell you until you had finished your exams. I really wanted to overrule her, but I didn't want to agitate her any more than she already was.'

'You've stolen our chance to spend more time with her, talking to her and looking after her, you're pathetic!' This is like a metaphorical slap across my face.

Jon then turns on me. 'It's your fault we ever came here in the first place, just to pander to your mid-life crisis. She might have been okay if we had just stayed where we were, instead of traipsing up here.'

'She wanted to move here just as much as I did – and she has been very happy here.'

But I am weak in my defence from the onslaught of their naked anger. I had not expected, nor been prepared for this virulent, two-pronged attack directed against me, so very personally. I understand that they must blame someone or something – but I find myself the sole object, the very manifestation of their anger, when it should be the tumour. Part of me feels I do not know my sons at all; their response is alien and hostile. I understand that they will soon lose their mother, who has always been there in their lives and that this situation is hard for them to bear. Verbally they are hitting out at the unfairness of it all and I am the nearest target, their convenient punchbag. They cannot imagine, nor accept, life without her being physically in their world, at the end of a phone or evident in an email, when they are in another part of the country.

When Sarah is lucid, she scolds me for bringing our sons home to her, against her clearly stated wishes – but not when the boys are present, which would support me. This makes me feel I am being attacked on all sides by relentless battering rams.

They are with her, so I leave them and go off on my own with Bess, to try to make sense of the anger I have been forced to absorb and to neutralise it. I reason that these things happen and are completely out of my control. This feeling of powerlessness is alien to me, as I have always been in control of my life and feelings. But I have no control over the emotions and irrationality of others – manifestations I find difficult to cope with.

The last few weeks have been fraught. Daily we see a marked deterioration in Sarah's condition. Even the news that the boys have passed their final exams does not penetrate the gloom. We are in no mood to celebrate. Sarah is now paralysed down one side of her body and her vision is further impaired. The boys take turns to sit at her bedside. They talk to her about their university lives, their hopes for the future and their memories of childhood but she often drifts off to sleep as they talk. Eventually the sleep periods became longer and periods of consciousness shorter. The local GP arranges for a nurse to come daily to make sure she is comfortable and to administer painkillers. The nurse shows me how to give her morphine, if she needs it at other times.

She has been in a coma for a few days, her life slowly slipping away, but we believe she knows that we are all there with her. The boys and I watch as she falls into a deeper unconsciousness, from which she never wakes.

Sarah dies quietly early the next morning, just after dawn, as the new day's birdsong begins. Devastated by the finality, the boys leave the room to deal with her death in their own way, which is to take themselves off into the hills and I know I will probably not see them for many hours. They will be unaware of their surroundings as they walk, blinded by the hot tears which sting their eyes. But in the background, they will feel the soothing comfort of the ever-present hills.

Meanwhile, in the bedroom, I lay down on the bed at Sarah's side for a while, holding her, stroking her hair and reminiscing out loud because I cannot bear the deathly silence in the room. I talk about how we first met, the things we have done and achieved together, as silent tears stream unashamedly down the sides of my face. I do not direct my anger at anyone, or anything – but am internalising a deep cleaving sadness. It has sunk into a dark unfathomable place in the darkness of my soul. I find that anger is exhausting and futile; I decide I will not let it eat away at me.

After a few hours in which I may or not have slept, I feel more in control and able to deal with practical things. I rise and dial the doctor's number. He calls at the house to confirm her death and issues a death certificate. Cause of death – 'Malignant brain tumour.' The words look stark and unforgiving as they are, written down.

Soon after the funeral, a private humanist affair, the boys leave home, telling me they have decided to go travelling for a while, to work their way around the world. They ask if I will buy them the air tickets as a reward for getting their degrees. What can I say? How can I refuse? The last thing I want them to do is go away, I need them to stay around for a while – but it feels they can't get away from me quickly enough.

Once they have gone, I am totally and utterly abandoned by Sarah and the boys. Only Bess stays close and tries to comfort me, nudging my hand to stroke her; maybe she also needs comfort. I finally accept that this is the way the boys are dealing with their mother's death and that they will come back when they are ready.

I try to keep myself very busy, although I often wonder what is the point of all this activity, or life even. I use industriousness to work through my grief, which is slowly eating me from the inside out. Stubbornly I do the jobs on the farm to the point of utter exhaustion, so that at the end of each day all I can manage is to collapse onto the bed in a deep exhaustive sleep.

Tonight, it is very stormy outside, a north-westerly howls around the farm buildings and blasts the trees in the foothills so that there is a constant background murmur. To distract myself from the ever-present lump of grief and loneliness which sits at my core, I take out the bundle of old letters, to recapture happier evenings spent with Sarah. My online research has located William Ffowcs' will, in which he acknowledges Evan as his illegitimate son and leaves him enough money to buy a farm. This is a huge breakthrough. I have already established that William and his ancestors are buried in Eglwysbach churchyard and that Evan's grave is next to the Ffowcs tombs. I had planned to visit the churchyard in Eglwysbach sooner – but when Sarah became ill, I put it on hold.

I pick up further clues in the will. My Evan was just plain Jones but when he inherited from his father, so he must have taken on his surname. Evan must have lived a very interesting life, having started off as an illegitimate son, living the life of a crofter to becoming a child labourer on a farm. Suddenly, due to his inheritance, he was a well-to-do farmer and the son of one of the noble families of the area.

Next, I pick up an even older letter, written in beautiful Copperplate, a bit more of a challenge to read than the Will. It was addressed to Elizabeth, Evan's mother and signed by William Ffowcs, Evan's belatedly discovered father. This therefore establishes the link between Evan and the famous Ffowcs clan.

Evan's paternal side of the family is really interesting. First, I decide, I will visit the churchyard and find Evan's actual grave, plus that of his father, William, who should be in one of the tombs. The more illustrious branch of that family is buried in Llanddoged Church so I will also visit there out of interest.

Finally, I re-read a letter written to Evan by Hugh William Ffowcs, son of Hugh, offering him half of his inheritance, and wonder if Evan ever accepted. He didn't sound the type who would, probably too proud. Maybe our family would now have been much wealthier if he had!

Doing this distracts me for a few hours and I feel my mood lift a little at the thought of having something to look forward to, even if it is a visit to a cemetery. I am also encouraged that I have managed to go back a couple more generations in my family tree – but sad there is no one to share this breakthrough with.

Early next morning, I am heading up the Conwy Valley to find the tiny village of Eglwysbach, which is surrounded by outlying farms. Then, I will also go to look for Llanddoged Church, which Google tells me is not too far away and probably accessed by narrow single-track roads around Maenan.

I find the church easily. It is just a tiny hamlet with one road running through it. It does not take me long to locate Evan's grave, which is just across from the main church door. On a flat purple gravestone, I read Evan Ffowcs Jones, of Glyn Abercyn. Catherine, his wife is named below and Elizabeth his mother, above. I make a mental note to bring some flowers from my garden next time I visit.

Evan's grave lies right next to the iron-railed and important looking tombs of the Ffowcs family. The engraved letters are very weather-worn, the names difficult to read but I can just make out the name William Ffowcs, seventeen-hundred and something, as well as Hugh Ffowcs and Frances Ffowcs, although their dates are difficult to pin down. I will need to look at Church Records for these. Although I have unexpectedly uncovered my link to this illustrious family, I am aware that these members never resided on my farm. However, I feel justified in following this lead wherever it takes me because it is interesting and according to manorial documents, it appears that my farm was once part of the family's vast estate. That said, this is a bit of a stretch, but there are no hard and fast rules and for the moment, it serves as a good distraction from my sadness.

Having taken plenty of photos for later analysis, I head off for Llanddoged. The church is very ancient and beautiful. On the back wall inside the church hangs a plaque evidencing the importance of the mainstream Ffowcs family. On the floor of the church there are some very ancient plaques, probably the resting places of even older Ffowcs family members which link back to one of the Royal Tribes of Wales. This will be a rich hunting ground for ancestral evidence, as I travel further back along the lines.

So engrossed am I in what I am doing, I have forgotten my

sadness for a short while but soon I come back to my harsh reality as I hear the church door handle turning in its rusty holder. Dusk is falling, so I gather all my precious evidence and head back to the car.

* * *

William & Elizabeth's Story

'But I don't want to get married to her or anybody else. I don't even like her. Get Hugh to marry her, he is the older son. He's the one who is supposed to produce the heirs in this family,' William shouted at his father with impotent rage.

'Why should I go and live in some God forsaken castle, in the middle of nowhere?' William, born in 1776, lived at the Hall with his renowned family. He loved his home more than anywhere and had no desire to live anywhere else; everything he wanted was here.

William and Hugh's father, also called Hugh, was becoming increasingly impatient and beyond irritated with his sons, who in their late thirties still showed no sign of settling down to start their own families. He was desperate for one of them, preferably Hugh, the older, to have an heir to carry on the family line. To Hugh's disappointment, his sons had failed to marry, possibly in passive defiance. He had introduced them to the daughters of the local gentry, as well as to those further afield but they seemed unable to form real attachments.

The brothers seamlessly ran the large estate, which spread out over at least two valleys. Their father found legal work much more stimulating than estate management and was Justice of the Peace for the district. He was also clearly the law within his own family. Deeply religious, he read dry Christian tomes and regularly ordered books on theology which enabled him to participate in stimulating religious debate, whenever he could find a worthy theological adversary. Recently, he had been plotting with yet another of his old friends for William to marry his daughter.

'What you want is of no consequence, you must marry well.' he said coldly to William, feeling that he had already accommodated his troublesome son far more than he should, then added sharply, 'You will marry her – it is your duty. There is a whole world outside this valley – you need to broaden your horizons my boy. I know what's best for you and that is my final word on the matter,' as he turned back to the paperwork on his desk.

William knew that when it came to major life decisions, there was no point arguing but he was determined to thwart him one way or another. He loved riding his stallion around the valley, or flying his hawk, accompanied by his lurcher. What William had really wanted was to run his own farm. He had seen the one he wanted, which was in the next valley. It had a wonderful position looking out to sea and had plenty of arable land with it and far enough away from his father. It was already owned by the estate but when William asked his father if he could run it personally, he had been told, 'Leave farming to the peasants – I have other plans for you; your tutor tells me you have a great aptitude for figures.' Despite it being the choice of most second sons, William did not have the temperament for the army nor the church. His father's insistence that he attend Oxford was driven by family tradition, as William's great-grandfather, grandfather, father, brother and numerous uncles had all attended the University. Education was extremely highly valued. On his final return home, William was tasked with helping his brother to manage the estate's tenanted smallholdings. His father had decreed that this would be William's role in life.

William was clearly still dominated by his father's strong will even when older and it still rankled. Feeling utterly powerless, he dramatically stormed out of his father's study, slamming the heavy ancient gothic door loudly, in an act of useless defiance. His faithful lurcher had skulked out quickly behind him, tail tucked passively underneath him, sure there was more trouble brewing. The altercation was heard practically throughout the Hall, so staff and retainers had scurried off to safe places to avoid any fall out.

'What's the matter with you?' His older brother, Hugh, found William where he had expected to, in the stables, furiously grooming his horse, his therapeutic antidote to dissipate the intense anger his dominant father engendered in him. The hound, now sensibly curled up in a safe dark corner on a piece of old sacking, looked up with wary soulful eyes. Holding the currying brush, William was wiping away furious, angry tears with the sleeve of his jacket. William knew it was useless to try to garner any sympathy from his brother but said, 'I don't want to leave here to marry some woman I don't even know. You are the one who will inherit everything, why don't you marry her.' Hugh shrugged his shoulders, 'She doesn't want me, it's you she's set her cap to. Can't understand it really, as I am far more handsome,' he said, smiling to try to lighten the mood.

They had learned when young that it was useless to try to reason with their father. Their mother had died whilst both boys were very young – she was now a distant and indistinct memory. This may have gone some way to explain why they both found it difficult to relate to the women they were introduced to and continued to remain resolutely unattached.

Later, sitting at the long oak trestle table, surrounded as they were by plaques of famous ancestors and suits of armour, Hugh senior said, 'Now that you have had time to calm down a bit, just take some time to think about how advantageous this marriage will be for you and the family. Her father is an extremely respected and wealthy Baronet.' William scowled at him – all he thought of was status.

Hugh's family was also highly respected in the community and in the class-ridden society of that time; this marriage would certainly elevate its position to the next level. But to William, it felt like a punishment, a banishment, the end of his life as he knew it, surrounded by strangers. Looking down at the food which had been served to him, he remained silent. Wrongly assuming William was coming around to the idea, his father continued, 'I have invited her and her father over to supper in a fortnight's time, so you had better be here to meet them and show them the respect due to them.' William looked up sullenly at his father but said nothing.

Early, next morning, William, on his thirty-seventh birthday, sat in his father's study, checking the monthly accounts. Hugh senior told him, 'You must ride out to Pant Ffynnon smallholding to find out why they haven't paid their rent for the last few weeks. The harvest was quite good last year, so they have no excuse. Tell them that if I don't get it by the end of next week, they're out!'

Glad of a reason to escape outdoors, William ordered the groom to get his horse ready. William was a handsome man, who cut a dashing figure in his fitted riding outfit and tan knee-length leather boots. He rode about eight miles across a rough mountain track into a remote area at the top of the next valley. Passing a tiny ancient church with its sacred well, he saw its graveyard and surroundings covered in a cheerful abundance of wild daffodils, which made him smile. He went up a steep stony track, as his hound kept pace beside him. High above, he saw seagulls dropping mussel shells onto rocks to open and eat them. He saw a herd of wild ponies grazing contentedly but they did not move away.

He had not had any previous dealings with the registered occupants, a Mr. and Mrs. Jones; they had always paid their rent on time before – but he decided to be very firm with them. Or so he thought.

On approaching, he saw a typical small, whitewashed, single-storey cottage, with a low, thick, overhanging thatched roof. Tucked away in the lee of a small hillside, it was sheltered from the fierce winds, which blew relentlessly this high up. He had watched estate thatchers working on roofs such as this. He knew that a layer of hazel branches was first placed on the rafters, then layered over with thick gorse branches, a natural insulation. The reed thatch was then laid onto this foundation and was very watertight. On the underside of the roof, sheets of calico were pinned up, to prevent bits of gorse falling inside the property and to keep out small rodents such as voles, which liked to hibernate indoors in the winter months. The main open living-cum-kitchen area of these cottages usually occupied the centre of the building. One whole outer side wall, usually made up of chimney breasting, served an open inglenook-type fireplace. Occasionally, built into the wall nearby, was a small dough proving oven. The fireplace heated the whole area and any children slept snuggly, head-to-toe, like peas in a pod, in the crog-loft, reached by a steep narrow wooden ladder.

As William got nearer, he saw a small lean-to cowshed, with a roughly-hewn three-legged milking stool outside the doorway and a cow cropping close by. On the other side was a small lean-to workshop, the usual farming implements hanging on its wall. Then, up against the workshop was a small hen house, its occupants picking away at the ground in the yard. Their heads bobbed up and down as they picked, causing their fleshy, floppy red combs to flap about their eyes. Their eggs were a staple food for the small farmer, with any surplus sold at market. Most smallholders depended on the proceeds of a calf, which the cow produced each spring, to live on for the rest of the year, whilst augmenting their income with whatever else they could grow. William saw they had a few sheep, the lambs yet to be born would later be sold, keeping back the better breeders to produce next year's lambs.

William sneeringly thought that he would certainly not like to eke out a living in such a hovel – but its position was breath-taking; it had long ranging views way out over the valley below and far out to sea. A place to stir the hearts of poets, he thought. Given the property's remoteness, he presumed that it had once been a shepherd's shelter. Fruit trees grew valiantly at one end of the paddock, grown bent by the prevailing winds, their boughs caked in green lichen. Next, a small vegetable plot, with rows of newly planted turnip shoots, as well as raised furrows which he guessed were potatoes. All around the property was common land, where their ewes grazed, heavy with unborn lambs. On William's approach, geese suddenly lifted their long necks, their heads like periscopes pointed in his direction. A stranger was approaching their property. They began their frantic, bottom-waggling walk towards William, while their gaggling noise alerted the occupants of the cottage of a visitation or possible danger. He thought sardonically that given the remoteness of this place, they were not called on to perform guard duty very often.

Casually he dismounted and tied the rein to the fence, which marked off a tiny front garden festooned with daffodils and bluebells. Looking decidedly out of place in such humble surroundings, he was blissfully unaware of how his life was about to change so utterly and completely. As he reached the front door of the cottage, Mrs. Jones appeared in the doorframe, having quickly removed her calico apron on hearing a rider approach. She smiled nervously and nodding humbly said, '*Dewch i mewn*. Come in. Please sit yourself down,' gesturing with her arthritically bent finger to an overstuffed horsehair chair – its faded blue, once-velvet covering, mostly threadbare. He wondered idly where this chair had come from originally, as it seemed incongruous in this setting, where he would have expected to see plain, rough-hewn, home-made furniture. Less unusually was the largish black Welsh Bible, placed on a small table, indicating they were good, God-fearing people.

William, aware that a quaintly formal etiquette should be observed when calling on tenants, believed it cost nothing to be civil. Once he had settled in the best chair, Mrs. Jones asked, 'Have you come far? Would you like something to drink and maybe a bite to eat?' With gravitas, he bowed his head in assent – it would be churlish to refuse their hospitality.

William glanced around the spotlessly clean parlour, as a small tray was placed on the table beside his chair. Laid with crisp fresh linen, next to an earthenware jug of home-made nettle beer and a glazed brown earthenware drinking mug, was a small plate of lightly browned Welsh cakes. William looked up languorously to see who had carried it in, and into the most beautiful face he had ever seen. Stunning, mesmerising eyes, which twinkled with mischief and fun, set in an oval-shaped face of pure symmetrical perfection, a pert nose and slightly-pouting lips. He just stared, drop-jawed and transfixed by the vision. Mrs. Jones noticed his reaction and remembering her manners, said, 'This is my daughter Elizabeth. I really couldn't manage without her. She's such a big help to me, especially now.'

Elizabeth gave William a shy curtsy. He felt a rush of blood to his head, aware his heartbeat was thumping loudly in his chest and surprised no one else seemed to hear it. He stared openly at Elizabeth, who flushed and looked shyly away, uncomfortable under his intense scrutiny. Mesmerised by her beauty and suddenly dry mouthed, he picked up the mug and gulped deeply at the nettle drink she had poured. Distracted, he suddenly found it difficult to concentrate on why he was there. He dragged his eyes away from Elizabeth and focused his concentration on Mrs. Jones saying, 'I have come to check why you have not been paying your rent.'

Suddenly she welled up and dabbed at her watery, red-rimmed eyes with a small handkerchief, saying, 'I am sorry to say Sir, that my dear husband died very suddenly of heart failure two weeks ago.'

It suddenly struck William that the women were dressed head to toe in black and the small sackcloth curtains at the windows were half drawn. Taken aback, he said apologetically, 'I'm really sorry to hear of your loss. Please forgive my insensitive intrusion and accept my deepest condolences.'

Mrs Jones tearfully nodded her acknowledgment. She wrung the handkerchief with her work-worn hands, their only adornment, a thin wedding ring, 'We are both trying very hard to keep things going but the funeral costs have eaten into what little savings I had.'

He realised they were proud people who did not like to be beholden to anyone and had probably never owed anybody money. He realised it would be hard to scrape a living on this small meagre plot, where the common pasture was not very good.

A small awkward silence ensued. William took another gulp of the nettle beer from the earthenware mug, to give himself time to think, then said, 'Because of the difficult situation you find yourself in, I am prepared to give you a little more time to pay.'

Both seemed overwhelmed by his statement and extremely relieved. William realised that they had been expecting a visit from his father's bailiff, who would have evicted them. Then there seemed nothing more to say. He took another quick gulp of the beer for his dry throat, then stood. Taking a long lingering look at Elizabeth and reluctant to leave her sphere, 'I will call again in two weeks' time, see what you can manage by then.'

As he headed for the door of the cottage, he turned around once more to take in Elizabeth's slender form, outlined by the light of the small window. Looking back once more, he soaked up her image and indelibly imprinted her forever into his memory. Then carefully ducking his head under the low door frame, he went out to untie his horse.

As he rode away, William's head was filled with Elizabeth. He fought the temptation to turn around once more, to be sure his eyes had not played tricks on him. But mindful of his official role and feeling strangely disconcerted by what he had just experienced, he rode straight on. Instinctively, he knew they would both be standing in the cottage doorway, watching his back as he rode away. Reprieved and relieved for now, Mrs. Jones turned to her daughter, saying sternly, 'I saw the way he looked at you but there's no point in you even thinking anything can come of it, so you might as well forget about him now. He is not for the likes of you.'

Elizabeth, amazed that her mother could read her mind so easily, was embarrassed, causing a flush to rise in her beautiful cheeks. She moved away to clear away the tray to hide her feelings of confusion and rising excitement. She had never met anybody quite like William before. With her lips she touched the rim that William had drunk from and from that day on, thought about him constantly; she knew an inexplicable, invisible thread had woven itself between them, tying them together forever.

Despite strong temptation, William forced himself to stay away from Pant Ffynnon as a test but the two weeks were the longest of his life. During all this time, he had not been able to get Elizabeth out his mind for one minute. She haunted him day and night. Her face floated into his mind's eye, smiling at him, head on one side, when he least expected it. As he worked, thoughts of her distracted him from the figures he was meant to be counting. He visualised her standing apprehensively in the parlour after she had brought in the tray and her sweet curtsy when introduced by her mother. He remembered the relief in her beautiful face and the frown-lines on her forehead melting away when he said he would give them more time to pay their rent. He remembered her slender but work-worn hands, as she carefully poured the homemade beer. He saw her thoughtful face as he bade them farewell. He also felt that something imperceptible had passed between them when they had looked at each other, which had now bound them together, forever.

In his emotional turmoil, William considered confiding in his brother, Hugh – then hesitated, preferring to keep this delicious knowledge to himself. He did not want his brother to metaphorically pour cold water over these nascent feelings, to accuse him of being foolish and of acting like a lovelorn adolescent. William knew that his father would never approve of her as a suitable match for him, as she was of a much lower social status and probably illiterate. In his lofty opinion, she would be a most unsuitable match for a son of his. But William knew that this was the first woman he had ever felt this way about and he wasn't a young, impressionable man. It seemed to him that something special but catastrophically unfamiliar to him had invaded his heart. It had triggered something deep within him, making him increasingly restless, making it imperative he saw her again.

Hugh finally asked William, 'What on earth is the matter with you? Why are you so distracted? Every time I speak to you, you seem to be a million miles away, sometimes you don't even seem to hear me.'

Finally confronted, William said, with a dreamy far-away look, 'I have met the most beautiful, bewitching woman I have ever seen in my entire life.'

'Where? When?'

'When I went up to check on why Pant Ffynnon had not paid their rent. When I got there, I met Elizabeth, who is the daughter. She is a lot younger than me but she is just pure loveliness. Old Mr. Jones had died suddenly of heart failure, so their rent money had gone in giving him a decent burial.'

Hugh responded, 'She must be something quite special to have addled your mind like this, but you know father will never approve of her. He expects you to marry this other woman. She is of your own educated and social status. She will bring some money into the marriage and provide the estate with heirs. You don't necessarily have to love the woman.'

But it was all too late for William to now agree to that sort of sterile arrangement. Once he had experienced and knew that this truly euphoric feeling existed, he was never, ever going to commit himself to a woman he did not love. Instinctively he knew that this sort of feeling only came around once in a person's lifetime. After a small considered silence, he looked directly at Hugh and said with emphatic determination, 'I know you are right but if I cannot be allowed to marry Elizabeth, I have decided that I will never marry anyone else, ever. Anyway,' he said, lightening the conversation, 'You're a fine one to talk, it's you who should be providing the heirs around here!' as he affectionately punched Hugh gently on his arm. Hugh grimaced, knowing the truth of this, shrugging his shoulders as he walked away.

After the longest two weeks of his life, William made his way eagerly up to the head of the valley to see Elizabeth and her mother. He had ingratiated himself with the cook who had prepared a hamper of foodstuff for him to take, to augment their supplies. He saw nobody to query the hamper and quietly left unnoticed.

Anyone who had looked at him as he rode up the valley track would have seen the joy in his eyes, the happy anticipation radiating out of him, channelling directly from his heart. A handsome figure riding astride his horse, with dark Celtic looks inherited from his father's side. He was oblivious of those he rode past or of the impression he made on them.

His spirit lifted further as the little cottage came into view in the distance, his stomach lurching in response. He rode carefully along the rocky track and finally arrived at the cottage. He was again greeted cordially from the front door by Mrs. Jones as he tied his horse up outside on the fence, ignoring the gaggling geese, which were belatedly dashing from around the side of the cottage to perform guard duty.

Mrs Jones beckoned him in, '*Dewch i mewn*. Do come in, we've been expecting you.'

Ducking his head as he entered under the low door lintel, 'I have brought you some food. I thought you may have use of it.' Mrs Jones' eyes lit up as she said, '*O, Diolch yn fawr iawn*. Thank you so much, we are indeed very grateful.'

His thoughtful gesture made this already emotionally fragile person, even more teary. Whilst this exchange went on, Elizabeth feasted her eyes on William and as he turned to hand her the hamper, she felt the same frisson of excitement as last time; he hung onto it a few seconds longer than he needed to, so he could soak her up.

'*Diolch*', she said simply, with a quick curtsy. He melted at the sight of her grateful smile, feeling the exact same sense of excitement and infatuation as the first time he had laid eyes on her. Attempting to break the spell between them, Mrs. Jones said, 'Please sit down. Elizabeth will fetch you some refreshments' – indicating to him again to sit on the best chair. He made small talk about the weather with Mrs Jones, while they waited for the tray to come. On her return, Elizabeth said to William with a gleeful smile, 'We are ever so grateful for the hamper of food – there is enough there to feed a small army!'

Mrs Jones' expression and tone turned serious as she said apologetically, 'I have managed to scrape together some but not all of the rent we owe you,' handing over a small cloth pouch. William wondered sadly what they had gone without, or had had to sell, to be able to give him this small amount. It was then he decided that he would quietly make up any disparity in their rent. Being mindful of their pride, he would take whatever they could scrape together, so that they did not fall further into arrears. He knew his father would be none the wiser as to where the balance was coming from, if he, William, personally collected the rent and paid in the shortfall. Plus, calling to collect whatever rent they had was a good way to go on seeing who he now considered to be, his Elizabeth.

* * *

That evening at supper, William plucked up all the courage he could muster, the surety of the love he felt for Elizabeth giving him confidence, and said bravely, 'Father, I know you meant well when you arranged for me to marry the Baronet's daughter – but I am adamant that I will not.'

His father, utterly exasperated and once again thwarted by his stubborn son, furiously stood up and swept the crockery off the table. William was shocked at his father's violent behaviour and sat there stunned, wondering then about his sanity.

'You dare to go against my wishes! What sort of son are you? I should throw you out!'

But William was far too useful to him as the keeper of his accounts. He stormed out of the room waving his fist, while threatening William to reconsider his decision. William did not now feel bold enough to tell his father the true reason for his decision, leaving that instead for another battle, further down the line.

William visited the isolated cottage regularly and as the early spring slowly warmed into summer, he fell more and more in love with Elizabeth. The trees now looked fine draped in their soft livery of shiny tender green leaves, which he likened to the delicate new love which was blossoming between them. The frolicking spring lambs ran around the stone-walled fields in playful gangs. Their mothers now looked up at William with little curiosity as he rode past – preferring to munch contentedly on juicy new grass shoots.

William, who by nature was usually open and honest, did not feel completely comfortable about deceiving his father but his need to keep seeing Elizabeth was far stronger than any fleeting pang of conscience. He did not expect to be recognised by anyone in this remote part of the valley as it was not the type of place people travelled through to get to some other place. Consequently, he felt safe visiting her there.

One particularly lovely summer's day, William said, 'Come, let's walk awhile by the stream,' wanting some time to be alone with her, to tell her how he felt. Her mother was busy in the corner of the room, working at the large spinning wheel, by the light of a small window. She was feeding it with the stretched-out tufts of twisted sheep's wool from the bag which her daughter had painstakingly collected off the thorns of gorse bushes and brambles around about, the tiny fibres around the yarn highlighted in the strong sunlight. The wool had been carefully washed until most of the natural lanolin and bits of gorse and bracken were removed. The thinly spun yarn Mrs. Jones produced was used to knit warm woollen undergarments for them both. When there was plenty to spare, they would crochet warm shawls for themselves in the dark evenings, when outdoor work had to cease. The main fleeces of the flock were usually shorn by a travelling shearer who then gave them a price for each one, depending on its quality.

Mrs. Jones looked anxiously over the top of her metal framed spectacles as the couple strolled away, hand in hand, towards the river. She sensed things would turn out badly for them – but knew their attachment was much too strong to listen to her warnings.

They walked a while, then he stopped, turning to look deeply into her eyes as if trying to reach deep into the centre of her being. To him, Elizabeth was endlessly delightful; he felt relaxed and revelled in her nearness. He felt a strange mixture of euphoria and oneness each time he was with her; time spent alone with her was the only time he felt completely whole, for the first time in his life. He said, 'Elizabeth, you are such a joy to be with. I am only truly happy when I am with you.' She looked shyly down at the ground and as her lovely smile spread slowly across her face said, 'I have been longing to hear you say those words.'

Elizabeth was ecstatic at his declaration of love and felt a flutter of joy in the pit of her stomach. She knew that she loved him utterly and was happy to know that the feeling was reciprocated. They strolled alongside the stream, completely content in each other's company, until it was again time for him to take his leave of her. During the next two weeks, Elizabeth thought about him constantly and ached longingly for the time she would see him, touch him, again.

When he arrived next time, Elizabeth said, 'Come, I've prepared a small picnic of homemade cheese, beer, and some apples, wrapped up in a gingham tea cloth. We can walk along the river and find a place to eat it.' They ambled contently along the stream; strong sunlight reflected on the surface of the dark water, like ever-moving spears of light. William watched, mesmerised and knew that she was the light which now danced on the surface of his soul. He did not articulate these thoughts – knowing them and being with her was enough; there was no need for conversation. He had said what needed to be said.

'Here will suit us well,' he said as they came upon a shady place under the cover of a gnarled old scrub oak. The tree's stunted and wind-slanted branches had grown only in the direction the prevailing wind dictated. Its thick roots exposed due to erosion, were clinging heroically to the bank. This tree overlooked a naturally formed pool, its blackness indicating hidden depth. It had been created millennia ago by large, smooth, now lichen-covered boulders, which had formed a barrier to the water's flow. Even before these massive boulders had come to rest here, they had been painstakingly ground smooth as they moved surreptitiously downwards, underneath a powerful glacier. On its relentless journey, it had also carved out and shaped the valley below, before melting and flowing out to sea.

Strong sunlight illuminated the submerged rocks in the shallows, giving them a speckled golden-brown colour. These camouflaged the spotted brown rainbow trout furtively darting about there, occasionally surfacing to feed off the flies which danced on the surface of the water with their long spindly legs.

Fragile harebells grew on the opposite bank, their delicate blue colour mimicking the light indigo colour of Elizabeth's eyes. Only the occasional bleating of milk-laden ewes was heard in that expectant stillness, calling back the lambs they had lost to the playful gangs, their heavy udders in need of relief.

Elizabeth, feeling the oppressive, windless heat of the day, suggested impulsively, 'Come, let us cool off in the pool.'

She ran ahead of him, uninhibitedly removing her heavy woollen skirt, then waded into the cooling water. William followed, having removed his boots and leather jerkin and was soon in the water beside her. The water's iciness initially took their breath away, imbuing a sense of exhilaration and euphoria. Gradually as they got used to the cold, the heat of their bodies cooled off. They emerged from the water refreshed and flopped down close together on the sheep-cropped grass to dry off in the sun.

Presently, Elizabeth sat up and spread the small feast out before them on the cloth. Contentedly, they munched their way through it, savouring every mouthful and moment. They idly watched bees flitting between the yellow blossom of the nearby gorse bushes, busily collecting nectar to make their honey. Apart from the occasional bleating sheep, acrobatic skylarks swooping then chirping high above them and chiffchaffs calling as they flew between gorse-bushes, there was an utter and complete silence. Even the wind, whose mournful sound was usually heard in the background around the hilltops, was absent that day. This haunting stillness could only be found high up in the empty hills, where even the noises from the valley below did not penetrate.

After a short nap, William, propped himself up on one elbow and turned to Elizabeth, 'I would be truly content forever if you would agree to be my wife.'

Elizabeth was surprised when he said this, but knowing William as she now did, believed he was being utterly sincere. Slowly she shook her head and his smile quickly faded. She was a pragmatist and a realist. She knew how rigid and unbending – and ultimately unforgiving the structure of their society was. She knew people of different classes simply did not mix in any real terms, never mind marry. Social status was everything for the ruling classes and the lower classes knew their place. If he did marry her, he would be disowned by his own family and class. She knew that she would never be accepted by them. She was aware that casual liaisons between the classes existed – but these relationships rarely resulted in marriage. Slowly she picked up his hand and intertwined her fingers with his. Knowing that what she was about to say would wound him deeply, she said as gently as she could, 'William, I do dearly love you

– but your family would never allow that to happen. Can't we just be content to be as we are?'

He opened his mouth to speak but before he was able to respond she said, 'Besides, I could not leave my mother alone here, she would not manage without me. She has only recently lost my father, so she would not want to lose me as well.'

'Please, I beg of you, don't deny me my dearest wish.' He did not want to hear that this beautiful woman, who had captured and woven her way around his soul, could not be his constant life companion. Dejectedly, he looked lovingly at her face and traced her high cheek bones with his little finger. He noticed that the sunlight was highlighting the blueness of her gold-flecked eyes, lined by thick fairish lashes. Her peachy skin, abundance of golden, curly but unruly hair and laughing sensuous mouth, only enhanced her allure. Imperceptibly, he cupped her face with his hand and leaned his face towards her, as if drawn by an irresistible magnetic force towards her mouth. He felt their lips meld in the sweet kiss which followed. Soon their bodies responded to the urgent need in the other and their limbs became intertwined.

Once William had recovered himself, he realised the enormity of what he had done. He hadn't meant for it to happen. He was ashamed and appalled – but on another level, ecstatic. Sitting up, he ran his hands despairingly through his hair. Heavy with guilt, he was unable to now look into her beautiful eyes, afraid he would see accusation there. Having been brought up within the strict boundaries of his father's and uncles' religion, he had been taught that only within the sanctity of marriage could such physical activity between a man and a woman be condoned in the eyes of God and civilised society. He could already imagine the 'fire and brimstone' vicar at the pulpit of the church, shouting aggressively at him, pointing his finger at him, while predicting he would be damned to spend eternity in hell. 'Fornicator!' William imagined himself sitting in the congregation, wanting the earth to swallow him up. This image brought another wave of shame. He covered his face with his hands and cried out in his anguish. But again, he felt the conflicting emotion as he believed what they had shared was beautiful and right. His body was again aching to hold her, to be comforted and to once again be entwined with hers.

Presently, she coaxed his hands gently off his face and kissed away the slow tears making their way down the side of his face. Then, turning his face to hers to make him look at her, she said, 'Please don't distress yourself so. I am just as much to blame for what has happened.'

Her words did nothing to ease or reassure him. 'I should have known better – I am supposed to be the more responsible one. I now feel heavy with the shame of knowing I should not have disrespected you and given in to my baser instincts.' Elizabeth soothed him, 'Hush my love, do not scold yourself so, all will be fine.'

Later, he made his lonely way back down the isolated valley towards the Hall. Now more determined than ever, he would tell his father about Elizabeth and insist that he marry her. Little did he realise then, how totally devastating the exchange with his father would turn out to be.

As he rode slowly in through the gates and past the Lodge, his eyes sweeping across the carefully tended grounds, he realised how lucky he was to live there. Looking up, he saw the Hall nestled majestically in its imposing position, looking out over the valley to the ridge of the next on the other side, where his true love lived. Much of the park land was dotted with ancient oaks, their trunks shielded by metal cages to protect from grazing sheep. Years ago, his father had created a little wooded dell, which flanked a small stream just below the house. William often sat there and daydreamed about Elizabeth.

The drive finally led around to the back of the hall, passing a tranquil, sunlit lily pond. The low, early evening sunlight shone on its surface, while blue, turquoise and red dragonflies flew just above it. Occasionally they landed on the shiny green lily-pads, where they liked to sun themselves, their gossamer wings extraordinarily beautiful in the sunlight.

His feelings were intense, his perceptions sharpened, as if he was seeing these things clearly for the very first time; as if he had woken from a long sleep and was seeing things through different eyes. He was in a state of high euphoria, visualising how truly happy he had been a short time ago and could be again if he had his wish to be with Elizabeth. But his love for Elizabeth was like tender unfurling leaves that could easily be stripped off their branches by a summer storm. He wondered if their love would be allowed to fully open and blossom, to grow strong, to withstand what he knew would come to test it.

Riding at the back of the Hall, through the beautiful, dressed grey-granite arch into the stables, he dismounted and handed the reins to the stable lad. Glancing around the stalls, he noticed there were strangers' horses in the stalls and suddenly remembered that his father had guests for dinner. He walked quickly towards the Great Hall and saw them mingling in the main reception area. He remembered he was expected to join them, so quickly ran up the stairs, unseen, to freshen up and change for dinner. His important talk with his father would have to wait for now.

William restlessly endured the guests and dinner. Yet another attempt by his father to get him interested in his friend's daughter, yet another potential wife. But he refused to be drawn into his father's little charade and gave the guests the deliberate impression that he was not interested. When they had finally departed, William went to the study to speak to his father, who turned on him. 'You could at least have made yourself a little more civil to our guests, instead of being boorish and rude.'

William knew that this mood did not bode well for the conversation he planned to have with him. Standing nervously facing him he said, 'Father, please just hear me out. I have met somebody who makes me very happy and I want to marry her. Her name is Elizabeth and she lives with her mother in Pant Ffynnon.'

This news was received by a deathly silence, while his father digested what had been said. Angrily he realised that his latest plot to marry William off to their dinner guest had failed yet again. Turning thunderously towards William, with spittle flying, his eyes bulging, he shouted furiously, 'I refuse to even discuss the possibility of you marrying this peasant woman and forbid you to ever see her again. I warn you, my boy, that if you do, I will cut you out of the family and out of my Will.' Pausing for breath, 'Can you even imagine such a peasant sitting down to dinner with the sophisticated people we had here this evening?'

William stood there stunned into speechlessness, a slow quiet anger beginning to build in him. After a pause, his father continued icily, 'You will never marry that girl. You have two options: I will buy you a passage on a ship to the New World, where you can make your own way in the world, or you can continue to work as my accountant. Forget about her. There is one condition if you stay here: you must never, ever see or speak to her again.'

At this forceful demand, William's face drained of colour and he slumped against a high-backed chair, as if his father's words had physically struck him. He was now in a state of shock from his verbal onslaught and threats, which contrasted sharply with his earlier euphoric mood. The cold reality was that his hopes were in tatters, his dreams destroyed.

William left the office in a daze and made his stumbling way to his own rooms in the east wing of the Hall. There, he threw himself face down on his bed. He was devastated by what his father had said and the ultimatum which he had spelt out with such cruel finality. The thought of not seeing Elizabeth again felt like a physical withdrawal pain, which was slowly turning into a heavy, tight numbness around his heart. He could not visualise his bleak, empty future stretching out before him – but from experience, knew that there was an inevitability about it all. His dominating, all-powerful father would be obeyed.

Being banished to a strange country held no appeal for him. His place was here. But he flirted briefly with the idea that Elizabeth might leave for the New World with him where status was less important. But she would not leave her mother, and his father knew William would never leave his beloved valley. What would his life be like if his father disowned him? Then with devastating clarity, he acknowledged his weakness, in the face of his dominating father. William knew he liked his comfortable life too much and should he become estranged from his farther, he would be unable to find other employment in the area. Life was so utterly cruel.

After a sleepless night, the realisation dawned that he and Elizabeth could not marry for the very reasons she had predicted with such clarity.

His brother Hugh had been hovering close by the study the night before, covertly listening to their angry exchange. Next morning, he went up to William's rooms and tapped gently at his door. Entering, he said 'I do think it's all a bit unfair – but I can also understand father's point of view. After all, we are the only two sons left to carry on the bloodline.'

A still angry William responded, 'Clearly our father does not want his precious bloodline tarnished with the blood of a so-called peasant!' Hugh saw there was no reasoning with him in this mood, so let him be.

Despite William's strong resolve when he had last left Elizabeth by the little cottage, his father's power over him was such that when he asked him the next day, 'Well, what's your decision?' William reluctantly nodded his agreement not to see her again.

Maybe a stronger man would have stood up to him – if he went against his father's wishes, he would have no money and no place to live. He had no property of his own. Neither was he trained in any way by which to earn a living. He knew that he couldn't live with Elizabeth and her mother as his father would evict them immediately, then they would all be homeless. He could and would not let that happen to her. These were the stark realities of his situation.

The days slipped by. The darkness of his future sank in around him and he became increasingly unhappy, morose and moody. Frustrated by his powerlessness and his father's intransigence, he sunk slowly into a deep depression. He functioned as an automaton without a soul, feeling no real joy, no real anything. William had only ever considered Elizabeth as his equal – but the irrefutable truth was that his family were slaves to the doctrine that everybody had their proper place in society. There was only black and white, no in-between and if you broke its rules, you would be ostracised.

Whilst in the darkest depths of his despair, he decided he must write to Elizabeth, explaining what had happened. He did not dare to go to see her, in case his father had him followed and their meeting reported back to him.

He waited for weeks for a reply from her – but none came. He wondered why. On reflection, he realised he did not even know if she could read his letter, nor write a reply to him. At other times he thought his father had prevented his manservant from delivering it to her. Occasionally, he rode up to a high ridge to look down longingly at the little cottage, hoping to get a glimpse of her – but never did. She had completely and utterly vanished from his life. Sometimes, it felt as if she had never been in it, that he had imagined it all. All that was left were fast fading memories and his thwarted emotions. This began to turn into a slow-burning, impotent anger, which turned in on itself and never dissipated for the rest of his life.

William continued subsidising the rent on their smallholding for years. He could not bear the thought of Elizabeth being homeless. Then, during a regular meeting with his father's agent, aware that William was subsidising their rent but sworn to secrecy, he was told, 'You don't need to pay it anymore, old Mrs. Jones died and Elizabeth seems to have left the cottage.'

William immediately rode up to the smallholding and was devastated to find that it was completely empty, bereft of any evidence of her. What little furniture there had been, including the faded overstuffed chair and the spinning wheel, had gone, sold off, maybe over years, to pay the rent. Elizabeth would also have had to pay the undertaker for her mother's burial.

There was nothing of her there now, just an empty shell which held his beautiful memories of their time together. William looked a forlorn, thwarted, round-shouldered figure, as he wandered aimlessly around the place, remembering how joyful his life had been with her in it. He walked down to the river, where they'd had their picnic that last eventful day. He sat there remembering how it had felt to kiss her, to hold her, to love her. He thought about where she might have gone. She may even be married by now for all he knew. Maybe she had been offered employment somewhere. He decided he must try to find out – but her trail was now a few weeks old. At least his father would not suspect he was searching for her; he would assume that William had forgotten about her.

* * *

Unbeknown to William, Elizabeth had borne him a son, nine months after the only time they had laid together. He came into the world one cold snowy dark February morning in the remote cottage, with only her mother's help. She named him Evan, after her father. Elizabeth had a great capacity to love unconditionally; she held no grudge against William for having left her to bring up their child with only her mother. Elizabeth cherished her little son, the one part of William which she did have. As he grew, he looked more and more like his father and her love for William remained constant over the years. Being in a remote area, few knew Evan even existed and the little family managed to scrape together a living with William's secret subsidy
.

* * *

The years went drearily by for William, without anything of any consequence happening until his father died very suddenly. He had not been ill and had seemed to be in very good health – but was found slumped over his desk one rainy afternoon, when the maid took in his afternoon tea.

When Hugh and William spoke with the doctor, he told them, 'I had been concerned about his health for some time, as he seemed easily fatigued. I discovered he had an irregular heartbeat, but he strictly forbade me to tell you two about it and you know yourself, he was not a man to be disobeyed!'

Later that evening, as they sat in front of the fire over nightcaps in the main Hall, William said, 'The only guilt I have is that I am not sad about father's death. I still hold a deep resentment towards him for spoiling my only chance of happiness with Elizabeth. I know our faith teaches us forgiveness – but I still cannot find it in myself.'

'Well,' said Hugh, 'You did say you'd never marry anyone else, even when father regularly reminded us we needed an heir.'

'Yes, it was the one way I could thwart him, as he had thwarted my life by forbidding me to marry or even see Elizabeth. All I feel towards him is a deep-seated resentment and bitterness.'

But William outwardly played the dutifully grieving son. Following protocol, they arranged a large funeral, reflecting their father's status. 'I will be relieved when all the formalities and me having to pretend to care are over. The only difference is that you now own everything and I have to carry on helping you run the estate!'

Once the dust of the funeral had settled, William decided to search for Elizabeth again. There was nothing to stop him now, except the passage of time. It was nearly fifteen years since he had seen her last and much could have happened during that time. She may not feel the same about him. She could be happily married with a brood of children but he really needed to know one way or another, so that he could finally put his mind to rest. But where on earth should he start looking for her?

* * *

Things changed drastically once her mother died. Elizabeth knew they had to leave their sanctuary to find employment, as William's father would never allow her to take on the tenancy. Even more so if he discovered she had an illegitimate child who was his grandson. She wondered if he would ever make the connection between her son and William. There was a definite likeness. His fury would surely know no bounds once he realised his precious blood line had been sullied by one of the lower classes.

Elizabeth said to Evan, 'I have decided that our best hope is to find live-in jobs where we at least have a roof over our heads. We are both healthy and we know how to work on a farm.' In the weeks following her mother's burial, she travelled out daily to the nearest villages to search for live-in domestic work. The cottage was now devoid of any furniture, the stock sold and they were getting desperate for food. All they had left were some clothes and a cooking pot with two wooden spoons. Elizabeth said to Evan, 'See what you can find out there in the vegetable plot. We may have missed something last time we turned it over.' Evan found nothing but a few old crab apples which they stewed. They slept that night on the earth floor in front of the fire, covered by her crocheted shawl, the crab apples cramping away at their stomachs. In the small hours of the night, Elizabeth, in her desperation said out loud, 'William, where are you my love, can't you see that your son needs you?' She decided then that they would leave the cottage for the last time tomorrow and search for work as they went. As dawn rose, she packed all they had into two bundles and sadly shut the door of the little cottage for the last time, leaving behind her cherished memories.

When they came to the nearest town, they made enquiries again and just as she was nearing the end of her tether, she spoke to a farm worker. 'There is a farmer on the banks of the large river, about five miles away from here, who's recently lost his wife. I've heard tell that he is looking for a domestic live-in servant, but he is miserable, bad-tempered and difficult to work for.'

Elizabeth thought this situation did not sound good but desperate times called for desperate measures. At least, she thought, given the man's alleged temperament, not many people would be clamouring after the job, so she might have a chance. Having been given the name and directions to the farm from the farm worker, they picked up their bundles and began their long walk to the farm.

They had already walked quite a long way. They were hungry and beyond exhausted when they were offered a ride on the back of a cart. Elizabeth was grateful, as it had started to rain quite hard. They threw in their bundles, climbed onto the cart and covered themselves with the cart's calico tarpaulin which smelt of hay. During the journey, Elizabeth thought about what she should say to the farmer about her circumstances. She needed to have a credible story, as he would probably not take her on as what she was, an unmarried woman with a bastard child. While sorting her mother's belongings, she had slipped on her mother's wedding ring to make herself seem more credible. Once out of earshot under the tarpaulin, Elizabeth took her son's hand in hers. 'I know I have always taught you that telling lies is wrong – but I want you to understand that this time we must, otherwise we will be without anywhere to live. So, I want you to say nothing. I'm going to tell the farmer that my husband, your father, has recently died and that we had to vacate our tenanted farm.'

Evan looked at her, slowly taking in this information. Having lived all his life with two adult women, he was mature and insightful; he had always behaved more like a grown-up than a child. He said to his mother, 'Whatever you think is best Mam, I won't say anything to anyone. I'll just get on with what I'm supposed to do.' She looked at him thoughtfully and knew it was a lot to ask but she had no choice. She hoped the farmer would not make any wider enquiries about them and in truth, there was nobody he could ask. Few people knew the farm she had left even existed, as it was in a very remote area, never mind its inhabitants. Having journeyed for most of the day, they were finally dropped off at the end of the farm track, just as daylight was fading.

The two walked the last few hundred yards down the potholed track to the farmhouse, clutching their bundles to their chests. They were greeted by the loud, aggressive barking of a bad-tempered sheepdog. Elizabeth was glad it was chained up, as it could have done them some damage. The farmer, equally bad-tempered, came out swearing angrily, '*Pwy sydd yna?* Who is there? What's the meaning of disturbing me at this time of night? Can't a man have his supper in peace?' Elizabeth then saw a young girl surreptitiously peeping out of a porch window to the side of the front door, to see who had arrived at the farm.

Over the racket of the barking dog it was difficult to make herself heard but as soon as the farmer shouted for it to shut-up, the dog stopped, whined, then slunk back into his kennel. Elizabeth tentatively began, 'I have been told that you are looking for domestic workers. My son and I have had to leave our farm because my husband passed away and they would not let me keep the tenancy. We can start work straight away. I have experience running a household and my son knows how to work on a farm. We have walked a very long way today to get here......' Her words finally petered out. She was exhausted and felt defeated – his discouraging, stony face glared at her and sapped her confidence. He looked at her with pure hostility and she was sure that he was going to turn them away. He looked at her up and down, with intrusive, insolent eyes. 'You have disturbed my evening meal,' he complained again but added grudgingly, 'You'd better go and sleep in the barn for the night,' indicating the direction of the barn with his arm, 'then we will discuss the possibility of work in the morning.' With that, he turned, re-entered the farmhouse then slammed the door hard behind him.

They made their way into the barn and collapsed onto the hay on the barn floor. Hunger and thirst gnawed at their insides. They had walked and ridden all day with no food and were feeling very light-headed. Given the farmer's attitude, they did not expect to get any sustenance but just as they were about to fall into an exhausted asleep, a young girl, about Evan's age, brought some bread, cheese and milk in a billy-can for them. Having placed these on the floor of the barn, she quickly darted away, as if she did not want to be caught. The food tasted like a feast and both soon fell fast asleep, satiated and safe for now – but who knew what the next day would bring?

Early the next morning, the farmer came to the barn. Without even a 'Good morning' greeting, 'My daughter Catherine runs the household; you will have to help her.' Elizabeth thought his daughter seemed very young to have this responsibility and hoped that she might be able to take the load off her a little. 'Your son will have to be a full-time farm servant, so will not be able to go to school. Your wages will not be much but you will get bed and board.' Elizabeth, who felt she had little or no choice in the matter, nodded her agreement. 'Get to the kitchen and start straight away.'

She was greeted by the young girl, who seemed to be better endowed with the social graces her father so clearly lacked. She said, '*Croeso*, Welcome. My name is Catherine and this is my younger brother, Richard.' Richard looked at Elizabeth with a sulky expression, believing this woman was here to try to take the place of his mother, the only one who had ever really understood him, whereas the reality was that she had spoilt him by stopping his father being so hard on him.

Over the next few days, Elizabeth fell into the routine of the place, which was very much like any other farm. Her informant was correct, Catherine and Richard's mother had died a few weeks ago. Judging by the farmer's attitude, Elizabeth thought that it must have been from sheer exhaustion. He was a very hard taskmaster who shouted at and bullied them all. If it hadn't been for the children of the farm and the fact that she and Evan would be homeless, she may not have stayed there. She was given a small damp room in the eaves and Evan was told to sleep in the hayloft of the barn. From having been close for so long, the only time she saw him now was at mealtimes. Evan helped with feeding, milking and looking after the animals. He was often scapegoated, shouted at or clipped around his ear for his supposed ineptitude. But he bore it all for the sake of his mother and to have a dry place to sleep and food in his belly. Having lived in such a remote place previously, he had not attended school anyway, so it made no difference to him.

The farm had a large dairy herd of Welsh Blacks and a flock of wiry Welsh sheep, which grazed on salt-marsh land on the banks of the large tidal river. It also reared the male calves for the beef market. The farm was situated at the high-tide reach of the river, close to the only bridge in the area to span the river. The situation of the farm was idyllic – but the work was hard. Near the bridge, a weekly farmers' market was held, where farm stock and produce were bought and sold. Before this local market was set up, the livestock from the local farms had for centuries been taken by drovers down to London to be sold. It was a tight little community where everybody knew everybody else, or at least their families were known, even if an individual member was not. Word soon got around that the farmer had a new woman working in his house and they laid odds on how long it would be before he married her. Unfortunately, this bit of gossip did not reach William, who remained oblivious to the fact that Elizabeth, the love of his life, was now living just a few miles away. This news did not reach his ears, as the locals only gossiped amongst themselves, not with gentry.

True to local expectations, after a barely respectful period of mourning for his dear departed wife, the farmer suggested to Elizabeth, 'I think we should get married. It would make your position here more respectable and you could do a lot worse than marrying me,' believing in his own mind that he was quite a catch but genuinely unaware of how deeply repulsive he was to her. She was totally taken aback by his suggestion. It seemed very sudden. Once she had gathered her wits, 'It is a big decision, I will need some time to think about it.' The farmer was shocked, he had not expected this response. 'There is nothing to think about, you should be grateful that I asked you. Of course, I would not carry on paying you once we were married.

Whilst thinking about the farmer's offer of marriage, Elizabeth remembered William's sweet proposal, which had ended in nothing. She remembered how she had felt about William, her first and only love and was loathe to even contemplate marriage to the farmer; she cringed at the thought of him touching her. She had to finally accept that William was lost to her forever – but she could not help remembering the sweet love they had shared, which had produced Evan. Sadly, she again wondered why he had never come to Pant Ffynnon to see her again. Wistfully, she said out loud, 'Where are you my love? You have forsaken me.'

Elizabeth then remembered back to just after her mother's death. While sorting through her possessions, she had found a letter,

241

its stamped wax seal intact. She was not able to make out the letters of the ornate copperplate writing so had quickly stuffed it in her bundle when they left Pant Ffynnon. She decided to look at it again when she had more time; her first priority was to find work and a roof over their heads. Elizabeth knew that Catherine was good with letters but still she hesitated to ask her to read the letter. The contents might contain something she would not want Catherine to know about, which could reveal her cover story. So Elizabeth still did not know the message it contained – yet another opportunity of reconciliation lost to the ill-fated couple.

Elizabeth realised she was in a really difficult situation. If she refused to marry him, he may very well order her to leave the farm and they would be homeless once again. So, after a few weeks of agonising indecision, she resignedly plucked up her courage one evening after supper and said to him, 'I will marry you.'

'Don't know what took you so long,' he said curtly, 'you should feel honoured.'

They were quietly married in the registry office of the nearest large market town and on their return, they just went back to work as usual. Later that night, there was none of the tenderness she had known with William. The farmer treated her roughly, grunted and then rolled over to sleep. She lay there for hours, eyes wide open staring at the ceiling, with sad tears slowly working their way down the side of her face and onto the pillow, reflecting on the cruelty of her life. She guessed that this was the lot of many women and comforted herself by thinking that she had at least known a different, more tender love with William and felt blessed that she had her son, Evan.

Elizabeth seldom left the farm as the farmer was very controlling of her. People locally knew he had married but few knew who she was. She just threw herself into her housework and put her hopes into the belief that at least Evan would one day be able to leave, to find work where his skills and abilities were appreciated.

* * *

After William found out that Elizabeth had vacated the cottage and believing that she might be homeless, he had searched everywhere for her and made endless enquiries. People were curious about why he was asking and what his interest in her was – but they did not associate the farmer's new woman with the person William was seeking. He searched for months among the towns and villages nearest to the remote cottage and tried to follow any trail from there – but it had gone cold.

Many months later, he was riding out to inspect the estate's properties. While tying his horse's reins to a post, he fell into conversation with a local man in the village nearest to Elizabeth's old cottage. '*Bore da*, I'm on my way out to Pant Ffynnon to check on the tenant, did you know the people who used to live there?'

The man, sucking on his clay pile, liked to reminisce about the past, now he was retired. Casually he said, 'I remember old Mrs Jones, her daughter Elizabeth and the young lad who used to live there – I used to go there to shear their sheep. Can't shear now with these old hands,' lifting his gnarled hands, deformed by arthritis. 'Well, she was a pretty girl, that one. The last time I saw her, *Duw*, it was a long time ago now, just after her mother died and she had to leave the cottage. She said she was looking for work. She asked me if I knew anyone who was looking for live-in domestic workers.' William's eyes grew wide as his hopes rose. 'I told her about that miserable old farmer on the banks of the River Conwy next to the bridge. He had recently become a widower and was looking for a live-in domestic.' As William stood listening to the man, his jaw visibly dropped, but he did not really register what the man said about a lad. He continued, 'She rushed off soon after I had given her directions to the farm – but I don't know if she ever went there to enquire or not.' William was stunned. This was the first piece of real information he had ever heard about Elizabeth in years and he decided that he would go to this farm to find out. He also rushed away from the same man while he was still speaking, just as Elizabeth had done years before.

Later, at supper, William told his brother Hugh about his

conversation with the man and Hugh said sadly, 'I don't blame you for still wanting to find her. I suppose I have mellowed in my old age. I've seen how miserable you have been all these years and I really regret that I did not support you more about the girl at the time. After all, it was really up to me to produce an heir. Father was much too harsh on you, my brother. There would have been no real harm done if you had been quietly allowed to marry Elizabeth, except perhaps to the family's standing in society. Even that would soon have been forgotten when the gossipers found someone else to talk about. But you know what our father was like when it came to reputation and obedience.'

Hugh continued in the same vein: 'I am getting older. You will be the main beneficiary in my will but who will it all go to after you?' – blindly assuming as he was the older, he would be the first to die. This was a rhetorical, seemingly unanswerable question. So, they just sat there in the ornate wing chairs, flanking the ancient fireplace decorated with the family's ancient coat of arms. The flames from the fire flickered on the faces of the two middle-aged bachelors, morosely shaking their heads about the extraordinary abnormality of their lives.

Early the next morning, William made his way optimistically down to the farm where Elizabeth might or might not be. He rode into the farmyard where he was met by a lad he assumed was the farmer's son. Acknowledging William as gentry, he touched the front of his cap and asked him deferentially, 'Can I be of assistance sir? My father is currently away from the farm, but his wife will be glad to invite you in and offer hospitality.'

William dismounted. He was led into the farmhouse through the front door and shown into a parlour, which due to its un-aired smell, felt seldom used. He was left there but was too restless to sit as invited. He paced the room impatiently for the farmer's wife to appear, so he could make his enquiries. Suddenly, as he turned, framed in the parlour doorway stood Elizabeth, the love of his life. He took a sharp intake of breath. She quickly grabbed the doorframe to steady herself at the shock of seeing her beloved William standing right there in front of her. He gently took her hand and led her to sit down on the nearest couch then sat down beside her. He gazed at her adoringly, soaking in the loveliness of her. She had hardly changed, except now, he believed, she was even more beautiful than she had been as a young woman. She had lost the youthful roundness of her face, which was now accentuated by high chiselled cheekbones. Her hair was still the same unruly blond mop it always was. Efforts had been made to tame it under a housewife's cap – but disobedient tendrils managed to escape. She was modestly dressed in a rough working-dress – but this did not hide the fact that she was still slender, probably due to hard physical work. It did not occur to him that she was the farmer's wife – he assumed she was a domestic servant, who he immediately intended to release from servitude, there and then, on this very day. He felt such a rush of utter joy surge through him that he was momentarily robbed of his ability to speak.

Elizabeth, equally shocked to see him standing there before her, had almost fainted with shock as the blood began to drain from her face. Once seated, she held onto his hands, not quite believing that he was here next to her. She studied him and thought he had aged a great deal. Unhappy lines were carved deep into his face around his mouth and his body had thickened a little – but she thought that the silver liberally sprinkled through his hair suited him, giving him an air of gravitas. Seeing him there next to her, confirmed to her that she had longed for him during the long, hard, lonely years. She had managed to keep her thoughts and emotions about him in check by putting them in a small safe compartment at the back of her mind, only bringing them out now and again to look at, to recount, examine, analyse and reminisce. The door of the compartment had suddenly burst open of its own volition and all the pent-up feelings gushed out in a torrent. They were both locked into this frozen tableau of re-recognition of their souls when the voice of a young lad on the cusp of adulthood broke into their reverie. He had appeared in the doorway, then went to stand resolutely by her side, as if to protect his mother. William's gaze turned upwards to look at him – it was as if he was looking at a mirror image of his younger self. The enormity of what he was seeing suddenly struck him and again he took in a sharp breath, as his heart thumped loudly in his chest. He thought, could this be my son? Elizabeth was first to recover. Dragging herself into the present, she said, 'Ask Catherine to send in some tea.' Realising this man meant his mother no harm, he quietly left and shut the door behind him. It seemed that no sooner had he left than the door opened once more and a beautifully laid tea tray arrived, brought in by the farmer's daughter, Catherine, who once she had put down the tray, curtsied respectfully to William and left.

When they were alone once more, he held both of her hands and said, 'I am so happy to have found you at last. I searched for you everywhere after you left the cottage – but you had vanished into thin air. I have wondered where you have been all these years and have thought tirelessly about what you have been doing since I last saw you in Pant Ffynnon. But at last, yesterday, I was speaking to the man who told you about the live-in job here, so I came straight here this morning.'

'I had to leave the cottage after my mother died because I knew your father would not be allowing me to continue with the tenancy, even though Evan would soon have been able to do the work of a man. Had he known about Evan, he would probably have thrown us out even sooner.'

William asked out loud and in wonderment, 'So the boy who came into the room, is he really our son?' Nodding her confirmation, he felt overwhelmed. He closed his eyes and shook his head in wonderment, 'To think that all these years I have had a son after all.' He then felt deeply saddened that they had not been a part of each other's lives, that he had not seen him growing up, nor provided for him.

'Did you not receive the letter I sent to you, explaining why I had not come back to see you?' She seemed surprised by this, 'I did not receive any letter from you. I thought you did not come because your father had forbidden you or because you no longer wanted me.' At this, he looked at her with such naked anguish. 'If only you had known just how much I had wanted you.'

'After my mother died, I did find an unopened letter when sorting out her belongings – but I had not seen it before then. When I found it, I did not know your handwriting, so did not recognise it as being from you. Of course, by then I recognised my own name on the envelope, so I don't understand why my mother had not given it to me, as I may have been able to find someone to help me read what was written in it. Very soon after I found it, we had to leave the farm, so I did not have time to do anything about paying someone to read it for me.'

He silently berated himself for assuming she would be able to read it, then felt a resentful flash of anger towards Mrs. Jones for withholding his letter. He thought sadly of a critical opportunity lost. He castigated himself, as he often did, for being weak in not disregarding his father's will. His younger self should surely have gone to see her himself, not just written the letter, which was a coward's way out and it was now obvious his words had never reached her.

William felt bereft at the utter loss of what his life might have been. Again, he felt waves of shame, remembering how weak he had been in the face of his father's insistence that he did not pursue Elizabeth and also a deeply frustrated anger towards himself for not standing up to him, as any man worth his salt would have done.

Elizabeth, meanwhile, alarmed that her whole security might be at stake, begged William, 'Please do not tell the farmer that he is your son. I told him that I was a widow to get this job. He might even throw me out of the farm if he found out that Evan was born out of wedlock.'

'Don't worry about that. My father is dead, there is nothing now to stop us from marrying. I would be very happy and proud to acknowledge the lad as my own son and to look after you both.'

He does not know. Elizabeth thought about the enormity of the cruel blow life had dealt them and the one that she was now metaphorically to hit William with. After a small pause, realising that what she had to say was going to wound him deeply, she took his hand and turned to him with a deeply apologetic expression and profound sorrow in her eyes. 'William, I cannot go with you now and I cannot marry you. I am already married to the farmer and did make my vows before God.' She saw the shock register in his eyes as she continued, 'It was purely a practical arrangement to make my son and me more secure. I could not refuse him as I believed he would once again have made me homeless. I do not love him and doubt whether he is even capable of loving me.'

William, having just a few moments ago finally found his one true love again, had felt his heart begin to soften, then slowly start to soar. But now William was shaking his head in denial, trying to shake away the meaning of her words. 'No. No. This cannot be right,' he said plaintively. He did not want to hear any more reasons why she could still not be his. His heart was now thumping. He was glad he was sitting when she had shared this devastating piece of news, as his legs would have turned to jelly – then he felt a tightening around his chest like a tight metal band. Once again, he was thwarted in his need to be with her and he could not bear it.

Presently, having calmed somewhat, he rose, round-shouldered and defeated once more. He stumbled quickly from the room, and through blindingly hot tears, found his way outside to his horse. He mounted and rode sadly away. From having longed to be near to Elizabeth, he now wanted to put as much distance as he could between them. Meanwhile, back in the musty parlour, the tea tray, untouched on the table, was the only witness to Elizabeth's total collapse, brought about by this further cruel twist of fate.

After finally finding her and experiencing a few hopeful moments of real joy at doing so, he felt his heart beginning to harden once more. He was angry. Why did she not tell him all those years ago that she was expecting their child? His whole life could have been very different, fulfilled and happy; he could have poured his love into her and their son. But once he had calmed down a little, he began to think more rationally. At that time, she had no reason to believe that his family would ever have accepted her and his child, or even that he still wanted her. He realised that she had to do what she thought was best for her and her son, given her reduced circumstances. Even if she didn't feel that she could tell him when Evan was born, he wished he'd found her when she'd first vacated the cottage, as he could have done something then to help her, even if his father was against them being together. If he had done so, she no doubt would not have felt obliged to marry the farmer and would now be free to marry him instead. And as for him having a son all these years, the very thought took his breath away and gave him some small comfort in the dark place he was again in. He'd had an heir all these years without knowing it, the heir his father had desperately wanted him to have but whose pride in all probability would not have allowed him to acknowledge. Other people, even the poorest, seemed to be able to marry the ones they love and live happy fulfilled lives even in their poverty, whilst he, not without means, had to live without his. His was a different poverty, a poverty of love, fulfilment and contentment.

Later, when William felt a little calmer, he realised if he tried to help Evan financially or even offer to pay for his education, it would reveal Elizabeth's true status as the mother of an illegitimate son. This in turn would cause bad blood between Elizabeth and her husband. He did not think Evan would leave his mother to the mercy of the farmer and come to live with him, his father. He seemed very protective of his mother and by all accounts the farmer was a deeply unpleasant man. He would at the very least take it out on her, or evict her because she had had a bastard child. The farmer would certainly take it out on Evan. But even if she was evicted, William could still not marry her, as she was already married. On reflection, William decided it was best to leave well alone, there were too many complications – except that all was not well for him. His poor heart was broken yet again, just when true happiness had, at last, seemed to be in his grasp. He felt suddenly very weary – and tired of life. He felt the old blanket of depression beginning to slowly envelop him once again. Maybe he would go to see his doctor for a tonic. He felt totally drained; he should not be dealing with this sort of emotional turmoil at his time of life, a time he should be settled and content.

William arranged to call to see his doctor for his tonic. The doctor welcomed him into his surgery saying, 'I am very glad that you have come to see me. Given the cause of your father's death, it would be just as well for me to check out your heart. We should probably get your brother checked out as well.'

The doctor began his examination. He asked many questions about his general health, then carefully listened to William's heartbeat through his Pinard horn. After he had finished, he scribbled down some illegible spidery notes then looked grimly over the top of his steel-framed glasses at William. He always believed in being straight with his patients, as dressing up bad news in flowery words did not help them on a practical level. 'I think it is best to be completely frank with you about your condition. Unfortunately, you seem to have inherited your father's heart problem and you need to be aware of your limitations. I suggest that you get your legal and household affairs in order, as it is impossible to tell when your heart will fail – but fail it will and it will be sudden and catastrophic.'

William took this in stoically. He was not afraid to die, he felt he had no real reason to live. But the news galvanised him into action. Glad to have something to focus on despite the gravity of the reason, he arranged to see his solicitor in order to draw up his will. He thought once more what a cruel world it was for some. He reasoned that even if Elizabeth had been free to marry him, their happiness might have been short lived. She may soon have become a grieving widow, given his condition but at least she would have been very well provided for financially – and he would have been blissfully happy during the brief time they might have had together.

As they sat down to dinner that evening, William said to his brother, 'I have some news for you. Seems like I have inherited father's heart problem and could die at any moment, according to my doctor.' Hugh was stunned, it had not occurred to him that it could be an inherited condition. He sat there speechless. 'More than that, I have finally found Elizabeth, after all those long years but it was all in vain, as she is married to the farmer she went to work for after leaving the cottage.' William let this sad bit of news sink in before continuing, 'Furthermore, she has a son, my son. His name is Evan.' Hugh looked up quickly and sat there round-eyed and open-mouthed. 'I found them both working on a farm, not too far away from here. Elizabeth didn't know that I had been searching for her and had married the owner of the farm, to keep a roof over their heads.'

Hugh shook his snowy white head from side to side. Beside himself with sorrow at this news, he was appalled at this cruel twist of fate. Due to their father's intransigence, three lives had been blighted – lives which could have been quietly joyful. He agreed that there was nothing they could now do to help Elizabeth, as it was all much too late.

William died sometime later, his poor heart weakened through being thwarted at every turn or because it was irretrievably broken twice during his lifetime. He had left most of his estate to his older brother Hugh but made sure that he had given his illegitimate son, Evan, a good start in life.

Hugh was devastated by the loss of his younger brother, as it was not the natural order of things to have a younger sibling predecease you. For the first time in his life, Hugh felt utterly alone, utterly abandoned, an orphan with the absolute grief and loneliness felt when a person has finally lost both parents and siblings. William was the last link with the family as it had once been. Hugh knew that it was unlikely he would ever meet anybody to quietly live the rest of his life with and needed to decide which one of his cousins or nephews should inherit the estate.

Part 6

I am excited by my recent discovery of the plaque in the little church which confirms my ancestral link to the esteemed Ffowcs family. This now means that I might be able to trace my family tree even further back, possibly into the Middle Ages, or even to the time of the Welsh princes. So, I set about forensically researching this link. When I first started this family tree research, I never in my wildest dreams imagined that I would be able to go so far back down my blood line or that it might be royal.

I have become utterly obsessed by it all. I read everything I can lay my hands on about the family's history, already extensively researched by others. I delve into their manorial history, I scan Parish registers in the local Archives, I examine in more detail the graves in the floor of the old church, check Oxford academic attendance records, tithe and land tax records and pore over any on-line reference I happen to find. I am now totally absorbed in it, so much so that I begrudge any time I must spend on marking assignments.

Carefully, I enter the names of those I have proved to be factual onto the family tree I am building. Who would have thought my ancestors had lived such interesting lives?

One morning, I pause and reflect on my recent behaviour. What is this manic activity all about? Is it part of the grieving and healing process by which I make myself so busy, I have no time to think about losing Sarah? I ask myself, am I filling in the unfillable void left by Sarah with other dead people?

Or is it part of my mental profile? Given my low mood before I left London and now this frantic energy, I wonder if I might be a bit bipolar. But can bipolar people even recognise this in themselves? Besides, I don't think you can be 'a bit' bipolar, it's either extreme elation or deep depression. I let out a big sigh and decide I need to read up on this sometime, but meanwhile it would be beneficial if I could just slow down a bit and stop being so obsessive.

I re-read the letter written by Hugh William Ffowcs to Evan, offering him half his fortune. I should also follow up on the names and dates on the family tombs. The name Frances, who I guess must be Hugh William Ffowcs' mother, intrigues me, as she had died so young. The date of her death was a few days after Hugh William's birth date. Childbirth deaths, especially from childbed fever, were far more prevalent in those days and I reflect on how sad it was for the baby to be sent away and blamed for his mother's death and to be brought up by his relatives in Bala.

* * *

Hugh and Frances' Story

Hugh mourned his younger brother, William, and missed him much more than he had expected. Sometimes, he would think 'I must tell William about that,' only to suddenly remember that he was no longer there to tell. He felt very isolated and his long dreary days were endless. To alleviate this aching loneliness, he decided to get out more and socialise. He had met and been introduced to many 'suitable' women over the years but none of them had appealed to him, and the older he became, the fussier and more set in his ways he was. So he tended to seek out his contemporaries to pass the time of day with, as he had decided long ago that he was too long in the tooth to look for anybody special – until one fateful day.

Recently, a new vicar had been appointed to the church which Hugh's family had always patronised, replacing their revered old vicar, who had passed away unexpectedly. At the Sunday morning service, Hugh sat alone in his own private family pew in the 'gentry' section of the church. The pew, which his family had owned for centuries, was flanked by the elaborate plaques which commemorated his esteemed ancestors. They had been buried under the flagstones of the church and busts of his forebears were mounted on plinths all around him. He gently warmed his feet on the small enclosed brass coal brazier, already lit by his servant, and was settling in for the Sunday service. Like his father before him, he was interested in ecclesiastical matters, enjoyed theological debate and usually enjoyed the sermons. Other members of the congregation sat in the pews in order of rank and social status. The most important people sat in the front, cushioned rows, the rich farmers and rich merchants behind them and then the tenanted and poor farmers and labourers with their children. Hugh's pew was furnished with well-padded, buttoned, richly covered deep red cushions, the farmers benches were lined with a type of thick red felt to take away the hardness of the pitch pine seats, while the poorest in society had no such comforts and shuffled uncomfortably on the hard seats. Many were undernourished and did not have the natural padding to soften the wood.

Hugh sat listening to the organist filling in the final minutes before the vicar appeared in his chancel, while his playing competed with the tolling of the church bell. Hugh idly scanned the pews opposite to see who was attending, when he spotted an attractive woman sliding into the vicar's family pew. Was this perhaps the vicar's wife? But when he saw how old the new vicar was, he decided that she must be his daughter, whom he curiously glanced at covertly during the service. Protocol dictated that he would be introduced to the new vicar and family on his way out after the service. He felt an unusual sense of anticipation. Although the new vicar had written a good sermon to impress his congregation on his first day, Hugh was hardly listening at all, as his mind was distracted by the intriguing occupier of the pew opposite.

Once the sermon was over, everybody stood to file out of the church but only after the processional choir, the vicar and then the gentry. The vicar was there with his daughter by his side. 'God bless you,' said the vicar to Hugh, who received deferential treatment, given he was the vicar's financial sponsor. 'Please let me introduce my daughter, Frances.' She gave Hugh a slight curtsy as he took her hand and kissed it, his eyes never leaving her face. Unusually, he seemed spellbound by this woman's beauty and her natural unaffected charm which made it easy to converse with her.

Frances was of average height, in her thirties and of slender build. She was very attractive in an unusual way, which Hugh could not quite fathom. He said with real sincerity, 'I hope you enjoy living in the area, please let me know if there is anything I can help with.' He noticed she was quick to smile. A wide bewitching smile, which transformed her face, reaching her large blue eyes which sparkled with intelligence, awareness, as well as humour. Frances replied, 'Thank you for your consideration regarding our comfort. It is much appreciated.'

Hugh was enchanted. He felt irrationally drawn to her and despite not normally being a man for idle chit chat, 'Please do come for tea one day next week, when you have had time to settle in.'

'We would like that very much indeed; which day would be convenient for you?'

'May I suggest Thursday at three o'clock?' The vicar, noticing the intensity of the exchange on Hugh's part, interjected, 'Thursday would suit us very well. Thank you.'

Frances obviously adored her father and they seemed to have a very close bond. Hugh wondered if this would be an impediment to getting to know her better. To the vicar, the invitation from Hugh indicated to those milling around that they were being socially accepted by the gentry of the local community. Some vicars, like Frances' father, although well educated, were relatively poor, living frugally off stipends provided by the church or rich sponsors like Hugh. One of the benefits of their occupation was that it gave them a certain status in society, responsible as they were for people's immortal souls. This allowed them to socialise with the gentry as well as minister to the poor. Hugh knew that inviting the new vicar to tea would not cause any speculation from the village gossips, as it was acceptable established social protocol at that time. The vicar was anticipating some stimulating theological debate but Hugh's anticipation lay elsewhere.

Thursday arrived. Hugh's guests rode up the drive to the Hall in their pony and trap. They were ushered into the impressive main reception room of the Hall, where Hugh was waiting for them, standing in front of a roaring fire. The vicar bowed his head reverently, while Frances dropped a small curtsy.

'Thank you for your kind invitation to visit you at your home.' They looked towards the large fireplace, adorned with the coat of arms of Hugh's family and around about them, as in the church, they saw statues on plinths, of Hugh's eminent family. Hugh pulled the golden silk cord by the fireplace and a parlour maid soon appeared with a tea tray with an array of delicious sandwiches and cakes, which she placed on a small table beside the guests.

Much of the conversation was led by the vicar and centred on religion and the historical achievements of Hugh's forbears. Eventually getting on to more personal topics, the vicar said,

'Eight months ago, I lost my sweet wife and sweet life companion to the good Lord, whilst my dear daughter lost the gentlest of mothers. She had been sick for a considerable time and Frances nursed her selflessly.' Hugh was glad to tolerate her father's monologue so that he could look at Frances. 'However, once she had passed away, we found we could not bear to stay in our last parish because of the sad memories the place held. When the unexpected opportunity to move here arose, we felt it would give us a fresh start. But I do feel selfish keeping Frances at home with me, when she should be out socialising with other young people.'

Frances demurred, 'I really don't mind father, I love looking after you.' Her father reiterated, 'But I worry about you, should anything happen to me'. Meanwhile, whilst half listening to the vicar's dreary tone, Hugh studied Frances at close quarters. She really was lovely. Her hair was fair, brushed into a simple chignon fashion which gave her grace and dignity. Her beautiful neck, which he felt an unfamiliar but irresistible urge to bury his face in, was flawless. Her sensuous lips gave way to the captivating smile, which was immediately reflected in her mesmerising blue eyes, framed by long curled lashes. He mentally feasted on her countenance and wondered at himself being so besotted with this woman so late in his life. Feelings such as this were new to him. Despite being an important local personage used to dealing with all sorts of situations, he suddenly felt a little out of his depth. He resolved then to visit William's grave later that day to tell him about her and through contemplative thought, get a sense of what William would say. He imagined that William would tell him to grab the opportunity with both hands, if she would have him. 'Be happy. Do not waste your life trying to fulfil our father's criteria of what is acceptable.'

Once they had left, he decided Frances was even lovelier than he had imagined and wondered at how at ease he felt in her company. He was smitten and wondered how he could arrange to speak to her without the irritating presence of her father. He thought about her all the time. She tormented his thoughts and he spent hours walking around his estate wondering what to do about the situation. Weeks went by when suddenly, in the middle of the night, he sat up in bed having had the most radical idea, which might be mutually beneficial to them all. He decided to first speak to her father on his own.

Hugh called at the Vicarage a few days later, on one of his regular walks through the village at a time when there were few people about. The vicar himself answered the door, suggesting that Frances was not at home. 'Do please come in. Frances has gone to visit a sick parishioner but should be back within the hour.' The vicar led him to his study, where he appeared to be in the throes of writing his next sermon.

After some small talk, Hugh looked directly at the vicar. 'I have a proposition to put to you. I am not a young man and I still need an heir to continue my ancient family lineage. I am unexpectedly taken with your daughter, so I am suggesting to you that we should marry.' The vicar stared open mouthed at this unforeseen turn of events. 'She would want for nothing and would be very comfortable should anything happen to me, and you would no longer have to worry about her welfare after you are gone.' The vicar, visibly shocked and surprised, appeared uncharacteristically lost for words. He stared off into the near distance while he digested this proposal and its implications. The only sound to be heard was the fire crackling in the hearth and the ticking of the study clock.

After a short while, which seemed like an age to Hugh, the vicar said thoughtfully, 'I can see that there is some merit in the proposal….' A short silence followed. He seemed to be slowly coming around to the idea, with the added attraction that Frances would be marrying into a very important family.

Hugh, as if reading the vicar's mind, reiterated that 'If Frances is agreeable to becoming my wife, she would have both security and status.' Tactically he let that sink in, then added, 'I would also ensure that you are not deprived of a housekeeper, by paying for a local woman to fend for you.' The vicar had a few reservations which he did not voice, mainly that Hugh was so much older, almost thirty years in fact, but it was not unknown then for rich older men to marry younger women. He was also concerned about being lonely but was comforted that she would always be financially secure if her husband predeceased her. The vicar was aware that Hugh had no heir, so knew that this would be a main consideration for the union, although to be fair, Hugh did seem quite smitten with her when they were first introduced and later when they visited the Hall. He also realised that a possible grandson could be a very rich and important man. Maybe, he thought, Hugh wanted companionship in his older years. Goodness knows, he had come to know what loneliness was since his own sweet wife died. The vicar had no idea that Frances was the first woman Hugh had ever felt really drawn to.

'Could I please have a little time so that I can consider the matter?' This was agreed and Hugh asked gravely, 'Please treat the matter with utter confidentiality. I will await your decision with hopeful anticipation.' They stood and shook hands formally as Hugh said his farewells. He walked back pensively through the village, believing the meeting had gone quite well. He took a shortcut through the fields back to the Hall, the open space of the countryside giving him space to think about how his future could be about to change. He knew he was a bit long in the tooth but was determined to be a considerate husband, should Frances agree to his proposition of course!

Frances was blissfully unaware of what the two men were plotting. It was not even a year since she had lost her mother and she was still in mourning. All she had left now was her father and she was happy just to take care of him and the parishioners. This was now her duty and she did not yearn for any other sort of life. She certainly had not considered marriage, as where would that leave her father? She did not think herself to be even attractive to men and was totally unaware of the spell she had cast over Hugh. Her childhood was probably considered unusual, with only adults for company, so she would make a perfect companion for a person such as Hugh. Her father had encouraged her to read widely and had also educated her himself. She was very interested in a variety of subjects and could hold her own in most discussions. Her main concerns were the plight of the poor, their lack of education and insanitary living conditions. She had been taught household skills by her mother, who was a gentlewoman who had married below her station in life, having chosen love over fortune.

Soon after Hugh and the vicar had had their first meeting, Hugh called at the Vicarage again. Her father called her to his study and asked her to sit down. She was totally unaware of how her life was to completely change from the one she was living and had envisioned. She sensed something unsettlingly formal about his request. However, she sat, her back stiff as a ramrod, hands folded neatly together in her lap. 'What is it father? Is something wrong?'

'That very much depends on how you feel about what Hugh has to say to you, daughter.' She immediately tensed and knew then that it was indeed something very serious indeed. 'It appears that he is very taken with you and has told me that he would like you to be his wife.'

Frances clearly in a state of shock uttered, 'I can't believe what you are saying to me. I don't want to marry anybody; I am looking after you ... it is my duty.' Hugh then rose from his chair and lifted her hand which he held with both of his. Kissing the back of it he said, 'Dearest Frances, would you do me the honour of being my wife?'

The Vicar, who did not want to be her burden, her responsibility, wanted her to have her own life. He said, 'But daughter, I won't always be here and who would look after you then, when you no longer have me to care for? You will have no home and no income. I acknowledge the age gap between you but if you marry Hugh, you will always be provided for, which will give me great peace of mind. I believe that he is genuinely fond of you and sincere in his request, otherwise I would not even consider this suggestion. Think about it at least, there is no rush, then let me know what you want to do.' Frances left the study in a daze and made her way to her bedroom where she paced up and down. In truth she had not given Hugh much thought after meeting him outside the church and during the subsequent visit to the Hall, so was really surprised when she had been called to the study to be told of Hugh's proposal of marriage.

Next morning at breakfast she said, 'I really don't want to leave you father, but if you think that I should go ahead with this plan and if it will give you peace of mind, then I will. I know that you worry about me and what will happen when you are no longer here, so maybe this is a solution.'

A few days later, the vicar called at the Hall to see Hugh. 'After much forethought and earnest praying for guidance from the Good Lord, we have decided to accept your proposal.' Hugh was elated but hid his inner excitement. Instead, he gravely took the vicar by the hand and shook it warmly, in tacit agreement of the arrangement.

Once Frances had agreed, she started to get used to the idea and plans were made. The requisite banns were read out in church on three consecutive Sundays. The first time the congregation heard them announced, it was visibly stunned by the news. Members turned to each other wide-eyed, jaws dropping, when the names were read out and the local gossips subsequently had a field day. Within no time at all, the village and surrounding valley was abuzz with the news.

Hugh and Frances spent time getting to know each other better, through a short-term courtship. Hugh was happier than he had ever been during his whole lifetime. He was besotted with her and he liked to think that she might become fond of him. He had looked

260

through the vault where the family jewels were kept and had chosen an engagement ring which had belonged to his grandmother. He also chose her rose gold wedding ring for the wedding ceremony. When he showed Frances the engagement ring, she protested, 'I could not possibly wear such an expensive and beautiful thing.'

Ignoring her protestations, he quietly slipped it onto her finger saying, 'You have made an old man very happy, Frances, I want you to accept it as a token of my love and the high esteem I hold you in.'

Hugh went ahead and made all the necessary arrangements and they were quietly married in the local church by the vicar. Frances wore her best Sunday clothes which were simple but to Hugh she looked wonderful. Neither of them had any close family who could attend, so two witnesses, high ranking retainers from Hugh's estate, were recruited for the task. After the service, a wedding breakfast was provided at the Hall by Hugh's staff. When this was over, Frances' father returned to his lonely vicarage, hoping fervently that he had done the right thing by his daughter. He wandered aimlessly from room to room, unable to settle to anything. He did not know why but he had a feeling of deep, impending doom.

Hugh at last tasted the sweet joy of love that his brother William had felt for Elizabeth but had been unable to fulfil, as he was forbidden to marry. Hugh, although having regretted his lack of support for William at the time, now felt huge remorse. Life might have been better for William, who could have felt this sweet contentment that he now felt, instead of the endless longing which had eaten away at him throughout his later life. He visited William's grave and told him all about Frances. He knelt in the mud at his graveside, praying long and hard for his forgiveness. Although his authoritarian father was long since dead, Hugh also felt a deep resentment towards him about the way he had treated William.

After the wedding, Hugh took Frances down to London. Whilst there, he said to her, 'I want to treat you to some travelling clothes and suitable dresses for evening wear.' She really thought she didn't need anything and that what she had was adequate – but he insisted. He took her to various dressmakers' shops, as befitted the wife of a gentleman. From there they boarded a ship and travelled to Europe to do a grand tour. They saw the sights in Paris, travelled through France, then toured the romantic cities of Italy. She was enchanted by what she saw, as well as enchanting Hugh. Frances wrote excited letters back to her father about all the wonders she had seen to assuage the pang of guilt that he had been left alone.

They travelled around the continent for a few months and by the time of their return, Frances informed Hugh she was expecting his child. They were ecstatic and started counting down the months. Hugh would not allow her to do anything which would endanger the baby, so she spent her days quietly in the morning room, reading or sewing. Worryingly, towards the end of her term, she began to have problems with intermittent bleeding and the doctor, who was there almost daily, ordered her to rest in bed for the duration of the pregnancy.

A few weeks later, it was clear that all was not well, despite the care she was taking and being given. Frances went into an early labour which lasted for many pain-ridden, anxiety-laden days. When at last a baby boy was born, the doctor was very concerned about the mother's weakened state. The bleeding did not stop as it should do, despite her legs being elevated. Hugh was glad about having a son but was very worried about his wife's deteriorating condition. He sat by her bedside continuously, praying and willing her with all his might to live, until the doctor became concerned about his mental well-being. He ordered him to find a wet nurse for the baby, more to get him out of the house and to think of something else besides Frances' precarious state. A young girl called Sali from the village, who had recently lost her own baby, was found and brought into the house, where she happily took immediate charge of the boy, who was named Hugh William, after his father and his brother.

After the birth, Hugh sent Frances' father a message announcing the baby's birth but warning him she was unwell. He came rushing to see her and blessed the child, his grandson. He visited daily and saw the deterioration in her condition. Realising his daughter was now gravely ill he began praying fervently on his knees by her bedside.

Frances lay there, drained of any colour except for two red patches on her cheeks, which indicated childbed fever. Her father gently tried to cool her fevered face with a damp flannel as she muttered gibberish in her semi-conscious state. He looked across at Hugh and said, choking on his anguish, 'What have you done to my own sweet girl? Why did I agree to this insane marriage plan?' Looking then at his daughter and stroking her face, he said, 'You would still be safe at home with me now if I had not been tempted by his offer. I was led by the devil into temptation. I was supposed to be making you safe and secure, not to be killing you. I will never forgive myself for my vainglorious decision. I will pray to the good Lord for forgiveness for the rest of my days.'

Sadly, by morning, Frances still had a high fever and slipped further into a deep coma. The doctor confirmed 'childbed fever' as she had abdominal pains and the infection caused a bad smell which permeated the air in the chamber. The windows were kept tightly closed, as she shivered uncontrollably. As well as the infection, he could still not stem the flow of her bleeding, despite his best efforts. As Frances' life force slowly ebbed away, she drifted inexorably away from those who loved her and were sitting and praying around her bedside. Hugh was desperately hanging on to her hand. His voice now raw with emotion said, 'Frances, I am begging you not to leave me. I know we have not known each other for very long but the short time we have been together has been the only time of true happiness and contentment I have ever known.' But it was all to no avail, he was powerless in the face of the malaise which had come over her. She had been so weakened by the long labour and birth that she had no fight left in her. By mid-morning, her father who had not left her bedside for hours, prayed for her immortal soul. It was all too much for Hugh to bear and when she finally slipped away, he broke down completely, sobbing uncontrollably and howling with the pain of his loss, while still holding her hand.

Frances' funeral was administered by her grief-stricken father, who conducted the church service and burial. Hugh, her now widower husband, stood forlornly by the damp, freshly dug grave, the earthy smell cloying and foreboding. He could not bear to think that that his once vibrant, warm Frances would soon be lying alone in the cold ground. Once over, as they walked side by side away through the graveyard, the vicar in his anger and grief turned on Hugh, attacking him with such vitriol that Hugh physically winced to protect himself from the harsh blows of the words.

'You have killed my daughter. We were happy as we were before you took her away from me. I hope you rot in Hell.' With that he strode away from Hugh, who stood there in shock. The vicar walked, head down, into the cold east wind and disappeared into the church. A few days later, the people of the village realised that their vicar had vacated the vicarage. Someone said they had seen him in the cold grey light of dawn, loading boxes onto his cart and riding away. He did not have the heart, nor even the faith to preach to them anymore and he was never seen nor heard of again.

As grief is wont to do, Hugh turned his anger at his loss of Frances towards the baby, which had lived, while she had died. He wished fervently it was the other way around and when he arrived home from her funeral, he could not bear to look at him and would not hold him. Hugh knew that Frances would be distraught that the baby was being rejected by his father after so tragically losing his mother. He could hear her voice in his head admonishing him for his callousness – but even this did not make him think kindly towards him. But Sali continued to carefully nurse him, so the baby was oblivious to his father's cruel rejection of him.

By the evening, Hugh could no longer tolerate to hear him cry nor even to be in the same room as him. He decided that he did not want him in the house to be a constant reminder of his loss, even though he was his heir. In his demented state, he thought illogically that the child did not even deserve to inherit his estates. It had killed his adored Frances and along with her, his only chance for happiness and contentment in his older years. He hardened his heart and decided that the child must go. He would not be able to bear to look at him as he grew up without thinking that he had killed his sweet mother, simply by being born. There was no one there to soothe him and tell him that his grief would eventually pass. By morning, he had decided that he would write to a cousin of his who lived in mid-Wales, married for many years but childless. He would ask if he and his wife could bring him up as their own. Soon he received the reply that they would be overjoyed to bring up his child.

Arrangements were made and soon the tiny baby, along with Sali, his wet-nurse, were sent off in a carriage to another home many miles away. Hugh never visited his son, neither did he write to him. He never invited him, nor was he welcome at the Hall for the duration of Hugh's life. Hugh received regular updates from his cousin on the child's progress but could not even bring himself to open them to read. Loath as he was, he appointed executors in the event of his death, to run his estate until his son came of age but only time would tell if his son would reject his estate, as his father had rejected him.

These two brothers who had wealth and privilege were unable to experience lasting happiness. William and Hugh, both having searched nearly all their lives, on finally finding their real loves, were fated. Despite their social 'status', both died of broken hearts and the sons they both begat late in life, grew up without knowing their fathers or their fathers' family. How ironic it is that when William's brother Hugh finally had an heir, he banished him to mid-Wales to be raised by God-fearing family members. This son found comforting solace in the study of religion and using his father's fortune, founded a school for the sons of disadvantaged families in Bala.

Part 7

Much time has passed since Sarah died but sadly my sons continue to shun me for not telling them when their mother first became gravely ill. They believe I deprived them of time they could have spent with her. This accusation saddens me deep inside, as there is no rationality in their thinking. But grief is seldom rational. It is loss, anger, denial and then hopefully, eventual acceptance. Following my earlier manic phase, I realise that I have probably been in a long, low depressive stage for some time. The loss of Sarah has left me devastated and bereft of human comfort. I seldom prepare a proper meal now, leave dirty dishes to pile up and sleep in an unmade bed. There seems no point to anything. Bess is bewildered and keeps looking for Sarah and the boys and won't let me out of her sight; she sneaks up onto my bed at night seeking her own comfort. To be honest, I think caring for her and the chickens is probably what keeps me going. We take long rambling walks among the hills, two forlorn souls, seeking something no longer there, out of reach. In the still silence of the hills, I listen intently for Sarah's voice on the wind and seek her soft touch in the gentle rain which falls on my face.

Returning from a walk one day, as I approach the back door, I am struck once more by the massive size of the boulders used to build the foundations at the back of the house and wonder if the building could originally have been a fort.

As a distraction from my low mood, I start researching when a dwelling could have first been erected on the site, guessing that the original building must at least have been built during the early Middle Ages. I read through the Chronicles of Gerald of Wales. Although he was not an authority on buildings and wrote at a later age, it gives me an insight into Welsh life during that period. At the university's library, I come across a very ancient map which shows there was some sort of building on the site in 1514 but the original could well have been earlier – much, much earlier. The boulders in the current

266

building may have formed part of an earlier construction as people generally used what was to hand, in the same way that the rocks from an old castle were often used to build houses within its walls.

It may have been chosen as a site for a stronghold due to its elevated position, as it would have been possible to see enemy invaders approaching; it would also have acted as protection during the lawlessness of the Middle Ages. Maybe the building was even commissioned by one of the Welsh princes to protect this area of the princedom.

It could have been built by a particular tribe or clan, to protect their livestock and family members from invaders and raiders of stock, produce and humans for slavery. There is no way of ever knowing for certain – but it is hugely satisfying to hypothesise on the subject. During this period, it seems Welsh life was not primitive by any means but consisted of well-organised, settled societies which were divided into three main social groups: upper class, freemen and peasants. The peasants were tied to the land and could not leave their village.

The practice of transhumance within the farming communities continued then as it had in ancient times, by moving stock from the lowland settlements in the winter to the rich upland pastures in the summer.

The upland farmers were freemen who supported the Welsh prince militarily, as well as ceding him some of their harvests. During the eleventh to thirteenth centuries, when I estimate the house was originally built, the Welsh were mainly rural – with just a few towns nearby the castle fortresses of the Welsh princes. In these towns, goods such as live sheep, fleeces and corn were brought in and all manner of household goods were traded. I try to imagine who would be living at the farm during that interesting period in history.

* * *

Gwenllian's Story

Tearfully, Alys said to her father Gryffudd, 'I don't think my mother is long for this world. I have tried most of my potions – but she weakens more each day. I believe what ails her is 'the wasting sickness' for which there is no cure.'

'Don't fret so, daughter. All we can do is keep her warm – there are some sicknesses which cannot be healed.'

She was desperately working on yet another potion and reached up for one of the many earthenware pots which held a variety of different herbs, tinctures and elixirs. Numerous bunches of herbs, such as thyme, comfrey, chamomile, lavender, borage and cumin hung down from the ceiling. She had tried everything, including a watercress tonic. She had tried an infusion of 'dail gron' – a fleshy round succulent leaf which grew on stone walls around the property. These were said to be good for bladder infections. But nothing was working – and she was in despair.

'I have failed to ease her discomfort and pain,' she said angrily, as she furiously pounded yet another concoction in her pestle and mortar. She left this to settle as they moved outside, towards the well-stocked herb garden. This had been planted many years ago by her long-dead *Hen Nain*, who had taught Alys her healing skills. She bent now to pick some fresh herbs for the potage she was preparing and carried them back to the kitchen, to add to the slowly bubbling pot.

A noise in the front courtyard told them that her brother, Dafydd, had now returned from his hunting trip and they reached the kitchen door at the same time. He placed a brace of birds on the table whilst saying, 'I saw some strangers up on the mountains this fore-noon but they were too far away to see properly. I hope they are not that group of reprobates I have heard tell of.' He turned to his father, 'Best send up more guards to the animals in the high *ffriddau* tonight.'

The night was uneventful, but in the morning their mother

began an uncontrollable coughing fit. Unable to take in a breath and despite Alys' frantic efforts, she died that morning. This was not unexpected – but the family and servants were absolutely devastated as she had been a god-fearing wife, mother and mistress to all her servants.

Alys realised that she would now be expected to take on sole responsibility for running her father's household, as well as supervision of her younger sister, Gwenllian. She resigned herself to the fact that she would not now have her own life; she was needed here. She fed the family, put fresh rushes on the floors and wove wool into yarn to make shawls, garments and blankets. She also became very skilful at making leather jerkins and shoes out of the treated animal skins.

The fortified farmstead and most of the surrounding land which the family owned, was the result of their fealty to a long-dead prince. It was situated in the foothills within the princedom of Gwynedd. It commanded an excellent defensive position, looking far out to sea and doubled as a protective fortress for their kinsmen in times of danger. Lookouts were permanently posted on the surrounding hills behind the property to warn of invaders. The house had originally been built by Gruffydd's ancestors, on the site of an ancient Celtic ruin. The massive smooth boulders of the tumbledown ruins had been re-used to build the back wall, which was impenetrably thick, and large boulders had been rolled down from the higher fields to reinforce it. This made the building defensively strong. Gruffydd had later added the upper floor, which had small, infrequent windows and narrow slits for firing arrows. In the lawless middle ages, they needed a stronghold not only to protect their animals from rustlers and invaders plundering their harvests but also to protect their women and children from being taken as slaves. Most of these invaders came on foot and horseback from across the English border but some came in from across the Irish Sea, while others were from even further afield across the North Sea.

The family lived on the upper floor, grateful for the warmth which rose from the animals below in one half of the building. There was a retractable ladder to the upper floor and once it was drawn up at dusk and at times of danger, no one ventured outdoors. The other side of the building at ground level was used for threshing and storing their corn. There was only one entrance, a door made of heavy oak, strengthened internally by drawbars, which slid back during the day into recesses in the wall. As extra security, they had built quelling holes, down which they could pour water, should the enemy try to burn down their door.

When Gwenllian was eight years of age, her father returned after being away for a few days and told her that he had arranged a marriage for her when she was older. Gwenllian was shocked. She had expected to spend her life here with her people in the house she loved. She brooded about this for a few days, then decided she would worry about it later, when it happened. She had a wilder spirit than her more docile elder sister and preferred the company and pursuits of boys rather than domesticity.

Years passed, and Gwenllian's mind was still closed to the arranged marriage, hoping that her father had forgotten about the arrangement or that her intended had been slain in battle. But it was not to be and in due time, the dreaded subject raised its head once more.

Gwenllian turned furiously on her father, 'You can't make me marry that repulsive man. He makes my skin crawl every time I see his sneering face. I warn you: he will not treat me well.' She stood there, her face contorted with anger and frustration. She was already dressed for horse riding, her waist-long hair plaited and threaded through with ribbon, to keep it off her face. She wore a long tunic with leggings, tied with braiding.

'You'll do as I tell you,' said Gruffydd in his Old Welsh – although he inwardly shuddered at the thought of the man being cruel to his daughter. 'The union will be of great advantage to our clan and will double the size of our territory.' Gwenllian just glared at him with her beautiful dark eyes and he felt a rare twinge of guilt. However, losing patience and in no mood for another argument with his headstrong daughter, he thrust his short sword into its leather scabbard and stomped out of the door of the homestead. Shortly, Gwenllian went out and mounted the horse the serf had prepared for her. She turned its head towards the hills and cantered angrily away. The feeling of freedom which riding gave her always managed to calm her down and by the time she reached the top of the track which led to the open hills, her anger had left her.

Last time Gwenllian went riding, there had been a daring daylight raid on her home. It had been a wind-free day up on the silent hills but as she made her way back down, she heard the lookouts sounding out a warning of approaching raiders. She wondered if she had time to get back to the safety of the house before the hatch was closed or whether to stay hidden somewhere safe. She decided to try to see what was happening below before making up her mind. Suddenly, she remembered there was a cave close by, where she hid her horse. Then she crawled on her belly over to a nearby ridge and lay down in the low growing shrub. She saw the raiders had almost reached the farm and that the people and stock were already safely inside. She felt safe where she was from the raiders. She watched as they milled around the settlement causing havoc, angry that their plan to surprise the occupants had been foiled. She watched as they set fire to a few of the serfs' huts and haystacks with their flamed torches. At the first sound of the warning horn, the serfs had melted into the surrounding background; they knew the safe places to hide until the raid was over. They did not want to be captured as slaves and taken to a foreign place even if they were already slaves where they now lived.

As she lay there, she noticed a crop of bilberries in the low-lying bushes next to her. Hungrily, she feasted on these while they rode around the stronghold. Suddenly she heard a twig crack behind her. Turning her head, she saw a young man approaching, holding his finger to his lips to stop her from talking, then quickly lay alongside her and looked down. 'What's happening? I heard the lookout warning as I was riding along the track over there, then saw you lying here; I wondered if you were injured or dead.' Appraisingly he said, 'Clearly, you are very much alive and have luscious blue lips!'

Gwenllian wiped her mouth with her sleeve then realised that her tunic was a probably stained now with bilberry juice. Her handmaiden was sure to scold her later. 'I didn't get back in time to get inside, so had to hide out here. Then, haughtily, 'What's your business up here anyway?'

'I am Rhodri, part of the Prince's retinue – his messenger, and on my way to deliver a report to the Head Abbot at the Abbey in Conwy. On my return, I will report this raid to the Prince and apprise him of details of the invaders.'

Gwenllian liked the look of this boy who she judged was roughly the same age as her. 'Where is your home then?'

Pointing westward to the large island, 'I hail from Mon, where my family farms and has lived for many generations. But I am no farmer, I prefer adventure.'

Lost in their conversation, they did not realise that the raiders had finally ridden away eastwards and as she rose to retrieve her horse from the cave, he walked alongside her.

'Shall I escort you back to your farm?' Gwenllian was quite smitten with him but thought it best that her father did not know about him, so declined his offer. She was pleased when he asked, 'Will we meet again?' – also aware of the growing mutual attraction.

'Meet here by this cave, one week from today, at midday,' she told him as she untied her horse's rein.

They met often during the summer and became very fond of one another. Although he was from a well-respected, noble family, she knew that nothing could come of it, due to the arranged marriage brokered by her father when she was younger – but she did not tell him of this. She was determined to enjoy her freedom while she still could.

After the raid, Gruffydd ordered roof repairs for the serfs' huts and a few days later, he was checking around the boundary of the settlement when he met up with Rhys, the overseer of his workers; 'All is well with the serfs?'

'Yes. The repairs have been carried out. There's a cockfight down by the river later but all is as it should be. What ails you, you seem in poor humour?'

'Women!' Gruffydd spat on the ground. 'My daughter to be exact. She's a stubborn vixen. Likes her own way but she will not have it on this matter. She will marry Rhoderic Mawr and that is that. Our security depends on it, we need to double our local militia, as well as gain more land for our flocks. It was all agreed years ago when she was a child. I do wish her dear mother was still here to guide her. She does not listen to her older and wiser sister. She's become way too wilful and needs taking in hand. I'm afraid the fault is mine, I have indulged her, let her have too much freedom and her own way too often – and this is the upshot,' Gruffydd said, shaking his old head sadly.

The overseer made sympathetic noises then changed the subject. 'What is to be done about this new wave of raiders?'

Gryffudd told him, 'I will be riding over to the Summer Court at Abergwyngregin to petition for a meeting with the Prince to discuss it. I have already sent a runner on ahead to request it. I will ask if he can spare more men to patrol the county boundary, to make our settlement and general area more secure. Good thing the livestock was hidden in the high pasture this last time – at least they didn't get away with much but I'm sure they will be back. The main culprit is the Earl of Chester, who leads these raiding parties. His English slaves are sometimes caught by our Prince, who then uses them as slaves himself. But some escape back over the border, taking back information about our strongholds, thus making us vulnerable. Perhaps it would be better to kill them instead.'

The Prince was a powerful warrior aristocrat. He led and was protected by his own personal military retinue, the Teulu. To counter invaders, he had ordered castles and strongholds to be built in strategic places to protect his population and their goods from these pillagers. He was considered a brave leader and revered by his countrymen. To him, honour and reputation on the battlefield were of utmost importance and at court, poets read out long eulogies, praising his gallantry, his bravery and recounting his many victories against the sworn enemies of Wales.

'Tell them to prepare the cart. Load up the goods I have put to one side for the Prince. I want an early start. Dafydd's in charge while I am away. I may be gone a few days, so I'll take Gwen with me to keep her out of mischief.' But that was a decision he was to regret for the rest of his life.

The overseer, Rhys ap Madoc was a handsome but reserved man. He displayed his status by being better dressed than the peasants – but not as well dressed as his master. While the peasants wore a coarse belted tunic, felt shoes and breeches, he wore a long cloak and flattish hat, which gave him an air of authority and distinguished him from the common man. He had loved Gwenllian since she was younger and longed to marry her himself but had never dared broach the matter with Gruffydd, who he knew had bigger, more ambitious plans for her. As the daughter of the clan leader, she was way out of Rhys' class but useful as a bartering tool for her father, who looked every bit the prosperous landowner in his leather belted jerkin and knee-high boots.

Gruffydd's family used their serfs and their captured English slaves to work their land. These lived nearby in a cluster of houses built of wattle and daub. The roofs were made of bundles of reeds packed closely together. The workers were tied to the land and were forbidden from leaving. They planted, then tended the crops, which they later harvested. They were not paid – but given food and shelter. Some of Gruffydd's harvest was given to the princely court in return for his protection. Any surplus goods, such as cattle, animal skins and fleeces, were traded in exchange for salt and iron with other clans in the area.

Gruffydd, with his black curly hair and piercingly blue eyes, was proud he could claim distant clanship to the Prince and was looking forward to meeting with him. He wondered if the Prince would be at the Summer Court when he arrived or away hunting with his hawk along the Caerneddau range. No matter, he would wait patiently for his return.

In the morning, the entourage set off early as planned. Gwenllian had cheered up, excited at going to the Court for the first time and glad to get away from the tedium of daily life. She thought excitedly that she might even see Rhodri there. Gryffudd looked sternly at her: 'Now I expect you to behave properly when we get there, as you will be representing our family, so I don't want any of your nonsense my girl.' Happy to be allowed to go, Gwen retorted, 'I will be as good as gold,' with no intention whatsoever of being so. Apart from her hill riding, she didn't get out of the family compound much and intended to make the most of this unexpected opportunity.

With the tide way out, they made their way west along the coastline on the Lafan sands, then turned inland at Aber. As the entourage finally pulled up to the entrance of the Royal Court, the guards stood and blocked them entering by crossing their long spears, then commanded, 'Stop, come no further. Identify yourselves and state your business here.'

'I am Gruffydd ap Rhys ap Morris ap Tomos,' announcing his pedigree proudly and with authority. 'I bring provisions for our noble Prince and seek an audience with him to discuss grave matters of security. He is aware of my intended visit.'

The guards conferred with their senior and eventually waved Gruffydd's wagons through, while insolently eyeing his daughter as they passed. All then had no idea just how devastating this visit would turn out to be.

At the end of a long tree-lined track, they came to a large open sunlit courtyard and pulled up. They were at the side of a large house, its walls covered in a lush green creeper and surrounded by more guards. Gruffydd ordered his drivers and henchmen, 'Stay with the cart and do not unload anything until you get your orders from me.'

Gruffydd and Gwenllian were duly escorted into the Great Hall of the house, then invited by the steward to sit at a long refectory table and offered beer, bread and cheese. They were told to make themselves comfortable and that the prince was out hunting but should be returning soon. The Prince was on a tour of his lands locally, making himself known to his people, so Gruffydd was fortunate that he did not have to travel any further to see him.

The Great Hall was impressive, with Gwenllian overawed by its size. It was a long room with a high timbered roof and wood panelled walls. These were adorned with the trophy heads of animals, caught by the Prince and his retinue. The floor was laid with large granite flagstones, covered with fresh rushes.

At one end, up on a dais, stood a long single-piece oak dining table. Running at right angles to that was another, even longer table, lined with seating benches. There were strict rules and etiquette at court about who sat where, as well as how they should behave. At the opposite end were screens, beyond which lay the prince's sleeping quarters. This was the realm of his bedchamber master and royal dresser.

Already in the Hall were other petitioners waiting to see the Prince. Gruffydd and Gwenllian socialised with them while they waited, discussing their mutual concerns. 'These raids are getting worse, the Normans and the Irish are becoming more brazen, even raiding in broad daylight,' said one clan leader who farmed land near the border. 'The Prince needs to stop this now or they will think they can get away with it. I lost forty head of cattle last week. They used to be safe up on the *ffriddau* but now...'

Gruffydd nodded in agreement and added, 'They need to be taught a lesson. We need to retaliate.'

Suddenly, as daylight was fading, there was a flurry of activity outside in the courtyard, indicating that the Prince had finally returned. His servants took the brace of partridge and the wild boar which were flung over one of the pack horses, into the Hall kitchen to be butchered.

As the Prince entered the Hall, his authority was instantly evident. Servants, retainers and guests alike all bowed deeply in homage to him. 'Please rise, fellow countrymen and ladies,' said the Prince, removing his richly embroidered leather falconry gloves. His appraising eye fell purposefully on Gwenllian, who disconcerted by his directness, looked demurely down at the floor. 'I am fatigued from riding now but later we will feast and be entertained. On the morrow, we can discuss your plights.' With that he disappeared into his own quarters behind the screens.

Servants started preparing the dining table for supper. Gwenllian watched in wonder as platter after heaving platter of food of all kinds was carried in and placed in a row, the full length of both tables. She said to her father in wonder, 'I have never seen the likes and there are foods I have never seen in my life before.'

'This is how the rich and powerful live, my daughter; they take what they want but will also share with their countrymen.'

The Prince then reappeared, splendidly dressed in red and gold. He sat at the top table along with his courtiers, while guests, retainers and entertainers sat at the longer table. The Prince's hounds curled up next to his feet. Gwenllian and her father were seated a few places down from the Prince, who occasionally stared at her, making her feel slightly uncomfortable but at the same time, flattered by the attention. Then, at the end of their table she saw Rhodri, who smiled at her. She hoped to get a chance to speak to him once the meal was over.

During this sumptuous meal, scraps and bones were thrown to the grateful hounds. Later, poets recited ancient Welsh battle victories. Harpists played hauntingly beautiful melodies, whilst the ale oiled the voices of tenors and baritones who sang of old hunting successes and lost loves. The Prince then turned to Gwenllian, who blushed furiously as he asked her, 'And what can you add to the entertainment this eve, pretty maid? Do you dance, recite poetry, sing – or all three? He smiled at his own wit while Gwenllian squirmed. Gruffydd volunteered, 'My Lord, if I may be so bold, my daughter Gwenllian has the finest soprano voice for miles around. She would be honoured to entertain you.'

The room hushed expectantly as she stood and walked nearer to the front. She usually had no qualms nor nervousness about being asked to sing but felt a little intimidated by the situation. However, she decided to sing as if she was alone, walking or riding the hills above her home. The audience was instantly captivated as she sang a story about an unrequited love and when it ended, there was rapturous applause and banging on the table, led by the Prince himself. This seemed to mark the highlight of the evening as the Prince then rose from the table, nodded briefly to his guests and headed once more for his screened rooms.

As Gwenllian was returning to her seat, she passed Rhodri, who whispered urgently, 'Meet me by the stables later, when all are asleep.' He had been doing a lot of thinking recently and had decided that he would ask her to marry him.

She sat down by her now beaming father. 'Well done, my girl, you did me proud.' The others then seemed to melt away, so on finding a small unused space near the door into the Great Hall, father and daughter lay down on their furs. Her father was quickly sound asleep, tired out by the excitement of the long, eventful day. Soon Gwenllian rose, slid back the drawbar and slipped soundlessly out of the Hall into the moonlit night.

When Gruffydd woke in the morning, Gwenllian's furs were empty. He was not too worried at first, as he assumed that she had gone for an early walk and waited for her to reappear. After a while he became anxious, as this was not like her. She was in a strange environment, so would not have wandered far. He started asking the guards if they had seen her – but none had. She was nowhere to be found.

Soon a search party was sent out and reported back that fresh horse tracks had been found near the falls, heading up the track in the direction of the lake above.

Speculation was rife that she had been kidnapped during the night. The guard at the Hall door, who admitted he had fallen asleep and conceded that she could have been taken without him being aware, was placed under guard. Gruffydd suspected he may have been bribed by another to turn a blind eye.

The Prince was horrified that such a thing should happen to guests enjoying his hospitality and vowed to do all he could to find her. The Prince was later told that one of the gate guards had gone missing but there was nothing to link this to Gwenllian's disappearance.

The search party was sent out again to follow the horse tracks further. They went up the side of the spectacularly thunderous Afon Goch waterfall and as they climbed, they felt the spray from the falls falling onto their faces. They continued to follow the tracks which passed by the feeder lake at the top. As they neared the foot of Drum mountain, the leader of the search party split them into three groups. One headed westward following the coast, one eastward along the old Roman road towards Caerhun and another went deeper south into the Caerneddau range. Visibility was excellent but they encountered nothing. One group saw a herd of inquisitive wild ponies – but their hooves did not match those found on the track.

At dusk they all returned, exhausted and empty-handed. It was a complete mystery; she had vanished into thin air. Gruffydd was in utter despair. He had sent word back to their farmstead for the overseer to search the area above the farm but to no avail.

Gruffydd spent a fitful night and decided to return home in the morning, as the Prince had assured him they would continue the search at first light and send word as soon as they had any news. Gruffydd ordered his cart be offloaded then set off for home, his plan to discuss extra border security now forgotten but probably even more necessary. He felt as if his own life had been raided and was deeply upset about Gwenllian's disappearance. He knew she was wayward but that she would not have gone away willingly.

Gruffydd searched and questioned people as he travelled along the coast on his way home but nobody had seen or heard anything of her. He was sure she was not on the coast but somewhere in the mountains.

Next day, a further search had yielded nothing. Rhys, the overseer, tentatively asked, 'If you could spare me from my duties, I will go and look for her again up in the hills.'

Without much hope but clinging to what little he had, Gruffydd nodded his agreement. She had been out for two nights now and even if she was still alive, the chances of her survival were growing slimmer. She could even be over the border by now, a slave, never to be seen again. Gruffydd was glad her dear mother was no longer here to experience this trauma nor to know this terrible loss he felt. He slumped into a chair near the hearth as a lurcher nudged his hand in comfort. Both her siblings were devastated by her disappearance and her brother also rode off to search for her.

Rhys, who knew the landscape like the back of his hand, set off immediately on his horse. He spent hours checking riverbanks, quarries, caves, ruins and called at every upland farm. He looked down crevices and searched rocky outcrops. He could not express his own feeling of loss to anyone, as no one knew of his deep feelings for her. As dusk fell and with his heart full of despair, he decided as a last resort to ride towards the ancient stone circle on the other side of the gorge. As he approached, he saw a body lying prone over one of the fallen menhirs. Can it be her? Hoping against hope, he sped up. Does she live? He dismounted and went towards her tentatively, for fear of frightening her. Her clothes were torn and bloodied, her hair matted – she was caked in mud.

Dismounting, then removing his riding gloves, he tenderly pushed her wet hair away from her eyes and said softly, 'Gwenllian, it's Rhys Madoc here.' There was no response and he thought she must be dead. Then he saw a small, weak pulse throbbing in her neck. She was only just alive and deeply unconscious. He could not leave her exposed to the night's cold while he went to fetch a cart. He had no option but to gently lift her onto his horse, cover her with his coat and begin the long walk back to the farmstead. Whatever had happened to her had been very traumatic. He noticed that her face was heavily bruised and that her nails were torn and bloodied. She must have put up quite a fight. Having been out for two nights on the mountain had worsened her already weakened condition, leaving her in a very bad way. Her nose was bloodied and swollen but that was not the only source of the blood. Her clothing was deeply stained in dark blood.

It was quite dark by the time they reached the farmstead – but he and his horse would know their way back blindfolded. Sombrely, as if carrying a very precious, fragile cargo, he carried her, still unconscious, into the house, then up the ladder to her chamber. Her overjoyed father and house servants followed.

'Leave her with the women now,' said her father, noting the loving look Rhys gave her as he lay her down gently on her pallet. 'The women will wash and care for her; you have done your duty and I will never be able to repay you enough.'

Later, Gruffydd asked the women, 'Does she wake? How is she?'

Alys said, 'We believe she has been attacked and violated – she was very bruised all over her body, her legs were covered in dried blood.'

Covering his face with his hands in despair, Gruffydd broke down and sobbed, deep racking sobs, for what she had suffered. He suspected the rogue guard had kidnapped her, taken her up the mountain, had his wicked way with her, then abandoned her, weak and helpless. 'Oh, my poor daughter, her strong spirit will be broken, if she ever recovers consciousness.'

Through the night, Gwenllian tossed and turned, and as she slowly emerged out of her deep unconsciousness, cried out to be helped. When she finally fully woke late next morning it was as if she had gone mute. When her father gently asked her, 'Who did this to you?' she did not answer; she had blocked the trauma out as it was too painful to recall and she felt too ashamed about what happened to her.

Slowly, she started taking the potions and the broth the servants brought her and she gradually regained her strength but not her former feisty disposition. She was broken, just as Gryffudd had feared. Rhys constantly asked about her recovery, confirming to Gruffydd his suspicion when he had brought her home. It was much more than a general concern; it was the concern of someone who loved deeply.

Gwenllian eventually tried to get back to her normal routine – but depression and apathy took hold. Within a few months, she was dismayed to find that she was vomiting on rising and soon the horrific realisation that she was with child caused her to have a relapse. The women, too afraid of Gruffydd's response, confided this to Rhys, having sensed his empathy for her and he agreed to break the devastating news to her father.

'I have grave news for you. Your daughter is with child.' This possibility had not even occurred to Gruffydd. Stunned, he said, 'What is to be done? We are all undone. Rhoderic Mawr will not now keep his side of the bargain to marry her if she bears the child of another.'

Apprehensively, Rhys cleared his throat and suggested, 'If you will permit me?' Gruffydd nodded his assent. 'I will ride over to Rhoderic Mawr and tell him that she has married another without your consent, so you can no longer keep your side of the bargain.' Gruffydd nodded disappointedly, 'We have no choice.'

'Also'– it was now or never – 'with your permission, I would like to offer myself as a husband to Gwenllian. I will care for her and the unborn child as if it were my own.'

Gruffydd turned to look at Madoc aghast, with dropped jaw. 'You? Marry my daughter?'

Rhys argued, 'No other would have her now – but I have always loved her and will treat her well.'

Gruffydd needed time to think about this. He stomped off, thinking Madoc was a cheeky upstart, an opportunist, but maybe he did genuinely love her. Slowly coming around to the idea, he thought it might be the only solution. She needed protection, someone to look after her, once he was no longer here.

Eventually, Gruffydd, grudgingly and unenthusiastically gave the union his blessing, while Gwenllian seemed apathetic and indifferent to the arrangement. It would take her a long time to get over her trauma, if ever – but Rhys had the patience of a saint. Her assailant was never apprehended – it was assumed he had crossed over the border.

Gwenllian never spoke with anyone about what had happened to her on the night of her abduction, even though it might have helped to apprehend her assailant. Neither did she ever sing again — her mind and spirit were irrevocably broken. She rejected the boy child she bore and it was left to Alys, the servants and Rhys to raise him, as he had promised her father he would. She never went riding in the hills as she had in the past. She did not stray far from the farmstead and only felt safe within the confines of her fortress home, built of large ice-age boulders.

Despite Rhys achieving his wish to marry Gwenllian, it was not a happy union. He was angry with her for rejecting her son, who they named Osian. So, Rhys poured all his love and energy into Osian and carefully tutored him on how to think both practically and strategically. He also schooled him in the arts of archery, sword-fighting, hunting and hawking, until he became a highly accomplished individual. When Rhys thought he was finally ready, he took Osian to the Princes Court at Aber and lobbied for an audience with him.

'Sir, please forgive my audacity in coming here today. May I introduce you to this fine, upstanding fellow. You may remember his mother, Gwenllian, sang for you on that fateful night, fifteen years ago, before she was abducted and violently attacked.' The Prince frowned and nodded his acknowledgment that he remembered the incident. Discomforted, the Prince said, 'Continue.'

'He is a very bright and able young man and would be a great asset to your Household, Sire.'

The Prince, considered this suggestion. If he agreed to take on Gwenllian's son, it would compensate in some way for what had happened to her whilst under his hospitality. 'If he is as bright as you profess him to be, I will offer to put him under the tutelage of my legal advisors. This will be on a provisional basis, depending on how quickly he learns.'

Osian, used this opportunity wisely and rose rapidly in the Royal Court. In the fullness of time, he became a valued advisor to the Prince, helping him on policy and formulating laws – his legacy to Wales.

Part 8

My grief continues to haunt me – but on balance, I have more good days than bad ones now. My heart is beginning to open up and feel some joy at little unexpected things. But I endure mostly long, empty days, my only companion Bess, who still wanders around the house looking for Sarah. As I do.

I recognised my manic phase for what it was: a desperate effort to escape my reality and fill in endless time. It has now passed and as spring arrives, my mood is lighter. Having done all the farm tasks, we tend to wander along the mountains behind the farm for hours and I find solace in their quiet beauty and wildness. A skylark rising, fluttering and singing up high lifts my heart, as does a glimpse of a heavily pregnant hare – a sign of renewal.

As spring moves into early summer, my spirit is soothed by the beautiful sunrises and sunsets. It begins to get light at about four o'clock now and the sun sets at about ten. But the time in between can be endless. When I walk, I welcome the squally rain showers, which help to wash away the sudden tears, triggered whenever I recall something Sarah had said or done, or see her face before me.

Sundays see me down at the cemetery, taking flowers I have grown in our garden. I sit by her grave and tell her what I have been up to – but she probably knows already. I cannot tell her about the boys. They are still blocking me; I cannot tell her how they are, where they are, what they are doing with their lives.

Bess and I walk wherever the fancy takes us. Sometimes I follow her, sometimes I lead. We cross boggy areas and walk the high ridges from which we can clearly see into the next valley. The old water reservoir, which used to supply the village, is an interesting feat of historic engineering with many of the workings still there. Higher still is an old quarry, where locals used to walk up to work. I wander about there and see slate heaps but wonder if at some stage they also found deposits of lead.

On another day, I discover an ancient burial cairn, high up in a desolate spot at the foot of Tal-y-Fan. I wonder who had built it, when and why. I suspect it is very ancient but as it is the only one around, I believe it was a one-off burial for a special person of an ancient tribe.

We enjoy the walk over to the famous stone circle, Meinir Hirion and the other, older, small circles just off to the right. Maybe these smaller ones were the prototype models of an earlier tribe. I sit there to soak up the atmosphere of the place and study the way it had been built and the type of stone used. Further along the range, I find the scant remnants of what may once have been a Bronze Age axe factory, now decimated by modern quarrying.

In early summer, we walk up to these circles before dawn to watch the wonderful sunrises and see the way the light filters in through the two main uprights, onto what could have been a central altar. I try to imagine the people who built these circles and consider their motivation. Given its sacred atmosphere, I believe it was a place of worship and although I'm not sure who or what they worshipped, their exactness in harnessing the light of the sun may indicate that they worshipped the sun, moon and the stars.

There are also random standing stones at various points on the hills, which I believe may have been some sort of traveller markers. This may indicate that the ancient people could have lived up on the hill tops if the climate was warmer then; or had travelled along the hills, because the coast route was impassable at high tide. I make careful notes of all these things which continue to inform my research.

Proper unbroken sleep continues to elude me. I wake at first light after an exhausted sleep of a few short hours. Without my research, my days would be unbearably long – but I am able to find plenty to do, to fill up the empty hours. At one very low point I even consider giving up the farm to return to my former life in the city – but I know in my heart that I could not bear to leave. At some point I had even darker thoughts but know that if I am to heal, it will be here in this place, not in some anonymous, overcrowded, unwelcoming urban jungle. So I stay to keep the place going, with the vague hope that my sons will return and want to live here one day; the thought that they may choose to carry on the family connection with the farm keeps me going.

During one of my very early morning meanderings on the hill just above the farm, I make a new discovery. The sun is still low in the sky but has cleared the craggy tops of the mountain to the east where it rises, creating long, early morning shadows on the ground. Away from the main path, I notice some lichen-covered boulders, among the dead, rust-coloured bracken. I think these boulders may have formed the foundations of a large hut circle, with a gap where the entrance would have been. This is an extremely exciting find. There are two long, now fallen stones, which may originally have stood upright in this gap, the entrance into the circular hut. The low stone wall may have housed small upright tree trunks, rising to a point in the centre. Turfs were then probably laid on these to form a roof. The circle itself is in a small dip in the land, not too far from the small stream which later runs through my fields below. I look at the ordnance survey map but cannot see it marked on there. Have I made a new discovery? I carefully take photographs of the site while the sunlight is still low and decide to use this material in my research. My instinct was sound when I suspected the ancients had lived close to my farm.

I sit by the stones for a long while, trying to imagine the lives of these ancient people and their reasons for choosing this site, until Bess whines for us to go. As I rise, I see the still-long morning shadows highlighting a row of ridges, possibly old crop furrows. Much of this furrowed area is covered with last year's dead bracken but the lines are clearly there. Is this where the ancients planted their seeds to grow corn or are the furrows the work of latter-day quarrymen, who cultivated potato patches here to supplement their meagre wages to feed their families?

The chance of finding such a site was a major motivation for moving here so I am thrilled about it. It will need very careful research. Through learning about the lives of these ancients, I feel that I am drawing nearer to them.

Once home, I search online for evidence of an ancient settlement in this spot and find none. I visit the university archaeological reference library for a more detailed map and discuss what I have found with specialist experts.

Then I return to the site and with the help of a colleague and proper geological surveying equipment, I map it out. Excited and enthused by my find, I write to several institutions and bodies, describing in detail the setting and hope they might be interested in funding me to do more research into this ancient site. All this takes time and it seems that in no time at all, it is autumn again. Analysing my find keeps me occupied through most of the long winter months as I wait for replies to my funding requests. Money is getting tight now, so I return to marking assignments.

Engrossed in my work one dark evening, I suddenly get a weird sensation that somebody is watching me from behind. The hairs rise on the back of my neck and I feel a sudden chill in the air. Discomforted, I slowly turn around to look by the back door and see a strange light fading away into the wall. I don't know what to make of it and wonder if it is a visitation by one of the former inhabitants. Suddenly I remember that a few months ago, I thought I had heard hobnailed boots marching up the front garden path and had envisaged soldiers. Then, more rationally, I tell myself that I must have imagined these things, pack up my paperwork and head off to bed.

Christmas comes and goes and by the time spring comes around again, I still have no word from either of my boys. They have frozen me out of their lives completely. I feel as if I don't exist. I assume they will have finished their travelling and will now be working. I make excuses for their shabby treatment of me, realising that the longer they take to contact me, the more difficult it will be for them to do so. I still try to call them occasionally, on their birthday and Christmas Day but they never answer. I leave them voicemail messages but they don't return my calls. It's time I accepted that I no longer have a family and just leave them be, as that seems to be what they want. There is just me and Bess now.

As the weather starts to warm up, I venture out to prepare the ground for the spring plantings and decide to turn over a section of land by the stream for potatoes. I had looked at this area as a possible vegetable patch previously when we first moved here – but my boys had decided to establish a vegetable patch near the barn, so I let them get on with it.

It feels good to be outside again, feeling the warmth of the sun on me. There is a feeling of renewal. From December, when the sun is low in the sky, the surrounding hills prevent the sun shining directly on the farm until February. Now that the frosts have finished, I fetch my gardening fork from the barn and set about turning over the ground. I have not been working for long when suddenly the fork hits something hard. Expecting a rock, I turn over the soil to reveal what I think is an ancient cutting tool, caked in thick mud. I take it to the stream to let the water slowly work away at the compacted soil and it reveals an ancient stone axe. Excited by this discovery, I continue to dig carefully. Within a few hours I have uncovered a cache of stone axes, cutting knives and scrapers, which would have been used by the ancients to kill, butcher and skin their animals. Having gently cleaned them, I leave them out to dry while I go to find suitable containers to store them.

I am utterly exhausted by the digging but exhilarated by my discovery. I will notify the authorities about this extraordinary find and am convinced this is clear evidence of ancient inhabitation here. It follows that there should be evidence of a dwelling or dwellings nearby. But try as I might, I fail to find anything. Maybe there was once but perhaps the stones have long since been used to build the stone wall nearby, which divides my two fields, or even used for the original dwelling where my house is now. Bursting with my news, I call my sons but as usual, they do not answer my calls. Again, I feel deflated. I have so much stuff now stored up in me that I want to share with them. I long to tell them about my finds, how the farm is, my roundhouse discovery – as well as how much I miss them, every single, achingly lonely day. The tears spring up quickly again, reminding me once more of my shattering losses.

However, thinking positively, I quickly make myself put the sadness to one side and allow myself to be inspired by my findings. I wonder whether the tools belonged to the original inhabitants of this valley or to some other transient group travelling through. I compare mine with those I found near the axe factory and see similarities.

Later, I dismiss the theory of a transient nomadic group, reasoning that they would not have gone to all the trouble of building roundhouses nor used so many tools. When these people came, they came to stay.

* * *

The Ancients' Arrival

Far back in the mists of time, eons before humans inhabited this once glacial, coastal valley, animals had roamed peacefully for thousands of years. Then one day, a ragged group of travellers, now way past exhaustion, arrived. The animal skins they wore were in tatters, their hair matted, their skin ingrained with dirt. Walking determinedly westward along the coast, they rounded the massive rocky headland and entered a vast and beautiful sandy bay. Behind it lay a deeply wooded valley, protected by a semi-circle of hills and further behind these, stood majestic, snow-capped mountains.

At the opposite end of the bay was an equally impressive headland – thereby forming the two ends of a semi-circle. The tide was way out now but this vast expanse of pristine sand would be hidden once more on its return. Feeling the warm sand oozing up between their toes and a soft sea breeze gently playing on their faces, their leader, Tor, scanned the valley for signs of human habitation. 'There doesn't seem to be anyone living here but we will have to travel inland to be sure.'

Walking forward onto harder sand, the receding tide had formed wave-like ridges which dug into their sore and tender feet, already ravaged by their epic journey.

'Is this our new home?' said Jana one of his twin daughters. During their long, arduous and often dangerous journey, they had sought somewhere safe and secure to live. They had endured prolonged, extreme hardship, often coming close to starvation – but they had forced their often-emaciated bodies to keep going. But now, with the seascape behind them and the landscape in front, the hardship lines etched on their faces slowly melted away, replaced by relieved, thankful smiles.

Being skilled trackers had ensured their safety and continued existence during their dangerous journey. Each day as the sun went down, they rested and ate, then set off again in that first dull glimmer of light which appears well before sunrise. Initially they had trudged on relentlessly, to put a vast distance between themselves and their former tribe.

This horseshoe-shaped valley seemed to beckon them to enter – to offer sanctuary. Would this be their safe, settled future and spiritual home? 'We have seen no other people for many moons,' said her sister Juno, 'No signs that people have settled this far west.'

'Of course, we cannot be sure no-one is here, until we carry out a survey of the area, but any inhabitants would surely have challenged us by now. They would see our dark forms moving along the beach if they had been watching from the hills,' said Tor.

Suddenly, he spotted an opening in the trees on the shoreline – an animal track running alongside the river which spilled out onto the sands. 'We'll follow this river up into the surrounding hilltops, from where we can scan the valley below.'

The river ran into a pool, formed naturally by a sandbank. 'If we use these smooth, rounded pebbles to build a wall for a fish-trap, it would provide a plentiful supply of fish,' said Jon.' These granite pebbles were in every conceivable shade of purple, lilac, blue, white and grey and ranged from small to very large. But these people had no knowledge yet of the weather patterns in the area; of the sudden violent storms in the mountains and the north-westerly winds which pummelled the sea and made the waves mountainous. They would need to learn quickly if they were to survive and thrive. If they stayed here, they knew they would have to spend the summer building up stores for the as yet unknown winter conditions.

Attached to their long spears using a paste of honey and tree resin, were barb-like hooks carved out of a hard, black stone. These they used to spear fish. Their other longer-handled spears also had the sharp pointed blades and were used to protect them from danger and to kill animals for food.

Surreptitiously, they had left their former tribal home and travelled resolutely north-west for many, many moons. They had learned of a plot by the leaders to sacrifice Tor's twin daughter, Jana and Juno, to their Gods. Tor already knew he was considered a troublemaker, as he frequently questioned their decision-making. He had realised that he and his family group would not be safe if they remained there. But now, here they were safe. He felt a surge of hope and well-being as he looked upwards to the valley in front of them. They would establish their own tribe and create a fair society, in which people were equal and the vulnerable protected, unlike their old one, where the few had procured power for themselves through manipulation, guile, superstition and mystification. They had told the tribe that the Gods were angry with them, as the herds of wild animals which roamed the plains had become scarce - and that sacrifices must be made to appease them.

* * *

Very early, one morning, Tor had indicated to his group they were leaving. In the ghostly, misty pre-dawn light, whilst others slept off the excesses of the night before, they picked up their few possessions and quietly stole away unobserved. Tor's mate Lal, his twin daughters, his best friend Jon with his mate, Soo, and Tor's elderly mother, a healer, silently walked out into the obscurity of a swirling early morning river mist. This ensured they were almost instantly invisible from the camp. Tor assumed it would be many hours before they were missed and hoped they would not be followed but they could not be certain how vengeful the leaders would feel, having lost their potential sacrificial offerings. However, despite their belief that they left unobserved, one sleepy person did notice but for his own reasons, chose not to raise the alarm.

They carried dried strips of meat with them, which they ate while walking and drank from their animal-stomach water carriers, careful to leave no tracks. They continued their relentless journey until well after sunset each day. They then rested for a few hours, wrapped in their animal skins against the chill of the night and set off once more before first light. This became the daily pattern of their days.

After many moons, they came across a distressed couple. Their facial features and language were different – but they communicated their needs well enough. She, Baa, was with child and through gestures, the male, Zor, begged to be allowed to join their group. Given the female's evident vulnerability, the group agreed. Tor's mother saw that Baa still had many months before her baby was due, so she would not impede their progress.

Despite Tor's sharp intellect, he was tolerant with those less so and kindly towards all. He exuded natural authority and was physically impressive. Taller than the average male, he had black hair, blue eyes and a swarthy complexion, indicating he originated from a southern European region. As a young man, he had been fascinated by the tales told by lone travellers and given the opportunity, had questioned them intently. He was told that few had ventured to a distant land mass far to the north, separated from the mainland by water. His plan was to head for this coast and one day they finally smelt and heard the crashing waves of the sea. As they walked over the tops of some sand dunes, they saw the sea and could just make out the mysterious land to the north on the other side.

They built strong rafts and Tor studied the ebb and flow of the tide. He decided to wait for not only a very calm sea but also an ebb tide. When the conditions were at last right, they dragged the rafts far out to the water's edge and climbed aboard in their allotted space, then plunged their paddles through the water with all the energy the rowers could muster. When they were well clear of the shore, they dropped to a steadier speed and continued like this for many hours, reaching the other side just before nightfall. Elated but exhausted, they did not notice the tiny distant speck in the water behind them but collapsed onto the beach and fell asleep. Next morning, without a backward glance, they set off on the next leg of their journey, which was to take many more moons.

Tor's mate, Lal, was shorter in stature and fairer. She was in her prime; fit and healthy, despite the privations of the journey, which had made the muscles of her body sinewy and taut. Lal's brother, Jon, and Tor had been inseparable since they were young boys and considered themselves brothers. They had learned to hunt together but Tor had always been the leader.

Jana had a strong, adventurous personality and was daring and fearless. She had spent her formative years hunting with the tribe's boys rather than staying near the camp with the women. She enjoyed hunting with a sling, which she learned to use with deadly accuracy and helped to keep the group fed. Her sister, Juno, who was quieter and more reflective, was learning the healing skills from her grandmother.

After rounding the headland, as had happened so often on their momentous journey, hunger gnawed away at their insides awaiting satiation – but safety always came first. They walked silently in a single file along the wooded animal path, alert to possible dangers. Moving furtively, spears at the ready, they passed through sun-dappled glades and heard the scuttling of small creatures in the undergrowth next to them.

On entering a clearing, they spied a herd of small deer. Tor raised his hand and the group instinctively froze mid-step while he drew back his spear and carefully aimed. It found its mark and a deer dropped to the ground, while the other animals scattered all around in panic and fear, their idyllic existence shattered. Tor said, 'Although this will provide food for us for the next few days, predatory animals could soon pick up the blood scent of the dead animal, so let's quickly unpack our skinning and cutting tools and butcher it. The animal's coat will be a welcome addition to our depleted skins and its bones will make good cooking utensils or tools, once dried and hardened.'

Others dug a shallow pit and gathered firewood from a plentiful supply of dead wood lying about on the ground from previous storms. Striking two flint stones together they started a fire in a bundle of dead grass and fine kindling. Once the wood had turned into coals, they placed the strips of meat to cook and enjoyed their first meal in the valley. By then, it was too late to travel further that day, so they pitched their crude tents, which were skins laid across their spears. Suddenly, a cool breeze picked up with the turn of the tide, so they built up the fire and sat around it, talking about their good fortune in finding this beautiful, empty place. Darkness eventually fell. Tor kept watch for a few hours while the others slept a deep, exhausted sleep.

At first light, to a cacophony of chattering birdsong, the group broke camp. They left the foothills behind and continued tracking upwards along the river, which wound its way to the higher hills. Occasionally they looked back to scan the valley below for any sign of human habitation but there was nothing to see.

The group looked at the granite-bouldered river which higher up was flanked on both sides by tall pine trees. The ground was carpeted with thick, verdant mosses and low-lying fan ferns. Dappled light from the low, early morning sun filtered in between the branches, creating a magical flickering effect on the surface of the water. Birds with silvery blue wings and orange breasts dived, orange beak first, into the deep dark pools; little reddish creatures with bushy tails scampered up the tall tree trunks and beautiful, long gossamer-winged insects hovered just above the surface of the water. Long-beaked birds pecked noisily away at the tree-bark, searching for insects. As they climbed, they looked down into the glen and saw where, over time, the force of the water had gouged out earth and stones until only the large, immovable boulders remained; where the land dropped suddenly, magnificent waterfalls fell into a black cauldron of frothy, peaty water.

Higher up on open grassland, the river narrowed as it neared its source. No trees grew here but grasses, heathers and low scrubby bilberry bushes grew in abundance. Any tree which did manage to seed and sprout was eaten by grazing animals, which devoured anything tender and succulent.

The brackishness of the water indicated it had recently travelled through a peaty bog area. Its rich, dark amber colour was even more noticeable when it cascaded over smooth boulders, blackened by the endless water – but where stones were exposed to the air, they were covered with luxuriantly green, springy, velvety mosses.

Soon, they came to a short waterfall. Large boulders some way in front of the waterfall had caused the water to dam, creating a deep, dark, fathomless pool. Tor said, 'We'll stop here, eat and wash.'

They plunged into the pool to rinse off the ingrained dirt of their epic journey. They felt exhilarated by both the iciness of the water and their new-found freedom. After, lying on the grassy bank by the pool, the breeze and sun dried them and a deep contentment spread through the group.

Setting off once more, the land now sloped steeply upwards. Tor's mother, who was struggling to keep up said, 'I can feel the pull on my pace now.' While everyone was deep in their own thoughts, they came silently over a small rise, disturbing a herd of wild mountain ponies. These scattered in all directions – but one mare was left behind. Prostrate on the ground and struggling to rise, her eyes were wide open with fear and pain. Copious blood around her hind legs indicated she was in the throes of giving birth - but the strength of the labour pains and her predicament prevented her escape.

Tor predicted, 'This may not last the night, predators will probably attack it.'

Juno, horrified by the thought of this helpless animal being ripped apart by wild cats or wolves, suggested, 'Why don't we help it to birth, then we might keep them both and tame them to be useful? It's obviously not a dangerous nor aggressive animal. Maa, please help me to get the foal out; it must be the same as a human being born.'

Maa was 'old school.' She could not see the point in wasting precious medicines on animals only good for eating. She reluctantly agreed to help but refused to touch it herself. As the group gathered around, Maa said to Juno, 'First try to see how far forward the birth is and get this down its throat,' handing her a concoction from her collection of herbs she had quickly mixed with water. 'I'll help,' said Jana. Between them, they coaxed the animal to swallow the draught. Within a few minutes, it visibly relaxed. Maa told Jana, 'Hold the animal's head and try to soothe it.'

Because the foal seemed to have become stuck and its legs were coming out first, Maa suggested, 'Tie thin strips of animal skins around the foal's legs and gently begin to pull, using the rhythm of the mare's contractions as a guide.' Suddenly it came out in a slithering rush, encased in a thin film of clear but bloodied membrane. Visibly repulsed, Maa instructed, 'Clear the stuff away from its nostrils and eyes.'

Revealed was a beautiful, mahogany coloured male, with a white mark down its nose and although weak from the hard labour, it was very much alive. Juno said, 'Get the foal to his mother's teats to suckle.' The mare was slowing coming around from the relaxant and was turning her head to her foal, her raspy tongue trying to lick it clean of birth matter. This stimulated the foal to move and soon it was trying to stand up on its spindly legs – an innate mechanism that caused a new-born to be quickly mobile, to prevent it being eaten by predators. It fell over at the first few clumsy attempts, which caused great amusement, then eventually managed to stay upright. Having put a rope around its neck, Jana now coaxed the mare into a standing position, allowing the foal to suckle more easily.

Tor was in awe of his daughters as they worked together as a team. He was impressed how Juno had taken control of the situation. She seemed to care for these animals while Jana was keen on the idea of training them to do her bidding.

Jana led the mare to the stream to drink and gently rinsed the blood off. It would not try to run off while the foal was around. She studied the foal, which had followed its mother. She could not believe how beautiful he was. She stroked both and spoke gently to them, to get them used to her. She plaited leather head harnesses with which she could tie ropes to tether them, then informed the group, 'From now on, one of us will always have to stay on guard over them, especially through the hours of darkness, until we build an enclosure. I will try to train them to carry things for us.' The group would agree to anything which made their lives easier.

Having concluded that the valley was not inhabited, they chose a site to erect a round-hut in a small dip next to a tributary of the stream they had followed. They used medium-sized boulders, which lay scattered around on the ground, to build a small round wall. During the previous millennia, these boulders had been ground smooth and scored, under the heavy frozen blanket of a glacier, as it made its way inexorably down the valley. Once the climate warmed, the glacier had retreated, leaving these boulders exposed – looking absurd and abandoned on the open plain.

'This shelter must be strong enough to protect us during the winter,' said Tor. 'We don't know what it will be like here. Once the pony pen is built, we need to fell some of the small pine trees we passed on our way here, so we can fit them upright from the wall to the centre, to form a roof frame. We can then cover the frame with turfs.'

As it was a warm night, they slept under the stars, close to the site of their prospective new home. Jana built up the fire and slept close to the mare and foal. The mare occasionally, half-heartedly tugged at her rope to get away from the humans but knew she could not leave behind her foal, also tied. The night was uneventful but they knew their luck might not last. The ponies needed a wooden enclosure to protect them, so they would set about felling the small pines with their cutting tools to form a stockade.

Exhausted by their work and with the ponies safely tethered, they sat around the fire. Jana had downed a large hare with her sling and they waited hungrily for it to roast on the spit above the coals. It was a beautiful evening and as the sun slowly started to sink, they watched the sky become streaked in a spectacular display of orange, pink, cerise and deep blood reds. Soon the dramatic gunmetal clouds above became spectacularly edged with a bright silvery lining.

* * *

A few weeks later, after exploring the area alone, Tor told them, 'I've found a type of rock which makes excellent axe heads and is easy to knap. I've also found a large cave near the rocky outcrop where we first entered the valley. It is well hidden and has a wide ledge with a large overhanging rock. At the back of the ledge, there is a smallish entrance into the cave. It seems to go quite deep into the mountain. From the entrance, I could look down onto the whole of the valley floor and the length of the beach and out over the sea. It would be easy to see if anybody enters the valley from there or if anyone is travelling along the mountain ridge above. Maybe we should live there when the weather gets cold.' Zor, the comedian of the group, responded with a wry smile – 'Pity we didn't find this cave when we first got here, we could have saved ourselves a lot of hard work building the hut!'

'This will be big enough for us all to stay in through the winter,' said Maa next day, clapping her hands gleefully as she entered the cave; she was tired of climbing up and down mountains. The cave offered security and shelter from the weather and it was also close to the shore for food. They set about clearing the inside, allotting themselves sleeping areas. There was plenty of space to store food to survive the winter in the cave but they decided they would spend their summers up at the round-hut where the ponies could graze on the long grasses.

The twins roamed the hills alone and together, exploring and finding new secret places unknown to the others. They swam in the deep dark pool, discovered when they first arrived in the valley. They took the ponies with them and tethered, let them graze lazily on the sweet mountain grasses. Other days they spent underneath a beautiful waterfall Jon had found. While drying off in the dappled sunlight after a swim in the waterfall's deep pool, Jana wondered how a place of such incredible perfection had been formed.

Within a few months, the foal was happy to carry small amounts in the paniers Jana had woven, placed on its back. She used him to carry the fruits, berries, fungi and nuts she collected, as well as an occasional small deer. Sometimes she felt she was being watched but thought that this could not be possible. Presently she shared this feeling with her father, who confirmed that occasionally he sensed the same, as he had on their journey.

Maa and Juno collected plants, herbs and spices and raided beehives dripping with honey, delicious to eat and useful in the preparation of medicines – and glue for fixing their spear heads. They knew a small smoky fire was the best way to make the bees sleepy while they raided their honeycombs.

Gradually the days grew colder. They closed the hut for the winter and moved to the cave. The ponies were safely ensconced in the nearby enclosure Zor had prepared. The foal settled but the mare would still try to escape back to her herd, given the opportunity.

Tor announced, 'Now we will build a fish trap. As soon as the tide begins to go out, we will start to build a wall across where the pool empties.' They were still building when the sea came back in and lapped around their ankles. Once finished, they stood back to admire their handiwork.

Jana went out at the next low tide to see if fish had been caught but was disappointed, as the wall had been breached. It was hastily repaired and made stronger. The next time, she rushed back to the cave, her woven basket full of fish. 'The wall has stood. I have flat ones with their face on the side, some silvery ones, a large vicious-looking eel and many I have never seen before.' The group enjoyed a fish feast that day, grilled on coals, and the trap provided them with a regular food supply through the winter months.

When weather permitted, they cleared a gently sloping area not too far below the cave, digging out bushes, cutting trees and burning stumps. All were involved apart from Baa and Maa, who prepared meals for the workers and collected firewood. The rest was set on fire to clear it and because they knew that plant growth was better where there had previously been a fire.

One day as they returned to the cave, they heard ear-piercing screams echoing around the walls of the cave well before they got there. Wringing her hands, Maa needlessly stated, 'Baa's baby has started. It's been going on for hours. She's very close now but the baby seems stuck. I couldn't fetch you because I couldn't leave her. My hands aren't strong enough and my fingers too weak to turn the baby.' Realising the urgency, Juno said confidently, 'I will do it.' So the men then melted away from the cave area, claiming other jobs which urgently needed doing.

'I've managed to turn the baby, but I don't think Baa has much strength left to push.' Later a subdued group huddled around the fire at the cave's entrance. Then, in the middle of one last blood-curdling scream, the baby's head finally appeared. With one final push, the baby slithered out, covered in a mixture of blood and a white waxy substance, onto the animal skins on the cave floor. Once its mouth and nose had been cleared of mucus, Maa placed the baby at Baa's breast to suckle. Juno, exhausted but pleased with herself announced, 'We have a healthy baby girl.'

There was jubilation. 'This is the birth of the first baby to our new tribe,' Tor declared. 'A good omen that the tribe will flourish and grow.' They discussed a name for the first cave baby. Suggestions were put forward but Ogof was finally agreed on and a celebration meal prepared.

Jana often took the foal onto the wide-open spaces on the sands. One day she decided to slide onto its back, reasoning that if it could carry goods, it could carry her. Surprised, the foal took off at a very fast gallop. Jana, jolted by the speed, leaned forward to grab his mane and pressed her legs tight against his flanks. After riding a long way, Jana was eventually thrown but not hurt. Exhilarated by the ride, she was determined to do it again soon. The pony soon stopped running and came back to where Jana sat on the sand getting her breath back. In time, the foal accepted her riding him, while Jana became more and more skilled at getting the animal do her bidding.

Following a very bad autumnal storm which had blown in during the night, Jana made her way down to the windy beach with the pony. These storms, from the north-west, were quite spectacular. The white-topped waves were enormous and crashed relentlessly onto the beach, creating a frothy yellowish foam, which was picked up then blown aimlessly along the shoreline. The wind was sometimes so strong that it picked up water and carried it in sheets of spray across the surface of the sea.

Jana and the pony ambled slowly along the tide line, engrossed in looking at the seaweed, wood debris and tiny delicate shells which littered the sand, picking up anything of interest. Looking up, she spotted a dark shape, bobbing about on the surf line. Having never seen anything like it before, she watched as it was bounced about and when it tipped sideways, saw there was something inside. The wind was blowing strongly towards the land and she wondered if she could try to get close to it or fetch the others. If the wind changed direction, it would be blown back out to sea. She feared the power of the sea but nevertheless decided to try. She tied one end of a long rope to her pony, the other around her waist, then started wading out towards it through the icy cold water. She needed to act quickly to be safe; some sands could suck you under, so she took great care where she stepped. As water reached the tops of her legs, she was suddenly walking up a slope and realised she was on a sandbank. The object was the shape of half an eggshell, covered in animal skins and other material she did not recognise. She saw a man lying curled up inside, so stretched to grasp the edge and pulled it towards her then turned and waded back towards the shore, towing it behind her. When she stepped off the sandbank, she was shocked to find that the water now reached her armpits. She commanded the pony to pull and with his help, managed to reach the safety of the beach. Jana knew she could have drowned.

Having seen her from the cave, Tor and Jon were running along the beach towards her with the others some way behind. She looked up when Tor shouted, 'That was a stupid thing to do, how could you take such a risk?' – more from relief than real anger. She knew she deserved his admonishment but was exhilarated by her own daring. As she lay on the sand on her back, recovering her breath, the others examined the object.

A man, either unconscious or dead, lay curled up inside. Reluctant to touch him, Jon poked him gingerly with his spear but got no reaction. 'I wonder where he has come from and how long he has been in the floating object......and why he was in it?' Tor remarked, 'He doesn't look like us. Is he dead or alive? Will he be dangerous?' They did not want to risk their Utopia by taking in someone aggressive. His body was curled around two bundles, tied up in skins. Tor said to Jon, 'Let's see what's in those.' They pulled one out, untied it and saw that it held some unfamiliar working tools made from a hard, cold material. They had an even bigger surprise when Jon opened the second bundle. It was an assortment of beautiful body adornments, made from a shiny yellow material similar to what they had recently found in their stream. The designs were unlike anything they had ever seen and wondered why this man possessed them. Sensing trouble, Jon quickly closed up the bundle and put it to one side.

Maa, last to arrive, elbowed the others aside: 'Let me check his pulse. Mmm. He's alive but too thin and weak to survive.' As with the pony, Jana and Juno begged their grandmother to help make him live. They gave him some water – but he choked on it, which at least confirmed he was alive. Reluctantly, Tor said, 'Let's lift him onto the pony's carrier and take him back to the cave.' He was intrigued by the man and wondered what his story was. The floating object could be useful, so they pulled it further up the beach and placed heavy stones in it. Tor picked up the bundle with the tools in, then quietly instructed Jon to take the other bundle and bury it somewhere; he did not want the group to start arguing over the ornaments. He told him to also bury the yellow metal found in the stream along with it. Jon split off from the group to bury the hoard while Tor and the rest followed the pony.

Jon buried them in the beautiful little glade where they had camped on the first night in the valley. Strangely, the subject of the adornments was never raised again but by contrast the tools were to prove useful and in great demand.

After carrying the man into the cave, they removed his wet skins; they placed him by a low fire on a bed of freshly cut grass and covered him with dry animal skins. Maa prepared a draught of herbs, which Juna drip-fed into his mouth but nobody held out much hope of him surviving.

Hours, then days passed, as he tossed and turned in his unconscious delirium. He moaned and cried out but they could not understand his words. Jana often sat by his side to watch and soothe him, talking to him as she would her ponies. She longed for him to live, more than she had longed for anything before but did not understand why. Maybe it was his vulnerability. She studied his features, different from that of her group. His skin was darker and his hair was blacker.

When he eventually opened his thick, black-lashed, startlingly blue eyes, it was Jana who saw the instinctive fear. 'Shoosh....' she said as he tried to rise in his panic. His body was too weak to resist her reassuring insistence that he lie back down. He seemed frustrated that he could not understand the words she spoke, nor could he remember who he was. He seemed to have no memory of how he had come to this place nor what had happened to him. They had chosen not to reveal to him how they had found him, nor about his possessions; gradually he came to accept his life was here now with them, where he felt safe.

'What shall we call him?' said Jana when he was strong enough to sit up. Soo replied, 'What about Erg? – the man with no memory,' and that is what he became known as. They told him their names and the names they used for various objects. Although he nodded and seemed to understand, he made no attempt to repeat the words. Jana wondered why this was the case, as she had heard him talk in his sleep. He seemed happy spending time with Jana and did not seem surprised that animals did her bidding.

The first time he eventually spoke was while out hunting with Jana, who was tracking a fat grouse. Realising that she was headed for a dangerous boggy area, he shouted, 'Stop!' Astonished to hear him call out, she forgot about the bird, happy he had finally spoken.

In time, he was accepted as one of them. He never spoke of his past nor did he ask about his bundles. They thought he was probably so shocked by what had happened to him or at what he may have done, that he had blocked out his memory, as it was too painful to remember. Or he may have chosen to keep quiet, knowing he had done something very wicked and would be rejected by the group.

Eventually, their shared passion for the ponies drew him and Jana closer and Tor could see their attachment forming. Some months later, Erg suggested they try to capture ibex and aurochs to rear for food. This had a mixed reaction – but Jana reminded them they had captured the ponies. They did eventually manage to capture some and used them for breeding, making them less dependent on hunting.

* * *

Rys woke suddenly in the cold misty light of pre-dawn, sensing quiet movement close by. Everybody around him seemed fast asleep, wrapped in their animal skins – but he saw a handful of people outlined in the blurriness, directly across from where he lay. They seemed to be slowly moving away from the main camp so were not there to attack. His curiosity aroused and his chance to go back to sleep gone, he rose; grabbing his spear and water carrier, he decided to follow at a distance. The group seemed to consist of five adults and two older children. The swirling mists began lifting as they moved further from the river and he was shocked to realise it was the family of his long-time friends, the twins. They seemed to be carrying all their basic possessions with them. Then he remembered the half-heard rumours about sacrifices and knew how fiercely protective Tor was of his daughters. He did not want the girls to leave; they were like sisters but he didn't want them to be in danger either. More recently, he had begun to realise that the feelings he had for Jana were more than just friendship.

As the sun rose, it began to burn off the river mists, making Rys drop further back to keep cover. He felt real sadness at the thought of losing his friends and wondered what he should do. If he returned to the camp to raise the alarm, that would only make matters worse. He could return and say nothing but the other more appealing alternative was to follow them. Would they allow him to join them? He knew his own family would not miss him. His older brother, his father's favourite, had made it abundantly clear he hated him and took every opportunity to be unpleasant to him. What did he have to lose, or rather, what did he have to stay for? He craved adventure away from the usual routine. After all, he reasoned, he would soon be making his own way in the world anyway. He decided to follow them. He dared not go back to the camp to pick up more belongings, as others may be awake and stirring by now. He had his spear, catapult in his belt, water carrier on a strap on his shoulder and the skin he had wrapped around him on waking. What he had would have to suffice.

Rys tracked them throughout the day. They did not stop; walking steadily, he assumed to allow Maa to keep up. By mid-afternoon he felt light-headed, having not eaten that day but was determined not to let them out of his sight. He drank deeply from his water carrier to keep himself going.

They finally stopped to rest for the night as daylight faded, so he settled down to wait. He dared not light a fire but knew he must eat soon or would not be able to continue. He had topped up his water carrier in a small stream he crossed earlier. So he sat very still in a small clearing, catapult in hand, waiting for small creatures to cross his path. There were plenty of animals which came out at dusk when they thought they were safe from airborne predators, so he hoped it was only a matter of time. He had to eat the small rabbit he killed raw – but it was better than being hungry. He was afraid to fall too deeply asleep and miss them setting off at first light, so only allowed himself a few fitful sleeps.

After many days of travel, it was clear that they were not returning. Rys thought Tor had seen him once or twice, so dropped back further but it gradually became easier to follow them now they were no longer so careful about covering their tracks.

And so the group, and separately Rys, continued to travel doggedly northwards. The group had a few skirmishes along the way with wild animals and other humans. Rys watched them fording streams and bravely crossing large rivers, then followed. On reaching a major channel he had watched as they built large rafts to get across. He built a small one on which he could follow. He had to wait a while before setting off and then keep his distance, so he would not be seen by them. He only just made it, his raft starting to come apart as he neared the shore. They did not notice Rys coming ashore a little way east of them. They rested for a few days after this momentous crossing. Rys was also glad of the rest and stocked up on food for the next part of the journey, as it did not look as if they intended to stop any time soon.

The weather was getting warmer, the days longer, so they travelled further every passing day. Finally, having crossed the next land mass, they reached the north-west coast. They crossed a large tidal river estuary at low tide then walked westward along the coastline. As they rounded a large rocky headland which jutted out towards the sea, they suddenly stopped in their tracks. Rys could not see the reason for this and wondered if they were facing more danger. He had to bide his time until he was able to make his way around the headland. Then he saw them turn inwards towards a wooded valley, walking along the banks of the river which spilt out onto the large bay. One by one they disappeared from his sight under cover of the trees.

Rys, not knowing whether this valley was their final destination, sought a secret place to stay nearby, as he could not yet pluck up the courage to reveal himself. He found a natural hideaway on the opposite side of the large glen. Nearby was a small lake for drinking and washing, and from his vantage point he was able to watch them building their round-hut. He longed to help and be part of their activity. He also longed to speak to Jana when he found her away from the others. But he was too afraid of what Tor would say, once he realised Rys had followed and been spying on them. Having hidden himself away from them for so long, it was now difficult to break the habit. However, one day, when Jana was on her own, his subterfuge was finally exposed.

* * *

They survived the winter and as spring approached, they were glad to see signs of the new growing season. Early buds and blossom appeared on trees and delicate flowers began to push themselves up through the soil. It was time to leave their winter cave and return to the summer hut, where the ponies could graze on the new tender grasses. Zor stayed behind for now with the breeding animals, until they had built a larger enclosure near the summer hut.

Jana had earlier been to check the hut was still habitable. 'I'm sure somebody has been living in our hut but there's nobody there now.' Tor replied, 'I think we should tell the others of our suspicions so they can be vigilant. But I don't think there is any real risk to us, as something would have happened before now.'

Making the most of the warm weather, they prepared rows to plant their seeds. Later, they sat around the fire, watching the beauty of the evening sky again, glad to be back in the hills. As the sun sank slowly into the sea, the sky lit up in the most indescribably beautiful colours. They knew now they never wanted to leave this glorious place, with every sunset different from the night before.

As well as an enclosure for their now domesticated animals, they built a wooden-staked enclosure to protect the plants, high enough to keep out most predators. Soon the tender green shoots began to thrive in the rich soil, warmed by the sun and fed by the light summer rain showers which blew in from the sea.

After being up in the summer camp for a few days, the mare began to get restless. Neighing and pulling at her ties, she finally broke free and cantered away. Jana was distraught at losing her. She tracked her down after a few days to her old herd, some distance away. Once Jana recognised her, she called out to her. The mare looked up but chose to ignore her. Wondering what she should do, she sat on a large boulder and observed them. The mare became restless, walked towards a stallion, then turned her back on him. Another stallion approached her, then both stallions got up on their hind legs to confront each other, spurning and biting. Jana watched, mesmerised by this strange behaviour which eventually culminated in one of the stallions mating with Jana's mare. Once it was over, Jana gently approached the mare again and she voluntarily walked back towards her. She praised her for coming to her, then looped a rope through the mare's halter and began to lead her back towards the hut.

As they walked away, Jana suddenly heard a thunderous galloping coming behind her at tremendous speed. She turned around and saw a very wild looking stallion bearing down on her, eyes ablaze. Uncharacteristically terrified, Jana froze to the spot. Out of the corner of her eye, she saw a figure running in from the side, intent on diverting the stallion, brandishing a spear and shouting. Close to her ear, she heard the swishing sound of a spear being thrown. It hit the ground just behind her, causing the rampaging pony to veer away. After calming down the mare, Jana, herself very shaken by the incident, turned to look at this person who had saved her life and saw a man who was vaguely familiar. As she studied him, he asked, head to one side, 'Don't you remember your old friend then?'

Realisation dawned. Jana recognised the face she had known when it belonged to a boy. 'It's you, Rys, what are you doing here?' His face was the same but different. It had lost its childish roundness and was more angulated. He had high hollowed-out cheekbones – but the soulful hazel-coloured eyes were still the same they had always been, although they now contained a new depth. 'Did you follow us right from the beginning?' Rys nodded, his head bowed down, ready for the tongue-lashing he expected. 'But what have you been doing since we have been in the valley?'

The deprivation of surviving alone during the trek and since, had sculpted his body into a swift, tightly muscled, efficient machine. He looked straight at her and said wearily, 'It's a very, very long story.'

'Well, you must come back to the camp. Don't worry, you will be quite safe from my father.' But Rys was still wary.

The stallion had now lost interest and moved away from the mare to graze. As they walked, Jana said, 'We suspected we were being followed and that there were others living here but had never actually seen anyone. Why didn't you just show yourself sooner?'

'I argued long and hard with myself about it but I was afraid your father would send me away or worse; the longer I left it, the harder it became. I have been very lonely and desperate at times. I knew I could never go back to the old tribe, even if I could ever find my way there. They probably think I left with you anyway because I disappeared at the same time. No-one will even care by now. I like the freedom here and have built myself a secret hideout. I had to learn a great many things just to survive. I love this place now and don't ever want to leave.' Jana had never heard Rys saying so much all at one time. He was obviously making up for lost time.

As they neared the camp, the inhabitants stopped what they were doing one by one and stared into the distance, from where two figures and a pony were approaching. Soon they recognised Jana bringing back the mare but who was the other figure? Only when closer did Juno recognise their old playmate, Rys. All were astonished.

Tor realised that it had been Rys watching them and sternly ordered him to tell his story from the beginning. Noting the tone of her father's voice, Jana interjected, 'Rys saved my life. When I was taking the mare from the herd, a stallion came right at me and it was only Rys' quick thinking that diverted it.' Now grudgingly in his debt, her father softened his attitude and encouraged him to begin.

'When I woke up on that morning, I saw people leaving. Being curious about who it was, I decided to follow, then realised it was your family. Soon I had gone too far to turn back; the others would have made me tell them which way you had gone. I guessed you left because of the risk to the girls. I had heard the rumours about what the leaders were plotting. So I decided to keep on following you as I had nothing to go back for. My step-father and step-brother hated me and made my life miserable.' Tor acknowledged that his stepfather was a very unpleasant man, who was plotting the sacrifice. Rys told them, 'I longed to show myself to you but the longer it went on, I just couldn't.'

Once Rys finished his story, Tor said, 'You are welcome to join the group.' Rhys was hugely relieved that his extreme loneliness and isolation were finally at an end. Had Tor been aware of his feelings for Jana, he may have hesitated, as rivalry could cause disharmony in a group.

* * *

The following spring, almost twelve moons later, the mare produced another male foal. Jana acknowledged the mare's instinctive need to escape to mate, so did not try to stop her, as she knew she could get her back eventually. In time, the captured herd was itself big enough not to need to find other ponies for mating.

Rys began to spend most of his time with Juno and before long they became partners. Tor observed his daughters settle into their relationships. He was proud of the self-sufficient women they had become. He discussed the idea of a mating ceremony marking the fact that they belonged to each other. A union meant the mingling of their spirits, so he decided it should be symbolised by the mingling of their blood. During the ceremony, the skin on their arms would be cut and their blood mixed together. This ceremony would be used by all joining couples in the future, preferably at a time when there was an abundance of food for a celebration feast.

Tor discouraged the use of fermented drink because it changed the way people behaved – but he was not against it being used on special occasions. Maa was tasked with producing such a drink. She and Juno gathered berries and placed them in a large animal skin, then crushed them by hand. She poured in warm water, stirred then covered it. After leaving it for a few days, the mixture started to ferment, due to the natural yeast present in the fruit. This in turn fed on the sugars in the fruit and turned it into alcohol. Maa hadn't made this for many years – but it tasted very good.

So, Jana and Juno were joined to their partners, Erg and Rys, on the longest day of the year and the feasting went on into the night. Jana had never tasted fermented drink before. She wasn't sure she liked it, as it had a very strong taste and made her head feel strange. However, the men appeared to enjoy it and she noticed that they became jovial, their stories even more exaggerated.

As the months went by, Jana noticed that her monthly bleeding had stopped and that she felt strange. She was nauseous in the mornings, found it difficult to eat anything and her breasts became sore. Her stomach began to swell a little and she guessed she was with child. Having watched her grandmother and Juno birthing the baby foal when they first arrived in this place, as well as Baa's baby birth, she knew what to expect. As the months passed, Jana became alarmed by how big she was becoming and had to leave more of her tasks to her partner, Erg. The twins discussed with their grandmother, who was now very old, about preparations for Jana to give birth.

They survived a third winter in the cave. In the early spring, Jana noticed on waking that her bed was wet. She said to Erg, 'I have strange pulling pains in my groin and my lower back is aching.' As these pains built up and became more frequent, she said, 'They are becoming stronger and seem to be squeezing my insides, until I can hardly breathe.' After a particularly powerful spasm, she told her sister and grandmother, 'My baby is ready to be born.' They gave her herbal drinks to keep her calm as the spasms became stronger, gently dabbing the sweat from her face. She could not settle to anything and paced around the cave.

After a few hours, she said, 'I need to push down and squat,' as she held on to a ledge which was close to their sleeping area. After another very powerful spasm, her grandmother said gleefully, 'I can see the baby's head. Just one more push now.' The baby slithered out onto the animal skins, then Maa cut the cord which joined the baby to Jana and tied it with animal sinew. She passed the baby over to Juno who gently wrapped it in the softest animal skins and handed it to Jana, announcing, 'It's a male child.' Although exhausted, Jana was happy but still felt a pulling. Maa gently kneaded Jana's abdomen to expel the afterbirth but the spasms became stronger again and she saw another baby's head appearing. Gently, Maa helped this baby's head and shoulders to come out. Jana felt she was being ripped in two, and with a final, monumental push, accompanied by unrestrained screaming, a second boy was born. Maa noticed that it was smaller and weaker but seemed lusty enough. Juno quickly cleared his airways, cut the cord, then wrapped it in soft skins and passed him onto Jana to suckle alongside his twin.

On studying them, Juno declared, 'They seem to be a mixture of both you and Erg to look at.' Both babies were now contentedly feeding on their mother's breasts and Maa knew that their suckling would help Jana's womb to contract and expel the afterbirth.

Juno went out to the waiting group, 'We have more twins, two baby boys.' Erg was ecstatically proud to be the father of two sons, as it raised his prestige among the group. They discussed what they would be named. After many, sometimes hilarious suggestions, the first born was named Enig, as he was full of spirit and the second, smaller, quieter was named Becan.

After being confined to the cave for a few days, Jana became restless to get out. She felt well enough to get back to her hunting. She devised special carrying baskets, fitted on to the mare's back, to take her babies with her and feed while she was out.

Given the twins were born in the spring, they had a good chance of surviving and soon fattened up on Jana's copious milk. Jana and Erg continued to live in the cave with the others through the cold winter months but talked of building their own hut. They chose the place near to the little stream where the group had camped on their very first night in the valley. Jana felt that this was a very special place. They would be well screened and equidistant from both the summer hut and the cave. Their new home slowly took shape and the family finally moved in once the weather warmed up.

Maa lived in the cave with Tor and Lal as she could no longer walk up mountains. She was easily exhausted and Juno worried about her. She tried to make her grandmother better using all the concoctions she knew but Maa was slowly fading, finally leaving only the husk of her former, formidable spirit. Sadly, Juno found her one morning, lying on her bed as if asleep – but she had died during the night. This was a big sorrow for the little community in the valley; it was their first death. They discussed how to bury her and the rituals they would use. Erg suggested they build a circle of upright stones high up in the mountains where they could bury all their dead inside, to protect them. Their spirits could roam the hill tops and speak to them through the winds when they were up there in the silent spaces. But this would take too long. Instead, they decided to create a cist in the ground and cover it with a mound of stones, so scavenging animals could not dig up her body.

Setting off early next morning, they found a remote peaceful place high up. They dug a long, deep hole then lined it with long flat stones. They walked back to the cave, where Juno and Jana had ritualistically prepared the body for the burial. They wrapped her in animal skins and put aside some food and water for her journey to the next world. They carefully placed her on a ladder of small pine trunks, so the men could carry her to the resting place, which was no hardship, as she was as light as a feather by the time she died.

A sad little procession followed behind the body, until they reached the burial site. Gently, they lowered her body into the sunken cist. Then each in turn spoke about happy memories and what she had meant to them,

'You were the gentlest caring mother a son could wish for. You made the great journey to this place without complaint and I thank you on behalf of our people for the care you have given them for so long.'

Juno said, 'Thank you Maa for what you have taught me about healing. Remember the day that the wild mare gave birth to the foal and you helped us? We would not have the ponies now if you had not. I will miss you more than I can say in words – but you will still be alive in our thoughts and actions.'

As they spoke, the sun slowly began to lower and they could feel the evening chill blowing in around them, reflecting the mood. The men gently lifted a large flat stone and placed it on the top of the cist. They covered this with the soil they had dug to make the hole in the ground and then the whole group covered the top with rocks, creating a cairn to mark the place.

* * *

The twins were now old enough to be left with the group while Jana went hunting. She soon reached her favourite hunting grounds, near a boggy area in the shadows of the high mountain where the wild hares ran. As Jana stalked a fat partridge, she was being watched by a repulsive, heavy-browed, wild-eyed man. His mouth was full of black rotted stumps, while coarse hair covered most of his body and face. Stealthily, he moved silently closer, into the shadow of a nearby rock. As she slipped a small stone into her sling and took aim, she was herself struck by his heavy club with such brute force, she fell to the ground, unconscious. As she came around, he was lying on top, suffocating and violating her. She tried in vain to fight him off, clawing at his body and face but was overpowered. She was in agony and felt that she was being torn in half. As she continued to struggle, he held her by the throat and hit her again, causing her to slip into merciful unconsciousness. When he had finished, he picked her up and threw her in the nearby bog, where the carrion and the worm would feed off her.

The sky turned threateningly black and thunder began reverberating around the mountains. Forks of lightning struck the ground. Suddenly afraid, the man ran off to find shelter. The stallion, panicked by the thunder, also ran off at a fast gallop. Torrential rain began to fall. Slowly, it washed away the blood from Jana's face, her unseeing eyes and ravaged body, then ran off diluted into the peat as her life force drained away. Soon the run-off from the rains on the higher slopes began to fill up the marshy peat pools. The water level rose until imperceptibly, Jana's body became submerged, sinking down into the deep, dark depths, enveloped in the acidic peat; in time, nature removed any visual evidence that Jana had ever laid there.

At dusk, Erg was concerned that Jana had not yet returned. Even if she had taken shelter from the storm, it had now passed – exposing a bright full moon riding high in the sky. Then he saw the stallion canter up to their hut and knew something was seriously wrong. The men set out immediately to search for Jana – but it seemed she had just vanished off the face of the earth; they never found any trace of her. They believed something very bad had happened, as she would never willingly stay away from her small sons. Erg was devastated at losing Jana and was left to raise his sons alone. Tor was a broken man and the sadness never left him. He had lost his mother and now one of his precious daughters, whom he had tried to keep safe by removing them from a known danger – only to bring her to an unknown danger.

* * *

Juno mourned her twin for the rest of her life. Whilst roaming the hills, she was soothed by familiar sounds; the mournful wind, skylarks twittering high up in the sky, the busily chirping chiffchaffs, the endless bubbling of the stream and even the sound of wolves far off in the night, lulled her to sleep. She often visited her grandmother's cairn and sat there telling her what was happening with the group; about her new healing discoveries, her successes and failures in treating people and animals. Juno told her she was teaching Awel, the daughter she and Rys had together, to be a healer. Juno wanted to believe that Jana was now with her grandmother and she asked them to care for each other's souls. Juno's son, Ulo, born a few years later, became one of the tribe's most important spiritual leaders.

Years passed. Some of the original group continued the practice of transhumance – spending the colder months on the valley floor, then moving up to the mountain plateau in the warm summer months to graze their animals. Only some of the older members still lived in the cave, the younger ones had moved out to populate the valley floor. They built small dwellings and cultivated the surrounding land. In this way, the valley floor lost its original wooded nature and small farmsteads became established.

Younger members gradually took over the running of the tribe, which still lived by the basic tenets Tor had established; all had thrived under his guidance to become a cohesive, caring population. On warm summer evenings, unable to sleep, Tor studied the night sky. He noticed the movement of the stars, recognising small groups were always in the same configuration and travelled in the same direction across the night sky. He noticed the time of the season when the larger stars appeared low in the sky then moved overhead as the night went on and in time realised there was a natural predictable pattern to it all. He recognised which stars were the first to appear on the horizon in the morning and to come out at night. When the weather was warm, the period of night darkness was much shorter. Whilst others took the seasons for granted, he wondered why the winter days were cold and short and the summer days long and warm. He concluded that the sun shone less on cold dark days but for much longer in the growing days – and guessed that the sun must be further away on the darker, cold days. He also wondered about the moon and felt it held some sort of power. His natural curiosity about everything and his insatiable need to understand the world drove him to study these things.

Tor was now very ancient. He sat for hours meditating on his favourite boulder, warmed by the heat of the sun. He thought about his younger self's life-changing decision to leave their tribe and embark on their epic journey. He believed his motives had been good and he was proud of the new tribe. His biggest sorrow was the inexplicable disappearance of his daughter Jana. He was very tired and wanted to let go. He would not always be around to mediate and guide the big decisions in the future, the youngsters would have to sort things out for themselves; he could think of several youngsters who would make good leaders – but the tribe would have to choose them for themselves.

As Erg had suggested at the time of Maa's death, they still

planned to create a special place; a circle of standing stones, where they could gather to pay homage and say thanks to the sun, giver of light and warmth. It would be used for their special ceremonies and for burying their dead. Tor had worked out when it would be the longest day of sunlight. He suggested that the stone circle be positioned to harness and focus the light from the sun at its centre point. He knew this dream would take many years to complete and it was unlikely that he would still be alive when they started building. So he marked out for them where that special point should be. However, he only agreed to do this on the condition that they were categorically forbidden from ever making any sacrifices, animal or human, there. Soon after, he was found dead, lying on his favourite boulder, having died as he slept, his work finally complete.

Jon died next of old age. He never disclosed to a single soul where he had hidden the hoard of golden ornaments found in the boat with Erg, so it lay undiscovered. Erg became a loner after Jana's disappearance – but Juno helped him to rear his twins. He found comfort in training the animals and was the one everybody went to for advice and animal husbandry. Having bred the wild animals at his suggestion, the tribe had a plentiful supply of food without the need to hunt. Many of the things that they discovered were accidental – but others were out of sheer necessity to make their lives easier. The tools they found in the boat with Erg had found many uses over the years. They were highly valued and once they had acquired the necessary materials and skills, were replicated. Later, someone discovered by chance that when the peaty soil in the marshy uplands was cut into squares and dried, it would burn for long periods. This gave them heat to cook their meat and kept their fires burning during the long hours of darkness – but they never dug anywhere near to where Jana's body lay and the mystery remained unsolved.

They began their stone circle, believing that a certain blue-grey coloured stone emanated special powers, and they travelled great distances to find the stones. The people were excited by the project and all threw themselves wholeheartedly into its construction. They had to learn many new techniques for building and transporting the stones, which was no mean feat. Large deep holes were dug to place them in, so they would stay upright.

Completion of the stone circle took many decades. They knew it would soon be the longest day of light of the year. They had built a central altar to capture and maximise the rays of the setting sun which streamed in between the pillars into the circle. In the evening it funnelled onto the altar from the west and in the morning from the rising sun in the east. They believed that this concentration of light held great power. They also felt powerful themselves in being able to direct this celestial power. During the inauguration ceremony, Tor's special input in its design was acknowledged, as well as his role as the original founder of the tribe. The circle soon became an important symbolic place, which indicated to others who were now inhabiting the wider area, just how powerful the tribe was.

The descendants of Jana's and Juno's children gradually spread over to the next uninhabited valley and colonised a large sloped area which became an important settlement in the uplands. Trade was established between tribes and meeting places were established, providing great social occasions. Young people would meet in these places and sometimes chose their future mates. Ceremonies to mark the joining of these couples were then held in the now established stone circle. The valley people made axes from the rock found at the top of the mountain near the far headland, which were sought-after, due to the pure craftsmanship which shaped them.

One evening, Juno sat outside her hut in the evening of her life, her eyesight not as sharp as it once was. She looked out to sea as the hazy sun started slowly sinking below the horizon, as she had done on countless nights before. The red sun illuminated the wispy cloud overhead and created a strikingly beautiful, streak-ladened sky of many colours. A vibrant line of shimmering red light fell across the surface of the sea towards where she sat. It seemed to be offering a pathway, inviting her to walk across it. She thought she fleetingly saw her twin, Jana, beckoning her to join her and knew she would not live much longer now. She was tempted to go but reluctant to leave this beautiful place of natural loveliness. She felt privileged to have lived here; she knew that this same wonderful vision would be beheld by the generations of people who would follow her – and was truly content knowing of that constancy.

The descendants of these original settlers thrived in the area for thousands of years. They intermingled with newcomers and invaders – and the population of the area continued to multiply. The genes of these first settlers were passed down through their descendants and may still be carried by some of today's fortunate inhabitants.

Part 9

Eventually, I secured the research funding and in due course produced a book on the subject; I am now a 'supposed' expert in my field. While packing away my laptop after giving a lecture, I turn and see that most attendees have melted away except for a woman I have not seen before. She asks me if I could answer a few questions. On impulse, and knowing the caretaker needs to lock up the lecture theatre, I suggest, 'Would you like to go to the university bar for a drink, then you can ask your questions?' She responds, 'Yes, I'd like that. My name is Liz by the way and I'm a mature student here, working in a similar field.' We walk across to the union bar and order drinks.

'So, what are you working on?'

'Mainly the symbolism of ancient Celtic civilisations. It's absolutely fascinating. For a start, did you know that the spiral is the oldest symbol of the Celtic culture? It's said to represent the sun. Others believe it represents the balance between inner and outer consciousness.'

Fascinated, I ask, 'Why did you choose that as your subject?'

'I know it's a difficult one, as there isn't much evidence about – probably because the Druids forbade the writing down of sacred knowledge. They had a tradition of oral history and could recite stories going back down the ages.'

'Do you like making things hard for yourself then?' She laughs and replies, 'What's life without a challenge?'

I find her fascinating. I feel myself physically relaxed in her company and enjoy her quirky, dry sense of humour. Last orders are called so I fetch more drinks from the bar; we move onto more personal territory. She tells me she had been married a long time ago but that she has been happily single for many years.

'And you?' Maybe she wants to know whether I am worth investing her time in.

'I lost my wife to cancer a few years ago. It's been hard but I find things are finally getting easier now.'

As we finish our drinks and I pick up my belongings, she asks, 'Would you show me where the cairn you found is? I would love to have a look at it.' We agree to meet up next weekend to walk up to the site.

* * *

By the time we reach the agreed meeting place, it has started to rain but this does not put us off. Once we have our walking boots and wet weather gear on, we set off at a brisk pace. I know the route like the back of my hand, so there is no chance we will get lost, even in this thick, low mist. At about the halfway point, we stop to catch our breath, before setting off once more. Conversationally, I tell her, 'The weather can change so quickly on these hills that sometimes you can experience the four seasons in the course of a day.'

Soon, the strong sunshine burns off the mist, causing ephemeral wisps of vapour to rise, twisting upwards from the ground, making it feel other-worldly. Visibility improves and suddenly we get a stunning view of the ridge ahead of us. We finally arrive at the cairn and I tell her what I know about it. I am gratified at last to share this with someone who seems just as enthusiastic as I am.

This first walk forged a real connection between us and as we got back to our meeting place, I offer, 'I can take you to see the Druid Circle, or as it's called in Welsh, Meini Hirion.'

'I'd like that very much – next weekend?'

We soon begin to spend more and more time together, meeting up often for walks, drinks or meals. I now feel lighter and happier than I have done for a long time and it's good to have something to look forward to. For the first time in a long time, I see a future for me, maybe with Liz in it if I'm lucky – but I believe I have at last turned a corner.

I still have not heard from my sons since they left home after the funeral of their mother. It has been years now and I really don't understand how they can continue to be so cruel. I have no idea about their lives nor where they are living. This continued estrangement is a huge sorrow for me, which I carry like a heavy weight around my heart. I wish they had been around for me, to comfort me and to share my achievements – as well as me sharing theirs. Liz asks me about my low mood one day, so I begin to tell of the deep grief I have felt at the loss of my wife, as well as the sad fact that that I am unwillingly estranged from my sons. She tells me to be patient, saying the boys will return when they have matured and are ready. It is probably pride which prevents them. Slowly, I realise she is becoming more and more important to me – but she turns down my suggestion that she moves in to live with me. She feels that when my sons do return, it would not be right for her to be there; she does not want them to think she is trying to take the place of their mother. So I leave it be. I must learn to be patient.

Life goes on pretty much as what passes for normal nowadays. I carry on with my research and tend the animals and the vegetable garden, which is my pride and joy. There is nothing more satisfying than going out to the greenhouse to smell that wonderful aroma which comes off tomatoes, to cut a lettuce and pick peppers I've grown myself, or to dig up new potatoes. It doesn't get any fresher than that! I have this romantic vision of myself working the land, just as my ancestors had done. I imagine that they would probably consider me a complete amateur – but grudgingly respect my efforts.

Today, I am gently hoeing my vegetable plot, removing the weeds which have shot up between the rows of lettuce after the rain. I sense someone's presence behind me. I turn slowly around and look up and see my son Robert standing a short distance away, silently watching me. He is no longer the boy who left me – he is a man – but I would know him always. He is holding a young child in his arms. Standing slightly behind him is a young woman. I am so shocked my hoe falls from my hand and I stand there open-mouthed. Robert, who is far more in control of himself than I am, calmly says, 'Hi Dad. How are you doing? This is my wife, Claire and here is your grandson, William.'

A grandson! I am elated, overwhelmed; I do not have the words to articulate the extreme joy and happiness I am feeling. All I can do is to walk up to them and take the child from Robert and hold him close, hugging him gently to hide my tears of joy in his soft hair. I am humbled that this child is also named William – but am told he is called Wills for short. Wills does not seem to mind me holding him and seems quite content in my arms.

Overcome with extreme emotion, I have forgotten how to be hospitable and suddenly remember my manners as a host. I hand Wills back to his father, pick up my basket of salad ingredients and usher them all into the farmhouse, while stutteringly offering refreshments. I ask Wills what he would like to drink, as we make our way into the kitchen. Robert gets a big tail-wagging welcome from Bess, happy to see her old walking friend again and gets a good rub around the ears which she appreciates, then she goes to get an excitable fuss off Wills.

Robert says approvingly, 'The place is looking good – don't you think so, Claire?' as he turned to her. I feel enormous pride at this – but am instantly deflated by him saying, 'But you've aged a bit. We called at the cemetery on the way up; the grave's looking very tidy down there. I felt it was time I made a pilgrimage to the old place, so here we are.' At long last – I think to myself.

We then talk for what seems like hours over a home-grown mixed salad, homemade bread and a few bottles of red wine, catching up on some of what we had missed out on. Claire takes Wills outside to look at the chickens in the yard, to give us some personal time to talk I suspect, to say what needs to be said. But I decide it is not a time for recriminations; this can be a new start, a second chance. I am just glad they are here.

When they return, I take Wills' small hand in mine. 'Come with me. I have a present for you – just over here, look. An original set of books written by your grandmother. You never knew her – but she would have been very fond of you. I'd like you to have them – but you must promise to look after them very carefully, mind, because they are very special.' At this, his parents look at each other with slightly teary eyes, while Wills is delighted with his present and soon settles down next to Bess to look at them.

Robert specialised in studying ancient antiquities in his final year at university and achieved a First Class honours degree. He tells me that having worked in the field for a few years, he set up his own company with an older, more experienced specialist, which involved identifying and dating ancient artefacts. I tell him I wished I had been more involved in his life and had been there for his graduation, now a few years ago, to which Robert mumbled a rueful, 'Sorry, I know I have been a complete idiot.'

'You're here now is all that matters.'

I tell Robert about my discoveries and the books I have written. Robert seems to be well aware already, so has obviously been following my work. I tell him that I have found numerous stone axes, spear heads and tools in the small meadow between the fields, indicating there had been some ancient occupation in the area. I tell him that I don't know why, call it intuition, but I have a strong feeling that there may even be metal artefacts buried underground on the land of the farm.

Robert fills me in on where he went travelling after graduating, then on his return about marrying Claire, 'Our happiness was compounded when our son Wills came along.' Claire interjected, 'But the one blot on our otherwise near-perfect existence was Robert's estrangement from you, his father. I would get so cross with him for not returning your calls. And when Wills was born, I begged him to get in touch with you. I told him he was depriving our son of knowing his grandfather and have tried to persuade him numerous times since then.' Robert, who had been looking at the floor, interceded, 'I knew I shouldn't have blamed you because it wasn't your fault – I realise that now but I was very pig-headed and the longer I left it, the harder it got to make the move. But soon after Wills was born, I began to realise how important the bond between a father and son is. Claire worked away at me and I gradually softened my hard stance towards you. I became a little more empathetic and understanding regarding your decisions at the time of mum's illness and now accept that you did not contact us sooner on her very strict instructions. Maybe I got my stubbornness from her,' he laughed self-deprecatingly.

I'm gratified and relieved to hear Robert saying these things and ask, 'Have you any news of Jon?' Are you in touch with him?'

'I am – but we don't see much of him as he travels all over the world with his work and seems to have a new girlfriend every time we speak to him!' I wonder at the reason for this behaviour. True, he was always the more extrovert of the two, whilst Robert was quieter and more reflective. I wonder if his mother's death has affected Jon's attitude to women, believing it was better to leave them before they left you. Robert, on the other hand, was already in a loving, supportive relationship when he lost his mother, which probably made her death a bit easier for him to deal with.

After our joyful and longed-for reconciliation, Robert and family begin to visit often. Soon, I introduce Liz to them, then I finally persuade her to move in with me. Robert says he guessed that I had stayed on the farm in the hope that they would one day return – but also for the satisfaction of living the dream I had had all those years ago, of moving to 'my ancestral home,' in the country.

Robert is slowly realising that living on the farm is now also becoming his dream and one day, during a conversation with me, says, 'Dad, I think you were absolutely right to buy this place. We all love it here and wonder how you feel about us moving in on you? This is very unexpected but not unwelcome. 'I don't need to be based in the city now as I can work from home and travel to where I need to be for work. It would be a great place for Wills to grow up, as whenever we tell him we are visiting granddad on the farm, he gets very excited.'

I know that Wills is happy when he's here and Claire seems taken by the place too. Wills is given little jobs, such as feeding the hens and he loves the responsibility of taking a basket to collect their eggs from the henhouse. He does it ever so gently, laying them carefully next to each other in the wicker basket, lined with straw. He has also declared that he is going to be a farmer when he grows up!

I am delighted by this suggestion and we agree that his little family should live in the main farmhouse. In the meantime, we will convert one of the outbuildings into accommodation for Liz and me. Plans are drawn up and the local planning department consulted. However, the process is not as straightforward as one would expect, many compromises on the design are insisted upon by the planning officer, who frustratingly often contradicts himself in terms of requirements.

Moving in and moving out day arrives. Much of the original furniture from the farmhouse is moved into the newly-converted accommodation, except for the large kitchen dresser, which seems to have been there since time immemorial; it is too big to get out through the doorways and too valuable to break up, so they are now happily stuck with it. Items such as Robert's tools of the trade as an antiquities dealer are put into storage in the barn, to be sorted out later. The ancient master carpenter's tools we inherited with the farm are also carefully stored away. We had later found an old carpenter's tool chest with the initials J.J. carved on it and guessed it was the same J.J. who owned the rose-gold fob watch. This seemed to indicate that he was the carpenter who used those very tools to build the old dresser. I like to think so anyway.

In no time at all, everyone settles down to the general rhythm of the farm. Wills oversees the chickens, letting them out in the morning, feeding them, collecting the eggs, then making sure they are all safely in the hen house at night. He started at the local primary school in the autumn and Claire has found a part-time job locally. The only fly in the ointment is that Jon remains estranged from me and I only learn about his life, second-hand through Robert.

One fine sunny day, while fetching a garden fork from the barn to do some gardening, I spot a metal detector belonging to Robert. Later, I suggest, 'It might be fun to have a go at using that around the farm. In all probability we will only find old nails, horseshoes and general household castoffs.' Robert agrees, 'It would be fun for us three to do something together and it might get Wills interested in such things.'

Next weekend, well-equipped with a fork, trowels, the metal

detector and wearing our wellies, we set off to explore around the farm. We work along the outside walls of the buildings of the farmyard and as expected, turn up a few old door hinges, bolts and old square-headed nails. To Wills though, it is all wonderful 'buried treasure' and he complains he has to stop when Claire calls us in for lunch.

Later we return to the serious work of 'metal-detectoring,' despite a light drizzling of rain. Robert suggests we try the meadow by the stream where I had found axe heads. We had identified these as having been made locally from the same stone found at the local Neolithic stone-age axe factory, about two miles away on the far headland.

I say, 'I'm not sure if this small meadow was inhabited in a later period but being near to running water, there is a small chance that it was, so we might find something.' Armed once more with the metal detector, we make our way to the site and spend happy hours working together. This was what I had yearned for – to work with my son and share our mutual enthusiasm for ancient artefacts. First, we check the lower section and dig up hinges, door locks, bolts, fencing nails and barbed wire. 'This must have been the farm dump, where the old farmers burned stuff they wanted to get rid of, which explains the concentration of metal things there.' But Wills is excited by every single find and happily takes them to wash off the dirt in the stream, except of course for the barbed wire! Then he lays out his treasure trove in the late sunshine to dry off. He has found an old tray to put them on. Digging generally, we unearth a few more axes and spearheads, which prove a bit more exciting than old hinges – but not for Wills.

Mid-afternoon, Liz brings us some home-made lemonade and biscuits – but we don't stop for long. Suddenly, the machine gives off a loud, continuous sound. Robert says, 'That's a pretty strong indication,' so we start to carefully dig. My hand trowel comes up against something hard. 'What on earth is that? It looks like metal, either bronze or gold coloured.' Wills, beside himself with excitement, runs down to the house shouting, 'Come quickly, Mum and Liz, we've found real treasure.'

We dig carefully and very gently brush the soil away from the shiny item. Soon, we realise that it is big and very, very ancient. We carry on the painstakingly slow work. Presently, Robert says what I am thinking. 'It could be one end of a gold torque.' We stand and look at each other in awe, almost too afraid to continue but itching to do so, as this could be a very significant find indeed.

Now with an audience of three fascinated, wide-eyed family members, I say 'The best approach is to cut out a square of soil which fully encases the object, then we'll clean the debris off it by the stream.' Robert asks Claire, 'Will you please fetch my camera so we can keep a record of the proceedings?' I remember about a large slate slab I had seen propped up against one of the farm outbuildings. 'Robert, I have the ideal thing to put it on while we clean it. Come with me so that we can carry it up to the stream.' Then I warn the enthralled audience, 'Don't you lot touch anything while we're gone!'

Robert takes photos with his camera and we take careful measurements. Once it is lifted out onto the slab, we gingerly work away at the packed soil around the artefact. After quite a few hours of back-breaking work – the once captivated audience having drifted away – we lift it out, still encased in its clump of soil and carefully place it on the slate slab. As we lift it out, Robert says, 'I think there may be more items underneath. What we are exposing is a massively important find.' I look at Robert and we are now totally in tune with each other, the bond mended, the rift forgotten. We work as one, cleaning up this thing we have pulled out of the earth. What is slowly emerging is, as suspected, a golden neck torque, no doubt extremely ancient. I observe, 'It's difficult to tell at this stage whether or not it's whole. Clearly, as we are suitably qualified to be doing this work, we should just carry on with it.' Using the pure water from the stream, we continue to wash the soil off slowly until it is completely free. What emerges is a beautiful, ancient, intact golden rope-patterned neck torque, of exquisite quality and workmanship.

Looking at it, I have not felt this excited since I attended the auction to buy the farmhouse – before I lost it! Again, I feel my heart thumping away in my chest. The fact that we have found this beautiful piece together, makes it even more special.

Now it is completely free of soil and before we carefully store it in an airtight container, we take photographs from many angles, using Robert's professional's camera. We are aware of the legislation and procedures regarding antique artefacts which are dug up. Her Majesty's Coroner, who will have to be informed and involved in its classification, would declare whether it was treasure trove. We record map references of the exact spot where it was found, the date and time it was found, the condition it was found in and then add our names as the excavators. We will need to take it to a special laboratory to be analysed, something that Robert says he will organise with his business partner.

Next morning, after a hearty breakfast, we set off once more to continue the dig, fortunate that the weather stays fine. During the day, we uncover a bonanza of gold artefacts such as rings, bracelets, brooches, headbands – a wonderful collection, a hidden hoard, secreted millennia ago. We also find a few random gold nuggets. I am curious about where the hoard had originated, who had made the items and why, and who had buried them.

One thing that puzzles me is the fact that the torque was higher in the earth than the rest of our find. I wonder if it has already been dug up once before in the past. If that was the case, why was it reburied? Alternatively, it could have been added to the treasure trove later. This is just pure conjecture.

Well, what a few days we have had! With the precious items safely and carefully packed away, we decide to have a celebratory meal, al fresco in the farmyard, seated around a large table. 'Do you remember, Robert, your mum saying when we first viewed the farm, before the auction, that this area would be an excellent place to sit out and have a glass of wine in the evening?' He nodded, glad of the shared memory as we all solemnly raised a glass to her sweet memory.

It is one of those glorious summer evenings; we are all are happily relaxed, tongues are loosened by the wine and the large red sun is just starting to sink below the horizon. We chat about taking the hoard to be inspected when Robert suddenly turns to me and says out of the blue, 'Why have you and Liz not got married? You are obviously made for each other and get along really well.' I was astonished. In his own way, he was saying that he would be okay with it. I tried to bluff my way out of my embarrassment by saying, 'I don't think she would have me!' as I looked smilingly, slightly questioningly at Liz.

To be honest, we had tended to rather play down our relationship, so as not to make them feel discomfited – but on the contrary, it appears that the exact opposite is the case. Robert is very comfortable with it and is giving the idea his blessing. Robert continues, 'We want you to be part of the family, Liz. Wills clearly adores you, so you must be all right!'

Suddenly we are all discussing the possibility, with all agreeing what a great idea it is. Liz doesn't seem to be unhappy about being put on the spot. It feels as if my family is asking her to marry me, so I turn to Liz and say, 'Well, what do you think? Should we?' There is huge jubilation and she seems unable to speak due to being choked with happy tears, so she just nods her head in agreement and I kiss her sweet lips to seal the agreement, which brings on more merry cheers.

This opens up a whole new field of discussion, such as where and when the wedding should take place. I sit and listen quietly to all these ideas. Eventually, they turn to me to ask what I think, rather as an afterthought. Having got over the initial shock of this sudden turn of events, I turn to my family, 'I would like to be married in the little Methodist chapel along the road, which my great-great-great-grandfather, Evan, built and would like to imagine that he and our ancestors would also be gathered there, looking on with approval,' adding, 'my only sorrow is that Jon will not be there.'

Later, I have an inspired idea. I had kept back one of the small nuggets of gold we found by the hoard. Next time I find Liz has left her ring in the bathroom, I secretly take it to the manufacturing jeweller's shop in the next town. The jeweller measures Liz's ring, then I ask, 'Can you make a wedding ring out of this?' handing him the nugget of gold. 'Could you also possibly make it in a Celtic design?'

The man looks at me over his half-moon glasses, then replaces them with an eye glass. Rolling it round between his thumb and index finger he says, 'This is pure Welsh gold, I thought it was only royalty who had rings made from this stuff. I would have to mix it with some copper of course to make it stronger but it can be done. In fact, I could make two wedding rings out of this if you want.' It has not occurred to me to have one made for me as well – but I quite like the idea of a matching pair. The jeweller then measures my wedding finger and tells me it will probably take him about three weeks to make them.

I wonder if this gold nugget had been found originally in my stream and buried with the other stuff to keep safe or had come from elsewhere. But it is strange that it had been buried in the same spot as the main hoard. Maybe a later farmer had decided to plough that area and stopped when the turned-over turfs exposed them. But why did he not dig them out? It would have made him a very rich farmer.

* * *

The big day has arrived. The food is already prepared in the farmhouse for the wedding reception. Although it is warm, we have hired a small marquee in case it rains. We have a couple of young people from the village in to help with setting up the buffet and later to clear up. It is to be a very small affair, just family, local friends, a few of Liz's friends and relations, together with a few old and more recent work colleagues.

Just before we leave for the chapel, the others having already left, I open the black velvet boxes and show Liz the wedding rings I have had made and hand mine to her. She is clearly very moved by this gesture, 'I am so lucky to be marrying you; you have been well worth the wait.'

'But I have another surprise.' I pull out a small box, then ask Liz to turn around. I take out Catherine's antique gold locket which we found in the hole in the wall. Very tenderly, I hang it around her neck and do up the clasp. Then she turns to face me, gently touching the locket, as she softly kisses me, with tears welling. 'Watch your mascara doesn't run,' I joke, 'I don't want to be marrying a panda!' Then I show her a small pocket in my gold brocade waistcoat and pull out the ancient rose-gold pocket watch, found with the locket in the wall. 'Well, it is a very special occasion,' I say, then leave to get to the chapel before her. Robert is waiting outside the house to escort Liz along the road.

Our guests are already seated in the little chapel and the organist is playing soft background music as I stand nervously waiting by the altar with my back to the congregation. As the music changes to Gounod's St Cecilia's Mass, a piece loved by both of us for being bold and celebratory, Liz walks slowly down the aisle, on the arm of Robert. Just before she joins me at the front, I turn around to look at her and see how radiantly happy she looks. As I turn back to face the front, I literally do a double take, because standing in the pew that Robert is now walking back towards, is his twin, Jon. What a shock! What a joy! It feels wonderful to see him there, as well as the fact that Liz has now arrived by my side. I just cannot stop smiling, even as we exchange marriage vows. A wonderful double celebration. I think Liz seems to have been in on this special secret, as she smiles sideways at me. My little circle is no longer broken.

Liz and I proudly lead our family and guests the few hundred yards back along the road from the chapel to the farmhouse. Passing locals bib their car horns in approval along the way. Once there, copious champagne is poured, toasts are made and guests help themselves to food from the buffet table. Robert then brings Jon over to me. There is nothing which needs to be said. We just hold each other, making up for the lost years of painful estrangement. I am whole once more. We know we will have a conversation about where he has been and what he has been doing but for now, Robert is tapping his glass with a spoon to gain everyone's attention. He makes his speech, welcoming Liz into the family, thanking Jon for coming, thanking everybody for being there and then wishes us a long, happy life together. This is the only speech I will allow so that we can just get on with our celebrations, eating, mingling and story swapping. It is a really wonderful and memorable day.

Jon tells me he flew in the day before with his partner Dorothy, who he calls Dottie. He explains that he works for a global charity, involving frequent international travel but he may soon return to London for a while, so we might see more of him in future. But these are just words; what is important is that he is here, so I stand there and listen and rejoice in his nearness. Jon is interested to hear about our uncovered treasure, which has been sent to be analysed, hopefully to identify the source of the gold which the ornaments were made from. There is general consensus by experts that it probably originated in Ireland, so not the same source as the nugget for our wedding rings which is identified as Welsh.

It seems it may have been possible that someone was crossing the Irish Sea, maybe in a coracle, when he got caught in a storm which blew him in towards the Welsh coast. Maybe it was being taken somewhere to trade or had been stolen from someone rich and important. One can only speculate on these things, which is endlessly indulgent, but whatever the reason, we will never know.

It is such an important find that it has been put on display in the National Museum, so that all can have the opportunity to view it. Although a small reward is paid, which has been put into a trust for my grandchildren's education, for me, the find is far more significant than any reward. It would be nice though if Wills wanted to be an archaeologist one day, once he had finished being a farmer of course!

* * *

Pondering about the ancient people who may have lived in the area, I reflect that since the beginning of time, people have moved around the world, looking for a better, safer life as they are still doing today. Some people just know when they are in the wrong place and seek a place which feels right. They move for economic, security, religious or ideological reasons; reasons known only to themselves, or simply so they can become themselves. There have always been idealists who are able to visualise how good life could be from an altruistic point of view. These people are driven to create a better world, believing that the world belongs to everyone; not to the few who own it due to an accident of birth, or through brute force, or manipulation of people for their own selfish ends. Some travellers are lucky enough to find the wide-open space they seek to settle in, whilst others do the opposite and move to smaller spaces, where they can earn a better living and be anonymous. But incomers are not always welcome and are sometimes seen by others as a threat, as their ways change the existing cultures. It is in the very nature of humankind itself to move, to improve and thrive. Some early humans were not content to live the way that their tribes did. They wanted something better. Modern men such as myself, also not content with my former life, craved space and quietude. Quality of life is far more important to me than status and money in the city. Others want different things at different stages of their lives, due to the changes that take place in their values and priorities as they mature.

Despite the sorrow of losing my beloved first wife, Sarah, I am glad I moved here and feel lucky enough to have been given a second chance at happiness with Liz. Unless you have known deep painful sorrow, how can you experience deep joyful happiness? I have also been given what I wanted – the opportunity to research the lives of the ancients, as well as my ancestors, which has made me feel very connected to them all in this beautiful place. I believe they were much the same as us today in terms of intelligence, resourcefulness and humanity. I like to speculate that my more immediate ancestors may even have originated from the first ancient occupiers but of course we would have to find an ancient's body in the peaty bog of the uplands to be able to get a DNA sample in order to prove that point!

Although the buried hoard was an extremely exciting, once in a lifetime find, what is a thousand times more important to me is the fact that I am now reconciled with both my sons and that I have a delightful grandson and a loving wife. All in all, I consider myself to be extremely privileged to be living the life I had craved a decade ago.

Often, just before sunset, I walk up to the site of the ancient roundhouse on the hill behind the farm, as others have done before me. The presence of the ancient people resonates down through the ages in this valley, the clues of their existence here are all around if one knows how and where to look. I sit there, sometimes alone, sometimes with one of my sons or Liz, looking out at the gloriousness of the sunsets. Like snowflakes, each sunset is unique, depending on the time of year and weather conditions. As the sun sinks, the cloud formation above often lights up spectacularly in all possible shades of red, orange and gold, pink, purple and indigo, deepening further as the sun falls below the horizon. There are no words adequate to describe these spectacular sunsets – one has to see them to believe them.

Standing here on my mountain vantage point where I know I belong, I am a deeply contented man. I look seaward and scan the length of the expansive sandy bay, between the two rocky headlands. As I do, I visualise in my mind's eye a small group of ancient, bedraggled settlers, coming wearily around the rocky headland onto the expanse of the beach. Then, looking up in awe, they see in front of them the beauty of this uninhabited valley and decide that, at last, this would be the home for which they had searched for so long.

Epilogue

Liz and I decide one lovely spring morning to go to Llangelynin Old Church to see the spectacular wild daffodils. Driving up through Llechwedd, I say to Liz, 'This is the area where Bob and his daughter Ellen used to live. We spot the Tabernacle Church and always a sucker for a graveyard, I say, 'Why don't we park here and have a quick look around?'

It was a lovely setting to be laid to rest in, on a grassy slope, looking out across to the other side of the Conwy Valley. We get out of the car and walk through the Victorian, cast iron gate, designed primarily to keep out stray sheep. We climb the path up a gentle slope, then spend time walking along the rows, reading out the predominantly Welsh names engraved on the mostly slate headstones.

Eager to help, Liz asks, 'Are we looking for any names in particular?'

'I suppose if we are very lucky we might come across a Robert and Anwen Jones; they raised Thomas' son Owen. We continue to scour the names and I find it endlessly fascinating to look at them and the clues the engravings give us about them, as I try to imagine what their lives would have been like.

Suddenly, Liz calls out, 'I've found a Robert and Anwen Jones but are they the right ones?' I catch up with her and carefully read the inscription. The dates seem to tally but when I read below that also buried is Ellen Jones, I am absolutely convinced that it is my ancestors' grave, otherwise it would be just too much of a coincidence. The grave is neat and well-tended with fresh flowers. 'Well, well,' I say, 'Fancy that, another bit of evidence for my family tree.' I take a photo with my mobile to download when I get home.

Satisfied with our discovery, we head back to the car as a light shower of rain begins to make its presence felt. It's still a bit of a pull up to Llangelynin so I suggest we drive just a bit further, park the car and do the rest of the journey by foot. I love these adventures with

Liz and I think again how lucky I am to have her companionship.

A little further up on a wider part of the road, near Llechan Isaf, we decide to park the car and start walking. It's quite a strain on the leg muscles in places and we stop for a breather near a pull-in to a farm. Casually, I read the name on the gate and am astounded to read that it says Pont Werglodd, Bob and Ellen's farm, where Owen was raised. It is a lovely little place with a bridge over a stream. I had heard tell that Ellen had been found dead sitting outside the front door, shelling peas. As I look closer, I see an old man with snow white hair, walking towards the front door from one of the outhouses. Looking up, he sees us and comes over to say hello.

'Lovely place you've got here,' I say.

'Yes, been in the family for years,' he replies.

'Some of my relatives used to live here a long time ago,' I tell him.

'Oh, what were their names?'

'We've just found their graves in the cemetery down the road, they were Bob, Anwen and Ellen Jones.'

He swoons and holds onto the gate to steady himself. 'And how are you related' he asks.

'Through Thomas, who owned Glyn Abercyn, and my great-great-great-grandfather, Evan, I reply. 'We live there now.'

'Well, goodness gracious me,' he says. 'What a small world, I am Owen, son of Thomas.'

* * *

Ffowcs/Jones Family Tree

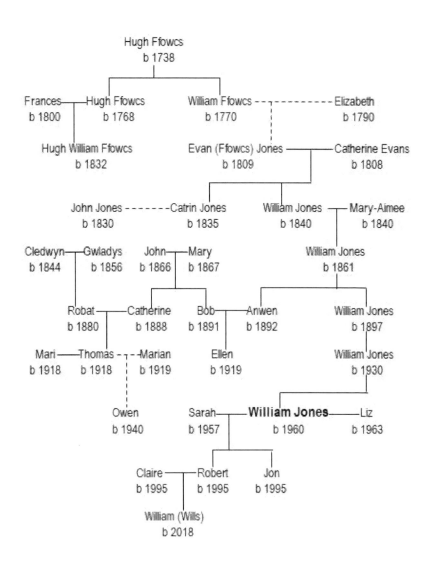

About the Author

This is a story, spun purely from my imagination, about the place I spent my childhood, early adulthood and have since returned to. The place I call home. As a child, I was lucky enough to have the freedom to wander around this valley and its surrounding hills, unhindered and safe, alone or with friends. It was a time when everybody knew who everybody was. Nobody worried where I was, knowing I would be back when hungry. I found my way around the wide, often windy hills, which wrap themselves protectively around this valley and discovered peaceful places, pretty waterfalls, caves and secret hideaways. I knew the places where the less common animals and birds could be found. I discovered unusual flowers and plants and which, once home, tasked myself with identifying. This activity took place against the backdrop of the ever-changing seasons, which brought with them their own particular changes and curiosities.

Books fed my imagination, which saved me from the tedium of closed-in rainy days, when the mountains mysteriously disappeared into their thick shrouds of ever-moving mist. But once the sun came out, I was soon out and about again. My surroundings stimulated my imagination to overflowing and knew no boundaries. I scared myself with irrational thoughts of witches who lived in caves, and mad but kindly hermits who lived in remote, tumble-down mountain cottages. At school, I wrote these imaginings into stories and they were sometimes chosen to be read out in class. This encouraged me to think that maybe one day I might write a proper story. This story, although fictional, was always going to be set in the place in which I grew up and roamed, because this is where I know.

Wandering the same valley and hills as an adult, I began to look at the place with grown-up eyes and started to imagine the people who may originally have inhabited this valley. I was inspired to imagine what their daily lives would have been like. I also wondered about the families who over the centuries had lived in my family home. Coincidentally, it was bought by my grandfather a hundred years ago in 1921, although my family had lived in the area for many years prior to this. The house probably dates back to the middle-ages, and I have spun my web of stories mainly around it. The one thing all the real and imagined families would have had in common, at whichever period in history, would be a deep abiding love for the valley, because that is what it engenders in all who are fortunate to inhabit it.

When the first inhabitants arrived, they began the transformative but necessary process by which they slowly changed the nature of the valley. From its former wooded state, it changed into land they could cultivate and on which to raise the livestock they had tamed. This process continued to shape the valley over many millennia. I imagined these first inhabitants had originated from southern Europe, carrying within them their need for a new, idealistic utopia, away from the restrictions, beliefs and structures of their former existence.

With these newly adult eyes, better knowledge and a continued love of the freedom of hill-walking, I began to see evidence of their existence, high up in remote places. The places they built their shelters, the areas they cleared to grow their corn, the pens they built using the smooth granite boulders which had been dragged down by an ancient glacier, to enclose their newly domesticated animals. I noticed the cairns they built to bury their dead and the upright stone circles where they worshipped their Gods. Those who know how to look, can see that the footprints of these former inhabitants resonate strongly down through the ages and can still be heard today. In my wanderings along the higher ground, I have also observed the pre-mating rituals of the descendants of the sturdy wild ponies that the ancients captured and tamed, and which today, still roam wild in the hills.

My stories are told through the prism of a modern-day inhabitant, drawn by the pull of the valley, in a desire to find his roots through ancestral links. With a specialist knowledge of pre-history, William strives to thread together and make sense of the lives of the first inhabitants and the occupants in the following centuries, their stories interwoven with his modern-day presence. Although devastated by personal events, he finally finds his own inner peace.

The valley is still loved and appreciated today as much as it was when first settled and as it has been throughout the ages. People move away, miss it and long to return through feeling the 'hiraeth', the nearest translation of which is a longing homesickness; it seems that when you leave, a piece of you stays behind. Others discover the valley and are motivated to move there to escape their relentless modern lifestyles in search of a slower pace, just as William's family does. Many more retire here from the industrial areas where they have made their fortunes, choosing to spend their later years in peace and tranquillity, surrounded by beauty.

What shines through all these ages is the deep love and commitment the valley engenders in the people who have the good fortune to be born and live there. I hope you enjoyed my story and that I have done the valley justice.

A Quick Favour

If you enjoyed this book, would you please take a moment to write a short review on Amazon so other readers can enjoy it too?

Please go to: https://eleri-thomas-k0e5y2.mailerpage.com or alternatively, just go the book on Amazon.

It really does help!

Thank you so much.

Acknowledgments

My heartfelt thanks to those who helped, supported, advised and encouraged me to write this book. I am grateful to those who read the earlier prototypes and others who gave their time to reading it as it neared completion. You are too numerous to mention but know who you are.

I feel fortunate to have such interesting and hard-working ancestors, who inspired some of the historical characters, although the stories I wove around them come from my imagination.

Special thanks to my long-suffering husband, who has read it more times than he cares to remember – and now knows all about self-publishing.

Also, gratitude to my wonderfully creative daughter-in-law, Megie, who drew the cover for the book.

Printed in Great Britain
by Amazon